A SMOKE TREE SERIES NOVEL

I0638510

THE HOUSE

OF

THREE

MURDERS

GARY J. GEORGE

TABLE OF CONTENTS

For Ginny. The very best part of my life.

A WORD ABOUT THE WAY THE AUTHOR USES
QUOTATION MARKS IN DIALOGUE

Dialogue in this novel opens with quotation marks, as is usual. However, what follows sometimes differs from convention. If the person speaks for more than one paragraph, I do not put quotation marks before each new paragraph; instead, I don't close the quotation marks until that person has finished speaking.

Chapter 1

CHARLIE

On November 2, 1960, Charlie Merriman, a young man of the Fort Mohave Tribe of Mojave Indians, was bored and restless when he met up with the wrong guy at The Palms. The Palms was on Front Street in Smoke Tree, California, a small, isolated town on the banks of the Colorado River, not far from the Mojave Reservation. Charlie liked the Palms. The owner, a retired Marine gunnery sergeant, ran a tight ship. Although he rarely called the police, there were few fights in his place. The reason? If one broke out, Mac was around the bar with a nightstick and sap, and he was not reluctant to use them. If you got in a fight, whether you started it or not, you were eighty-sixed for a week. No exceptions.

The Palms was a cavernous, old-fashioned place with a high, hammered-tin ceiling and bad lighting. A big swamp cooler ran all summer, and ancient black ceiling fans kept the air moving. Every morning Mac scattered sawdust on the cement floor. Then he put bowls of peanuts salted in the shell on tables and along the bar. All day and into the night, beer drinkers ate the peanuts and threw the shells on the floor of the dimly lit room. At night after closing, he swept the sawdust and peanut shells off the floor, then seined the mix through animal cage wire nailed to a frame. On a good night, he would find ten to fifteen dollars in change and paper that had been dropped by careless drunks. He also had a clean floor for the next day.

The Palms was quiet that Wednesday afternoon. There were a few railroaders, just in off the line, having a beer before heading home. And there were the three women from the reservation. Charlie thought of them as the village *brujas,* and he hated to see them in town. They were the kind that gave the Mojave a bad name in Smoke Tree. They were drinking up their Bureau of Indian Affairs money. They would keep drinking until they passed out or went broke. They typically wore loose-fitting, shapeless dresses until they got dirty; then, they put on clean dresses over the dirty ones. When they had on so many dresses they could hardly waddle, they walked into the river and began peeling off dresses and throwing them up on the beach until they were naked. Then they hung the dresses in the bushes and sat on the bank while they dried.

Charlie was not a heavy drinker, so he was still nursing his first beer when Sixto Morales walked in and sat on the stool next to his. He caught the odor of talcum powder, cheap cologne, and sweat. Sixto was 5'10" and 225 pounds of cruel intentions and malicious anger. His big head, with its deep black eyes, long black hair, and badly scarred face, sat atop a body designed to inflict pain and create mayhem. His broad shoulders and thick chest supported massive arms and tapered to a surprisingly narrow waist. The knotted forearms jutting from his guayabera shirt were covered with tattoos that featured daggers, skulls, big-breasted women, and random splatters of blood. His powerful thighs made his Levi's look like they had been painted onto his legs.

Sixto seemed to have been born looking for trouble. He often found it. His juvenile record, put together in three states, was the stuff of legend. He had already been in prison twice as an adult for strong-arm robbery and assault, even though he was only in his early thirties. There had been other assaults, and everybody knew it, but the victims often refused to press charges or became forgetful when the trial rolled around, and they had to face Sixto in court. Except for the high school football coach, who had once boxed semi-pro as a heavyweight, everyone in Smoke Tree, including the law officers, was afraid of Sixto, whether they admitted it or not.

You did not get up and move when Sixto Morales sat down next to you. Not if you wanted to get out the door in one piece. Sixto was easily offended: for all his power and menace, he was a man of delicate sensibilities when it came to possible snubs. Charlie stayed put.

"*Ya'at'e'e'h,* brother," said Sixto, who wasn't even part Indian.

"*Buenas dias, hermano,*" replied Charlie, who wasn't even part Mexican.

Sixto stared hard at Charlie, trying to decide if he had been insulted. Before he could make up his mind, Mac came down the bar. "Hey, Sixto, I thought I eighty-sixed you."

Sixto stared at him with angry, sullen eyes. "A week ago Sunday, Mac. My time is up."

"Yeah, well, I'm thinking of making a new rule for you." Mac paused. "In fact, I just made it. The next time I eighty-six you, it's a month before you can come back. I'm tired of you making trouble every time you have a couple of beers."

"Let's go get us a table," said Sixto to Charlie. "We're too close to this *hijo de puta.*"

"What'd you say?"

"Hey, five years you've owned this bar. Learn a language, huh? Half your customers are Mexicans." He took Charlie by the arm and led him to a table by the jukebox. There was a mural of Lefty Frizzel painted on the wall. It was autographed.

After they sat down, Sixto yelled, "Hey, *Senor* Mac, bring me a beer."

Mac looked at him a long time, then drew a draft beer and brought it over. "That'll be twenty-five cents."

"Start me a tab."

"I didn't know you had a sense of humor, Sixto. No quarter, no beer."

Sixto slowly opened out the wallet hooked by a chain to his belt. He fished out a wrinkled dollar and put it on the table. "And bring one more for my buddy Charlie here."

Mac went off with the dollar and rang up the sale. He drew another beer and brought it back to the table with the change. Sixto picked up his change and said, "Hey, hombre, this beer is so damn good; why don't you fetch me another one?"

"You're not done with the first one."

"Yeah, but I'm gonna be pretty quick, and the service is not too good in here."

Mac walked behind the bar and punched the "no sale" key on the ancient cash register. He took Sixto's dollar out of the till. He brought it back to the table and stuffed it into Sixto's pocket. He picked up the two beer mugs and took them to the bar. He came back to the table, his face red, his mouth tight and white beneath his mustache. He was carrying his sap and his nightstick.

"All right, you've got your dollar back. Now get out. And this time, you're out for a month."

Sixto stood up, his hands opening and closing at his sides. The only sound in the room was the squeak of the old fans hanging from the ceiling. "You think you can take me with just that sap and stick, jarhead?"

"No doubt in my military mind. If you're not out that door in one minute, I'm going to break you into small pieces and have you rendered for your ugly fat. Now get moving. And take Charlie with you."

"Hey, Mac, what did I do?" asked Charlie.

"You sat down with this creep."

Sixto stood silently for a moment. Charlie could see him weighing possibilities behind those dead eyes. Then he laughed and turned away. "Come on, Charlie; let's get out of this dump. This man don't want our business. He don't like wetbacks or savages."

As he went out the door, he turned back and yelled, "Hey Mac, thanks for the free beer!"

Outside on the sidewalk, the bright sunlight hurt Charlie's eyes. He began to walk away. "*Adios,* Sixto. *Hasta manana.*"

"Nah, come on, *vatolo*. Get in the car. I'll give you a ride out to the Indian Village."

Sixto's '51 Mercury, with its grinning shark grill, was angle parked at the curb. It was painted a dull, primer gray. The chrome gleamed in the late afternoon sun. "Geez," thought Charlie. "Even the guy's car looks mean."

Charlie got in, and they drove down Front Street, turned in front of the depot, and merged with the westbound traffic on 66. But instead of staying on the highway, Sixto turned and drove across the railroad tracks on the north side of the depot.

"Sixto, what's up? I thought you were giving me a ride to the Village."

"What you gonna do there? Sit in the dirt? Let's go have some fun."

He stayed on the street until it turned into a dirt road and merged with the dike road along the river. Sixto turned south and then went over the bureau bridge into Arizona.

"Where we headed?"

"We're going to the Oatman Hotel. They got a lady bartender up there makes a drink called a Cointreau cooler. Taste's great going down, but it'll put hair on your chest."

"Indians don't have chest hair."

"You will after you put down a couple of these babies."

Sixto turned off the dike road that ran up the Arizona side of the river and headed east toward the Black Mountains. It was colder in the mesquite and tamarisk thickets. Charlie could smell the familiar river bottom smells of alkali, tamarisk, cow dung, and brackish water pooled in irrigation ditches.

Charlie fell asleep for a moment, then woke suddenly when they turned onto the badly washboarded road that went up the hill toward Boundary Cone. They left the river bottom farmland and thickets behind and entered a creosote-covered desert landscape. The washes they crossed were full of broken volcanic rock and stunted cactus.

Just to the north of Boundary Cone, they turned onto the remnants of Old 66 as it rose up the hill from Topock, Arizona. By the time they got to the old gas station on the outskirts of Oatman, they were surrounded by volcanic boulders and stands of teddy bear cholla. They came around the final curve before town and drove through ugly piles of reddish-mud-colored tailings leftover from Oatman's gold rush heyday of the late 1800s. As the road straightened and they left the mounds of tailings behind, the shacks and mine shafts of the ghost town spread out across the hillside in front of them.

Misfits who had washed up on this distant shoreline of civilization lived in some of the shacks. No one in Oatman asked where you came from, and many of the people went by first names only. Very few of the old shacks had electricity, but people squatted in them anyway. Hundreds of burros, the descendants of pack animals left behind by the old prospectors, wandered over the hillsides and through the streets.

Sixto pulled up in front of the Oatman Hotel, one of the few buildings on the town's main street that was not boarded up. When Charlie got out of the car, he could smell burro dung and mesquite-wood smoke. A cold wind kicked up dust, and an old Coca-Cola sign hanging under a covered walkway on the other side of the street squeaked on its hinges as it flapped in the breeze. Somewhere on the hillside, someone was playing what Charlie thought of as old-time music. Since there was no electricity in those shacks, the scratchy record was playing on a wind-up Victrola.

They went in the hotel and turned to the left into the bar. There was a woman behind the bar smoking a cigarillo. She was a handsome, statuesque lady in late middle age, made taller by the undershot heels of her cowboy boots. She was wearing Levi's and a white western shirt with mother-of-pearl snap buttons. Her hair was piled high on her head, and she had a Navajo squash blossom necklace on the outside of her shirt. She did not look very happy to see Sixto Morales.

The only other person in the place was an old man at the other end of the bar. He was asleep with his head turned sideways on his folded arms. An ancient straw hat lay on the bar next to him.

"What'll it be, gentlemen?"

"Two Cointreau coolers"

"Your *compadre* there looks like he might be a little underage, Sixto."

"Oh no, ma'am," said Charlie. "I'm twenty-one." He pulled out his wallet and showed her his driver's license.

She looked at it carefully. "Okay, four months is as good as forty years when it comes to being legal to drink."

She turned away and began to make the drinks. She filled two tall glasses with crushed ice and then added tonic water, rum, vodka, and red liqueur. She put maraschino cherries on top of both drinks and turned and set them on the bar.

"Two dollars."

"Run me a tab."

"You know better than that. I ran a tab for you once, and it took me six months to get paid."

Sixto grunted and got out two dollars, then drained his drink in a series of continuous gulps. He banged the glass on the bar.

"Two more. And this round's on you, Charlie."

★ ★ ★

Four hours later, it was dark outside, they were out of money, and Charlie was drunk for the first time in a very long time. Sixto made one more attempt to start a tab without any luck.

They went outside. All the buildings on the deserted street were dark. They could see lights flickering here and there in the windows of the shacks on the hillside behind the main street. The dim lights had the yellowish cast of oil-burning lamps.

"Maybe you shouldn't drive. You might get a drunk driving."

"Hey, Geronimo, think there's a highway patrolman within forty miles of here?"

"I guess not."

"Then shut your face and get in."

When Sixto hit the dirt road that went down the hill toward Smoke Tree, he mashed down hard on the accelerator. They flew down the hill with rocks banging hard off the undercarriage of the Mercury. The moon was well up behind them. It chased them down to the river bottom. At the bottom of the hill, instead of continuing toward Smoke Tree, Sixto turned north.

"Where we going?"

"Up through Bullhead and over the dam to Searchlight."

"What for? We're broke."

"Know a guy there. Works in the cage at the casino. He'll give me an advance on chips. We can cash some at the coffee shop and get something to eat, and then play craps with the rest. I feel a lucky streak coming on."

Charlie had no choice other than to ride along. He had made his first mistake when he got in the car outside The Palms. He should have walked home to the Village, but he was stuck now. As they drove north, he looked out the side window at the big moon racing them up the road.

Bullhead in 1960 wasn't much. There were a few waterfront cabins and docks along the river. The gas station and a liquor store across the street from each other at the crossroads of two dirt roads formed the rest of the town.

Sixto pulled off the road into the dirt parking area next to the liquor store, an ugly, square building made of unpainted cement blocks. There were two spotlights over the door angled to light up the parking area.

"Why are we stopping?"

"Cause I'm hungry."

"I thought you were broke."

"I got enough for a couple of candy bars. I gotta eat something."

They got out and started toward the building.

"Hold up a minute," said Sixto. "Be right there. I think I dropped some change on the floor."

He went back to the car, pulled open the door, and leaned inside.

"Got it," he said when he came back.

They went into the store. The man behind the counter reading the Las Vegas Review-Journal was middle-aged and slender. He was wearing tan western slacks with a big belt buckle and a white cowboy shirt with a scrolled pattern across the shoulders. He had on a cream-colored Stetson.

"Once you cross the river, it's nothing but cowboys," thought Charlie.

"Pick us out a couple good candy bars and get a bag of Fritos," said Sixto.

Charlie walked over to the candy rack. "What kind do you like?" he asked. Then he realized Sixto wasn't with him. He turned and saw him back by the beer cooler. The man behind the counter was watching Sixto intently.

Sixto disappeared from view, and Charlie thought he had bent down to get something out of the bottom of the cold case. Then he heard the heavy door to the cooler box open.

"Hey," yelled the cowboy, "you can't go in there."

But Charlie heard the heavy door slam shut, and Sixto came toward the counter carrying a case of Lucky Lager. The man started to say something, but Sixto slammed the case down hard on the counter.

"Uh-oh," thought Charlie. "We're in it now."

"Did you get our candy bars and chips?"

"Not yet."

"Well, get them, *vato*. And grab us a bunch of that beef jerky and a can of them mixed nuts. Come on, man, hurry up!"

Charlie did as he was told and put everything on the counter.

"Get a couple packages of them Twinkies, too. They go real good with beer." Sixto winked at him. His mouth was smiling, but his eyes did not look friendly.

The man rang everything up.

"That'll be …" he began.

"That'll be nothing," said Sixto. Reaching under his shirt, he pulled a .45 automatic out of the waistband of his Levi's. Sixto pointed it casually at the man. "No, that's wrong. That won't be nothing, *senor* cowboy *grande*. That'll be everything in the register. *Manos arriba!*"

The man didn't move.

"Jesus! That means 'hands up.' Don't any of you gringos speak Spanish?"

Charlie could see the perspiration beading on the man's upper lip and smell the odor of fear that suddenly filled the room. He saw the man's eyes jerk down and to the side.

Sixto pulled the hammer back on the .45. The click sounded to Charlie like a key locking a cell door in an old western. The man's eyes went wide. "Don't even think about it. Open the register with one hand. Pull all the bills out of each tray with the same hand and pile them on the counter. Leave the change in the register."

The man did as he was told. His face looked bloodless under the fluorescent lights.

"Get one of those big paper bags there. And do it real slow. I could get nervous and shoot if you scare me." Sixto laughed a cruel laugh. "Now put the money in it.

Good. Now grab hold of that cord that hooks the phone to the wall. Hey! Don't pick up the phone; just get the cord. Good! Now, give it a big yank and pull it out of the wall.

Put the other stuff in the bag," he said to Charlie. "Hurry up. We've got a train to catch.

Lift the counter with one hand and come out here," Sixto said to the man. "Come on, come on. We're in a hurry here."

The man complied, lifting the counter with one hand while he kept the other hand up and then putting the other hand back in the air.

"Lay down on your belly where we can see you." As the man stretched out on the floor, his Stetson fell off. He started to reach for it. "Aww, your cowboy hat fell off. Don't worry about it, Roy Rogers; I'll take care of it for you." Sixto stomped the hat flat.

"Hey! Don't turn your head to the side. I want your nose right on the floor. That's right, in the dust. Watch him. If he moves, kick him in the head."

Sixto went around behind the counter and removed a short-barreled revolver from a shelf. He stuck it in his pocket and came back around.

"Listen to me, *pendejo*. We're going out the door. If I so much as see your ugly white face, I'm gonna start shooting. You better not come near that door before you hear us drive away.

Pick up the beer and the bag, and let's go."

Charlie put the bag on top of the case of beer and picked it up. They went out the door, and Sixto hid the gun under his shirt. As they walked through the dirt in the front of the store, he said, "That guy's on the floor in there pissing his pants. I've seen his kind before. He's not going to risk his butt for his boss. *Pinche* cowboy!"

But Sixto was wrong. The man he had just robbed was the owner of the store. He was also a veteran of World War Two and Korea who had been at both the Battle of the Bulge and Chosin Reservoir. The man had another gun in his office, a .357 magnum. When he retrieved it, he pulled the door open and started shooting. The gun sounded like a cannon. Charlie saw Sixto's shirt puff out in front of him as if the wind had blown through his body. He went down on one knee.

But he was no quitter; Charlie had to give him that. Even as Sixto was folding, he pulled the .45 from beneath his shirt, pivoted on his knee, and let go. The big gun shattered the glass door and blew chunks of cement and clouds of dust out of the blocks around it. The man disappeared. While the gun was going off, the world around Charlie slowed to a crawl. He could see the spent shells ejecting in graceful arcs from the side of the .45 and spinning toward the ground. He could see the barrel rise and then fall with each shot. The puffs of concrete seemed to blossom like cement flowers from the building.

Then it was over, and the world sped up again. He could smell gunpowder and cordite. His ears were ringing, and the sound of the big gun was still roaring in his head. He dropped everything on the ground and was turning to run when he heard Sixto screaming at him. He turned back to see the .45 pointed his way.

"Hey! Hey! *Conejo!* Where the hell you think you're going?"

Charlie's voice sounded far away. "I'm heading for the river. I don't want any part of this."

"You're already part of it. Now help me to the car. I'm hit bad. That *pinche* cowboy punched one right through me. Help me to the passenger side. And bring that paper sack."

Charlie did as he was told. When he managed to help the big man around the car, he opened the door. "You get in first," said Sixto. "And slide across. You're driving."

As Charlie slid across, the man appeared in the doorway and fired two times. One of the rounds shattered the windshield and took out the rear view mirror, blasting glass and metal all over the inside of the car. Sixto crouched down behind the open door and let go with three more rounds. Charlie could hear things breaking inside the store. The man disappeared again.

Sixto got in and pulled the door shut with a groan. "Start the car. The key's in it. Get us out of here before that clown comes back out."

Charlie started the car and spun out onto the road. As the tires caught on the asphalt, he heard the big gun boom again. Something hit the back of the car with a thunk.

"Man, if I wasn't hit, I'd go back there and kill that *cabron*. Head for the dam. We've got to get across before he gets to a phone and gets the word out."

"But you're hurt. We've gotta get you to a doctor."

"*Buey!*"

Charlie looked over. Sixto had the gun pointed at his side.

"Drive to the dam or get blown out the door. Your choice, *ese!*"

"God," thought Charlie, "I'm gonna be lucky to get out of this alive. Why didn't I walk away from this crazy man this afternoon when I had the chance? Oh, yeah, I was bored."

It was less than three miles to Davis Dam, but Charlie smelled steam, rubber, and hot metal as they approached. He looked down at the temperature gauge. The needle was moving toward the red.

"That guy must have put one through the radiator. We're getting hot."

"Just get us out of Arizona. Don't stop."

They drove across the dam into Nevada. Steam and smoke began to come through the vents.

"Turn onto the dike road and head downriver."

"I don't know how much farther this thing will make it."

"Take it as far as it will go. We gotta get out of sight. Turn off the headlights."

There was enough light from the big moon to see well enough to drive. Charlie couldn't see the temperature gauge with the dash lights off, but he really didn't need to. They weren't going to be driving much farther.

"Take that little side road there," said Sixto.

Charlie turned onto the narrow dirt road. Within a hundred feet, they were surrounded by mesquite thickets. Terrible sounds were coming from the engine compartment. They drove another mile or so, and then the car lurched a few times and stopped.

"I believe the engine has froze up."

"Yeah. We're going to have to walk from here. Get over here and help me out."

Charlie came around the car and opened the door. Sixto was rummaging in the glove compartment. He retrieved a box of .45 cartridges, a roll of nylon cord, a knife, and a flashlight and put them in the paper bag with the money and the food. He handed the bag to Charlie and then struggled to get out of the car.

"Gimme your hand. Come on, pull me up."

When Sixto got to his feet, Charlie could see blood on the seat where he had been sitting.

"You're going to have to help me here. I don't think I can walk very far on my own. But you listen to me! I'm hurt bad, but I ain't dying, so don't get any funny ideas about trying anything or running off."

They set off down the road, Sixto with his left hand over Charlie's shoulder and his right holding the .45, Charlie with the paper bag clutched in his left hand. Charlie had to admit that Sixto was one tough *hombre*. He didn't complain or moan despite the terrible wound that was soaking the right side of his shirt and Levi's with so much blood it glistened in the moonlight. Every once in a while, he let out a "*cabron*," but that was it.

They walked very slowly for a long time, with frequent stops for Sixto to rest. Finally, they came to a driveway that turned west off the road. They followed it. It was a long driveway, but eventually, it brought them to an abandoned house. Charlie could see a windmill rising above the house, the blades catching the moonlight as they spun. They went inside.

"Gimme the flashlight."

Charlie reached into the bag, found the flashlight, and handed it to Sixto. He turned it on.

"Now go on ahead of me, but real slow. Don't get more than a step or two away."

The flashlight had weak batteries. By the pale light of the beam, they could see nothing in the first room but a broken stool. They went toward the next room.

"Put your right hand on top of your head and open the door with your left hand.

Now go through the door and stop and put your other hand on your head."

After Sixto came through the door, he stopped inside the room and pointed the flashlight and the gun at Charlie.

"Push that door closed behind us. And don't try to duck around it!"

The room they were in was bigger than the first one. It seemed to be some kind of dining room and kitchen combination. As Sixto shone the flashlight around the room, Charlie could see a sink on the left-hand wall. There was an old-fashioned iron pump next to the sink.

Sixto gestured for him to move to the opposite wall, and then Sixto put the bag down and came over next to Charlie.

"I want you to get this shirt off me. But remember, this gun will be pointed at you the whole time."

While Charlie unbuttoned the shirt and pulled it off over one arm and then the other, Sixto was very careful to transfer the gun from hand to hand and keep it pointed at Charlie. Once the shirt was off, he gestured with the gun for Charlie to step away. He kept gesturing until Charlie was all the way in the corner.

Sixto angled his flashlight so he could see his injury. It was a through and through, but the exit wound was terrible. Even in the dim light from the weak beam, Charlie could see the bullet had taken big chunks of Sixto with it on its way out. He had lost a lot of blood and was still leaking. Even from across the room, Charlie could smell sweat and dust and blood.

"It don't feel like that bullet hit any bones. But it tore something loose inside of me."

Sixto gestured with the gun again.

"Take yourself over to that sink and see if you can find something that'll hold water. I'm dying of thirst. And don't walk out of the light, or I'll shoot you."

Charlie went to the sink and looked around. He found a small pan with a broken handle. He held it up for Sixto to see.

"Don't just show it to me. Fill it up and bring it here."

The pump was stiff with rust and clanked and groaned. Charlie pumped for a long time before anything came out. Finally, rusty water began to emerge from the spout. The water splashed onto the floor because the sink was no longer connected to a drain pipe. He pumped until the water looked better, then rinsed the pan and filled it. He started to take it to Sixto.

"Not so close, *ese*. Sit it on the floor and back up."

Sixto waited until Charlie had moved away. Then he put the flashlight on the floor and came forward and picked up the pan. He drained it in one long swallow.

"I'm going to toss it to you. Catch it and fill it up again. Then bring it back here and put it down in the same spot."

Sixto backed up and waited, then moved forward and picked up the pan and drained it again.

"One more time."

"I don't think you're supposed to drink a lot of water when you have a belly wound."

"How do you know?"

"Uh, I saw it in a movie once."

"Well, *chorro*, that's just great. You saw it in a movie. It must be right then. Jesus! Just fill the pan and bring it back."

Now get some for yourself. But no tricky moves. When you're done, put the pan in the sink and get over there in the corner and sit down."

When Charlie was sitting, Sixto moved to the opposite corner with the paper bag. He pointed the flashlight at Charlie.

"Now listen good. I'm going to pull the clip out of this gun and slide it to you. Then I'm going to slide this box of bullets over. I want you to put as many bullets in the clip as it will hold, then slide the clip and the box back to me. And remember, I've got one round in the chamber and another gun in my pocket. If you do anything stupid, I shoot you. Lots of times."

Charlie thumbed .45 cartridges into the clip until it wouldn't hold anymore. He slid the clip and then the box back to Sixto. Sixto slammed the clip back into the gun.

"Okay. You did good. Now I'm going to give you my knife and this cord. Cut me ten pieces of it. Make them all about three feet long. And don't fancy yourself some kind of a *cuchillero* just because you have a knife. That blade is no match for this gun."

When Charlie had finished cutting the pieces, Sixto told him to slide the knife back. Sixto put his foot on it. "Now listen to me. I don't trust you. I think you're a little *conejo,* and you'll run if you have the chance, so you' ain't getting no chance. I'm hurt, and I need some sleep, so I'm gonna tie you up, so I don't have to watch you. I'll untie you in the morning."

"What if I have to pee?"

"Piss in your pants. I don't care. You *Indios* all stink anyway. Now roll over on your stomach and put your hands behind your back. And don't turn your head to look at me."

Sixto got on the floor behind Charlie with some difficulty. He tied Charlie's feet first. He used two lengths of the cord to make it secure. Then he used two more lengths to bind Charlie's hands. He moved away without getting up.

"Now turn on your side and scoot around so you're facing the wall."

When Charlie complied, Sixto joined the ropes tying Charlie's hands and feet with another piece of the cord. Then he rested. Charlie held perfectly still.

"I'm going to go across the room into the corner and get some rest. I've got the gun and the flashlight. When I was in prison, I had to learn to sleep with one eye open. If you move any closer to me than you are right now, I'll shoot you. Guaranteed." He turned off the flashlight. He didn't say anything else until morning.

In a dark room, on a dusty floor, hog-tied, with the nylon cord biting into his wrists, Charlie Merriman began the longest night of his young life. His first thoughts were about the events that had unfolded from the moment Sixto sat next to him in The Palms. Then he thought about what would probably happen next. He could not see a way that things would turn out well for him. Why had he ever agreed to get into this loser's car?

His mind was spinning, and his thoughts were a jumble. He couldn't seem to make a plan. Earlier in the afternoon, he had been a young man without much future. Now he was a young man who might have no future at all. What a mess! What could he have done differently?

Charlie had been a good student in high school: one of the few good students from the Village. His teachers had encouraged him to plan on going to San Bernardino Valley Junior College after graduation. His counselor had taken it a step further: she had found financial aid for his books and living expenses.

What these well-meaning people didn't understand was that he couldn't leave the Colorado River. White people called his tribe the *Mojave,* but his tribe called itself *Pipa Aha Macav,* "the people of the river." The Colorado was the source of all life. It was the center of creation. The old ones taught the children from their earliest years that to leave the river for extended periods was to cut themselves off from life. Those who did this, the old ones taught, would die inside. They may continue to move around and eat and drink and breathe, but they would not really be alive.

So even if it were possible to go to a college close enough to the river valley to be able to return frequently, what value would be gained from going? He would still have to move back after he finished in order to stay close to the source of life and close to his tribe and his ancestors. And there were only two jobs to be had in Smoke Tree for Mojave Indians. The women could get minimum wage work as maids in the motels that lined 66, working for white people who did not respect or even like them. They cleaned up after people who stared at them like they were animals while leaving their rooms like pigsties when they checked out. The men could get minimum wage work on the railroad, doing the incredibly hard work of repairing tracks and roadbeds in 120 plus degree heat that sometimes warped the rails.

No one in Smoke Tree would hire a Mojave to do anything else, regardless of his or her level of education. He knew. He had seen it before. Had seen the young women come home with their A. A. degrees and search in vain for any work other than as a maid. He had once seen a motel owner haltingly read the instructions on the back of a bottle of cleaner to a young woman with almost enough units for a Bachelor's degree.

Disjointed thoughts and fears kept Charlie awake most of the night. He finally managed to doze but was jolted awake by the agony of his cramping thighs. He managed to keep from crying out, afraid that Sixto would start shooting. Later he fell asleep again but had terrible dreams.

Dreams were important to the Mojave. They believed it was through dreams that special gifts and powers were bestowed. But important dreams could only be achieved after trials and fasting – not on a floor covered with mouse droppings in an abandoned house, the hogtied, terrified prisoner of a crazy and evil man.

★ ★ ★

The pitch black of night had given way to the dark gray of false dawn before he really slept. The house was filled with light when he awoke to the sound of his tormentor's voice.

"Hey, *Indio,* wake up. Get me some water."

At first, Charlie was confused, but then the events of the previous day and night came rushing back. "You're going to have to untie me."

"Slide over here. I hurt too bad to go that far."

Charlie wriggled his way across the floor until he got close enough for Sixto to cut him free. Once he was loose, Sixto told him to scoot away before he got up. When he had moved away, he got to his hands and knees and then crawled to the doorway so he could hold onto the frame to get on his feet. His thighs screamed in agony when he straightened up.

He went to the sink for water. Sixto had him bring the water over, set it down, and then back away before he picked it up. He gulped it down and gestured with the pan for more. In the light of day, his exit wound looked like someone had chopped a chunk out of him with a dull ax. The wound was bleeding and seeping, and Sixto was in pain. He grimaced every time he moved.

He finished the second pan of water. The pan dropped from his hand. He stared at it. Then he fumbled in the bag beside him and dragged out a piece of jerky. He put it in his mouth and started to chew. He gagged and spit it out. Then he pulled a package of Twinkies from the bag and cut the cellophane with his knife. He ate half of one and then tossed it away.

"Tastes like crap."

"Sixto, I got to pee. I held it all night."

"No way you're going outside. Go over in the corner by the sink where I can see you. Piss on the wall or something."

When Charlie was done, he turned around.

"Come over here and sit in the corner where you was last night."

Charlie spent the morning in the corner watching Sixto suffer. But no matter how bad the big man must have felt, he never closed his eyes or put down the gun. He just sat with his back against the wall and stared out of his deep black eyes at the empty room, his feet splayed in front of him, blood and matter oozing from his wound. Around noon he turned his head and looked at Charlie.

"Stop staring at me. You ain't gonna get a chance to jump me. I'll shoot you before you get on your feet."

"Sixto, we can't just sit here. You're hurt. You've got to let me go bring back some help."

"Hah! That's great. The Indian goes for the cavalry. I let your skinny butt out that door; I'll never see you again. Just let me be. I hurt, and I need to think. I'll think of something. I been in bad spots before."

Around mid-afternoon, Sixto's bowels let go. He groaned in agony, and his wound began to bleed heavily again. He filled the room with an odor so foul that Charlie had to pull his shirt up over his face to keep from gagging. Sixto's breath was coming in pants. His head was canted at an odd angle. Finally, his breathing slowed, and he closed his eyes for the first time that day.

Charlie sat and watched him for a long time. He could no longer hear Sixto breathing. Charlie wanted very badly to be out of that room. Away from the crazy man with the big gun. Away from the crazy man with the terrible injury that would have killed anyone else hours ago. Away from the awful smell.

Sixto remained motionless. Flies were beginning to show up. They buzzed around his pants, where liquid was dripping on the floor. They crawled all over his wound. A fly landed on Sixto's face and explored the drool from his mouth. Still Sixto did not move.

Finally, when the flies were crawling all over the crazy man's body, Charlie leaned over sideways and slowly, quietly, got onto his hands and knees. Carefully, watching Sixto intently every moment, he began to push up onto his feet.

Sixto opened one eye. Charlie froze. The eye swiveled and glared at him.

"Who said you could get up, *pendejo*?"

"Uh, just stretching my legs. I'm getting cramps."

"What you're going to get is dead if you don't sit back down right where you were. You were going to sneak off, weren't you? That's just like a stinking Indian. Sneaking around. Well, I'm going to have to rest some more, so I'm going to tie you up again. Get on your belly and scoot over here."

As Charlie inched himself across the room, the hole in the middle of the .45 Sixto had pointed at him got bigger and bigger until it seemed like he was looking into a drainpipe. The stench got stronger. It was so powerful it made his eyes water. He thought he was going to vomit, but he choked it back because vomiting was a sudden move that might get him killed.

"Turn on your side. Face away from me. Scoot toward me until I tell you to stop.

Stop! Now listen to me, you skinny little Indian." He stopped and took several ragged breaths. "Sometimes, while I'm tying you up, I will have to put this gun down. But you won't know when. And even if you guess right, I can pick it up and shoot you before you can turn around."

Charlie lay on his side while Sixto tied his hands. He used two pieces of cord again. When he was still using the first piece, Charlie thought he sensed a moment when he could chance a move. The instant the thought crossed his mind, Sixto stopped.

"Damn," thought Charlie. "This guy is some kind of *brujo*."

"Get those bad thoughts out of your head, little red man. They can get you killed."

Sixto didn't say anything for a long time. Then he went back to work. When he was done with Charlie's hands, he had him inch along the floor till he was perpendicular to Sixto with his feet against Sixto's side.

"No, no, don't bend your knees. Keep your legs straight. I'm not having you kick at me. Uh uh."

Sixto tied his ankles. Charlie noticed he only used one piece of cord.

"He must be getting very tired," Charlie thought.

"Now move again until you're next to me."

Charlie did as he said.

"Now bend your knees and pull them toward your chest. Even if you do try to kick me, you can't do anything else, and I'll just shoot you." Sixto's voice was getting weaker, and he gasped between words.

Sixto tied the cords holding Charlie's hands to the cord binding his feet. Charlie was hog-tied on his side when he was finished, just like the night before. The countless flies that had been attracted by Sixto's wound and stink now crawled over Charlie's face. There was nothing he could do to stop them. They crawled inside his nose, and if he opened his mouth to get a deep breath to blow them out of his nose, they climbed into his mouth. He gagged, thinking about where they had been.

Sixto had tired himself while tying Charlie. He said nothing for a very long time. Charlie lay silently. He cursed the flies, Sixto's odors, and his own stupidity. But he was happy about one thing: Sixto had left the pocket knife open and lying next to his leg.

Nothing changed for the rest of the day. Charlie was trapped on his side, terrified, trussed, and harassed by the relentless flies. The day was perfectly still. The windmill did not turn. He couldn't even hear birds outside. He never heard a car passing on the road. Although it was November, it began to get hot in the house. He was very thirsty. But at least he was not hungry. The incredible stench in the airless room had killed his appetite.

Sixto never spoke again. He groaned now and then and grunted occasionally. He must have developed an infection because Charlie could feel heat from his body.

★ ★ ★

Late in the afternoon, Charlie heard the gun fall to the floor. Sixto made no response to the sound. As the daylight was beginning to fade, his breathing became more ragged. Sometimes he sounded as if there were an obstruction in his throat. As the final hint of daylight disappeared from the room, Charlie heard what he thought was Sixto's final breath.

At first Charlie wasn't sure. He quietly spoke Sixto's name. No response. He said it louder. Nothing.

"Hey," he yelled at the top of his voice. "Hey, Sixto. Wake up Sixto!"

Again, no response. Still, he listened intently for some sign of life. Then he realized the room was different somehow. He yelled again. The sound was muted, flat and empty. He was alone. Sixto was gone.

As the room darkened, the flies disappeared. There were no more bugs crawling on his face and into his nose and mouth. But the smell didn't go away. If anything, it got worse.

Charlie scooted closer to Sixto's body. He remembered approximately where the knife was, but it still took him a while to locate it since he was trying hard not to touch the corpse. Finally he got hold of the knife. Once he had it, he squirmed and wriggled until he was as far away as he could get.

But his difficulty was just beginning. He quickly learned he couldn't do much with the knife. He certainly couldn't use it to cut the cords binding his wrists. After a lot of trial and error, he managed to maneuver so that the sharp edge of the blade was at the right angle against the cord tying his ankles to his wrists. By holding the knife tightly and jerking his feet, he could make the knife rub against the cord and hopefully begin to fray the nylon a strand at a time. But the cord was thick, and the knife wasn't very sharp. Plus, the movement was very tiring and made his shoulders ache. He had to stop often to rest.

More and more frequently, his wrists cramped up, and he couldn't hold onto the knife. Then he had to start all over: squirm around, pick up the knife and struggle to get the sharp side angled against the cord, and start jerking around like a fish out of water again.

Chapter 2

AEDEN

When my friends and I were young, we did not understand the importance of the past. We thought when something happened, and there were no immediate consequences, the event simply disappeared, much like an image rapidly receding in a rear-view mirror. We were unaware the past could leave dormant roots waiting deep beneath the surface to put forth tendrils that could wrap themselves around the future.

As I grew older, I began to learn that lesson. But I was a slow learner. It was years before I fully connected the chain of events we unwittingly set in motion the night we burned down the House of Three Murders. The fire itself was a silly accident, but what should have been a harmless mistake changed the lives of all of us and ruined the lives of some.

On Thursday, November 3, 1960, at twenty minutes after five o'clock, a full moon rose above Boundary Cone, a dead volcanic remnant south of Oatman, Arizona. Although it was November, the temperature at sundown had been over eighty degrees. In the cloudless sky, the moon lifted huge and brilliantly yellow above the twisted basalt forms of the Black Mountains. As it rose, it bathed the isolated Mojave Desert town of Smoke Tree, California, on the west side of the Colorado River in a soft, warm glow. The closest town of any size was Las Vegas, over a hundred miles to the north.

In the moonlight, the town looked almost pretty. It wasn't. Smoke Tree was a dry, dusty, drab, cobbled-together collection of railroad housing, low-income projects, and an odd mishmash of privately owned homes of no particular design or merit. The only uniform architecture was provided by two small, nondescript housing tracts built cheaply, without grace, style, or landscaping, on the west edge of town.

As the moon lifted higher, I watched it from a sharply raised berm just across the street from our house. The berm marked the southwest edge of the newer of the two tracts in Smoke Tree. When the developer had finished grading the three-street subdivision out of the rock and sand of the desert and building the houses, he pushed all the extra dirt into a four-foot-high berm on top of everything he didn't want to pay to haul away: lumber, drywall scraps, empty paint cans, wiring, chunks of concrete, pieces of rebar and discarded section of conduit. He marked the three streets in the tract with ugly signs made by welding sheet metal to posts. The street names were crookedly stenciled in black paint.

On the west side of the berm, a large gully dropped down into the Mojave Desert, rolling away to the west. The desert, unimpressed by the little town, lay patiently waiting in the darkness for the place to crumble and disappear and for the next few million years to pass by. As I stood on the berm looking down on my neighborhood, bats and nighthawks flew over my head into town to hunt bugs flying around the streetlights.

I was listening to hear Johnny Quentin come up Jordan Street hill in his '52 Ford coupe. At first, I could hear only neighborhood sounds: the murmur of a television, a sprinkler oscillating in a neighbor's yard, a dog barking somewhere down the street. From the desert behind me, I heard the yipping and howling of the pack of coyotes at the base of Bump Hill, a half-mile west of town. The sound was carried on a soft breeze coming out of the northwest. From farther to the west, I could hear the deep thrum of diesel locomotives dragging a long freight train up South Pass.

Then I heard, far away, the sound of a flathead V8 winding hard in second gear, then dropping into third. I pictured Johnny racing up the hill, his eyes moving back and forth between the road and his rearview mirror, checking for the police trying to catch him speeding. The sound grew in volume as the car approached the top of Jordan Street, then ratcheted down to popping and snapping as his glass packs caught the back pressure when he crested the hill and lifted off the gas. As his car flashed past the deserted Little League park and the first house at the top of the hill, a phone was probably lifted off the hook as Mrs. Crooks dialed the police station to tell them 'that darn Johnny kid' was speeding past her window again. By the time his car made the two turns that brought him up our street, the noise had dropped to a low, resonating burble.

The coupe approached our house, and I walked off the berm. I could see Johnny's face reflected in the greenish glow from his dashboard lights, his long hair glistening with Brylcream. I knew his comb would be in the pocket of his white T-shirt.

I crossed the street and got into the car.

"Where we going first?"

"Pick up Judy."

Judy was Johnny's girlfriend. She had transformed Johnny from the relaxed, easy-going guy I had hunted, fished, and played sports with since junior high school into someone different. He was still my best friend, loyal and good-hearted, but he had changed in many ways. He was obsessed with Judy. She was not only the most important thing in his life, she completely dominated it. He hung on her every word and gesture. He worried constantly that she would grow tired of him and find someone new.

"Then what?"

"Places to go, places to roll."

As Johnny let out the clutch, I reached over and turned on the radio. As usual, it was set on KOMA out of Oklahoma City, the only rock and roll station strong enough to reach our town. The Drifters were singing, "There Goes My Baby." I liked that one, since it seemed my baby was indeed "moving on down the line." A year older than I, she had left for college in August, and already her letters were dwindling. I cranked up the volume. We drove slowly down the hill toward town. The Drifters continued their sad song, and a breeze blew through the open windows.

"Why so slow?"

"Old lady Crooks probably called the cops when I blew by. Officer Sutcliffe will be parked in a driveway at the bottom of the hill, hoping to catch me."

Sure enough, just before we reached Broadway, we saw a black and white in the driveway of a vacant house. It was parked well back in the shadows.

Johnny laughed. "These guys are so predictable."

At Broadway, we made a right turn and drove slowly past a long stretch of old houses. Soon we came to the town's only traffic light. At that intersection, the traffic on Route 66 merged into Broadway. As usual, it took a long time for the light to turn green: 66 traffic took priority over town traffic. When it changed, Johnny let out the clutch and we moved on into the downtown.

It was odd to move from a small-town street into the flow of Route 66, a major highway, even though it was still "Broadway," our main street. With the exception of cars that had turned north toward Las Vegas as they left Barstow, all of the eastbound traffic from the Los Angeles area funneled through Smoke Tree. Entering 66 was like paddling down a tiny creek that flowed into a big river.

We drove through town with the 66 traffic. The gas stations, restaurants and courtyard motels were all one-story buildings. The only exceptions were Milner's Market, the Central Hotel and the Majestic Theater. Then the business district was behind us, and there were houses on both sides of 66 again. The ones on the east side were small, wood-frame houses. They were all painted the drab, yellowish-orange color of a Santa Fe Railroad reefer car, but they were well maintained and had neat, clipped yards.

After we passed them, the road turned southwest to parallel the Santa Fe tracks coming in from the east. A switch engine was clanking around the rail yard, making up a train with a string of reefers from the ice house: fruit and vegetables from the coast re-iced to go east. I could see water dripping from the cars and smell the sharp tang of citrus. With the tracks on our left, we drove past more service stations. There were small motels and a couple of bars on the right side of the highway before we drove up the hill toward the south edge of town. Just past the top of the rise, we turned off 66 onto a street that led to "the heights."

Nearly everyone in Smoke Tree worked for the Santa Fe. Most of those who didn't either had jobs related to the traffic on Route 66 or worked for the school district. The heights was home to the few families in town who had any significant money. The homes on the flanks of the heights were owned by local doctors, dentists, lawyers and the more successful merchants in town. Their homes were almost all ranch-style.

At the crest of the heights was the ornate house where Judy McPhearson lived. The fronds of the tall fan palms lining both sides of the house whipped noisily in the wind. Directly in front of the house were two huge cottonwood trees. Backlit by the lights on the front veranda, their leaves were just beginning to turn golden yellow.

We pulled into the circular drive. Johnny shut off the engine and opened his door.

"Just honk the horn and get her out here so we can go."

"Are you kidding? Her old man expects me to come in and ask permission to have his daughter go out with me. You'd better come in too. Mrs. McPhearson's probably peeping out between the curtains right now, and she'll want to know who you are."

I got out and we headed toward the house. As we walked, I saw Johnny undergo a transformation. Between the time we left the car and the time we climbed the steps to the door, his usual confidence evaporated. His relaxed, easy gait was gone. With every step his shoulders inched a little closer to his ears, and his head dropped lower.

Johnny took a deep breath, let it out with a sigh, and pushed the doorbell. A "Big Ben" chime sounded from deep inside the house. Heavy footsteps approached and Benedict McPhearson pulled the door open. I had seen him a few times in his expensive car, but never up close. He was a big man with sandy hair, a sunburned face and more stomach than he needed, but even though he was overweight, there was nothing soft looking about him. There was nothing friendly about him either. He looked past us to the driveway.

"Johnny, that piece of junk had better not leak oil on my driveway. Those flagstones cost more than your car."

"Nossir, she's tight. Never leaks a drop."

He stepped back and pulled the door open. "Come on in."

We walked into the house. There was a large vestibule that led to a staircase. There were rooms on either side of the staircase and the hallway continued toward the back of the house. The room to the left was a dining room. I could see a massive table surrounded by at least ten chairs, towered over by a gaudy chandelier.

We entered the huge room on the right. One side of the room was open to the staircase. Inside the room were a number of overstuffed, wingback chairs and two large couches. Both couches had coffee tables in front of them. There were magazines neatly arranged on each of the tables. I could see *Life, Look,* and *the Saturday Evening Post.* There were oil paintings on the wall. A woman was sitting in one of the chairs. She lifted her eyes from her Reader's Digest Condensed Book.

"Good evening, Johnny."

"Evening Mrs. McPhearson. How are you?"

"Fine, Johnny, fine. Aren't you going to introduce me to your friend?"

"This is Ade."

"Ade? What an odd name!"

"It's Aeden, Mrs. McPhearson, Aeden Snow. Everybody calls me Ade."

As if I weren't standing there, she said, "Benedict, do we know Aeden's family?"

"No."

"Why don't you boys sit down and visit a while? I am just so curious about the lives of the people who live in this town."

"Eileen, they don't want to talk to grown-ups. They want to be on their way. Judy! Hey Judy! Get on down here. Your Homecoming King is here."

"Isn't that exciting, Aeden? Johnny and Judy are royalty: homecoming king and queen."

"Yes ma'am. I guess it is."

I heard a door close somewhere upstairs and then saw Judy McPhearson come skipping lightly down the stairs, a smile on her face. All her best features were on display. She was stunning. Her beauty was so overwhelming that she was hard to see. I know that sounds crazy, but it was true. I usually tried to look at her obliquely so she would not think I was staring, because so many boys did stare at her. But even when I looked at her head-on, it was as if I saw her through some sort of hazy mist and could not quite bring her into focus.

★ ★ ★

Judy had an angelic look. Her cascading blonde hair and blue eyes set slightly too far apart gave her a startled, innocent expression. Her skin was flawless, with only the faintest hint of freckles over the bridge of a nose perfectly proportioned to her face, a nose that set off full lips and a well-formed chin. All this and a body that was the stuff of male adolescent fantasies. And yet, there was a coldness to her that set my teeth on edge.

Case in point: when she first came to Smoke Tree High, a lot of guys asked her out. She refused every time she was asked. Then Stanley Appleton, a good-hearted boy in our class who was just a little slow, thought the new girl might be lonely. He walked up to her at lunch one day and said, "Hello, Judy, I'm Stanley. I think you're just the prettiest girl in the school. I don't know why you don't have any dates. Would you like to come out with me to the pictures?"

"The pictures?"

"A movie show."

"Are you for real?"

"Yes. They have some real nice movies. I don't have a car, but we could meet there. I'd be glad to buy your ticket and some popcorn."

Judy stared at him for a moment in disbelief.

"I don't know what makes you think I would ever want to go out with you. Keep away from me."

She turned and walked away, leaving Stanley staring after her with sad eyes.

But my opinion of Judy McPhearson was not one held in common with others. The boys at Smoke Tree High School were in awe of her. They turned into simpering, loose-jointed idiots in her presence. No matter how hard they tried to appear cool and casually unimpressed, all she had to do was speak to one of them, and he became unhinged and tongue-tied. Grown men would sometimes stop in the street when she passed and stare after her. I had seen this more than once, despite sharp words from their wives.

Johnny could maintain his poise in her presence. He could even feign a slightly disinterested, oh-so-what attitude when she spoke to him. And Johnny saw everything in life as a competition. I think he saw getting Judy to go out with him as some kind of a challenge. I was standing next to him when he asked her at lunch one day if she'd like to go driving in his car. It went like this:

"Judy, why don't you come out with me some night?"

"Come out where?"

"Oh, nowhere, in particular, just driving around. Aren't you a little tired of sitting home alone on top of that hill every night? It's time you stepped out some evening."

I think she was so amazed she could not flatten him with a single flutter of her eyes that she said "yes."

But Johnny's nonchalance was an act. He had rehearsed his speech in front of a mirror until he had it down pat. In spite of that, I think he was surprised when she accepted. And her acceptance started the high school romance of the decade in our little town. That was in March of our junior year, but it was five months before Judy's parents even knew their daughter was "dating" Johnny, though it was a stretch to say their encounters were real dates.

Judy only had one friend, and that was Linda Bergstrom, my girlfriend. Most of the girls at Smoke Tree High were either intimidated by Judy or jealous of her effect on the boys. Linda was neither, so she and Judy got along. When Johnny and Judy had one of their "dates," they would drive down to Topock and back, listening to rock and roll on KOMA. On those nights, Linda would pick Judy up at her house and take her to the old road that led to the ice house. Johnny would meet them there.

After Johnny and Judy drove off, Linda would drive across town and meet me near the Foster's Freeze. She would park behind the stand and get into my car, and we would drive "laps" from one end of town to the other, waving at the other kids who were doing the same thing. Then I'd take her back to her car so she could meet Judy on the ice house road at a pre-arranged time.

For Judy, it was all a game, something to do to pass the time in a boring little town. I suppose it amused her to be dating the most popular guy at Smoke Tree High. It was different for Johnny. He fell hopelessly, helplessly in love with her the first night they went riding in his car.

I don't know how long it would have taken for Johnny to meet Judy's parents if Linda hadn't graduated in June of '60. When she left for Westmont College in Santa Barbara in August, Judy lost her cover story for leaving the house at night. By late August, Judy realized she had to break the news to her mother and father that she had a boyfriend. She was worried about how they'd react, but it went pretty well. They invited Johnny over for a barbeque on Labor Day weekend, and Johnny, who could be very charming when he put his mind to it, won over Mrs. McPhearson. Benedict was not impressed at all but knew he was out-numbered, and he accepted Johnny as not-the-most-terrible temporary escort for Judy.

But it was a grudging compliance. Benedict McPhearson had big-ger plans for Judy than getting involved with Johnny Quentin. I don't think it was Johnny, in particular, he objected to – I think he just saw Johnny as the pick of a pathetic litter. Benedict had decided Judy was going to USC in the fall. Not just to study there but to meet a young man of substance and promise, someone who would be worthy of Judy in a way that none of the Smoke Tree boys could be.

This disdain for the locals was part of the McPhearson mystique. They had shown up in Smoke Tree at the beginning of our junior year in high school. It was early October, and school had already started when Judy enrolled. One day the McPhearsons weren't in Smoke Tree; the next day they were. They blew into town like an Indian summer dust devil and reshaped the hierarchy of not only the school but the entire town.

Their arrival solved a mystery that had captivated the town gossips since May of the previous year. Benedict bought the Swanson place at the top of the heights before anyone in town knew it was for sale. The sale was handled by an out-of-town realtor, and no one in town had any information about the buyer. The Swanson place was, far and away, the grandest house in Smoke Tree, but Benedict had it torn down! The only things left were the two rows of fan palms and the two massive cottonwoods.

Between the palms and behind the cottonwoods, a contractor from the coast built an exact replica of the Kimberly Crest French Chateau built in Redlands during the California Victorian period. The house, with its asymmetrical roofline, was made entirely of unpainted cement, giving it a stark and harsh appearance in spite of the ornate design. It had multiple towers and spires and impossibly-steep roofs. The only colors were provided by the green shingles on the steep roofs and the faux-gold metal caps on the spires decorated with tri-color pennants. On the northwest side of the house, the builder recreated the Kimberly Crest carriage house as a garage.

The contractor was told to reproduce the sweeping expanse of concrete that fronted the Redlands chateau and include the fountain in the center. However, Benedict did not have him make any attempt to recreate the lush grounds and extensive walkways of the original project that stood inside an orange grove in Redlands. The McPhearson chateau simply sat flush with the surrounding desert without as much as a flower bed or a blade of grass surrounding it. In front of the chateau was a circular flagstone driveway. Branching off the circular drive on the east was a narrow strip of concrete that looped around the house to the ornate garage.

The finished project was as out of place as an orchid in a dry lake bed. On a hot summer day, the chateau looked embarrassed. On a cold and windy winter day, it looked depressed.

The McPhearson family itself was an enigma to the town. Benedict and Eileen did not mingle with the townspeople. They were mailed many invitations. They declined them all, but the local social set never stopped asking. They had their groceries delivered by Milner's market. They bought their clothes and took care of their personal grooming and medical needs in Las Vegas. There were rumors that Benedict had made his early money in the trucking business and then quietly bought into a number of the big casinos in Las Vegas, but those rumors were never substantiated and probably never would be. In the 1950s, the mafia ran Las Vegas. Prying into the unofficial ownership of a Las Vegas casino was not a good idea.

The only contact Benedict had with the locals was at the gas station. His entire exchange consisted of: "Fill'er up with ethyl. No, I don't want you to check under the hood. How much do I owe you? Keep the change." He always had a pair of the newest model Cadillac Eldorados. They were always the same color: a custom, candy-apple red, bought no one knew where. Benedict would simply leave town alone in one Eldorado and come back a day later with a newer one.

This aura of mystery drove everyone in town crazy. There was endless speculation about where the McPhearsons had come and why they had moved to Smoke Tree. The speculation was fueled by the fact that there were sometimes two very large, very quiet men at the McPhearson house. In winter or fall, the men wore navy blazers, khaki pants, and highly-polished loafers. In summer and spring, the blazers and shirts and ties were replaced by Hawaiian shirts.

The men would appear a few days before the McPherson family went out of town. While they were there they were rarely seen outside the house, and never downtown. One of them would stay at the house while the McPhearsons were gone; the other would act as the family chauffeur. As they drove out of town, Benedict would be sitting in front with the driver: Mrs. McPhearson, and Judy in back.

When Benedict took Judy to Smoke Tree High to enroll her, he demanded a personal meeting with the superintendent of the district. The only news anyone could pry out of Lettie, Superintendent Symington's secretary, was that Benedict had made it very clear he would sue the district if any information about his daughter was leaked. To make sure the superintendent knew he meant business, he carried a letter addressed to the district from the senior partner in the biggest law firm on the West Coast.

But what really settled the issue was that Superintendent Symington considered Smoke Tree a stepping stone to a political career at the state level. Benedict somehow knew of this, and in his meeting with the Superintendent, Benedict dropped some powerful political and financial names along with assertions about serious help down the road if his wishes were met.

After the meeting, the word went out from Superintendent Symington to his secretary and to Principal Flowers that the McPhearson file would not be available for inspection. Superintendent Symington examined the transcripts himself and pronounced Judy a junior in good academic standing at STHS. The file itself disappeared into his office.

From the beginning, Judy had a strained relationship with the girls at Smoke Tree High. None of them, with the exception of Linda, were ever invited to the McPhearson house, and any attempts they made to get close to Judy were rebuffed. After Linda left for college, Judy was even more isolated. I think that isolation made her relationship with Johnny more important. She accepted me as Johnny's pal and talked to me at school from time to time, but although she pretended we were friends, I knew we really were not.

★ ★ ★

As Judy reached the bottom of the stairs, her mother spoke.

"Show me your outfit, dear."

Judy turned in a slow twirl, her plaid, three-quarter-length skirt dropping over bobby socks. Her shoes were saddle oxfords. She had Johnny's letterman's sweater on over her blouse.

"Dear, are you sure that's dressy enough? After all, you are the homecoming queen."

"Certainly Mother, we're just going to a bonfire."

"I know, dear. I just want you to be seen in the best light."

"Enough, Eileen. She's dressed okay. She wants to go, don't you, sweetheart?"

"Yes, Daddy, we do have to get going. Good night, Mother. Good night, Daddy."

"Have a good time, sweetheart. And Johnny, home by ten. This is a school night."

"Yessir — by ten, sir."

"Nice to meet you, Mr. And Mrs. McPhearson." But they had already forgotten me.

And we were out the door. As we walked down the steps, Johnny underwent the earlier transformation in reverse. His step grew lighter, his shoulders moved to their normal position, and his head came up. He moved with his natural grace. It was obvious Benedict McPhearson intimidated Johnny.

I opened the door, tilted the passenger seat forward, and got in the back. Judy got in the front and slid to the middle. Johnny closed the door for her, got in, and started the car.

"Ade, sit up front with us."

"Yes, Aeden, come on up. It's hard to talk to you when you're back there."

"No, I'm good."

Johnny laughed and started the car. I noticed there were no extra revs to make the glass packs pop and crackle. He just let out the clutch and idled out of the flagstone driveway onto the street.

"So, where to, people?"

"We don't have to be at the field for the bonfire before seven-thirty. Let's just take a ride."

"Okay. I'm going to stop at Renee's for a minute. Missed dinner tonight."

Johnny missed a lot of dinners. His mom died when we were still in junior high, and he and his dad lived in an old, two-story wood-frame house that echoed with Mrs. Quentin's absence. Cleaning was minimal; meals were hit-and-miss. His dad mostly drank and listened to Hank Williams and Lefty Frizzel records. Johnny came and went as if he lived alone.

We pulled into the parking lot at Renee's on Broadway.

"Judy, anything for you?"

"A root beer float would be real nice."

"Ade?"

"Nothing, thanks."

Johnny got out and walked with his rolling, athletic gait to the window.

Judy turned toward me, one side of her face in shadow, her head backlit by the orange neon sign of the burger stand. It occurred to me that she was as beautiful as any of the movie stars we saw at the theater on Saturday nights.

"Ade, have you heard from Linda?"

"Less and less. She told me she would be coming back for homecoming, but that was a couple of weeks ago. I guess we have a date for the dance tomorrow night, but I'm not sure anymore."

"I've had a few letters. She sounds very happy, and she seems to be very excited about college. She just *loves* Santa Barbara. You must know that she always wanted to be out of Smoke Tree?"

"Yes, I knew that. She doesn't seem to be homesick."

"No, she doesn't."

"Judy, is there something you're not telling me?"

"I think she may have met someone special. She's mentioned this one guy a few times now."

That's what I had been afraid of. Shot out of the saddle from four hundred miles away. I realized Judy had enjoyed telling me about Linda's new guy.

Johnny came back with a sack of burgers, a coke, and Judy's float. Grease was already bleeding through the sack. He set to work on the burgers, making each of them disappear in three bites. I sat in the back seat, absorbing what Judy had told me. I wasn't surprised, but that didn't make it any easier. The night seemed sadder and less interesting.

Johnny finished demolishing his dinner, wadded up the wrappers, and stuffed them into the sack.

"So, where should we go?"

Judy didn't answer for a few minutes, just spooned the ice cream out of her float and stared out the window at the cars rolling by on 66. She finished her last bite of ice cream and handed the mug to Johnny. He got out, threw the sack in the trash, and took the mug up to the window.

When he came back, she said, "Let's skip the whole thing."

Looking back, I think he was hurt that she didn't want to go. I know he liked to be seen with her – liked for them to be seen as a couple in public. I think he had been looking forward to the ceremony of it – the king and his beautiful queen lighting the homecoming bonfire. But he didn't say any of this. He could never deny her anything.

"Sure, it's stupid anyway. They can light the bonfire without us."

"So, what are we going to do, Johnny? Everybody's going to be at the field for the bonfire: Coach, Principal Flowers, the team. If we don't show up, they'll wonder where we are."

"Let's get out of town. We'll go up River Road and out to the old Boy Scout camp. We can go to water-gauge beach and watch the river roll in the moonlight."

"Sounds romantic, but not for three people. I'm a third wheel here. Just drop me home."

"Oh, come on, Ade. Come along."

It occurred to me Judy didn't want to be alone with Johnny under the moonlight. But Johnny never argued with her.

"Forget that third wheel stuff, Ade. We're all going."

Johnny pulled out of the lot, and we joined the stream of traffic moving north on Broadway. The black and white that had been hiding at the bottom of Jordan Street hill passed us going the opposite direction. Johnny waved. Officer Sutcliffe didn't.

We stayed on Route 66 as it moved north beyond the city limits. Two miles out of town, 66 veered due west, but we turned off the highway and continued north on River Road. We passed Sunset Beach and entered a stretch of low desert hills. Occasional houses appeared, desolate-looking places surrounded by salt cedars, abandoned vehicles, and collections of junk. People living lives even more isolated than the people in the little town.

The road twisted and turned through hills and gullies. Creosote bushes and ghostly white bursage flashed by on both sides of the road. Johnny tried to drive the Ford as if it were a sports car, going hard into the corners, downshifting and accelerating coming out of the curves. But it was an overweight, underpowered Ford coupe that yawed and pitched like a bathtub in heavy seas.

After ten miles, we arrived at the top of Piute Wash, a deep, wide, and sandy arroyo that flooded when heavy rains fell in the mountains to the northwest. I thought Johnny would lift off the gas at the top of the bluff overlooking the wash, but he didn't. He kept the throttle wide open, and after a nearly vertical drop of three hundred feet, we were going over seventy-five when we hit the bottom.

The weak suspension couldn't handle the impact. The frame bottomed on the asphalt road, sending showers of sparks into the air. Somehow, he kept the car from flying off the road into the sand, but we careened from lane to lane while he fought the steering. Judy shrieked. I banged my head against the roof and bounced all over the back seat. By the time the car was under control, we were leaving the wash and entering the river bottom. We passed the Warren ranch on the east side of the road.

Instantly everything changed from a wide-open desert to dense stands of tamarisk and mesquite. The temperature dropped ten degrees, and the humidity rose sharply. The road changed from sub-standard blacktop to dirt and sand. A cloud of dust began to billow behind us. But just to call it dust doesn't do it justice. The river bottom was filled with millions of years of silt from Colorado, Utah, and Nevada that had settled out of the wandering Colorado River. As fine as talcum powder, the silt would hang in the air for a long time after a car passed.

We came to an intersection of dirt roads in the river bottom. Johnny slowed and took the road that ran off to the right. We were, by now, deep into the mesquite thickets, the thorny trees so close together and low to the ground that it was nearly impossible to walk between them or crawl underneath them. The moon, which had risen farther above the horizon, filled the sky with a pale, opaque glow, casting eerie shadows under the mesquites. Occasional salt cedars leaned on either side of the road, their long needles ghostly in the moonlight.

We broke clear of the mesquites and turned north on the road that bordered the river, the mesquites now forming a wall on our left. After a mile, the thickets began to recede farther and farther from the road. I knew we were getting close to the spot where the very southwest corner of Nevada touched the California border at the Colorado River.

We came to a clearing. Large salt cedars surrounded the area but opened to the edge of the river. There was no one at the camp. Johnny let the car roll to a stop and turned off the engine. The cloud of silt that had been following caught up with us, falling softly on the car. Johnny and Judy rolled up the windows, but I could already feel the grit between my teeth. The only sound was the popping of the manifolds as they cooled and the murmur of the river at the bottom of the embankment.

When the dust had settled, Johnny got out. Judy slid across the seat behind him. I pulled myself out of the other door. Johnny walked over to the cut above the river and scrambled down the steep embankment. Judy followed. I stood above them, looking down at their upturned faces.

"I'm going to take a walk up the road. Don't go off without me — it's a long walk home."

I turned and headed north on the road. On my right, the Colorado hurried past, deep and dark, gurgling noisily as it fought to erode the bank. To my left were the salt cedar trees, and beyond them, the mesquite thickets. The musty smell of the ancient silt in the damp river bottom surrounded me. As I walked, I scanned the road ahead for sidewinders.

Before long, the salt cedars fell away, and I was in the open. The road I was on turned onto the dike created by the Bureau of Reclamation when the Colorado was dredged and captured inside what was essentially a very wide and very deep ditch. Outside the cover of the trees, the moon was brighter, and while the world around was more visible, it had a mysterious cast. As I walked farther up the road, there was a slough on the left side of the road. The slough had been created by water that had leaked out of the main channel over many years. The bank nearest me was lined with reeds and cattails, while on the other side desert willows competed with tamarisk for possession of the shore.

I came to one of the many small turnouts in the dike road – a small projection about thirty feet long that jutted into the river. These projections were all along the river. They were lined with boulders to break up the speed of the river and keep it from eating away the banks and escaping the engineered channel.

I walked to the end of the turnout. I looked around the base for snakes and then took a seat on a large rock. I sat there listening to the constant gurgle of the river and watching the moon climb higher above the Black Mountains in Arizona. Every now and then, I could hear a fish jump out in the river or hear a beaver slap its tail in the slough behind me.

I thought about a lot of things. I thought about Linda and her new boyfriend in Santa Barbara. I thought about my friend Johnny, in way over his head in a relationship with someone who loved only herself. I thought about her mysterious family suddenly appearing in our town – a family that was secretive and intensely private.

After a while, I stopped thinking about anything in particular, but troubled images flickered through my head as I looked across the eddying and swirling river. The Arizona shore lay bathed in moonlight two hundred yards away. Over there were many more mesquite thickets and much more empty space. There was not a single light between the far bank and the distant mountains. I listened to the music the river made as it flowed and curled around the rocky point where I sat. I could see the sand churned up by the current and smell the cold water. An occasional bat swooped down and snatched a bug from just above the river.

I don't know how long I sat there, but the moon had moved much higher in the eastern sky by the time I got off the rock. When I got back to the camp, Johnny and Judy were in the car. Johnny was stretched out across the front seat, his feet sticking out the driver's side window, his head in Judy's lap.

"If Benedict McPhearson could see you now."

Johnny sat up. "Don't even joke about that, Ade."

"Hey guys, what now? Back on Preston Field, they've given up on us, and the bonfire is going. We could ease back into town, and nobody would notice."

"Why hurry? You don't have to be home for a while. We've got this perfect night on the river bottom all to ourselves, and I just thought of something we could do. Aeden, have you ever heard of the House of Three Murders?"

"I've heard of it, but I don't know where it is."

"It's not far from where we are right now."

"Oooh, that name puts a chill up my spine. Who got murdered?"

"Let me tell you the story the way I heard it from my dad. It was a long time ago, back in the 1920s. The Santa Fe was running steam then. My dad says this was a real railroad town. The Santa Fe was even more important than now. There was a big roundhouse that was busy around the clock, and there was a Harvey House at the depot. Everything looked different. The river hadn't been dredged yet, and it would flood some years: flood out the whole river bottom and half the town.

Anyway, there was this guy. His name was Sven Thorvaldsen. He was a brakeman. He bought this piece of land, forty acres, on the west edge of the river bottom. People didn't usually buy land right on the river in those days because sometimes the floods were so big that afterward, the river would be in a completely different place. You know how the border between us and Arizona is the middle of the river? Well, sometimes after these floods, people who had been living in Arizona found themselves living in California and vice versa.

Anyway, this Thorvaldsen guy buys forty acres and puts down a well. There's water out here in the bottom – that's why all the salt cedars and mesquite and cottonwoods. The water's full of alkali and doesn't smell or taste very good, but you can drink it and not get sick. So he drills. He gets a stock tank and a windmill. He builds a little house. He builds a corral out back and buys a couple of horses to ride. He gets a steer or two. Fancies himself a bit of a cowboy. He builds a pigpen, too, and gets a couple of hogs. Gets some chickens.

This is not easy work, but he does every lick of it himself. He's a quiet guy and keeps to himself. He doesn't have many friends. He hauls everything out here all the way from Smoke Tree in an old Model T truck, driving a road that's nothing but dirt and sand and rocks.

It takes him a couple of years to finish. Of course, there's no electricity and no indoor plumbing, but he doesn't mind. He lives out here alone another year or two, and then the Depression hits. In those days, if you had enough seniority to hang onto your job, you were in the tall clover because you had income. And Thorvaldsen has the seniority. He has a job paying good money in hard times, and he can buy things he couldn't have afforded before because everything gets real cheap.

By now, Hoover dam has been built, and he doesn't have to worry about floods, so he buys another ten acres right on the river, close to here. He's sitting pretty, but he's lonely out here, so he gets himself one of those mail-order brides from Sweden."

"Wait a minute. I thought all that mail order bride stuff was in the old West."

"The way I heard from my dad, the Depression hit Europe really hard, even harder than here. So these big families all of a sudden had too many mouths to feed, and they were always trying to get rid of a few.

Anyway, Thorvaldsen ends up with this young Swedish girl, blonde hair down to forever, blue eyes, great figure, a real looker. When she gets off the train in Smoke Tree, Thorvaldsen just about falls over. He can't believe his eyes or his luck. Lord knows what he looks like to her, a big homely guy in his forties with bad teeth.

So he puts her up at the Harvey House for a couple of days, just until they can get the license and have the justice of the peace marry them. In the meantime, every train crew in town gets a real good look at her in the dining hall, and believe me, they are interested in Miss Sweden.

After a few days, they get married, and Thorvaldsen hauls her off to his house on the edge of the river bottom. This is early April, so it's not bad out here. The big winds that blow down the river out of the north are over, and the terrible heat hasn't hit yet. She settles in.

I guess she was a farm girl back in Sweden, so she doesn't much mind slopping the hogs, feeding the horses, and gathering eggs. I don't know what she thinks about the occasional sidewinder that crawls up on the porch or comes right into the house, but I guess she does all right. The way I heard the story, she even gets a good garden going and plants a few posies around the house.

Then it gets to be summer. Nothing this gal has ever seen prepares her for the awful heat of July and August. There are days, sometimes four or five in a row, with the temperature over a hundred and twenty and made worse by the humidity in the river bottom. Of course, there's still no electricity out here, so she can't even have a fan to move the hot air around inside the house. At night when she lights an oil lamp to try to read, the temperature within a few feet of the lamp goes up another five degrees. She probably thinks she's died and gone to hell.

It isn't long before she wonders why she's ever come here. And it isn't made easier by the fact that her new husband is a jealous man. He knows all about the remarks some of the guys had made about her good looks, and he isn't about to tempt anyone further by taking her into town unless it is necessary.

But he has to take her to town at times to buy clothing or supplies or see the doctor or the dentist, so people in town do see her from time to time. It's a little town like it is now, but even more cut off from the rest of the world. So anything at all that happens in town gets talked about, and anything about this beautiful Swedish girl, Liska is her name, is big news and gets chewed over and spit out and chewed over some more. My dad says the way he heard it, it was hard to tell who was worse, the men or the women.

But there's one guy, Bobby Schoen, who decides to do more than talk about her. He decides to drive out and see her. He considers himself something of a ladies' man. He works in the dispatch office, so he knows which men are on a crew headed west to Barstow or east to Williams and knows how long they will probably be gone. So, one night, when Thorvaldsen is on the mainline for Barstow, he fires up his Model T and heads out the river road. Nobody knows anything about what happens that first time, but I like to think he starts out here with a box of chocolates melting on the seat beside him and maybe a flower or two.

Whatever happens, Bobby Schoen soon becomes a regular visitor to the little house. Every time Thorvaldsen catches a trip that will keep him out of town overnight, Bobby heads out here. Apparently, Liska is so glad of the company she completely forgets to mention the visits to Sven. Well, you can't keep a secret long in a small town, and pretty soon, people know where Bobby is headed when he drives west every time Sven is gone. Heck, the lady at the drugstore, even reports whenever he buys another Whitman's Sampler.

It isn't long before Thorvaldsen hears the whispers. When you're on a twelve-hour rest layover in Barstow before you can catch the next job home, there's not much to do but play cards and talk. Maybe he even makes an extra effort to hear once he starts noticing the card room suddenly goes quiet whenever he walks in. Or maybe somebody who enjoys stirring up trouble slides a note under his door one night. Anyway, he hears about what's going on.

Now, this Thorvaldsen is a methodical man. Getting a child bride from Sweden is far and away the wildest, craziest thing he has ever done. He is also a jealous man. He's a lot older than his wife, and he knows other men are interested in her. And he knows she's bored and lonely out on the river bottom all by herself, and now he knows someone is showing up out there whenever he catches a trip. Another thing about Thorvaldsen: he's generally a calm man and slow to anger. But while he's slow to come to a boil, when he finally gets mad, he stays mad, even though he doesn't say anything.

He starts looking for little signs that Bobby has been out to his place – tire tracks different than his in the long, sandy driveway, cigarette butts (Bobby smokes cigarettes, Sven smokes a pipe, Liska doesn't smoke at all), or anything in the house that he hasn't brought home. His detective work doesn't uncover much. The sandy driveway doesn't hold much of a tire track, and Liska won't let Bobby smoke because she knows Sven has a nose like a bloodhound. When Bobby brings her chocolates, she burns the box and the papers before Thorvaldsen gets home. If Bobby brings wine, she makes sure he takes the bottle with him.

But even though he can find no hard evidence, Thorvaldsen knows. Liska, who has never been real enthusiastic about sex, becomes even less interested in her wifely duty. And she's nervous. She is afraid her husband will find out, but she's lonely, and Bobby's nice. She knows a secret like hers won't last long in a gossip-starved town like Smoke Tree, so she constantly keeps an eye out for any sign that Sven knows.

But anyone who played poker with Thorvaldsen during those lay-overs in Barstow could have told her that Sven was a hard man to read. You could study his face, his hands, his eyes, and his mannerisms and never be able to tell whether he had a full house or a busted flush. So, weeks pass while Sven and Liska circle each other, both looking for signs.

Bobby Schoen, unlike Liska, thinks Thorvaldsen is a dense, unsuspecting Swede. Working at dispatch, he never sat in on one of those Barstow poker games. He's so sure Sven knows nothing that he begins to drop little hints and winks when the subject of the beautiful, river-bottom bride comes up in conversation. Of course, the more Bobby hints, the more whispers get back to Sven, and the more he seethes.

Thorvaldsen could have forgiven a lot. He is essentially a good man who loves his pretty wife and could perhaps even overlook her cheating. But what he cannot take is being thought a fool. Nor can he bear the idea that Liska might leave him for Bobby and move into town and leave him alone again on the river bottom. So, he decides to put an end to the snickering behind his back and his fear of losing his wife to Bobby.

One night in early September, when he is chalked up on the extra board, he catches a job on an eastbound freight. It's nine o'clock at night when the train pulls out. Thorvaldsen is on the caboose as the rear-end brakeman. As the train clears the yard and pulls onto the main line, Sven steps off of the caboose and throws the switch. He gives the engineer the 'highball' with his lantern and steps up onto the rung of the caboose, but he doesn't stay there long. Before the train picks up speed, he steps off again and begins the long walk back to his truck.

Johnny stopped talking.

"Well, go on, Johnny. What happened next?"

"My dad told me everything I've just told you, plus some more, but he was short on details about the end of the story. I have added in the missing details in my own version of what happened that night.

I think Sven sits in his truck for over an hour, thinking things over and giving Bobby time to get a good head start. Then he starts toward home. There's a full moon, just like tonight. When Thorvaldsen gets back to his place, it's after eleven o'clock, and the moon's almost directly overhead in a cloudless sky. It was over a hundred and ten that day, and it's still close to a hundred degrees. He parks his truck a long way from the quarter-mile driveway that leads to his house. He walks down the road and up the driveway in the moonlight. There are dark shadows under the mesquites and salt cedars, but the moonlight is clear on the road and shines down on the tears that begin to show on his cheeks when he sees Bobby Schoen's car parked in front of his house. He pulls the .40 caliber revolver from the waistband of his work pants.

As he nears the porch, he hears laughter and music. Bobby has apparently been bringing a wind-up Victrola and dance records on the visits. Sven walks quietly onto the porch and looks through the screen door. There's an oil lamp lit on the parlor table, and beside it is a half-empty bottle of Tokay and an open box of chocolates melting in the heat. Bobby and Liska are dancing. Bobby's wearing only his underwear. Liska is naked. Liska's face is happy, and she's laughing at something Bobby said.

Thorvaldsen opens the door, and as their startled faces turn toward him, he says, "Good evening to you both." Then he shoots them. The first two shots put them down. He shoots each of them two more times. Then he puts one more bullet in the gun and walks through the house into the backyard and out to the horse corral. He sits down and leans back against one of the railroad ties he had strung with barbed wire so many years before and shoots himself in the head."

When Johnny ended the story, we sat there in silence, each of us thinking about the tale. The river looked like a ribbon of mercury under the bright moon. Somewhere out in the channel, a big fish flopped. The moon cast shadows under the salt cedars.

Judy broke the silence. "Good God, Johnny, what a horrible thing. What a strange life. That poor woman!"

"What about the guy," I said. "His life just fell apart around him."

"Yes, but my goodness, what a thing to do. He spies and plots and plans and then just shoots everybody? Didn't they have divorces in those days? I mean, a double murder is pretty extreme, don't you think?"

"Three murders," said Johnny. "Remember, Thorvaldsen killed himself too."

"Yes, and if he was going to do that, why didn't he shoot just himself in the first place? Darn it, he was going to be dead anyway. Why should it matter to him about the other two? He wasn't going to be around."

Johnny and I looked at each other. What could we say? Judy was right, but neither of us had ever considered that Thorvaldsen would leave the other two alive. The two of us had just been treated to a glimpse into the difference between the way Judy saw the world of relationships between men and women and the way we did.

"So, here's my idea. Why don't we go take a look at the old place, kind of get a feel for the story?"

"Sounds kind of creepy to me."

"It's just a house, Judy. Houses can't hurt you. You read too much Edgar Allen Poe at Halloween."

"Do you think you can find the place at night? Everything out here looks different than in the daylight."

"Yeah, I can find it. My dad showed me the driveway when we were out there hunting quail last season. I remember there are two really big salt cedars on either side of the driveway at the turnoff."

"Okay. It's either that or head back to town."

"Then let's do it."

We drove back to where the road forked at the edge of Piute Wash and took the road that went straight into the mesquite forest. The salt cedars Johnny remembered were huge. They must have been fifty or sixty years old, and the trunks were twice as big around as a fifty-gallon drum. The trees were less than twenty feet high, but they had heavy limbs with dense needles. More of the massive trees lined a narrow driveway that ended abruptly in a clearing, and there was the house.

We parked in front and sat waiting for the silty dust to settle before we got out of the car. Johnny shut off the engine and turned off the lights. The incredible silence of the desert night immediately surrounded us. As we sat there, the wind suddenly kicked up, and an old windmill that glinted in the moonlight behind the house began to turn.

Time had not been terribly unkind to the place. Even though it was over thirty years old and had been forgotten and neglected after the murders, the lack of rainfall and the dry, desert air had helped preserve it. Thorvaldsen had done a good job of putting the house together. However, vandalism had left its mark even though the place was well off the road. In the moonlight, it was obvious that the windows were gone. The front screen door had been torn from the jamb and was propped sideways on the porch. The front door hung askew on its hinges and partially open.

After the dust settled, Johnny stepped out of the car. Judy slid out her side, and I pushed the seat forward and followed her. As we stood there looking at the house, the wind began to blow harder, and the leaves of a big cottonwood to the right of the house began to ripple. The windmill caught the rising wind and began to spin faster. It made a mournful, grinding noise as the disconnected pump shaft rattled and flailed inside the metal tank.

"Whaddya think, Judy? Wanna go inside and look around?" Even though the night was still warm, Judy hugged herself and shivered slightly.

"You don't think there's any blood or anything still in there, do you?"

"Nah, I'm sure all that stuff is long gone."

"Then let's go in."

Johnny opened the trunk and got a flashlight, but nothing happened when he tried to turn it on.

"Dead batteries."

"Well, that's that then. I'm not going in some creepy old house without a light."

"I've got a bunch of fusees."

It was a fact of life in Smoke Tree that trainmen who worked on the Santa Fe stole railroad flares, called fusees. They looked like highway flares, but they had a sharp metal stake on the bottom so they could be jammed into railroad ties. They burned hot and bright and were good for all kinds of things, like lighting barbeques and burning out wasp nests.

Johnny got two of them. He handed one to me. We walked up the driveway, onto the porch, and slipped through the partially-open door.

★ ★ ★

It was much later and very dark when the knife finally shredded the last nylon strand, and Charlie Merriman could straighten his legs. Blessed relief! He flexed his legs repeatedly to get the circulation going again. Finally, they began to tingle. He dropped the knife and rolled onto his back. He turned his head and looked toward the outline of Sixto's body, now visible in the gloomy light leaking into the room from the full moon.

Then he heard something unbelievable: the rumble of an engine and then tires crunching. A car was coming up the driveway! He had no idea who it could be, but he was very sure he didn't want to be tied up and helpless in this room when whoever it was discovered Sixto's cooling corpse!

He heard two car doors slam. Then he heard voices, but he couldn't make out what they were saying. One voice sounded female. Suddenly the wind kicked up, and the windmill began to spin, the disconnected shaft banging in the metal tank.

His hands and his feet were still bound, and he had to get moving! He struggled to his feet by pushing himself upright in the corner and almost fell down. His legs were not yet completely awake. Once he was sure he could stand, he bent and tried to slip his arms down around his hips. He fell over sideways, landing hard on his shoulder and banging the side of his head. But he had an idea.

"Thank God I'm skinny," thought Charlie. Staying on his side, he managed to slide his hands down below his hips. Then he rolled onto his back and jackknifed his body, pulling his heels between his hands, practically dislocating his shoulders in the process. With his bound hands now in front of him, he picked up the knife and began to saw on the cord tied around his feet. Because he had leverage, it went much faster. As he cut and scraped, he could hear the people talking outside. There seemed to be three of them.

When he was almost done, he heard footsteps on the porch. Then there were people in the house with him!

As Charlie finally cut through the cord and began to unwind it from his feet, he heard a scratching sound. A deep red light appeared beneath the door. As someone walked toward the door, Charlie took off. He yanked the door open and hit the ground running. Then his feet got tangled in the trailing cord, and he went down. He got up and ran again. He could see an old corral by the light of the full moon. He skirted it and kept going until he got to the edge of the mesquite thicket.

★ ★ ★

"By the way," said Johnny, "I forgot to mention that the house is haunted by Liska's ghost."

"Let's get out of here!"

"May not be a good idea. The outside is haunted by Thorvaldsen's ghost. He prowls around out there to keep Liska from leaving him."

Johnny pulled the striking cap off a fusee and scratched it across the top. Immediately the room was filled with a brilliant, blood-red light, revealing a room, apparently some kind of parlor, bare of anything but a broken stool. Smoke from the fusee began to fill the room.

There was a closed door that led to another part of the house. As we started toward it, we heard fast-moving footsteps from the back of the house. Then a door slammed loudly.

This is one of the places where my memory of the details gets a little mixed up, but what happened next goes something like this. Judy, who was a step or two ahead of Johnny, wheeled in panic, almost knocked Johnny over, and ran screaming for the front door. When she turned, Johnny, afraid that the burning material from the fusee would get on her, lifted it high over his head. When he did, globs of the burning chemical splashed onto his T-shirt and burned right through it. He yelped in pain and flung the fusee away. Judy continued screaming as she went out the door and across the porch. Thinking she had been burned too, Johnny whipped off his shirt and went out the door to help her.

For reasons I still don't understand, I opened the door to the back of the house, trying to catch up with the person who had run away. As

I went through the kitchen, I saw an old sink and an iron pump looking like some sort of metal monster looming in the red light from the other room. There was something big in the corner, but I didn't stop to look at it.

The back door was closed. I pulled it open and went out onto the back porch. The moonlight revealed a small yard, a dead chinaberry tree, and a big corral made of railroad ties and barbed wire. There was no one in the yard. The only sound was the rattle and clank of the windmill shaft.

I realized I was holding a railroad flare. I ripped the top off and struck it to life. Holding the flare ahead of myself, I stepped down off the porch. I could see footprints in the soft sand by the light from the flare. The prints veered away from the porch to skirt the corral. I followed them.

★ ★ ★

Clutching the knife, Charlie Merriman dropped down and began to crawl into the thicket. The mesquite thorns tore at his face and hands as he burrowed his way forward. When he was about ten feet into the mesquites, he began to see the red glow behind him. He stopped and held perfectly still. He held his breath, sure that whoever was out there would hear the pounding of his heart. The light didn't seem to get any brighter, but it seemed to be swinging from side to side as if someone were trying to peer into the thicket.

I stayed on the tracks for almost thirty yards before they led me to the edge of the mesquite thicket. I could tell the person I was following had dropped onto hands and knees to crawl under the low-lying branches of the mesquites. The limbs were so low and the trees so dense I couldn't believe anyone could actually get through there. As I stood there peering into the mesquites, the fusee went out. I became aware of a noise behind me.

When I turned around, I realized the House of Three Murders was on fire. Flames were shooting up through the roof. My first thought was that we had to put it out. I ran three or four steps before I realized that there was no way we could stop it. As I watched, sparks flying off the roof landed in the dead Chinaberry tree. Within a few seconds, it blossomed into a giant ball of flame. That's when I knew we were in danger. If the wind picked up further and spread the embers into the mesquite trees around the house, we could be trapped.

★ ★ ★

The red light disappeared. Charlie carefully turned his head to look back the way he had come. There was a different light now, and it was growing brighter. He could smell smoke.

Something was on fire. Were they trying to burn him out? Why would they do that? Charlie knew that if the flames got to the thicket, he would be burned alive. Frantically, he scrabbled and twisted around, disregarding the thorns cutting his face. He went back the way he had come. When he got to the edge of the mesquites, he could see someone silhouetted against a fire. The house was on fire! Then a big chinaberry tree in the backyard exploded into flame. Time to get out of here!

He got to his feet and moved as quietly as he could toward the figure. The soft sand muffled the sound of his footsteps, and the growing roar of the fire helped. When he got six feet from the figure, he turned the knife sideways, raised his bound hands over his head, and ran at the man. He struck him hard between the shoulder blades. The man went down, and Charlie ran past him around the north side of the burning house. He peeked around the corner of the front of the house and saw a shiny, dark-colored Ford. He ducked back and crawled north through the mesquites until they thinned out a bit. He got to his feet, turned west, and headed for the edge of the river bottom, trying to keep ahead of the fire.

★ ★ ★

Before I could move, I was struck a violent blow to my back that sent me sprawling. I landed face down in sand, mesquite beans, and mesquite thorns. Pushing to my hands and knees, I saw the back of a figure running around the side of the corral. Before I got to my feet, the figure went through the yard and disappeared around the left side of the house. All I registered was long, dark hair, a long-sleeved shirt, and Levi's.

I started running. I went past the corral and around to the front of the house. When I got there, I saw a strange tableau by the light of the burning house. Johnny was clutching his T-shirt to his chest with his right hand. He had his left arm around Judy's shoulders, and he was trying to comfort her, even though she was not hurt. As I went toward them, Judy was wailing in anguish.

"It's all ruined. It's all ruined. My dad will kill me. He's going to find out we didn't go to the bonfire. Oh, this is terrible. This is just terrible. I never should have come out here with you."

"Johnny, we've gotta get out of here. There's a big dead tree in the backyard, and it's on fire. If the sparks blow into the mesquites, we could get cooked."

Even though we were in danger, Johnny carefully led Judy to the car and opened the door for her. As she got in, I was already climbing into the back seat. Johnny got behind the wheel. He started the car and turned around. As we drove down the long driveway, I watched the roaring fire through the back window. We took the road back to the pavement and then through the wash and up the hill. No one said anything. At the top, Johnny pulled onto the shoulder, and we got out.

We stood together in the moonlight. The fire was already huge: maybe twenty or thirty acres in flames. The glow of the fire was reflected on the bottom of the white smoke cloud hanging in the air. I looked at Johnny and Judy. Judy was shaken. Her eyes were wide, and tears were streaking down her face. Johnny was suffering. He pulled his T-shirt away from his chest to reveal terrible burns. There was an especially deep one right over his sternum.

"Johnny, have you got motor oil in the trunk?"

"No," he said absently.

"You've got to get something on those burns. Motor oil is almost as good as Vaseline."

I went to the front of the car, unlatched the hood, and propped it open. The chrome on the engine gleamed in the soft light. I pulled the dipstick and walked back to Johnny.

"Give this a minute to cool, then rub it on the burns. It's better than nothing." Johnny grimaced in pain as he daubed oil on the burns. "Clean them with your shirt. Try to get some of that junk out of the burns, and then put some more oil on them."

Johnny worked carefully, avoiding the deepest burn. When I turned to Judy, I realized her lips were moving, but I couldn't hear what she was saying. She was still looking toward the fire as she spoke. I moved closer to her. She didn't seem to see me, and I don't think she really saw the fire either. She was whispering to herself, "I'm dead, I'm dead. My dad's gonna kill me. I'm dead, I'm dead."

I turned back to Johnny and held out the dipstick. He daubed on a little more and then pressed his T-shirt to his chest.

"What happened back there?"

"The fusee burned me. I threw it away and went after Judy. I thought she'd been burned too."

I noticed he didn't mention Judy crashing into him in her panic.

"Where did you disappear to?"

"I went through the house to see about those footsteps."

Johnny looked at me with an odd smile. "What made you want to do that?"

"Darned if I know."

"You're crazy! You know that, don't you? Did you find anyone?"

"Not at first. Then I went out in the back. I found footprints in the sand and followed them to the edge of some mesquites. But I didn't go any farther. Whoever it was had gone through the thicket."

"Jesus, Ade, I didn't know anyone could get through there. Must have got cut and scratched to pieces."

"I tried to see someone back in there, but my fusee burned out. That's when I heard some noise and turned around and saw the fire. I thought we should put it out. Then I realized we couldn't, then the dead chinaberry tree caught on fire, then...." I stopped, realizing I was rambling.

Suddenly Judy spoke.

"God, Ade, you are so stupid."

"What are you talking about?"

"Johnny came out to help me, but did you pick up that, that, that doohickey and get rid of it? No, you ran off the other direction and let that house catch on fire." Her voice rose to a shriek. "Look what you've caused. Now we're all in trouble."

I ignored her and said to Johnny, "Did you see someone come around from the back of the house?"

"Yeah, you! Hollering about getting out of there."

"I mean around the other side."

"No. Did you, Judy?"

But Judy was staring vacantly toward the fire again. She didn't answer. In fact, she didn't seem to even hear the question.

"Anyway, while I was standing back there looking at the house, someone came up behind me and knocked me flat. By the time I got up, he was disappearing around the corner of the house."

"Know who it was?"

"No."

"Remember anything about him?"

"Long hair, long-sleeved shirt, medium tall, Levi's, that's all I got. But there was something familiar about the way the guy moved. I can't put my finger on it, but maybe it'll come to me."

I suddenly became aware of a new sound – far away but moving toward us – sirens!

"Johnny, we've got to get off this road. Sirens coming."

I ran to the front of the car, jammed in the dipstick, and slammed down the hood. Johnny was in the front seat by the time I finished, but Judy was still behind the car, staring off in the direction of the fire. I ran back and grabbed her by the arm. "Come on, we've got to get out of here. Police coming."

She wheeled on me; her eyes frantic. "Police? We can't let the police get us." She yanked her arm away from me and ran into the desert.

I caught up to her. "This way. You can't stay out here. We've got to get you home." She let me pull her back to the car. I shoved her inside and climbed in after her. Johnny had the car rolling before I got the door closed.

"The turnoff to the Allyson place is just ahead on the other side of the road. There! There! Take that road."

Johnny spun the wheel, and we hit the dirt road. As soon as we got about a hundred yards off the road, he shut off the lights and stopped the car. Just as he did, I saw flashing red lights coming fast on the highway.

"Everybody down! Don't let them see us." We collapsed into a jumble below the windows. The only sound in the car was Judy's voice. "This is terrible. This is terrible. We're gonna get caught. I know we are."

The vehicle with the flashing lights went by. We all sat up. Johnny reached for the ignition.

"Hold it," I said and rolled down my window. In the distance, I could hear another siren. "Start it up and drive down this road without turning on the lights. We've got to get farther off the highway. I'm sure people on the hill can see that fire from town. They'll be headed out here. Someone might recognize your car. Let's just sit tight for a bit."

We ended up waiting almost an hour. During that time, dozens of cars flashed by on the highway behind us. Finally, a few minutes passed with no cars.

"Okay," said Johnny. "I hope that's it. We'd better get out of here before they start coming back." He backed up and turned onto the highway. He drove slowly forward. We were all aware of the red glow on the horizon behind us.

No one said anything until we got close to town. Judy was hunched forward, her face in her hands. Johnny didn't put his arm around her because he had his left hand on the wheel, and his right hand was pressing the T-shirt against his chest. When we got off River Road and merged into the 66 traffic, I could see by the light of the oncoming headlights that he was sweating and grimacing in pain.

"We've got to get you to the hospital. That big burn is really nasty. It could get infected. I don't know what kind of stuff is in those things, but some of that junk is way under your skin. You need to get it out."

Judy sat up straight.

"No, no! We're not going to the hospital! It's way after eleven. I'm already in huge trouble."

"It's all right Judy. I'm headed straight to your house."

"I think we should go to the hospital, but you're the driver. We can go after you drop Judy."

"You can't go to the hospital. You can't, you can't! Don't you see? If you go, everyone in this trashy little town will know about it before morning. My dad's no dummy – he'll put it together. I know he will. If he's been outside, he's seen the fire from our hill. The next two houses down the hill from us are doctors. If my dad hears you went to the hospital, he'll connect it. Right now, I'm just in trouble for being out too late, but if he ever finds out we started that fire........."

"Judy, forget about yourself for a minute. Johnny has to go. These burns are serious. Someone who knows what they're doing has to look at them."

"Ade, it's okay, really. No sweat, Judy — I can handle it."

There was no point in arguing. I wasn't going to change his mind with Judy in the car giving him the big tears. Johnny was so obsessed with her that he was blind to how little she cared about him.

We drove through town and up the long hill to her house. As we approached the driveway, I told Johnny, "You stay in the car. You can't put that T-shirt back on, and you can't show up without it."

"Yeah, but Judy's old man will have a fit if I just drop her off and drive away."

"I'll take her up."

"What will you say if he comes to the door?"

"I'll think of something."

We pulled into the driveway. It seemed like days since we had parked on these flagstones — not just a few hours. As I got out and opened the door for Judy, the driveway lights came on. Benedict McPhearson was standing on the brightly-lit, second-story veranda, looking down at us. Judy got out without a word to Johnny or even a glance at him.

By the time we went around the fountain and climbed onto the porch, Benedict had come downstairs and was opening the door. "It's damn near midnight. You were supposed to be home by ten." He stopped and stared at me. "Where is Johnny?" He turned to Judy. "Why is his friend with you?" Benedict was looking over her shoulder, trying to see into the car.

Judy started to speak, but I interrupted. "Johnny's not feeling so good, Mr. McPhearson. Something he ate. Boy, he was throwing up all over the place. We stopped at the drugstore to get something for him. Then we sat in the park for a while 'cause he was afraid he'd throw up in the car."

"That's right, Dad. He's really, really sick." She brushed past her father and went through the door, leaving him on the porch with me.

"I don't like this, whatever your name is. When I say have Judy home by ten, I mean ten. I don't care how sick Johnny is."

I held up my hands. There was nothing I could say that wouldn't make things worse. I hurried down the steps and jogged to the car. Johnny was rolling as soon as I closed the door. Benedict stood on the porch, his arms crossed on his thick chest, staring after us. He looked like a bodyguard.

"What did you tell him?"

"Told him you were sick."

"What'd he say?"

"You mean besides, 'you're late getting Judy home?' Not much. He wasn't worried about your health."

"What'd he say to Judy?"

"Nothing. She snuck past him while he was yelling at me."

"Good. Maybe he'll leave her alone."

We came out of the heights and waited to turn left onto 66.

"How're those burns?"

"Hurt like crazy."

"Let's drive to the hospital. There must be someone there who has seen people burned with a fusee before. Someone will know what to do."

"No way, Ade. Judy is right. It wouldn't be five minutes before the story got around town."

"Okay, I can see you've got your mind made up. Let's go to your house, and I'll help you clean up the burns. You can't do it yourself. Is your dad in or out?"

"He's out. Caught a trip this afternoon. Won't be back until to-morrow."

We drove to Johnny's house in silence.

In the bathroom light, the burns looked worse. The material had burned him from above his belly button to his chest. The biggest splotch had landed on his sternum and burned almost to the bone. While I was getting some supplies from the medicine cabinet, Johnny wet washcloths and began to clean the burns, letting out a moan from time to time.

Johnny was a tough kid, but he screamed when I poured peroxide on the burns. Sweat popped out on his forehead, and for a moment, I thought he was going to faint. I stood back and watched the peroxide bubble in the wounds while Johnny rocked back and forth, his breath hissing in and out. I saturated a gauze pad with Mercurochrome. "Okay, buddy, this is going to hurt even worse, but we've got to make sure the burns don't get infected."

"Give me a minute." When his breathing had slowed, he closed his eyes. "Okay, let'er rip."

I doused the wounds with the Mercurochrome while Johnny twisted and shuddered. By the time I was done, the little bottle was empty.

"Just let me sit here for a minute."

"The bad part is over. I'm going to tape some gauze pads over the burns to keep them clean.

How are you going to put your shoulder pads on for tomorrow night's game? They're going to lace right over the worst burn."

"Don't worry. I'll get them on. All you have to worry about is not dropping the ball when I hand it to you. Come on, I'll take you home."

Johnny got one of his dad's flannel shirts and put it on.

When he dropped me at my house, my mom was up reading a book. I tried to breeze through the room. I didn't want to answer questions and was afraid my clothes smelled like smoke. "Goodnight, Mom. I've got to get to bed."

"You're late. I was getting worried."

"I was over at Johnny's. We were getting ready for a big chemistry test. I sort of lost track of the time." I was ashamed of how easily the lie rolled off my lips.

"Well, you'd better get off to bed. You've got a big game tomorrow night."

I was relieved when she said that. It meant she hadn't seen the fire. Luckily for me, when my mom stuck her nose in a book, *our* house could burn down, and she wouldn't notice. In my room, I took off my clothes and shoved them to the back of the closet. Until I sat on the edge of the bed to take off my socks, I didn't realize how tired I was. I really wanted to just get in bed and sleep for a week, but I forced myself to take a shower so I could wash the smell of smoke out of my hair. When I was done, I crawled into bed and fell into a deep and dreamless sleep.

Chapter 3

AEDEN

The next thing I remember is my dad banging on my door. He was always the first one up at our house. Mom, on the other hand, often slept until eleven in the morning or even noon. I got dressed and picked up my letterman's sweater for game day. By the time I got down the hall, my dad had cleared his dishes from the table and washed them. The black skillet he cooked his breakfast in was still on the stove, but he had wiped it out with a paper towel. He was at the table with what was probably his third cup of coffee. He loved his morning coffee.

"There's two slices of ham left in the icebox. You can fix yourself a sandwich or fry up some eggs. What time did you get in last night?"

"Late. Mom was up reading, but you were already in bed."

"I can't seem to keep my eyes open past nine o'clock anymore."

I heated a slice of ham in the skillet, then wrapped it in two tortillas and headed for the door with my schoolbooks.

"Big game tonight, huh?"

"Yes, sir. Homecoming, and a tough team."

"Well, good luck. I don't think I'll be there, though. Hate to miss it, but I'm fourth out, and no one will trade with me. Everyone wants to see the game. I'll probably catch something before evening."

I went out and got into my car, a '39 Plymouth with a six-cylinder engine. It had enough steel in it to build a tank but only eighty horsepower. It could barely get out of its own way, but it was reliable. I had been working my summer job at the service station when it was towed in. The radiator had been leaking, but the traveler kept driving, hoping to make it to Smoke Tree before it quit. He didn't. I bought the whole mess for forty dollars. We took it to Johnny's backyard and went to work on it. Turned out the engine had survived. We replaced the blown head gasket and a few burnt valves. We found a radiator for it at Zack's junkyard. I had a car.

By the time I got to school, I was almost late for first period. I walked into chemistry class a few seconds before the bell rang. The room smelled of chemicals and chalk dust. As I sat down in the back, I realized the other students had turned around to stare at me. I also noticed that Judy did not turn around and that Johnny's seat, right behind Judy's, was empty.

The bell rang, and Mr. Shaver had started handing out the tests when Johnny walked in. "Nice of you to join us, Mr. Quentin."

"Yessir, sorry to be late. Car wouldn't start." He took his seat. When he sat down behind Judy, she didn't turn around.

"Uh oh," I thought. "Trouble in Loveyland."

"All right, ladies and gentlemen, you may begin. No notes or books on your desk and eyes on your own paper only."

As I worked through the test, my mind kept drifting. Now that I was fully awake, images from the night before kept pushing valences and electron exchanges out of my head. I realized Johnny and Judy were probably having the same problem.

When class ended, I was the first person out the door. I waited outside for Johnny. When people stopped and tried to talk with me, I just shook my head and said, "Talk to you later."

Johnny came out. Judy wasn't with him.

"Man, she's shutting me out. She won't talk to me. She just sat at her desk until I gave up."

"Well, she's going to have to talk to us. We've gotta put our heads together. People are looking as us funny. Rumors must be flying."

The door to the classroom slowly opened, and Judy stuck her head out. When she saw Johnny and me, she started to turn back. I stepped over and pulled her out the door.

"Listen, Judy, I don't know what you're thinking, but the three of us have to talk and talk right now. We've got to get our story straight and stick with it." Although she looked nervous and withdrawn, she nodded her head. By then, Johnny had joined us.

"We're going to have to cut second period, and we can't leave campus. Where can we go? The library won't work."

Johnny snapped his fingers. "There's nobody in the band room second period."

"Let's hurry. If we're not out of sight before the bell rings for second period, we're sitting ducks."

We hurried to the band room; a separate building set away from the other classrooms. As we got closer, Mr. Jenkins came out the door. He walked past us without a glance, in a hurry to get somewhere. As soon as he was well past us, Johnny pulled the door open, and we stepped inside.

I didn't turn the lights on. The blinds were closed, leaving the room a little gloomy. I could smell dust and the light oil the brass players used on vales and slides. There was a tuba and a drum kit on one of the risers. The other instruments had been put away. Johnny and Judy sat on the bottom riser. I stood at the podium where Jenkins conducted. The bell rang for second period.

"Have either of you talked to anyone at school about last night?"

"No," said Johnny. "I was late to school"

"What about you, Judy?"

She gave a tiny shake of her head.

"People noticed the fire last night. They may even have been able to see it from the football field. I'm sure people noticed none of us were at the bonfire. So what's our story?"

There was silence for a few minutes. Finally, Johnny spoke. "We've got to keep Judy out of this. We can't let her dad find out she was there." Hope came into Judy's eyes. "My old man won't be happy about it if he finds out what happened, but he really doesn't care a whole lot about what I do, so I'm not worried on that score. What about your folks, Ade?"

"My mom would have a conniption fit for sure. Dad can be pretty cool about some things. I don't know about this one."

"That settles it. We cover for Judy."

"All right. Here's our story, unless one of you can think of something better. We picked up Judy and stopped for a burger. I'm sure someone saw us there last night. After we ate, we drove around for a while, and Judy got sick, so we took her home early. How's that sound?"

"That might work. Her mom and dad are too stuck up to talk to anyone in town. Nobody else knows Judy got home late, and I didn't go to the hospital so nobody knows I was burned. But that leaves a problem. What did you and I do? Why didn't you and I show up at the bonfire after we took Judy home?"

"I don't know yet. We'll think of something. Right now, this is all we need. We'll put something together at lunch. Anyway, this is all Judy needs to know. This makes it very simple for her." I turned to her. "Have you got that, Judy? We picked you up and went for a burger. We drove around. You got sick. We took you home early. That's why you weren't at the bonfire. You don't know where Johnny and I went after we left you at home. Got it?"

Judy seemed to be two or three beats behind the conversation. She looked dazed. I wondered what kind of scene she'd had with her parents last night or at breakfast. What had she told them? What did they suspect? Had she stuck to the story I tried to sell her father on the portico or the veranda or whatever in the world they called it?

Judy looked up at me. Then she looked at Johnny. She gave an almost imperceptible nod of her head and got up and walked out the door. Johnny got up to go after her, but I grabbed his arm. "Let her go, Johnny. She needs time to think about all this. Besides, she knows all she needs to know. It's best if she doesn't know the story you and I come up with for not being at the field. If she doesn't know our story, she can't get it wrong."

Johnny sat back down. "Yeah, I guess you're right. But we better get out of here. Jenkins could come back any time."

I opened the door and peeked out. Judy was nowhere in sight. I didn't see anyone outside. A student in one of the classrooms across the way would have to stand up to see over the windowsills to spot us. That left the teachers. We could only hope none of them were looking toward the band building when we came out.

We went out the door and hurried behind the building. The shop classes faced the back of the band building, but all the sliding doors were down. We ran across the open space and went behind the buildings. This was a favorite place for students to try to sneak a smoke, so Vice-Principal Fertig sometimes checked there between classes. With everyone in class, he wouldn't be coming this way.

"Man, Rosassen is going to be mad when we don't show up for class."

"That's right, but not until he finds we're not absent from school today."

"But it's game day. He knows if we're not in school today, we can't play tonight. And he knows there's a big game."

"Are you kidding? Rosassen doesn't even know this school plays football. He's so busy thinking about the beauty of the formula for finding the volume of a cone he has to be reminded to eat lunch! We can probably make it to noon before people start trying to pin us down about last night. Let's wait here until just before the bell rings for third period and then get to class a little late. Same thing for fourth period. As soon as fourth period ends, make a run for the parking lot. I'll meet you there. We'll take my clunker and leave your car in the lot. Between now and then, try to think of somewhere we can go where we won't bump into people from school. We'll work a story out at lunch."

We stood behind the buildings, not talking, each of us thinking our own private thoughts. I'm sure Johnny was thinking about Judy. I was thinking about the guy who had knocked me down. When the bell rang for third period, we waited for a few more minutes and then started toward our next class. Halfway across the open space, we saw Fertig headed our way. He was wearing his usual outfit: tweed sport coat over a plaid shirt with a bolo tie, heavy slacks, and highly polished shoes. He looked at us curiously.

"I didn't know you boys took shop," he said.

"We don't," said Johnny and kept walking. Fertig turned to watch us go by.

We walked into American History just as the tardy bell rang. Heads turned to look. I took my seat. Johnny walked to the seat behind Judy.

When he sat down, she did not turn around. Looked like the freeze was still on in spite of our talk in the band room.

Mr. Miller launched into a discussion of the upcoming election. On Tuesday, the nation would elect a new president to replace Dwight Eisenhower, that good, gray man. The last debate between Vice President Nixon and Senator Kennedy was over. The race had started with a big lead for Nixon, but Kennedy had begun closing after the first televised presidential debate in history. That was the one where Nixon looked like a used car salesman in need of a shave. The race was now a dead heat.

But no matter how hard Miller tried, he couldn't get the class very interested, although a few of the girls commented on how "dreamy" John F. Kennedy was and the fabulous clothes his beautiful wife wore. When the election failed to interest us, he turned to the battle of Gettysburg. He didn't have much luck there either, except for some mild interest from some of the boys about the number of Confederate soldiers who were slaughtered in Pickett's charge up Cemetery Ridge.

Finally, the bell rang. Johnny and I hung back as the classroom emptied. We pretended we wanted to discuss the Civil War with Mr. Miller. The only thing I could remember about the whole affair was the Emancipation Proclamation, so I asked him how he thought that had affected the outcome of the war. I thought Mr. Miller was going to faint with excitement over having someone stay after the bell rang to ask questions. We exited just in time to make Mr. Sorrento's class before the bell rang.

English was my favorite class, and Mr. Sorrento was my favorite teacher. But I couldn't stay focused. Unanswered questions about the previous night swirled around in my brain, mixed with worry about what might happen next.

After what seemed like an eternity, the period ended. I hurried out the door with Johnny right on my heels. We were the first people out of the parking lot. We were on our way down Canaan Street hill before either of us spoke.

"Where we headed?"

"Can't go to Lulu's or the drive-in, but I gotta have something to eat. There was nothing at home for breakfast. I found some Cheerios, but when I poured them in the bowl there was a big roach in the box. Kinda killed my appetite."

"How about the Jade? Nobody goes there at lunch. It's all older people."

Johnny nodded. We drove to the restaurant and pulled into the lot. As we walked in, the owner, Mr. Lee, waved at us and smiled. He was a friendly guy, and he liked us. Whenever we caught a snapping turtle while fishing for catfish, we took it to him. He loved turtle soup.

We usually sat at the counter, but this time we headed for a booth in the back. Hazel, who was the only waitress we had ever seen at the Jade, didn't even bring us menus. "Hi, boys. The usual?" The usual was an open-face roast beef sandwich, with fries on the side and a vanilla coke. We nodded. We waited until she walked away.

"How are those burns?"

"They hurt. I didn't get a lot of sleep."

"Can you play tonight?"

Johnny stared at me like I was an idiot. "Of course, I can play!"

"Johnny, I've got a bad feeling about this. I'm getting nervous."

"Don't sweat it. It's not as bad as all that. Tell you what I'm worried about. Did you see Judy this morning? She won't even look at me. I tried to give her a note in third period, and she wouldn't take it."

"Yes, I saw her. Let me tell you, you're not the only thing she isn't seeing. She has a funny look. Like one of the people in that 'Body Snatchers' movie."

"I wonder what went on in that big house after we dropped her off last night. I'll bet she got the third degree. I don't think her dad bought that story you told him for a minute."

Hazel came back with our food. "Anything else for you lads?"

"No'm."

"What brings you boys in for lunch? Can't remember ever seeing the two of you at noon on a school day."

Johnny put on his most winning smile. "We missed you, Hazel. Just couldn't wait until the weekend to see you." Hazel swatted at him with her little towel.

"All right, don't tell me then. But say, good luck tonight. The whole town's pulling for you. Seven and oh! That doesn't happen very often." She walked away.

Johnny turned his attention to his roast beef sandwich. My best friend loved the roast beef sandwiches at the Jade, and it was a wonder to watch him eat one. First, he pushed the gravy off the roast beef so he could save it for his French fries. Then he cut the sandwich into four equal pieces. Once he had done that, he ate the entire sandwich in four huge bites. As soon as he was done, he spooned the gravy on top of the fries, then covered them with catsup and mustard and ate them in giant forkfuls.

Hazel came back and asked us if we wanted refills on our cokes. "No charge," she said. "But don't tell Lee." She always said that, and we knew Lee liked us and didn't care if she gave us a free coke. And she knew we knew.

When we had our refills, I looked at the clock above the pie case. We had twenty-five minutes before fifth period.

"Let's get our story straight about last night. We dropped Judy off at about seven. Then what did we do?"

"Drove around?"

"That's not good enough. No, it's got to be something a little wild, so we don't come across as trying to be too innocent."

"I don't know. Say we went out to Zack's wrecking yard and stole a starter motor for your crappy car."

"Whoa. Ease up on my car. Best forty-dollar car in town."

"That's what I mean."

"Just a minute – got an idea. You know that liquor store by the old gas station outside Oatman?"

"The guy that'll sell to anyone?"

"That's the one. Here's our story: we drove up there after we dropped Judy, and we bought a six-pack. Then we drove over by Boundary Cone and drank it."

"That might work. We could act proud of it if our friends ask, and it's bad enough we wouldn't want to tell any adults unless we had to."

"And it puts us on the Arizona side of the river. Even better, we can say we saw the fire and wondered what it was, but by the time we got back to town, it was late, and we went home."

"I don't think anything's ever going to come of this, but what if it does? What if someone goes up to check on our story?"

"That's the best part. Nobody's going to believe the guy who owns the place. He's been lying for years about selling to kids. They'll think he just doesn't want to admit he sold to us."

"Got it!"

"Okay. That's our story, and we stick with it. We let the guys on the team know it. Once they hear it, they won't bother us about last night. But we don't tell adults that story unless push comes to shove. If they have to drag it out of us, they might believe it. And it's best not to tell Judy. She's going to stick with her story, and she doesn't need our story mixing up her head."

"Fine by me. We'd better go."

By the time we got back to school, it was almost time for class. We hurried across the parking lot. We went past the auditorium and under the long overhang that fronted the history and English classrooms, then turned into the west entrance of the science building. We walked down the interior hallway and into the back door of the biology classroom. Students were already sitting on the stools at the high tables used for dissection of things that didn't smell good. Once again, heads turned, and I could hear whispered conversations. I sat down at my stool just as the bell rang.

Mr. Gustafson, wearing a lab coat over his white shirt and tie, began to talk about cell division, illustrating the steps on the blackboard. I realized much of my anxiety had drained away. At least we had a plan. We had a story that would stand up under questioning, if questions ever came. Mr. Gustafson went through the phases of cell division as I parsed our story, looking for holes. It wasn't perfect, but I felt better.

Sixth period had been canceled for the football rally, and everybody headed for the auditorium. Johnny walked next to a silent Judy. Seve Zavala, our left end, fell in beside me.

"Where were you and Johnny last night? Didn't see either of you."

"We were on the way, but Judy got sick, and we had to take her home. Johnny didn't want to go to the bonfire without her."

"Oh, yeah. So, what'd you do?"

"Drove up to Oatman and got a six-pack."

"At Zito's? Man, that guy will sell to anybody."

"I guess the ABC doesn't get up there that often. So that's the guy's name, Zito?"

"Nah – I don't know his real name. We call him Zito 'cause he has a face full of pimples. But we don't call him that to his face. We call him, "Hello, sir," and "thank you, sir." Don't want to make him mad. He might stop selling to us."

"Good idea. At least it's a place to buy beer."

"You know, they made me come up and light that bonfire 'cause Judy and Johnny weren't there. Johnny owes me for that one!"

When we reached the auditorium, we moved to the front rows saved for the team. As we were sitting down, Superintendent Symington, a pompous and overbearing man, walked on the stage and tapped on the microphone.

"Students, please stand and join me in the Pledge of Allegiance."

When that was done, he motioned to the side of the stage, and the cheerleaders came running out and took us through a couple of cheers. Then the superintendent came back out onto the stage.

"Students, we are here today to rally the Smoke Tree Scorpions on to victory in tonight's homecoming game. These outstanding young men have compiled a perfect record of seven wins and no losses. That is an amazing achievement. But now, they face their toughest challenge of the season.

We are a small school in the middle of a vast, empty desert. We are hundreds of miles from the major metropolitan areas of our state, where playoff decisions are made. We play as an independent, so we do not get an automatic invitation like league champions do. And we play teams from Arizona and Nevada as well as California. Many of the C.I.F. commissioners are not even aware of the scores in those out-of-state games.

But tonight, we have a game with a team they are well aware of. That opponent is Sunset Crossing High, and they are from West Covina. Sunset Crossing has a six and one record, and they play in division two. That's two divisions higher than Smoke Tree. They are big, they are strong, they are fast, and they have no intention of riding over two hundred miles to lose to a little school they've never heard of. But they are in for a terrible shock when they encounter the swift and deadly

Scorpions of Smoke Tree High School. Winning this game will assure us of a post-season playoff berth.

We must have this victory. Like David facing the mighty Goliath, like Perseus facing the deadly Medusa, we face a daunting challenge. But I know our young men are up to it, and you know it too. And you are all going to be at the game tonight! All of you. Making more noise than you've ever made in your lives.

Now I give you the coach of the Scorpions, Coach Dean Lucas. Coach Lucas!"

Coach Lucas walked across the stage as the students roared. Coach Lucas was a popular figure. A former tight end at Oregon State, he was still, in his forties, a superb athlete and, unlike most of the adults in town, in great physical condition. He was the only head coach I had ever known in my high school football career, and I liked and respected him. So did the other guys, even though he worked us to exhaustion in practice. His August practices were legendary, and a lot of guys who came out for the team quit before September. There's something about an afternoon practice when the temperature is over a hundred and eighteen that weeds out the faint-hearted. Every year Johnny and I said we weren't going to go through that again, but every year we did.

But he was a straight shooter. He was fair and played no favorites. If you worked hard and performed, you played. If you dogged it, even for one play in a game or in practice, you were on the bench. There were no prima donnas on the team. And if you were a second or third-stringer and we were well ahead, you got into the game so you could earn your varsity letter. Coach Lucas didn't try to run up the scores. This caused friction between him and a superintendent who was determined to have a championship football team so his district would get noticed.

"Afternoon, kids. I don't have much to add to what Superintendent Symington has told you. But I will tell you this – these boys are ready to play. No team, anywhere, is fitter than this team. These boys will give you all they've got – and they've got a lot. There is no quit in them. They will put their best game on the field tonight, and I don't think these city boys who are coming out here to do some cherry-picking can match them. But they need your help. They need you in the stands, stomping, and screaming and letting them know you're behind them all the way. So, are you behind them?"

The students rose to their feet and screamed.

"All right then, let's bring those boys up here!"

We climbed the stairs onto the stage. I stood at the end of the row. Johnny stood in the middle of the front row. The whole time we were assembling on the stage, the students kept yelling and whistling.

"All right, all right, all right! That's what the boys and I like to hear. Now I want our co-captains to come out here and say a few words. You all know them. You've watched them for three seasons now. Quarterback Johnny Quentin and left end Seve Zavala."

The noise level went up. Johnny stepped to the microphone. At a muscular six feet, with gray eyes and light brown hair, he was the best all-around athlete in our school. As the quarterback of the football team, the point guard on the basketball team, and a fireball throwing pitcher, Johnny was a guy who liked to be in control of the action. That control carried over into other parts of his life. A natural and composed speaker, he had none of the "aw shucks" mumble of the usual high school jock. As I watched him, I thought, "This guy is special. He's smart, he's a great athlete, he has style, and he connects with people. He could be a congressman or a senator or the governor someday. But he doesn't know it, and he wouldn't believe it if you told him.

"Thank you! Thank you all! Just be sure to make that much noise tonight. This team is counting on your support. I know the stands will be full, but if you can't find a seat, stand in the dirt, 'cause that's the way Smoke Tree Scorpion fans are: not afraid of a little dirt! Let's give this team from L.A. an introduction to Smoke Tree Scorpion football they'll never forget. Let's show them we don't give a darn how they do it in L.A.!"

The students erupted again. Johnny stood there calmly smiling, waiting for the noise to subside. He instinctively knew better than to interrupt the positive energy the guys behind him were soaking up.

"Now, here's my good friend and the toughest man on the football field, Seve Zavala."

Seve dwarfed his quarterback. At two hundred and thirty-five pounds, he looked like just another big, slow guy. But in track season, he not only threw the shot put, he also ran the high hurdles with great technique and good speed. The picture of Seve gliding over the hurdles had to be intimidating to the guys who knew they'd have to face him on the football field in the fall. Seve banged on the microphone a couple of times. Then he cleared his throat.

"Hey!"

"Hey," yelled one of the students.

Seve looked surprised. He tried it again, louder.

"Hey!"

"Hey," roared the entire student body.

"Okay then."

The students laughed.

"This is a big game tonight. Big deal. I guess pretty much everyone has heard about it." He laughed nervously, then paused and shifted from foot to foot. "Well, I sure hope you can come and make noise and cheer and everything. We'd sure appreciate it." He turned and walked back to his place in line. Johnny went with him.

Coach Lucas stepped back to the microphone. "Let's get those cheerleaders back out here!"

The cheerleaders came back out and brought the pom-pom girls with them. They did another cheer. The auditorium rocked with noise. Then Mindy, the head cheerleader, came back over to the mic.

"As you all know, last night we had the big homecoming bonfire on the football field. The homecoming king and queen were supposed to light the fire, but they weren't there. And I know some of you are wondering why and maybe a little upset with them? Well, I found out at lunch today that Judy got real sick last night, and Johnny had to turn around and take her back home, and then Johnny didn't feel right going to the bonfire without her. So, I'd like to remind you that the home-coming dance will be after the game tonight. That's why we're having the rally in the auditorium. The gym is all decorated for the dance, and by the way, the dance committee did a great job with the decorations. The theme this year is 'stardust.'

Johnny and Judy will be there to lead the first dance. So, before we close the rally today, let's get them up on the stage. Judy? We're so glad you're feeling okay today, and we want you to get on up here with Johnny and the team."

I could see Judy in the third row of the senior class section. She was shaking her head and looking like she wanted to disappear into her seat.

"Come on," said Mindy. "Get on up here. Don't be shy. Let's give her a big hand, everybody. Homecoming Queen Judy McPhearson."

The girls on either side of Judy were pulling her out of her seat. She stood up and was pushed to the aisle. As she walked toward the stage, Johnny went down the steps to meet her. He took her hand and brought her up on the stage. The students cheered. Johnny smiled and looked happy. Judy looked like she would rather be at the dentist.

"Good Lord," I thought. "That story we made up is working. Judy must have told some of the girls." Well, at least she was sticking to it. Now Johnny and I had to stick to ours, even if we did get in a little trouble about the beer.

The high school principal, Mr. Flowers, who was always overshadowed by the superintendent, was finally allowed out of the wings and onto the stage. "Please stand and join with me in singing the Smoke Tree High alma mater."

The students rose and sang the song. When the final phrase faded away, Mr. Flowers dismissed the assembly.

As the students filed out, I could see Judy trying to pull her hand away from Johnny. It was obvious he didn't want to let her go. He was trying to talk to her, but she shook her head and pulled free. She hurried down the steps, leaving Johnny looking after her. His smile was gone.

Before I left the stage, I talked briefly with a couple of the guys on the team. I felt a little less anxious. Judy's story was in circulation, and Mindy had given a solid reason for Johnny not being at the bonfire.

I went out to the parking lot. As I headed toward my car, I saw Judy getting into her father's Eldorado. Neither one of them was talking as they drove away. Johnny caught up with me.

"I don't know what's up with Judy. All she says is, 'Leave me alone. Just leave me alone. I'm in enough trouble already.' I asked her if we were still going to the dance after the game. She said we had to. Had to! Like it was punishment. She told her dad it wouldn't look right if we weren't there, and he said okay."

"Don't let it get you down. You can talk to her at the dance. She'll come around. You'll see."

"I don't think so. I think this has blown us up."

"Give her time. In the meantime, we both have a game to think about.

I'm going to call Linda's house. She said she'd be home for home-coming the last time she wrote to me. But that was a while back, and now I'm not sure she'll show up. See, you're not the only guy with girl-friend problems. See you later."

I drove downtown to a payphone to make the call. Whenever I called a girl from home, my mom managed to hover in the vicinity. When I dialed Linda's number, her mother answered.

"Hi, Mrs. Bergstrom. It's Ade."

"Oh, hello, Ade. So good to hear from you. How have you been?"

"Just fine, Mrs. Bergstrom, and you?"

"Oh, just the same, you know. I read about you in the paper, Ade. You're having a wonderful season, you and the rest of the boys. Just wonderful. I'll bet you could get a scholarship."

"Is Linda home yet, Mrs. Bergstrom?"

There was a pause.

"No, Ade. She's not here." There was another silence. "I hate to have to be the one to tell you this: she's not coming. She told us last weekend that she wasn't. I told her to call you and tell you. I know you two had a date for the homecoming dance. I'm so disappointed in her that she didn't call. We raised her better than that."

"I know you did, Mrs. Bergstrom. It's not your fault."

"We've always been real fond of you, Ade. I guess these things happen when people go away to school."

"What things are those?"

"You know, meeting someone new. I guess she didn't tell you that either?"

"No ma'am, she didn't. I haven't heard from her since the begin-ning of October."

"Oh. Oh my. I don't know where Linda's head is. Up in the clouds, I suppose. Yes, she's met someone. He's going to take her to meet his parents. I'm sorry."

"Nothing to be sorry about. I'm very happy for her. I hope it all works out."

"I'm going to demand that she write to you and explain herself. That's the responsible thing to do."

"That would be one of those 'dear John' letters, wouldn't it? Please don't. I'm sure I'll bump into her sometime."

"Ade, I know you're disappointed."

"Well, goodbye, Mrs. Bergstrom. Thanks for letting me know. You're a real nice lady."

"Goodbye, Ade." She started to say something else, but I hung up so she wouldn't hear my voice break. So that was that. First love, first major heartbreak.

Suddenly, Smoke Tree seemed as confining as the phone booth. I got in my car and headed out of town. I crossed the Santa Fe tracks just north of the depot. I stayed on that road until it turned to dirt and ran along the river and south to the Bureau of Reclamation Bridge.

Just short of the bridge, I parked on the dike and walked down through the tamarisk thicket to the beach. I could smell the alkali dust from the city well site across the road. The Colorado was running fast and flat under a clear blue sky. I walked up the beach to one of the promontories that jutted into the river. I sat down among the rocks that formed the revetment. I could hear the gurgle of water as it hit the up-stream side of the point and bounced off, part of the water heading back into the main channel and part of it circling behind the downstream side of the point. The river, a startling, deep blue, looked smooth but fast. I could see large, circular spots where the churning water was bringing billows of sand to the surface. I could hear the whirring of the wings of the little gray birds flitting through the tamarisks. The sun was behind me. It was warm on my back, but there was a chill in the air coming off the river in front of me. I could smell the cold water and the dusty tang of the tamarisks.

I started thinking about Linda. I let my mind run that direction for a while, then realized I was starting to feel sorry for myself. I willed myself to stop. Getting weepy wasn't going to change anything.

I looked across the river at the thick bushes crowding the Arizona shore. I could see the rip-rock stacked on both sides of the bridge pilings and smell the creosote that coated the crude timbers and planks of the wooden bridge. I heard a vehicle with a defective muffler coming up the road behind me. It hit the planks on the bridge, and they began to tremble. I looked up to see an old, green Ford pickup moving slowly across. There was something painted on the side, but I couldn't make it out. As the planks rumbled louder, the swallows that had built their mud nests up under the bridge began to swoop and flare over the river.

The truck crossed the center of the bridge. I could see the spot below the plank roadway where a local man had painted "B. Jones was here" in bright orange. The same guy had painted the same thing on flat surfaces all over the desert, sometimes on beautiful rock formations. I couldn't understand why anybody would want to do that, but I sure wished he would stop.

When the truck had crossed and turned north toward Bullhead, I lay back on the rocky ground and stared straight up into the sky. When I closed my eyes, I could see the red behind my eyelids. Some of the pressure of the hectic, troublesome day began to slip away. As I relaxed, I became aware of the sound of my breathing and the beating of my heart.

But then I began to see a slide show of the night before: the old abandoned house, the windmill spinning silver in the moonlight, the half-open door hanging askew on the hinges, Judy slamming into Johnny in her haste to get out of the house, the metal pump on the sink, the chinaberry tree bursting into flames.

I saw the back of the guy who had knocked me down. I knew there was something about the way he moved, but I still couldn't place him. I sat up and tried to define what was so familiar. It was like trying to catch smoke.

The sky, which had been cloudless, was beginning to fill with horsetails. The color of the river was changing from deep blue to grayish-green. The north wind, which could blow hard enough from January to March to strip the bark from the trees along the waterway, began to pick up. Three mud hens landed on the river in front of me and began diving and bobbing back up. A swirl of starlings spiraled into the sky from a stand of tamarisk across the river.

I climbed down the rocks to the edge of the fast-moving water and cupped my hands, then splashed ice-cold water on my face. I leaned down, supported myself on two smooth rocks at the water's edge, and put my mouth in the river. I sucked in deep drinks of pure, sweet water.

I rinsed my hands and ran them through my hair. I walked to the top of the point, thinking about the guy who had knocked me flat at the House of Three Murders and wondering why he had been in that particular place at that particular time.

★ ★ ★

In the locker room that night, when Johnny undressed, he had a T-shirt on under his plaid shirt. He kept it on when he put on his shoulder pads, leaving the shirt he called his good luck shirt in his locker. He had worn the lucky shirt for every game of our undefeated season without ever washing it.

I saw the pain in his face as he laced the pads across his sternum. He saw me watching him. He made the "o.k." sign with his thumb and forefinger, but we both knew he was in for a tough night.

We left the locker room and headed to the field. As we ran down the cement steps, it looked like half the town was there. The band was sitting on folding chairs on the track to make room for more fans in the bleachers, but there were still a lot of people standing in the dirt. Dust was billowing high into the air, and bats and nighthawks were flying around the stadium lights, feasting on bugs. I could smell popcorn and hotdogs.

The Smoke Tree cheerleaders were in front of the stands. As we came onto the field, they turned toward the visitors' side of the field and chanted: "Hello Sunset, what do you know? Smoke Tree wants to say 'hello.' H-E-L-L-O, hello!"

The stadium p.a. system blared out, "Here they are, your 1960 Smoke Tree High Scorpions."

On our first series of downs, Johnny dropped back to pass on second and long, and the protection just broke down. The defensive end from Johnny's blindside crashed through, and when Johnny squared up to throw to his left, the guy drilled him chest high. It was a clean hit but brutal. How Johnny managed to hold onto the ball, I'll never know, but when the play was over, he didn't get up. I ran over. He was curled on his side, clutching the ball, tears streaming down his face.

"Can you get up?"

He shook his head. "Not yet," he said in a choked voice. "Gimme a second here."

The Smoke Tree fans were completely silent. They knew what it meant if Johnny was out of the game. He was the heart of the team, the guy who made it all work. The ref waved for an official time-out. The volunteer physician for all our games, Doc Hayden, jogged onto the field, his tie flying and his glasses bouncing on his nose. He knelt beside Johnny.

"What is it, son? Where does it hurt?"

"Everywhere. But I'm okay. I can get up." And he did, but because of the injury timeout, he had to leave the field for one play. The backup quarterback came in, and we went into the huddle.

"What's with Johnny?" asked Deke, our fullback.

"He's okay. He'll be back. Right now, let's not do anything stupid. Quarterback draw, on two, and for God's sake, hang onto the ball."

"Hey," said Bobby Quayles, a sophomore who thought he was Smoke Tree's answer to Johnny Unitas, "let's run a pass play."

"You heard Ade," said Seve. "Just do what he says. Quarterback draw on two. Break!"

We picked up a yard or two but had to punt. And that started a game that became a slog. We stopped Sunset Crossing on their first series. They had to punt. When Johnny came back into the game for our next series, his face was white and pinched behind the single bar on his helmet. When he threw, his passes had none of their usual zip and accuracy.

That left the running game, but their defense was tough. Neither the other halfback nor I could get much beyond the linebackers. Estaro was more elusive than I, but not as fast, and our line wasn't opening the big holes he was used to seeing. He had little room to shift and juke. I could hit the holes faster, but I was just a straight-line runner with no real moves. Even if I cleared the linebackers, the defensive backs, now aware Johnny couldn't pass well, were collapsing on the ball. I couldn't get that one step I needed to be gone.

But our defense was tough too, and Sunset Crossing couldn't get untracked. As a result, neither team could get beyond mid-field. When the first half came to an end, we had a scoreless tie.

At halftime, Coach Lucas was calm, as he always was. He praised the defense for its hard work and drew out some blocking adjustments for the offense.

"Johnny, what's wrong tonight? You're late with the ball every time. It's a wonder you haven't been picked off."

"Dunno, coach. My arm's dead."

"Well, their right side defensive back is beginning to jump our routes. He's number twenty-six. No more passes to that side tonight unless they rotate him. We'll pick on the other guy. He's not as sharp. Short routes – nothing deep."

"Okay, coach."

"Now, boys, Superintendent Symington is out in the hallway. He wants to talk to you before you start the second half."

A groan went up. Superintendent Symington had talked to us once before at halftime. By the time he got done lecturing about the Peloponnesian war and Caesar crossing the Rubicon, we didn't know if we were supposed to play football or write an essay.

Coach smiled. "But I told him he can't come in."

There was a cheer. We headed out the door and onto the field with smiles on our faces. Coach Lucas was a smart guy.

But the third quarter was more of the same. Neither team could do much. It must have been a boring game to watch, but no one left the Smoke Tree stands.

At the beginning of the fourth quarter, I had my shining moment in high school football. The Sunset Crossing Crusaders were starting to move the ball. Their front line was bigger than ours, and they were slowly wearing us down. I was playing my right-side defensive back position. As one of four players on our team who played every down on both offense and defense, I was sucking wind.

Sunset Crossing had the ball on our thirty-four-yard line when it happened. At the snap of the ball, their left halfback began to loop to his left with the quarterback trailing him. Suddenly, I knew what they were going to do. The quarterback was going to pitch to the halfback! It was my job to cover the left end for a possible pass, but I let him go by and sprinted toward the play. Their quarterback never saw me. It was a designed pitchout all the way. I was across the line of scrimmage when he shoveled the ball toward the halfback. I plucked it out of the air without breaking stride. No one had any chance to catch me. We kicked the extra point. It was seven nothing.

We kicked off, and their return man made some nifty moves and brought it back to the fifty-yard line. I thought we were in trouble, but on third down, their quarterback fumbled the snap and was lucky to recover it for no gain. When they punted, their punter shanked the ball. It went out of bounds just past the line of scrimmage.

When we went into the huddle, Johnny looked at Seve. "I've only got one good pass in me. Can you get a step on the linebacker on a slant?"

"Believe I can and throw the ball. I'll get it."

Johnny faked Estaro into the line, pulled up, and hit Seve with a hard, flat pass. Seve was a step past the middle linebacker and turned up field. Our right end hit the outside linebacker, and their defensive corner never had a chance. He saw Seve coming toward him with a full head of steam and dove at his knees. Seve straight-armed him and took off down the right sideline. The safety took an angle on Seve but miscalculated. I don't think he had ever seen anybody that big who could run that fast. Seve was gone. Extra point. Fourteen nothing.

Then the game went back into grind mode. Those two quick scores took something out of the Crusaders. They never recovered the momentum they had started to establish. Their defense continued to hang tough, but their offense kept going three and out. Frustration began to set in. There were questionable hits and penalties and lots of anger.

With less than five minutes left in the game, we were on the Sunset Crossing hash mark on second down and long near midfield. Johnny handed off to me on a routine twenty-two crossbuck that went nowhere. Well after the whistle blew, the right-side linebacker came across the line and hit Johnny at full speed. Johnny went down hard. Flags flew all over the field.

Seve ran to the play. He pulled the Crusader off Johnny and slammed him to the ground. The head referee picked up his flag and threw it again. All hell broke loose. There were fights all over the field. The Sunset Crossing bench emptied. On the other side of the field, Superintendent Symington got in front of our bench and yelled, "The first player who crosses this sideline will be suspended." He was nearly trampled.

It took the referees, all the coaches, and the reserve policemen ten minutes to restore some kind of order. For every fight they stopped, another one broke out. Johnny was still not up. Then the Smoke Tree fans began to spill out of the stands and onto the field. There was potential for an ugly incident. The coaches and policemen, and some of the teachers surrounded the Sunset Crossing team. The Crusader bus drove onto the field, and their team got on. The bus drove off the field, down the hill, and onto Route 66 without stopping. Smoke Tree wants to say goodbye!

When we went into the locker room after the game, Coach Lucas tried to be mad at us for the fighting, but he couldn't keep the smile off his face. He gave up and congratulated us on the win, especially the defense. He cautioned the offense not to be down on themselves. He told us that the character of a team is only revealed when things are not going well. He told us we had been tested and not found wanting.

Then he paused for a moment. "I'm going to tell you something now I didn't tell you before the game. We should never even have been playing these guys. Their enrollment is almost four times ours. They're a private Catholic school, and they recruit players from all over Los Angeles by giving them free tuition and housing. I can't tell you, boys, how proud I am of you for going toe to toe with them. You fought them to a standstill. Go home and get ready for the dance and enjoy yourselves tonight. And hey, let's take a day off. You've earned it. No practice on Monday!"

Everyone cheered. A day off from practice was unheard of. As coach walked out of the room, he tapped me on the shoulder and motioned for me to follow him. We went down the hall into his office.

"Sit down, Ade."

I sat down in front of his desk.

"I want you to know you about gave me heart failure when you dropped your coverage and took off for the line of scrimmage. If their quarterback had looked up and seen that end uncovered, it would've been six points. Want to tell me what you were thinking?"

"I can't explain it, sir. All of a sudden, I just knew what was going to happen. I knew what the play was going to be as soon as the halfback started to move."

"Well, I should have you running laps all week for breaking coverage discipline, but whatever you were thinking turned out to be right. But for God's sake, never, ever do something like that again."

"Okay, coach."

"Now get out of here. I'll see you next week."

When I got back to the team, Johnny was sitting in front of his locker, taking his cleats off. He put on his street shoes and then put his cleats, shoulder pads, and helmet in the locker. He gathered up his street clothes and headed for the door. I stopped him.

"Hey, bud, how you feeling after that last hit?"

"I'm all right. I missed the fight though. The guys were telling me about it. Everybody I talked to knocked down at least two players on the other team. I'll see you and Linda at the dance."

"I'm not going. Linda didn't come home. She's still in Santa Barbara."

He gave me a long look and shook his head. "Well, you could come stag. Might be some ladies would want to dance with you, now that you're a bona fide football hero."

"No thanks. I'm going to the mountains for the weekend. I'll see you Sunday night. By the way, nice pass."

"Thanks. And nice whatever that thing was that you did. Did coach want to talk to you about it?"

"Yeah."

"What'd he say?"

"Told me to never pull a stunt like that again."

"That's what I thought he'd say."

By the time I got home, it was almost ten o'clock. Mom was lying on the couch reading a book.

"How did your game go?"

"We won."

"That's nice. Did you make any points?"

"Yes, I made some points."

"Well, good for you."

"Is Dad out?"

"Yes. He won't be back until tomorrow."

"I was going to drive to the mountains tonight, but I'll wait 'til morning. I know Dad doesn't like you to be here alone at night."

"You should go to the dance with your friends. You don't have to miss it just because Linda didn't come home. Don't let her ruin your senior year for you. Go and have some fun."

"No, I don't think so."

"Are you going to be all right? I know you must be feeling bad."

"I'll be okay. Really. I've got to get to bed now. I'm going to get up early and get started."

"All right. I'm going to sit up and read. If I fall asleep on the couch, wake me when you get up."

I went down the hall to Dad's "extra room." I unlocked the gun rack and got out my single-shot twelve-gauge and zipped it up inside its case, then put my Winchester .22 pump in a smaller case. I put a box of Peters low-base six shot and a box of .22 shells in my hunting vest along with my pocket knife. I carried everything into my room and leaned the gun cases against the wall behind the door. I got my sleeping bag out of my closet. It smelled of wood smoke. I stacked my homework and school books on top of it.

I got undressed and climbed in bed. I thought about Linda and was sad again. Then I thought about picking that ball out of the air, and I didn't feel as bad. I told myself to wake up at 4:30 and rolled onto my side, and went to sleep.

Chapter 4

CHARLIE

On Friday night, while I was playing a football game that would soon be forgotten by everybody but the people who were part of it, Charlie Merriman was walking down a dirt road in the river bottom. He was heading for home. He was very hungry and very worried. His world was unspooling around him. He was listening hard for vehicles so he could get off the road and not be seen if one came by. His face and hands were covered with gouges and deep scratches from the mesquite thicket he had crawled into behind the abandoned house.

The night before, once he had knocked the man down and run away, Charlie moved away from the house. He was working on the cord around his wrists by the time the sheriff's cars and the spectators showed up. While they were coming in from the south, he was moving: first off to the north and then to the west. He reached the edge of the river bottom and climbed up onto a low hill where he could watch the fire. He knew he was in trouble but didn't know what else he could have done.

He estimated it was well after midnight by the time the fire was abating and all the vehicles had left. He watched the fire for a while longer and then fell asleep on the hill.

When he woke up on Friday morning, he walked back toward the house. The salt cedars along the driveway were still standing even though some of the needles were singed. Nothing could fully burn those things. Otherwise, there was devastation in every direction. The fire had burned through the mesquite thickets behind the house all the way back to the desert hillside at the edge of the river bottom where he had slept. It had burned the house to the ground. The only things left standing on the property were the water tank, the windmill, the charred railroad ties in the corral, and the salt cedars. The broken shaft of the water pump was still clanking against the side of the empty tank. Buzzards were circling in tight spirals high above.

As Charlie walked back down the driveway to the road, he saw a dust plume rising in the distance, then heard a car coming. Charlie was up inside the foliage of a salt cedar by the time the sheriff's department car arrived. The deputy stayed for a long time. He looked around behind the house and picked up something. He looked at the outline of the old corral, marked by the charred remains of the railroad ties. Then he began to poke through the debris from the house. Suddenly he stopped and bent down. He hurried over to the cruiser and talked on the radio.

Later, another sheriff's car arrived. A tall man with the high cheekbones and obsidian-black eyes of an Aztec warrior got out of the car. His sharply tailored uniform showed the lean power of his body. Charlie realized it was Lieutenant Caballo, the substation commander everyone called Horse. The other deputy came over to report. The two of them walked into the ashes of the house. A while later, another car drove up. A man in civilian clothes talked with the deputies and then walked into the debris with them. The three of them stood there talking for a long time.

An hour later, an ambulance came. The driver and his helper got out a body bag. Under the direction of the man who was probably the coroner, they put Sixto's remains into the bag. They zipped up the bag, dragged it to the ambulance, and got inside. The ambulance drove away. The coroner left.

Lieutenant Caballo and the other deputy put on gloves and walked around in what had been the interior of the house. The lieutenant kicked at the pipe holding the water pump where the sink had been. He gave the handle a couple of pumps. The other deputy picked up the pan Charlie and Sixto had used. Lieutenant Caballo came up with the pieces of Sixto's .45. Apparently, the rounds in the gun had cooked off and blown it into separate chunks. Charlie didn't like to think about what the .45 cartridges and the rounds in the other gun in Sixto's pocket had done to his body.

The deputies drove away. Charlie stayed in the tree for a long time. He wanted to be sure no one was coming back. He would have stayed up there even longer, but a stream of red ants found him. He climbed down and took off his shirt, and brushed them off. Then he pulled down his pants and brushed off the rest of them. When he thought he was rid of them, he walked north toward where he and Sixto had abandoned the car.

The car was still there. He couldn't tell if anyone had examined it. There was oil puddled beneath the front. When he walked behind the car, he could smell gasoline. "Damn," he thought, "that cowboy could shoot! We were lucky this thing didn't catch on fire."

As he stood there looking at the car, he heard a vehicle coming. He hurried into the mesquite thicket beside the road. An old, yellow pickup came around the bend a few minutes later. The truck slowed as it passed Sixto's car. "Castillo Ranch" was painted on the side in fading letters. Fifty feet past the Mercury, the truck stopped. Charlie heard the gears grind as the driver put the transmission in reverse. He backed up and got out of the truck. He walked around the car, bending over to peer in the windows. When he got back in the truck, he turned around and drove back the way he had come.

Charlie moved deeper into the mesquites. They weren't as thick here as they had been around the house, and he could make his way between them. Finally, he came to the edge of the backwater to the west of the river. He knelt down, cupped his hands, and tasted. It was brackish but drinkable. He drank his fill. It tasted of fish and decaying vegetation.

He moved back into the brush. He saw mud hens paddle by. Then some teal landed in the water. They left and were replaced by widgeon. Later, a single quail moved out of the brush ten yards from him. It stood off the water's edge and then called softly. An entire covey came out of the thicket single file and drank at the water's edge. When a scorpion ran across Charlie's hand, he jerked to shake it off. The covey exploded into flight. They flew over the water and circled away from him.

He stayed near the water all day. He hadn't eaten for a long time, but it didn't bother him a lot. He had been hungry many times before. Several times he moved back to the edge of the water and drank. In the late afternoon, he thought he heard vehicles on the road, but he wasn't sure, and he didn't go to look. Soon after that, he fell asleep.

When he woke, the moon was above the rim of the Black Mountains. He estimated the time at about eight-thirty. He decided it was time to go home. He wanted to consult with the old ones. They could explain what he had to do to have the dream that would give him his *sumach a'hot*. Once he had his "special gift," he could find a way out of this trouble.

He took one final drink and went through the mesquites to the road. He followed the road to Paiute Wash and then turned west up the wash toward the Dead Mountains. He intended to walk far enough so no one would connect him with the events in the river bottom and then turn south over the open desert. It was a good night to walk the desert under a full moon and breathe air that didn't smell of smoke and dead bodies.

Chapter 5

AEDEN

It was dark when I came awake. I turned on the lamp and looked at the clock. It was 4:30. I got dressed and laced on my hunting boots. I carried the guns, my vest, and a heavy jacket down the hall to the kitchen. I peeked into the living room. Mom wasn't on the couch. I went back to my room and got my sleeping bag and my homework. I picked up a towel on my way past the bathroom.

I opened the back door, turned on the porch light, and went out to the carport. I found the wooden box I used when I went to the mountains. I put pancake mix, dried milk, eggs, bacon, salami, cheese, peanut butter, bread, two potatoes, Crisco, coffee, and brown sugar into the box. I put the towel on top of the food. I took everything I needed outside, put it in the trunk of the car, and locked up the house. I had to choke the car to get it started in the chilly morning air. By five o'clock, I was headed down Jordan Street hill.

I merged with the light westbound traffic on 66 and crossed the railroad tracks. I stopped at the West End Shell. The attendant filled my tank with gas and washed my window. After I paid, I pulled around the side and went into the coffee shop. I smelled coffee and stale cigarette smoke. I sat at the counter. Bacon was cooking on the griddle behind the order window. The bleary-eyed waitress stubbed out her cigarette and came down the counter with her order pad. I ordered a cup of coffee and a side order of hash browns. I heard them sizzling on the griddle before the waitress even hooked the order on the wheel.

Back on 66, I turned on the radio. Roy Orbison was singing "Only the Lonely." I drove out of the city limits with the stream of traffic headed toward South Pass. When the two-lane blacktop began its steepest climb, the Hollywood Argyles were goofing their way through "Alley Oop." I turned off 66 onto 95 toward Las Vegas.

I crossed Paiute Wash, the smoke trees ghostly in the false dawn. I drove through Klinefelter, a wide spot on the road where an abandoned motor court sat huddled and sad inside a stand of massive salt cedars cupped by low, red hills, the paint peeling off the stucco walls and the roofs collapsing in on themselves. I passed a short section of cattail reeds, desert willows, and tamarisk shrubs lining a ditch filled with water from a spring bubbling out of the hillside farther back up the wash. I could smell hard water and the rank odor of algae growing among the reeds.

I left Highway 95 just before it crossed the Santa Fe tracks at Arrowhead Junction and turned onto the old, pre-war alignment of 66 toward Goffs. In front of the service station at the junction, three old, gravity-fed Mobil gas pumps with glass measures on top stood in front of an ancient, dark-green wood-frame building. There was a screened-in porch running across the front.

The man who owned the station lived in rooms behind the store. His name was Hugh Stanton, and Johnny and I sometimes stopped in to talk with him and buy a soft drink. I was pretty sure he'd be sitting on his porch, watching the light come into the sky in the East. As I got out of the car, I could smell the creosote coating on the railroad ties in the track bed and the gasoline and motor oil that had soaked into the dirt next to the pumps over many years.

I went up the steps and pushed open the screen door. The porch smelled of coffee, dust, and desiccated, sun-dried wood. Mr. Stanton, thin, almost to the point of emaciation, was sitting on a metal folding chair. He was dressed in his usual outfit: gray canvas pants, olive-green T-shirt, long-billed, green cap, and high-top boots. His almost-black eyes were buried in a face full of lines and creases. He broke into a smile when he saw me.

"Good morning, Ade. Step on up here."

"Good morning, Mr. Stanton. Getting ready for the sunrise?"

"Sure am. Got my morning coffee and my special toast."

Hugh Stanton's 'special toast' was a strange concoction. He stripped the tiny green leaves off of creosote bushes, mixed them with mayonnaise and Tabasco Sauce, and then mashed them into a paste he spread on toast.

"Care to sit with an old man a minute?"

"Yessir. Thought you might be out here. And you're not so old, Mr. Stanton."

"Eighty-four this past October. Eighty-four."

"I don't mean to be nosey, but I've never asked you how long you've lived here."

"Come out here in nineteen and thirty-four. My brother and his wife and me lived in the Oklahoma panhandle on our pappy's farm. He left Arkansas, where he had been a tenant farmer, in the 1800s. Told us he got tired of farming for other people. In Oklahoma, he homesteaded 160 acres. He was proud of that farm because he was part Chickasaw, and he never would've had no chance to own property in Arkansas.

"Well, Ade, we had some good years on that farm, but they come to an end when the Depression hit. Grain prices went way down, and the size of the crop went right down with the prices. Then the dust bowl hit, and we lost our farm to the bank. It broke my pappy's heart. Killed him. We were going to go back to tenant farming, but he died before we could find a place. So my brother and his wife and me come west in an old jalopy, like lots of other folks back then. I was fifty-eight years old. Nothing left for me in Oklahoma, so I thought I'd see California. Like to never made it. It was a terrible trip. Terrible hard. Well, sir, we was just about out of money when we stopped here, and the man who owned the place, a man about as old as I am now, had a sign up for help wanted, a rare sight in the Depression. Said he was too old to run the station.

I took the job, even though it paid next to nothin'. There warn't no minimum wage in those days, you know. It was the free room and board that drew me. My brother and his wife headed on toward the coast, and I never heard from them or of them again.

I been here ever since. When I started here, the old man's business was already drying up pretty bad because the gov'ment rerouted 66 over South Pass in' 31. He mostly got old cars with poor people who thought their junkers couldn't make it over the steep hill, so even the people who did come by here didn't have no money, no way. Well, sir, I saved almost ever cent the man paid me, even though it warn't much. In '38, I bought the place from him for three hundred and fifty dollars: the land, the well, and all."

He paused a moment and ate a piece of toast, and drank some coffee.

"I've owned her free and clear ever since, and I have everything I want right here. In the day, I watch the trains and cars go by, and at night I listen to the radio: KOA out of Albuquerque mostly. Some wouldn't like it, but it's a good enough life for me. I never wanted much, and I have everything I want right here." He laughed and drank more coffee.

"You must have seen a lot of changes in your time."

"Nossir, Ade. Look out there in front of us. Highway, train tracks, Paiute Wash, Dead Mountains. None of that has changed a nickel's worth. When I first come out here, I climbed up to the top of that mountain there and put my name on a note I left in a Prince Albert can. The note asked anybody else who ever come up there to add their name. Well, I climbed up there again when I turned seventy and hadn't nobody been up there. Leastways if they had, they didn't leave no note or take the can. It was still there. Nossir, the only thing different is the freights come up the hill hooked to diesels now instead of steam locomotives. I got to tell you, I surely miss that steam whistle blowing wild and lonesome for the crossing on a cold winter night. Surely do." He paused again. Shook his head.

"Say, the last couple times you've been through, your friend Johnny hasn't been along. You two have a fallin' out?"

"No, Mr. Stanton, Johnny's in love. He spends most of his free time with his girlfriend."

"In love. Well. I hope she's a good'un. He seems a fine lad."

"He is, Mr. Stanton. He's a good friend and a good guy."

"I hope this girl does right by him."

"Thank you. Hope so too. Thanks for the story. You always have something interesting to tell me when I stop by. I'd better get on up the hill."

"Stop by any old time, Ade. Always good to have you come in and say hello."

I pulled onto old 66 and started the fourteen-mile drive to Goffs. The road began to climb almost immediately. On the right side of the road, the Santa Fe roadbed loomed fifty feet higher than the highway. Creosote bushes and white bursage lined the edge of the road and spread all the way up to the tracks. On the left was a broad section of Piute wash, filled with white smoke trees turning pink in the rising sunlight. Clustered around the bases of the hundreds of trees were remnants from countless flash floods: humped clumps of brush, piles of stones, and the root balls of small trees. The wash smelled of creosote and dust. With the rising sun, KOMA began to dissolve into static. The only time Smoke Tree could get a radio signal was at night. During the daylight hours, even the 50,000-watt stations couldn't reach us in the middle of the Mojave.

The road curved slightly to the north, and I passed the four-wheel-drive-only road that went underneath the railroad tracks where they were spanned by a concrete bridge. The road, a wagon trail in the 1880s, meandered away to the north toward the remains of Fort Piute. Old 66 shifted to the west and began to climb again. A small range of volcanic mountains rose on the horizon as I drove up onto a plateau above the town of Goffs. I could see the water tower beside the tracks at Goffs, standing like a sentinel guarding huge piles of railroad ties massed to the south of the tracks.

I drove past the Goffs store, crossed the railroad tracks, and turned off old 66 onto Lanfair Road. I passed the abandoned adobe school-house with its tile roof on the west side of the road. On my right was the long row of rusty and dented mailboxes that served the houses, mines, and ranches scattered far and away over the expanse of Lanfair Valley. I crossed a cattle guard, and the blacktop ended. I was on a badly washboarded road moving over a broad plateau that gradually inclined to the north. I could see the Providence Mountains far off to the west and the bulk of Hackberry Mountain to the northwest. To the north lay my destination: the New York Mountains. My old Plymouth felt like it was shaking itself apart on the bone-jarring road.

The landscape around me began to change. Bayonet yucca and buckhorn cholla were now mixed in with the creosote and white bursage. I could see an occasional hackberry bush alongside the road, its green leaves tinged on the edges with yellow and red. The leaves would be completely red by Christmas. On the crossbar of a telephone pole, I saw a golden eagle. Two miles down the road, I saw another. Teddy bear cholla, golden, fuzzy, harmless-looking, and painful to tangle with, appeared on both sides of the road.

To a lot of people, the land I was driving through looked empty. It looked crowded with interesting things to me. The bones of the earth were there to see. There were interesting plants capable of surviving extreme heat and bitter cold and interesting animals with incredible coping skills.

As I pulled even with Hackberry Mountain, the road dipped down into Vontrigger wash. I decided to look for the covey of quail that often watered in the early morning at the water tank farther down the wash. I pulled over and stopped. The dust cloud that I had kicked up began to settle around the car. It smelled different than the dust out in the river bottom – dryer and cleaner somehow. I opened the trunk, got my shotgun out of the case, and put on my vest.

I walked down the wash toward the tank. The sandy bottom was thick with desert willow and cat's claw. The biggest willows were blighted with olive-green mistletoe. The large clumps of bladder sage interspersed in the willows had turned dark brown with the coming of fall. I saw deep green Mormon tea and the fuzzy white of mulefat. There were bayonet-spiked Mojave Yucca mixed with reddish barrel cactus on the hillside.

As I approached the water tank, I could see the blades spinning in the sunlight. I could hear water from a metal pipe spilling into a cattle trough. A raven, black and shiny as hot tar, rose croaking from the railroad-tie corral. I walked past the water tank to the abandoned roadbed of the Nevada Southern Railway. The railroad had once connected the small town of Barnwell, on the northwest face of the New York Mountains, to the Santa Fe tracks at Goffs. I climbed to the top of the roadbed. Neither the rails nor any of the ties remained. I looked east at the black and red volcanic rock of the Vontrigger Hills and beyond them to the Piute Mountains.

I stood there, scanning the creosote, white bursage-and-cactus-filled terrain. I could see no movement, nor did I hear quail talking while they fed on the seeds from last spring's flowers and grass. I sat down where the tracks had once been. A shadow streaked across the ground in front of me. I looked up into the deep blue sky. A red-tail hawk was flying in sweeping circles above me. If there were quail, they would be crouched under cover, holding perfectly still. There would be no quail hunting as long as the red-tail was there. I headed back to the car. A lot of hunters I knew would shoot red tails when they could. They claimed it left more quail for them to hunt. I never shot at hawks.

I got back on Lanfair Road. After more dips and curves in the wide, sandy wash, the road rose up and headed directly north again, paralleling the old rail bed. The road was smoother now. I was in the middle of a vast expanse of Joshua trees. A few miles up the road, I stopped at the lonely phone booth at the intersection of Lanfair and Cedar Canyon roads. It was the only phone between Goffs on the south, Searchlight, Nevada on the north, and Baker, California, fifty miles to the west. "What the heck," I thought. "I might as well get this over with."

I pulled over and went into the phone booth. Since there was no one waiting, I left the door open. I picked up the receiver and turned the crank on the wooden box.

"Operator. Where are you ringing from?"

"Windmill two."

"Is that the phone booth in the middle of the desert?"

"Yes, ma'am."

"Where do you wish to call?"

"Santa Barbara, California." I gave the number.

"I know there's no coin box there. How do you want me to bill this?"

"To my home phone number: EB6-2700."

"Thank you. Connecting you now. Please ring off when you are finished."

The phone rang for a long time before someone answered. I realized that people probably didn't get up early on Saturday mornings in Santa Barbara.

"Westmont College, Page Hall."

"May I speak with Linda Bergstrom, please?"

"I don't think Linda's here today, but let me check."

The girl put the phone down. I could hear the echo of her footsteps on a hard floor as she walked away. There was no other sound. Outside the phone booth, a dust devil bounced through the Joshua trees. I heard the girl's footsteps returning.

"Linda signed out for the weekend. The sheet shows her destination as Carmel. Do you want to leave a message?"

"No, thank you."

I hung up and cranked the handle to ring off. I stood outside the phone booth and let the desert silence surround me. I felt like crying.

The dust devil blew itself out in the distance. I got back in my car, thinking it was best this way. "Let it go, just let it go," I told myself. "Don't get hung up on this." It was an easy thing to tell myself.

As I continued north, the New York Mountains grew larger on the northwest horizon. I passed the headquarters of the OX cattle ranch, and then the Castle Peaks rose up to the northeast. The number of Joshua Trees began to decrease. By the time the road bent west to the turn-off for Carruthers Canyon, it was almost eight o'clock.

At the mouth of the canyon, the air grew colder, and the landscape began to change again. Junipers, pinyon pines, and scrub oak began to outnumber the Joshua Trees. Fall-blooming shrubs like rabbitbrush and snakeweed were covered with golden-yellow blossoms. I rolled down the window to take in the high-country perfume of blue sage, big sage, and Great Basin Sage. I was back in the beautiful, lonesome mountains of the Eastern Mojave.

Turning into the canyon, I shifted down into first gear. I crawled slowly up the barely-visible, rutted, and washed-out road that ran up the canyon's west side. I was climbing steadily now. It was getting colder. Slowing almost to a walk, I turned west on the rough track that led into a short, side canyon and Lee's Camp.

Lee Hoskins was a good friend of the family. He had inherited thirty acres of land, originally a mining claim, from his father. Lee built a compact adobe house with a tile roof next to the mining cabin his father had built. Lee plastered the inside of the house and white-washed the outside.

Inside, the adobe was comfortable but utilitarian. The cement floors were bare. There was a good-drawing fireplace and a wood-burning stove. There were rough cabinets and a galvanized metal sink with a water pump that pulled sweet water from the artesian spring out back. The sleeping arrangements were Spartan. There were army cots in the sleeping room. When we used the place, we brought our own bedding or sleeping bags. Lee had dug a root cellar deep into the hillside behind the original cabin. There was an old, insulated icebox in the cellar that would keep meat, cheese, eggs, and butter relatively fresh, even without ice.

Lee Hoskins had never married. He was a kind and somewhat shy and reclusive man, well-liked but reticent. Dad was his best friend. The two of them hunted and fished together. Lee was often at our house for dinner and at holidays. While I was growing up, I spent a lot of time at the place he called "Lee's Camp" with Lee and my dad, and mom.

As soon as I could drive, Lee gave me my own keys to the padlocks on the front and back doors and the root cellar. He told me I was welcome to use the adobe anytime. The only rules were to leave the place clean and lock up.

I pulled up next to the adobe and got out to unpack my gear. I could smell the pungent odor of the burnt sage the hot muffler had dragged across as I drove up the brush-covered, primitive track. I unlocked the padlock on the front door and the one on the door to the root cellar. I put the food in the old icebox.

I rolled out my sleeping bag on one of the cots. I checked the firewood box. There was wood for the fireplace and the wood-burning stove. I noticed mice had been in the adobe since the previous weekend and chewed up some of the newspaper used to start fires.

Once everything was put away, I went outside and climbed the steep canyon behind the adobe. The really cold weather hadn't set in yet. Mojave Green rattlesnakes could still be active, so I was careful about where to step and did not put my hands anywhere I couldn't see as I climbed and scrambled up the steep hill.

There was a great view from the bluff above the steep side canyon. To the southeast, I could see Spirit Mountain near Davis Dam, Boundary Cone at Oatman, and well beyond that the Hualapai Mountains southeast of Kingman, Arizona. To the southwest were the Whipple

Mountains near the edge of Lake Havasu. It was a huge, almost entirely unpopulated and mysterious expanse. Out there were peaks and washes and gullies where no human foot had ever stepped. To the north, I could see the 7,900-foot peak of the New Yorks, the highest point between the Hualapais and Mount Charleston outside Las Vegas.

My father had started bringing me to the mountains when I was just a child. Few people from Smoke Tree came out here. Most of the ones who did were hunters who only came for opening day of quail or deer season. But we came up year-round.

When I got older, we began to stay at Lee's Camp over the weekends. Lee was often there, but even if he couldn't come, the adobe was always available to us. Lee was very interested in everything that grew, flew, walked, or crawled here, and there were books in the adobe about the desert. Lee taught me to identify hundreds of desert plants and shrubs.

The New York Mountains and the Providence, Mid Hills, and Granites to the southwest resonated with something deep inside me. I don't know why. Later in life, whenever people asked me where I grew up, I answered, "Smoke Tree, California." But the picture that appeared in my mind when I said those words was not the town. The image I saw was the high desert mountains of the Eastern Mojave.

I sat on top of the hill and watched the sunlight paint the land with shadows and change the colors of the desert below me from brown to ocher to burnt umber. As I sat there, I reviewed the events of Thursday and Friday. I thought of the person who had knocked me sprawling, then ran away from me at the House of Three Murders. Once again, I struggled to call forth who it was, but once again, I could not.

I scrambled down the hill to the adobe. Even though the sun was now high in the sky, the cut canyon was still in shade. It would be almost noon before sunlight struck the red-tile roof. I got bread, salami, peanut butter, and cheese from the root cellar and made two big sandwiches at the sideboard by the old sink. I carried them to the crude, rough-hewn table and set them next to my schoolbooks and homework. I ate my sandwiches and drank cold water that tasted of the iron pump and the minerals of the hillside behind me. I knew hunting would not be good until the sun tilted to the west, so I got started on my homework.

* * *

By late afternoon, I had made a good beginning. I set my books aside and picked up my hunting vest. I removed the 12-gauge shells from the loops and got my .22 pump out of the case. I put my knife and a box of .22 shells in my pocket and set off toward the main canyon.

As I moved south toward Carruthers Canyon, I made an inventory of the plants thriving among the live oak, juniper, and pinyon pine. I saw the deep red of Indian paintbrush mixed with apricot mallow. There were tiny white blossoms on the Wright's buckwheat. In the shade created by the tilting sun, evening primrose and datura were opening pearly blossoms. When I reached the center of the broad canyon, I could see the peaks of the New York Mountains. On the flanks of the mountains, I could see the southernmost stand of Rocky Mountain White Fir.

It was a glorious late afternoon, the sky an amazing blue. The perfume of juniper and resinous pinyon pine mixed with sage filled the air. Sticky snakeweed, wooly desert marigold, Cooper's Paperflower, and turpentine bush were all blooming golden yellow. I also came across many of the large mounds of fallen cholla balls ingeniously piled up by packrats to make coyote-and-bobcat-proof nests.

I reached the east side of the deep canyon. I turned south toward the Pinto Mountains that lay between Carruthers Canyon and the boulder-strewn valleys and hillsides of the Mid Hills. I had come out to get a rabbit for my dinner, but I was doing more gawking than hunting in the crisp, clear air, even though almost every twenty yards, a cottontail rabbit would streak off through the brush or up the hillside.

Near the mouth of the canyon, I started to cross back over. I flushed a big covey of quail that had moved into the seed-rich wash at the edge of the sunshine. I stopped after they exploded out of the brush. I sat down on a big rock to listen. For a long time, all was quiet. Then I began to hear the males begin their distinctive calls to re-form the covey. Then I heard the hens talking as they hurried through the brush. Once the covey had re-assembled and moved off to the south, I continued to walk.

It grew colder as the sun tilted on the western horizon. By the time I reached the western edge of the canyon, it was in full shade. The temperature began to plummet. There were more cottontail now. They were feeding along the hillside in the fading light. I waited until one ran partway up the steep canyon hillside and stopped next to a Mojave Yucca. I shot it, gutted it, removed the head and feet, and stripped the fur off the small body. I slipped it into a plastic bag in my vest and headed home for dinner. I turned for one last look down the canyon. The dusk was turning the distant mountains a deep purple, and the wind was rising.

The sun had set by the time I reached the side-cut canyon. Even though it was only dusk in Carruthers Canyon, it was dark at the adobe. I got some newspaper and kindling and started a fire in the wood-burning stove. As soon as the kindling began to burn, I pushed the slider forward toward the chimney and stacked bigger pieces of wood on top of the small fire. The fire began to grow, and I opened the vents.

I wiped out the old, black skillet with a paper towel and set it on the stove above the firebox. Then I filled the Coleman lantern with white gas, turned the adjustment, and pumped it ten times. I lit a match and stuck it through the hole to ignite the mantle. When it caught, the lantern began to hiss. It soon filled the adobe with a bright, white light. I adjusted the feed and carried it out to the root cellar so I could find the Crisco, coffee, and potatoes.

Back in the kitchen, I got the rabbit out of my game bag and rinsed it under the pump. I cut it into six pieces and rubbed it down with salt. While I waited for the stove to get hotter, I put three big cups of water in the blue enamel pot, added coffee, and set it on the stove. Then I spooned Crisco into the black skillet. When it had melted, I put in the pieces of rabbit. While the rabbit was cooking, I washed two potatoes and cut them into pieces. When the rabbit was done, I pulled the pieces out of the skillet and set them on a piece of paper towel to drain. I put the potatoes in and began to turn them as they cooked.

Before the potatoes were done, the coffee boiled. I took the pot off the stove and added some cold water to settle the grounds. I moved it farther from the top of the firebox so it would stay hot but not boil again.

When the potatoes were done, I pushed the skillet to the side of the stove and poured Tabasco sauce and catsup on them. I put the pieces of rabbit back in the skillet and carried everything to the rough table along with a big glass of cold water. I was very hungry.

When I was finished, there was nothing left in the skillet but some bones and grease. I opened the door and threw the bones far out into the night. They would be gone by morning: the coyotes would see to that. I cleaned the skillet with paper towels, then tossed them into the woodstove, where they quickly burst into flame.

I banked the fire and got a mug of coffee and one of Lee's Zane Grey novels. To conserve white gas, I lit one of the big oil lamps and shut down the Coleman lantern. I sat down at the table to read. Despite drinking three mugs of coffee, it wasn't too long before I could barely keep my eyes open. I gave up on the book.

When I went outside before going to bed, the cold air had settled into the bottom of the cut canyon. I stood for a while, enjoying the sweet perfume of the pinyon-wood smoke from the stove. The nearly-full moon was well up in the eastern sky, and I could see my breath condensing in the night air. There was a big ring around the moon.

Back inside, I lit a candle and blew out the oil lamp. I carried the candle, some matches, and my coat into the sleeping room. It was much colder there. I dripped some wax on the floor and propped the candle in it. I put my jacket over the bottom of my sleeping bag to keep my feet warm. I got undressed, climbed into the bag, leaned over, and blew out the candle. I was very tired. Starting the day at 4:30 and ending it with a long walk over rough country had wiped me out. But it was a good kind of tired.

As I settled down to sleep, I could hear coyotes yipping out in the main canyon. Two different packs were calling to each other. As I tried to count the number of different voices, I drifted off to sleep.

★ ★ ★

I dreamed I was running on a broad plain under a winter sky and a late afternoon sun that was beginning to tint the western horizon Mercurochrome. I was in Lanfair Valley, surrounded by Joshua Trees, yuccas, and creosote. I wore sandals of woven yucca fibers lashed to my feet by straps of twisted agave. I was on the old Mojave trail.

I was running with a group of young men. They were all Mojave. Our only coverings were rabbit skins bound to our loins. I was breathing hard as I struggled to keep up, but the others were laughing and talking as they ran. We were running to the Pacific Coast over the Mojave Trail to trade for seashells. We carried turquoise and silver the tribe had traded for with the Hualapai, who had in turn traded with the Navajo and Hopi.

The trail dropped off the plateau down into a wide expanse of a sandy wash. The deep, coarse sand made running difficult. We rose up the far side of the wash and climbed to the top of the hill at Rock Springs. When we could see Table Mountain on our left and the beginning of the pinyon and juniper-covered Pinto Mountains on our right, we were joined by a group of young men of the Chemehuevi tribe. Without stopping, we traded some of our turquoise for a bundle of beautiful arrows bound with a leather thong.

As we ran on together, we were joined by coyotes. They ran on our right and left flanks, silent and intense, their eyes filled with the fantastic colors of a late afternoon sky now flaring deep red. The Mojave, the Chemehuevi, the coyotes, and I ran past Round Valley, through the Mid Hills, and down into Cedar Canyon. In the depths of the canyon, there was a huge boulder beside the trail. A mountain lion lay atop the boulder, its yellow eyes fixed upon us, its tail twitching back and forth as we ran toward it. The Chemehuevi fell away to return home. The coyotes stayed with us, though they gave the boulder a wide berth. Once we passed the cougar, they closed back in on our flanks.

We climbed to the top of the canyon and ran down the sun as it fell away from us through a western sky that was now the deep purple of a terrible bruise. The full moon rose up behind us. The coyotes continued on as our outliers, their backs straight, their tails lifted, and their noses pointed straight ahead as they ran with their heads entirely still in the effortless trot of the little cousins of the wolves.

The silent and implacable rotation of the earth in the deep black void of pitiless space turned us away from the sun and carried us into night. The smell of the desert changed. The tang of creosote gave way to the cool scent of sage. The wind coming out of the north picked up and blew colder.

When we started the long ascent of Cima Dome, one runner surged ahead. He had a peculiar lope as if he were pushing off harder with one leg than the other. As he moved ahead, he turned toward us and ran backward, gesturing for us to catch up, his face filled with laughter and the joy he took in the capability of his body. Using reserves I didn't know I had, I pulled away from the others. As he ran backward in front of me, I drew near to him. His eyes were so black, I thought I would see the silver moon mirrored there. Instead, I saw red and yellow flames. Silhouetted against the flames was a spinning, silver windmill.

I woke up. The room was pitch black and bitterly cold. For a few moments, I was still caught in the dream. Then it began to fade. But I knew there was something important I had to recall. I closed my eyes and strained to catch the wisps. I remembered running, but neither where nor to what purpose. I held very still. Bit by bit, I pulled back the pieces of the dream. It was like fishing something out of a deep, black well with a bright and shining silver thread tied to a hook made of the whitest bone. The prize the thread pulled toward me was the figure that had run backward ahead of me in the moonlight. The figure grew larger. The face expanded and filled my mind. My breath caught in my throat. Charlie Merriman!

I unzipped the sleeping bag and sat shivering on the edge of the cot in the freezing room, thinking about the running figure at the House of Three Murders. I felt around on the floor, found the matches, and lit the candle. I got dressed and went into the kitchen with the candle. The stove was still warm. I worked with the Coleman lantern and got it lit, then put chunks of wood on top of the coals in the stove. They began to burn almost immediately. The resin was popping as I closed the firebox door.

It sounded like hard rain was hammering the roof. I pulled open the door. Cold air rushed into the room. It was sleet, not rain. Small pieces of ice plummeted out of a black sky. The first storm of fall had come to the high desert mountains of the Eastern Mojave.

Chapter 6

CHARLIE

Charlie did not make it back to Mojave Village until well after midnight. He had walked west for hours up Piute Wash before turning south and crossing both the railroad tracks and Highway 66. When he was miles south of the highway, he turned due east toward the Village. The almost-full moon was very bright in the night sky. Charlie could see the creosote-dotted hillsides and sandy washes as he moved along the path he had chosen. He was very careful where he put his feet because he could not see the small, insidious ground cactuses. He was very thirsty.

He crossed 66 again just above the Village. Although he tried to shield his eyes from the oncoming headlights to keep from losing his night vision, once he was across the blacktop, he stumbled like a drunken man on the shoulder. He cautiously moved a distance away from the road and stood with his eyes closed for a long time before he went on.

He got home and let himself into the small cottage. He went to the kitchen for a long drink. Smoke Tree water was full of alkali and tasted terrible, but tonight he was grateful to have it. Charlie was very hungry, but he knew he had fasting ahead of him if he were to have the dream that would reveal his special gift. He had a two-and-a-half-day head start, so he didn't open the refrigerator door, afraid he would not be able to resist eating something.

His mother was in bed, breathing heavily, exhausted from another long day of cleaning rooms at the Travel Lodge. Charlie went past her door and into his room. He undressed, got into bed, and fell asleep immediately.

He jerked awake in the pre-dawn hours. When he first opened his eyes to the grayish-blue light outside his window, Charlie thought he was still on the floor of the house with a dead man in the corner. His muscles ached as though he were still hog-tied. He sat on the edge of the bed for a long time, trying to purge the image of Sixto's corpse out of his mind.

After a while, Charlie lay down and tried to go back to sleep. He heard a dog bark somewhere in the Village. There were no other sounds to disturb him, but his mind began to churn through the events of the last few days over and over again. He could not sleep.

Charlie got up and dressed quietly. He shivered in the cold. His mother was still sleeping soundly when he looked into her room, her coal-black hair spread on the pillow. He wrote her a note explaining he was on his way to see one of the old ones and slipped out the door.

In the gray light, the fifty tiny cottages on their fifty-by-one-hundred-foot lots could have been a feudal peasant enclave huddled out of sight of some arrogant, medieval lord. Some of the houses, like his mother's, were well maintained. Others were so neglected they appeared to be abandoned, but there was a family in each one. Charlie walked past the tribal office and the community hall. The Village was quiet as he moved through the poorly-maintained, narrow streets.

Charlie was headed for the last cottage on the southeast edge of the Village where one of the old ones, Hera anyai, lived. Known to the white people of Smoke Tree as Webster Charles, his Mojave name meant "flash of lightning." The name referred to his quickness of mind and the suddenness of his revelations. He was a singer of the old songs and keeper of the old myths, one of few such men still alive. Many of the Pipa Aha Macav sought him out for advice about the right way to undertake important tasks.

Even though the sun was still not up, Charlie found Hera anyai facing the Black Mountains on a folding chair in his neatly-raked dirt yard. Charlie knew the grandfather had cataracts. He wasn't sure how much the old man could see of the world around him, but Charlie knew Hera anyai could see deep into the spirit world. Not wanting to startle him, Charlie stopped a respectful distance away to call a greeting, but the grandfather spoke first.

"Good morning, Herow heilhevow. What brings you to me before the sun?"

"Grandfather, I have come to you for advice. I am in serious trouble because of the actions of another. The other has since died, leaving me with the consequences of his actions. I have come to ask you what I must do to visit the dream world and receive my *sumach a' hot*, so I can use my special gift to guide my actions."

"You have done the right thing by coming to me. Many of our young men are losing touch with the world of their ancestors, the world of Pipa Aha Macav. Come and sit next to me. While I wait for the sunrise, let me think about the proper steps for you to take."

Charlie moved into the yard and sat cross-legged in the dirt next to Hera anyai.

"I like to feel the heat of the sun on my face as it rises above the mountains in Arizona. My sight is failing me. My world grows dimmer with each passing year. It cheers me to see what light I can each morning even though it is fading."

Charlie and the old one sat silently side by side for over an hour. When the sun was well above the rim of the mountains, Hera anyai spoke.

"Walk with me to the river, Herow heilhevow."

He held out his left hand. It was bony, calloused, and covered with liver spots but strong for all of that. As Charlie helped Hera anyai to his feet, he put his hand behind the grandfather's elbow. The arm was thin but full of gristle and tendon that spoke of surprising resilience. It was less than twenty-five yards to the river, but it took almost ten minutes to get there. The grandfather walked slowly and carefully, picking his way through the rocks. He was wearing Levi's and a worn, red Pendleton shirt buttoned to the collar. As usual, on all but the coldest days, he was barefoot.

When they arrived at the river and moved to the end of an outcropping, they both sat facing the sun. Behind them, they could hear the sounds of the Village waking up: dogs barking, radios playing, doors slamming, cars starting, an argument breaking out somewhere. Even though the sun was warming the frigid air, the temperature was only in the high thirties.

There was no wind. A lone boat droned past on the smooth river. A man steered from the back, guiding it upstream. Charlie could see a fishing rod hanging over the edge of the boat. Hera anyai did not speak until the annoying sound had faded away.

"Tell me all that has happened."

Charlie told everything, from the time he walked into the Palms until he arrived at Hera anyai's cottage. He spared no detail. When he was finished, the grandfather sat quietly with his eyes closed and did not speak for a long time. When Hera anyai opened his eyes, he recounted the entire tale exactly as Charlie had related it; the old one was one of those with the long memory, and he had total recall of the spoken word.

When he had finished, he asked Charlie, "Is that everything that happened?"

"Yes, Grandfather."

"Think back over all the days. Are you sure you have told me all?"

They sat quietly again while Charlie compared the events of the days to the tale he had told the old one and the tale the old one had recited back to him.

"Yes, Grandfather. I am sure. I left nothing out."

"Herow heilhevow, you have become entangled in the world of people who are not Aha Macav. And in a serious matter. A man was robbed. Another man is dead. A house has been burned. Since Horse knows about this, he has talked to other law people. Now they know of it too.

Horse is a smart lawman. He will put these things together in a manner that will explain to him what has happened and who was there. It will not be long before he knows your name. When he knows it, he will come for you.

You must be prepared before Horse finds you. Although many paths through life are revealed to the Aha Macav through dreams, you are right in thinking an ordinary dream is not enough. You must indeed dream the dream that reveals your special gift to you. You must know what you must know before Horse, and the other law people take control of your life."

"I understand, Grandfather. I came to ask what steps I must take to have this dream."

"You say you have eaten nothing since the afternoon of Wednesday?"

"Yes, Hera anyai."

"Since that is so, once you have fasted until at least sundown on Tuesday you will be ready. But fasting alone will not be enough. When the time comes to sleep the sleep that will bring the dream you will dream, you must be in a certain place. And you must have been certain other places before you arrive at that place. And getting to those places must involve difficulty. This is the way of our ancestors.

I am one of the few remaining with the long memory. I am one who knows the old songs and stories that we must never lose, lest we cease to be the Pipa Aha Macav. I tell you this, Herow heilhevow because I have known of you in the Village for many years. You and one other boy. I have hope that you and this boy will someday carry the songs and stories so they will not be forgotten."

"Who is the other boy, Grandfather?"

"His taken name is Thainaack whoree. He is the boy who had the terrible sickness and now must have a wheelchair to move about.

It is my hope that you may both someday be singers of the long memory. That is why I am going to sing this song for you. It is a ceremonial song, and while many have heard part of it at funeral ceremonies, very few have heard the whole song. Listen carefully, for I paid a great price to learn it.

When I was a young boy in the school the white people made us attend at Fort Mojave, I was beaten often and terribly for refusing to forget our language and for trying to learn the songs of deep memory. At that place, the first offense for saying only a single word of the Pipa Aha Macav was five lashes with a leather whip. Every time after that cost more lashes: many more. I said many of the words of the Aha Macav and said them often. Because I was defiant, I was forced to live on bread and water from the time I was twelve until I was eighteen and could leave that awful place. I truly believe that is why I did not grow to be as large as my father and grandfather before me."

Hera Anyai closed his eyes and began to chant softly, so softly Charlie had to lean very close to the old one to hear the words. As Hera Anyai chanted, the sounds of the Village faded away. Charlie heard only the chanting and the sounds of the river as it rushed past the Village in its effort to reach the Sea of Cortez, a journey it could no longer complete because the river was doomed to die in the sands of Mexico because of dams built and water stolen by white people.

The song Hera anyai chanted was the creation song. The song told how Mutavilya had appeared at Avi Kwa'ame, the sacred mountain, in First Time and created the world and created the clans and named those clans. The song told how Mutavilya had started with clan names from the above-things: the skies and things of the skies, including the small birds of the sky, and the heavens and things of the heavens. How he then moved to the earth-things: the desert and mountain animals and plants. How he finished with the water and the below-earth things. After the clans had their clan names to pass on to their children, Mutavilya gave the people the rules for living.

However, the people struggled to survive in the world of his creation, so he sent his son, Mastamho, to teach the people how to live. Mastamho took a stick and drew a crooked line in the desert. That line became the river. Mastamho taught the people how to plant crops, capture the animals of the valley and harvest the fish of the river. Thus the people became known as the Pipa Aha Macav: the People of the River.

After some time, a terrible sea serpent made its way up from the Sea of Cortez by way of the river Mastamho had created and threatened the existence of the Pipa Aha Macav. Mastamho met the sea serpent at Huqueamp Avi and defeated it in a great battle. Mastamho then stayed with the people for a while longer, providing for them while they mastered the skills he had taught them. When his work was finished, Mastamho changed himself into a nighthawk and flew away.

When Hera anyai stopped chanting, the sun was halfway between the horizon and high noon. With some difficulty, he got to his feet and made his way down to the river's edge, where he drank long and deep before returning to sit beside Charlie.

"Herow heilhevow, the first part of your trial requires that you go north to Avi Kwa'ame, the place where Mutavilya summoned the people he had created and gave them the names of the clans. That place is where Mastamho stood when he made the river. You must go there on foot and see the world from where Mutavilya and Mastamho saw it."

"Grandfather, that is a very long way. The sacred mountain is in Nevada. Since I should not be seen near the river until I complete these tasks, I must go through the desert. How will I find enough water on my journey?"

"Today, when you leave the Village, take a part of the path by which you returned home last night. But when you reach Paiute Wash, instead of turning east toward the river, turn west and follow the wash until you come to the place the white people call Klinefelter. Do you know where the spring is in the hills there?"

"Yes, Hera anyai."

"After you leave Klinefelter, continue moving west until you are a mile above the highway that leads to the place where foolish people leave all their money before returning home in sorrow. Then turn north. In ten miles, you will come to a place where some white people made a deep hole in the ground, thinking they would find oil and be rich. They found no oil, but they found water. It bubbles out of the ground there. The water does not taste good like the beautiful water at Klinefelter, but you can drink it, and it will sustain you for the next part of your journey.

From the place of the hot water, turn east until you come to Avi Kwa'ame. There are many springs there in the canyons. You will have no trouble finding water. You must climb Avi Kwa'ame before sunset.

Once you have stayed on Avi Kwa'ame overnight and been blessed by the rising sun, return from Avi Kwa'ame by the same route you used to get there. Once you cross the big highway, instead of turning east to return to the Village, turn south and travel to the maze. While you are moving south, water will be very hard to find until you get to the river again, so stay close to the Sacramento Mountains until you come to Eagle Pass. Take the path partway through the mountains. On the south side of Eagle Peak, there is a spring. It is a very small spring and very hard to find, but I will draw you a map. Once you get water there, go southeast to the maze.

Very few know that what remains of the Maze is but a small piece of what once was. Once there was a huge figure. The figure was created by stones carefully set into the earth by our ancestors. The feet of this giant figure stood at the edge of the river, and the head was at the edge of the maze. The maze itself is all that now remains.

That figure was Mastamho, the Savior of the Pipa Aha Macav and the son of the Creator, Mutavilya. In his outstretched arms, he held the huge body of the evil sea serpent he had slain to save our people. Mastamho held the sea-serpent up to the opening of the maze to keep the bad ones inside.

When Pipa Aha Macav die, their spirits enter the maze. There they wander for some time. Those who have lived good lives leave their small sins behind in the maze and then enter the Spirit World and live there forever. Those who have lived bad lives are trapped in the maze and cannot enter the spirit world. They are doomed to wander inside the barren maze, even though they are in sight of Huqueamp Avi, the entrance to the Spirit World, the place they long for.

When the railroad people came, they built the railroad over Mastamho's body. When the highway people came many years later, they built the highway over Mastamho's legs and feet. Because Mastamho had been disfigured, the elders removed the rest of him, leaving only the maze.

While the sacred figure is no more, Mastamho is still there in spirit. No railroad and no highway can destroy sacred ground. The sacred ground waits for the time when the white people and all their creations have melted into the desert, leaving the Pipa Aha Macav to live in the ancient way. That will take some hundreds, or perhaps some thousands of years. It does not matter. We will be here still when the white people have destroyed themselves, and all their creations have turned to dust.

To have your special dream, you must go to the place where Mastamho's feet stood at the water's edge. The tamarisk growing along the river will shield you from the view of those passing close by on the highway. In that place, you must continue your fast. When the sun is going down on the final day of your fast, you must submerge yourself in the river and cleanse yourself of the events since Wednesday and the events of your trial.

Once you have done that, you will be ready to go into the tamarisk thicket and lie down to have the dream that will reveal your *sumach a' hot*. When you awake, the world will still be dark. You must return home with nothing more to guide you than the light of the remaining moon.

You must go all these places on foot. You must fast the entire time. You may not take a blanket with you to warm yourself during your trial. You may take only the clothing you are wearing now. This trial will be very hard. At times you may think you cannot complete it. I have faith, Herow heilhevow, that you can.

Come back to my house with me now. I will make you a map you will need to find the spring at Eagle Pass. Also, I have a special water carrier for you. Speak to no one from the time you leave my house, especially not white people. I will visit your mother today and tell her what she must know.

When you return to the Village, come to me. I will have food for you to break your fast. When you have eaten, we will speak of your dream to understand what you have been shown."

Charlie and Webster Charles walked slowly back to Hera anyai's cottage. Village life was in full swing at noon on a Saturday, and the sight of the nearly-blind old one accompanied by the young Charlie drew curious glances.

The cottage smelled of mesquite smoke, chili powder, herbs, sweat, tobacco, and old man. Hera Anyai made the map and bent over it with Charlie to make sure he understood the landmarks. Then Charlie waited while the old one went into his tiny bedroom. Hera anyai returned with an ancient clay pot.

"Herow heilhevow, this water carrier was the only thing of my father's that remained from his funeral pyre when he was burned in the old way. This should have been destroyed also, but the fire served only to make it stronger. Years later, I made the leather carrying straps on it from the hide of a wild pig I killed. The stopper is carved from mesquite, the tree of life for our people. It is fitting you should carry this. Bring it back to me if you can."

"I will, Grandfather. And thank you for honoring me with it."

The old one and the young man went into the small kitchen. Hera anyai filled the container with water from the sink and handed it to Herow heilhevow.

The old one put his hands on the young man's shoulders and stared into his face. Herow heilhevow looked into the old one's cloudy eyes in turn. He was not sure how much Hera anyai could see but was sure the old one had a deep sense of his young heart. Finally Hera anyai spoke.

"Go, Herow heilhevow. Go now. After you cross the highway, stay away from the town. Remember, it is especially important for you not to talk to white people if you are to keep your dream untainted."

Charlie walked through the Village streets. He ignored the greetings called out to him as he passed, leaving several people staring curiously in his wake. He left the Village and moved steadily west under the bright blue sky until he came to Highway 66. He stood by the side of the road a long time, waiting for a break in the traffic: a young, hatless Mojave man wearing Levi's, a flannel shirt, and a lined Levi jacket and carrying a clay jug.

Once he was across 66, he continued steadily west. He passed the rodeo grounds and crossed the Santa Fe Railroad tracks in the low hills to the west of the empty corrals. After that, he continued west for more than five miles, following the reverse of the path he had taken the previous night. He then turned north toward Paiute Wash. Once again, he had to cross both highway 66 and the Santa Fe tracks. By the time he was in Paiute Wash, his water carrier was empty, and he was weary and very hungry. He turned west toward Klinefelter and trudged on, determined to fulfill the tasks set out for him.

Shortly before sundown, he was just to the east of Klinefelter. Because the railroad tracks had turned north away from the highway just before the junction of U.S. 66 and U.S. 95, he had to cross both the tracks and highway 95. The sun had set by the time he was across. He continued west in the purple of twilight until he reached the place where there was water. A rusty, two-foot pipe jutted out from a hillside above a sandy wash. A constant stream of ice-cold, sweet water gushed from the pipe, splashing onto the rocks and sand below. He filled his water carrier and drank deeply and gratefully. He found a smooth place farther up the wash and scooped out holes for his elbows and hips. Taking off his Levi jacket, he lay down and pulled the jacket over his upper body. As the sky darkened, he could hear coyotes calling from far up the wash. Within minutes he was asleep.

Chapter 7

AEDEN

Sunday morning was bitterly cold. The storm had moved on, leaving behind a fantasy world beneath a sky of such intense blue it was almost indigo. There was half a foot of snow on the ground when I went outside. I walked down the road out of the side cut and into Carruthers Canyon. The snow-covered the pinyons, junipers, live oaks, holly oaks, Manzanita, and hackberry. As I walked out toward the middle of the canyon, I moved cautiously. There was broken rock and uneven ground hidden beneath the snow.

The only thing moving in the world of white were pinyon jays wheeling and calling above the canyon floor and occasionally landing on the snow-covered trees. A startling blue against the snow, their loud cries echoed through the clear, cold air. The only other sound was the crunch of the snow beneath my boots. I walked through the frozen landscape for half an hour and did not see another creature moving on the ground. My feet frozen, my ears and nose stinging from the cold, I returned to the adobe.

I built up the fire in the stove and cooked a big breakfast of pancakes, bacon, and eggs. I made syrup from brown sugar. The cowboy coffee warmed me from the inside out.

After breakfast, I cleaned the griddle, the black skillet, and the syrup pan. I packed all the food that was left into the wooden box and set it outside the front door. I had to let the fire in the stove burn down further so I could remove the coals before closing up the adobe. I took a final cup of coffee to the table and went back to work on my assignments.

By the time the sun was directly overhead, the fire had burned down, and the room was cold. I loaded everything into the car and came back inside. I rinsed out the coffee pot and my mug. I shoveled the coals into a bucket and dumped them behind the outhouse. I made one more check of the adobe and then put the padlocks on everything.

I had to remove the air cleaner and squirt starter fluid directly into the carburetor before my car would start. I crept along. The hillside was completely covered with snow, and I could not be sure exactly where the road was. I was afraid I might lose the track, drop into an unseen depression, and get stuck or punch a hole in the oil pan. Several times I had to stop the car and leave it idling while I scraped away snow with a shovel to find the road.

When I reached Lanfair road, the going was easier. The main road was broader and straighter. The glare of the snow was blinding under the bright sun. I passed cattle on both sides of the road. They looked miserable in the cold. By the time I reached the solitary phone booth, the snow was beginning to melt. At the junction, instead of continuing south to Goffs, I turned west onto Cedar Canyon Road. I felt compelled to stand on the high plain where I had run with the Mojave through the Joshua Trees in my dream.

I stayed on Cedar Canyon Road until it made a short jog to the north. I stopped and got out. A raven lifted off from a nearby yucca with a load croak. It seemed a timeless sound. I walked away from the car and stood for a while in the frigid air, an insignificant figure alone on a vast plain. I heard the sound of a jet high above me. In the cloudless sky, I saw it streaking south, a single white contrail scrolling a line behind it. Probably an F-100 from Nellis Air Force base outside Vegas.

I stood until the sound faded into the vast silence. The contrail began to dissipate. Soon it was gone, leaving no trace. Out here, far from the power lines, the highways, and the railroad tracks, it was as though the fighter had towed the modern world away with its long, white tail.

The silence left behind bespoke the existence of another world entirely; a world I was to someday find was elsewhere extant. In the distance, the raven croaked again. The sound seemed essential and filled with meaning and much more important than the noise the jet had made.

I got back in the car, returned to Lanfair road, and headed for Goffs. I quickly left the snow behind. By the time I got to Vontrigger wash, a dust cloud was billowing behind me. The desert had swallowed the previous night's moisture as if it had never fallen. I thought about stopping to hunt, but I had to be at work by six o'clock. All the way down Lanfair road, I kept looking in my rearview mirror at the snow-covered New York Mountains, feeling, as I always did, that I had left some essential part of myself up there.

When I reached Smoke Tree, the temperature was in the 70s. When I walked in the house, Mom was in the kitchen cooking Sunday dinner.

"Hi, Mom. That smells great."

"Roast pork. Your dad's favorite."

"Is Dad in?"

"Yes, he got back late last night. He got up at the crack of dawn this morning, as usual. He's back in the extra room doing something. He marked up around noon, so he'll probably go back out this evening."

I went down the hallway to talk to Dad. When I looked in, he was asleep. He was stretched out on his recliner, a copy of "Desert" magazine on his chest. I went back outside and unloaded the car. I piled everything by the back door and started bringing the items in the house.

"Aeden, Johnny called this morning. Asked me to tell you he had to talk to you when you got home."

"Probably about girl trouble. He and Judy had an argument about something. I'll call him later."

I took my sleeping bag and the guns down to my room. Dad was still asleep, so I put the guns in my room and went to take a shower. A lot of desert dust went down the drain.

By the time I finished and got dressed, Dad was sitting at his desk.

"How was the hunting?"

"I didn't hunt much. Shot a rabbit for dinner, but that's all. I looked for the quail at Vontrigger on the way up, but a red-tail was flying, so no luck. Then it snowed last night. Nothing was moving in the canyon this morning but pinyon jays. But it was a good trip. The snow was really something."

"Very unusual this early. Might be a cold winter. Heard you boys won the game Friday night."

"We did. We got a little lucky."

"Everybody in the crew office was talking about a fight after the game."

"It wasn't after. It was during. The refs stopped the game, and their bus drove on the field to pick up their players."

"Well, eight wins, no losses. I believe that's the best Smoke Tree High has ever done. By the way, the guys were also talking about some boy who scored a touchdown for the defense."

Mom stood in the doorway.

"Dick, dinner's ready. Ade, come on."

"Be right there, Mom. I've got to run a rag over the guns before I put them in the rack."

"That can wait. Dinner now, guns after."

During dinner, Mom and Dad talked about the election. Dad was a very strong union guy, so politics got talked about a lot at our house. Dad liked Kennedy, but Mom was worried about a Catholic being president. I'd heard it all before, but I liked hearing them talk about it. I liked the way they could be on different sides but still discuss it and even joke about it.

By the time dinner was over and I had cleaned my guns, it was time to leave for work. I didn't want to call Johnny from home because I thought he probably wanted to talk about Thursday night.

Sunday through Wednesday, I had a part-time job working at the Union '76 station from six o'clock until closing at eleven. The job paid only minimum wage, but during the winter months, the traffic on 66 was usually very slow after eight o'clock. That gave me time to do homework during my shift. The owner didn't object as long as I took care of business.

I got to the station a little before six and told the day guy, Bob Coleman, I would take over. He was glad to knock off early. He liked to walk down to Front Street and have a beer at The Palms before going home.

I had a little flurry of business between six and seven. I pumped gas, cleaned windshields, checked fluids, and made change pretty steadily for an hour. Then, as if someone had turned off the passenger car traffic switch, the number of cars dwindled. The truck traffic kept right on rolling, but we didn't sell diesel.

By seven-thirty, I was sitting at the desk where I could watch the aisles, surrounded by the oily smell of fan belts, radiator hoses, and tires stored in the office. I called the Whiting Brothers station.

"Whiting Brothers. Johnny."

"Hi. Mom said you wanted me to call."

"You missed all the excitement. Our fire is the talk of the town. You there by yourself?"

"Yeah."

"Okay. Here goes. They found a body inside the house."

"A body? You mean some old bones?"

"No. Recent. My dad is friends with the coroner. He told Dad the burned-up guy was Sixto Morales."

"Sixto? I thought he was too mean to die. And what do you mean 'burned up'? He was alive when the fire started?"

"They're not sure yet. The fire burned the body, but not so bad they couldn't tell he had been shot, too."

I didn't know what to say, so I didn't say anything for a while, just sat there watching bats chase bugs around the light beside the station. I was suddenly very cold.

"Ade, this is all getting very weird, very fast."

"For sure. And here's something else to think about. While I was up at Lee's Camp, I realized who it was knocked me down behind the house. It was Charlie Merriman."

"What was Charlie Merriman doing hanging around with someone like Sixto? Doesn't seem like those two would be buddies. And why were either of them at that old house?"

Just then, the island bell dinged as a car drove into the station. "Gotta go, Johnny. Got a customer."

"Call me when it gets quiet. It's dead out here on the west end."

"Okay"

And then I had one of those unusual nights where I stayed busy; however, I couldn't tell you what I did. The whole time I worked I was thinking about what Johnny had told me. I didn't get time to call again until almost ten o'clock. He picked up on the first ring.

"Whiting Brothers, Johnny."

"It's Ade. Sorry I didn't call sooner. It got real busy."

He started right in. "I'll tell you what I'm worried about. I'm afraid Judy will get pulled into this. She doesn't need that."

"And I'll tell you what I'm worried about. You and I burned down a house. The fire drew a crowd. The next day a body was found in the ashes, and nobody is sure whether the person was alive or dead when the fire started. And now everybody in town is talking about it. This is not going to go away. Smoke Tree hasn't had this much excitement since they closed the roundhouse."

"That's why I want to make sure Judy doesn't get dragged into it."

"And I want to know what Charlie was doing out there. How does he fit into all this? And why did he knock me down and run away?"

"How do you know it was him? You told me you didn't see his face."

"I had a dream last night. It woke me up. I saw his face in the dream."

Now it was Johnny's turn to be silent. Finally, he spoke.

"Well, that's it then. You saw him in a dream. Boy. Come on, Ade."

"He was there. It was Charlie. But who shot Sixto? And why?"

More silence.

"Bud, I gotta hang up. Mr. Garrett will be by in a minute to close up."

"Want to get together after work?"

"No, I'd better get home. Besides, I need some time to think about this. I'll tell you what. Let's get to school a half-hour early tomorrow morning. We can talk then. Maybe your dad will know something more by the time you get home."

"No, he marked up mid-day. He'll probably be out when I get home."

"My dad too. Maybe they'll catch the same job. Anyway, see you tomorrow morning."

I hung up and sat there listening to the buzz of the fluorescent lights. I could see trash blowing down the highway in front of the station. The wind brought the smell of the desert into town. I thought about Charlie Merriman.

Charlie was a senior when I got to know him. He held the school record for the mile, but it was not his natural distance. Because of a birth defect, Charlie's left leg was shorter than his right, so much shorter that when he stood up straight, his left heel would not touch the ground. He had an odd, rolling gait, almost like a high-speed limp.

Because of his handicap, Charlie's top speed for the quarter-mile was sixty-eight seconds. But there seemed to be no limit to his endurance. He could run sixty-eight second quarters back-to-back almost indefinitely. His school record for the mile was four minutes and thirty-two seconds. But if high schools had run the two-mile, I have no doubt he could have kept on knocking out those sixty-eight second quarters for another mile.

I watched Charlie run many races that year. Regardless of the conditions: heat, cold, high wind, no wind, he ran every race in four minutes and thirty-two seconds. Every one. He was like a metronome. As soon as he crossed the finish line, he would be laughing and joking and patting his competitors on the back while some of them were down on all fours gasping for breath.

At ten forty-five, Mr. Garret came by to help me close up. Together we wheeled the racks of motor oil, the windshield wiper display, and the tires in the rack into the garage. He turned off the compressor that ran the lift, and we pulled down the garage door and locked it.

Mr. Garret counted the money in the register and made up the bank deposit. We went outside, and he locked the front door. I followed him to the bank and watched while he put the money bag in the night deposit box. The entire time, he never mentioned anything about the events at the House of Three Murders. Maybe not everyone had heard about it.

By the time I got home, it was nearly midnight. Dad was out. Mom was reading a book. I went into the extra room and finished a couple of minor homework items. I showered and got into bed. It was nearly one in the morning. I was very tired, but I lay awake thinking about Sixto dead in the fire and how much trouble we were in.

Chapter 8

CHARLIE

Charlie awakened before sunrise to soft but steady rain. His face and clothing were wet. He was cold through and through. He shivered as he struggled to his feet. He pulled on his Levi jacket and began to walk in circles to warm himself. In the distance, he could hear diesel locomotives pulling a long freight up the hill from Smoke Tree. The freight was on the section of tracks that paralleled highway 95 and crossed Paiute Wash. Even over the sound of the passing train he could hear the water gushing from the big metal pipe and splashing on the rocks below.

He picked up his water carrier and took a long drink. Moving down the wash to the gushing pipe, he topped off. Because Hera anyai had instructed him to stay a mile west of 95, he moved west up the wash before he turned north. Within a half an hour, the rain had stopped.

By the time the sun was above the horizon, he was crossing Old 66 west of Arrowhead Junction. On the other side of the road, he scrambled up the steep embankment and stood on the tracks for a while, looking out over a huge expanse of brown desert dotted with creosote, white bursage, blackbrush, and yucca. To the northwest, he could see Avi Kwa'ame reaching into the sky. He estimated the distance he had to travel to get to the top of the mountain at about thirty miles. He felt much better after his deep and dreamless sleep, although he was a little stiff, either from waking up wet or from his two long walking stints. He had been three and a half days now without food. He took a long drink from his water carrier, scrambled down the embankment, and set off at a steady pace.

By noon, highway 95 was still on his right, but Avi Kwa'ame was almost directly to his east. However, he still had not found the place people had drilled for oil, and he was getting low on water. He was beginning to fear he had walked past it when he saw an incongruous sight. Poking up between some creosote bushes thirty yards ahead of him was something very green. As he walked closer, he realized he was seeing cattail reeds in the middle of the brown desert.

When he got to the well site, he could see the cattails were growing around a square, cement cistern. The cistern was full, and a steady outflow of water was spilling over the sides. Indian rice grass and ferns were growing around the edge of the puddles where the cattails were rooted. There were tracks from many different animals and bird feathers around the puddles.

Charlie sampled the water. It was hot and tasted of sulfur, but it was drinkable. He drank the last of the good water from the hillside spring. He submerged the carrier in the hot water until it was full. He set the carrier on the ground and got undressed. Holding onto the sides of the cistern, he eased himself into the hot water. His feet did not touch bottom. Hooking his elbows over the sides, he relaxed in his own mineral water spa.

After a long soak, he pulled himself out. He sat naked on the edge of the cistern, letting the light breeze dry his skin. Off in the distance, he could hear the occasional truck or car passing on 95. There was a light breeze, and the long, trailing webs of balloon spiders streamed high in the air, glinting in the bright sun.

When he had dried off and dressed, he felt much better. The ache was gone from his left leg, the one that sometimes acted up when he ran long distances. Although he was still hungry, he felt like a new man as he turned due east toward Avi Kwa'ame.

After he crossed highway 95, Charlie saw the dirt road that passed to the south of Avi Kwa'ame on its path to Davis Dam. As he walked, he was careful to stay well to the north of that road. As he approached the sacred mountain, the broad plain on which he was traveling began to rise. The plant life was changing: while creosote, white bursage, black-brush, and yucca still predominated, he began to see Mormon tea and purple sage. A little farther ahead of him, there were large stands of teddy bear cholla and golden cholla.

As the sun tilted to the west at his back, he reached the pass that led up between the peaks. He began to climb into the pass, and as he did, he found juniper, pinyon pine, and great basin sage. Moving through the tangled grapevines that gave the pass its name, he saw cottonwood trees, the quaking gold of their autumn colors highlighted by the setting sun. His ancestors had carved petroglyphs onto some of the rock surfaces. He saw the rock with the bighorn sheep and two animals that looked like antelope.

The jackrabbits that had sprinted well ahead of him on the lower desert gave way to cottontails. He heard quail calling as he climbed, and once, he saw a flash of tawny fur disappearing in the boulders far above him: possibly a mountain lion. He found a flowing spring halfway up the mountain. He filled his water carrier. He was glad he didn't have to drink the sulfurous water anymore.

Avi Kwa'ame was over a mile high and would not be an easy climb. The face of the mountain was very steep, and the pass was filled with huge boulders that he had to climb around because they were too big to climb over, and he was already exhausted by the distance he had covered since sunrise.

The air grew steadily colder. He knew he was in for a long night with below-freezing temperatures. As he neared the summit, he found a spot nestled within a circle of large boulders well protected from the wind blowing out of the north. There was coarse sand, and the ground was relatively level. As he had the night before, he scooped out indentations for his elbows and hips.

He reached into the watch pocket of his Levi's and pulled out a book of matches. "The Palms" was written in green ink on the cover. He had no idea why he had picked them up, but he was glad to have them. He began moving through the pinyons and junipers, picking up fallen branches. By the time the sun was disappearing behind the Piute range, he had a substantial pile of wood. He foraged under the pinyons for pine cones to help start his fire. Using his pocket knife, he stripped the bark off branches and stacked it with the pine cones. He would be ready to start a fire when the night grew cold.

Before the moon rose, there were more stars in the clear, cold, black sky than he had ever seen in his life. He sat staring at the profusion in wonder until exhaustion overtook him, and he slept, his Levi jacket spread over his chest.

Chapter 9

AEDEN

On Monday, Johnny and I were the first students in the parking lot. We walked out behind the gym and sat on the cold concrete steps that led down to the football field. There was an early morning bite in the air, and the grass on the field was brown. I could smell the smoke from someone's fireplace. The wind was scouring dirt from around the empty bleachers and blowing it into the salt cedars on the south side of the field. Looking north, I could see the Colorado River Valley all the way up to the Chalk Cliffs in Nevada. A flock of starlings wheeled in a circle around the field and then settled onto the grass. They looked like a handful of licorice drops.

"So the guy who knocked you down was Charlie Merriman, and his face came to you in a dream?"

"That's right."

"Want to tell me about it?"

"Not really. It sounds silly in the daylight."

"But we have a problem."

"We do. Sixto was in that house. All those years that house sat there empty, and then suddenly Sixto and Charlie are in it the night we show up?"

"Weren't very lucky, were we? The first question is going to be, was he alive when the fire started? I don't know if they can tell one way or the other, but if he was alive, I killed him when I started that fire, Ade."

"And if he wasn't alive, then who shot and killed him? Charlie Merriman? I can't believe that. So, if Charlie didn't shoot him, who did?"

"And where's Charlie?"

"Johnny, we're the only people who know Charlie was there."

"I wonder if he knows we were there. I mean, do you think he knew it was us?"

"I don't know. This is big. People don't get shot around here every day. The Smoke Tree Weekly will have a big story. Somebody knows something about this, and it will come out. In the meantime, what do we do?"

"We try to find Charlie and talk to him. Find out what happened."

"Okay. Billy Braithwaite lives in the Village. I'll try to catch him before class and find out if he's seen Charlie."

"Good idea."

"How's it going with Judy?"

"I tried all weekend to call her. No luck. Either her mom or her dad answered every time I called, and every time they told me she was not available and hung up. Finally, they told me to stop calling."

"How did it go at the dance?"

"When I went to pick her up, she was standing on the porch waiting for me. My God, you can't believe how beautiful she looked! But her dad was with her. He brought her to the car and opened the door. When she got in, he came around to my side and banged on my window. When I rolled it down, he said, 'I don't trust you to do what Judy tells you, so I'm telling you. In two hours, she's going to tell you it's time to bring her home. Do it. Straight home. No stopping. Believe me, boy, you don't want my friends to come looking for you. Ade, that black Chrysler Imperial was in the driveway, and the two guys with blazers were on the porch staring at me.

While we drove to the dance, she sat as far away from me as she could get. Would've sat outside if she could've. No matter what I said to her, she would not speak. We went to the dance and danced a few times. She drank some punch and ate some cookies, and she talked to some other girls. Then we danced some more, and she said, 'It's time to go home'".

All the way back to her place, same deal. Would not talk. I needed to find out what she was thinking before I took her home, so I stopped at the bottom of the heights. When I stopped, she got out of the car and started to walk up the hill, wobbling all over the place in her high heels, dragging her formal in the dirt. I had to promise to drive straight to her house before she would get back in the car. When I pulled into the driveway, her dad was standing on the porch. The blazer twins were standing beside him. He came down the steps and opened the door for her. She got out. He slammed the door. He never looked at me. Never said a word. Not 'goodnight' 'kiss my royal red fanny,' nothing. And that, good buddy, is how it went at the dance."

I got off the steps and dusted off my Levi's. "I'm off to see if I can find Billy."

Billy Braithwaite and I had played together when we were in first and second grade. But as we got older, we played together less and less. Then, in the fifth grade, Billy was hit with polio. Terrible luck because the polio vaccine was almost ready. We heard about his illness, but because we didn't see him in school for a long time, we thought maybe he had died. Had he been white, his illness would have been the talk of the school. But because he was just another one of those kids from 'the Village,' I am ashamed to admit we didn't give him much thought. That's just the way it was in Smoke Tree.

When junior high started, he was suddenly back in school, but he was in a wheelchair. We heard that he would never walk again. And he was changed in other ways. His smile and good nature, and energy were all gone. He was quiet and studious.

One evening at the dinner table, Mom and Dad were talking about changes for the Mojave. Apparently, there were negotiations underway between the federal government and the Mojave about a new constitution for the tribe. When Dad talked about the negotiators for the Mojave, I was surprised to hear that Billy's mother, Betty Braithwaite, was one of the leaders. By the time we were freshmen in high school, the new constitution had been approved, and Betty Braithwaite was on the tribal council.

I went out in front of the school to watch for Billy. The north wind was gusting across the campus in cold bursts. After a few minutes, I saw an old, pre-war Chevy sedan pull up to the curb. Billy was sitting in the passenger seat. His mom was driving.

Mrs. Braithwaite got out of the car and came around, and opened the back door. The back seat had been removed. Billy's wheelchair was sitting where the seat would have been. She pulled it out and set it on the sidewalk. She opened Billy's door and helped him swing his legs out from under the dashboard.

I moved forward.

"Can I help?"

Mrs. Braithwaite finished adjusting Billy's legs. He had one hand on the dashboard and one hand on the back of the car seat. He looked past his mother at me.

"Who are you?"

"Aeden. Aeden Snow. Everyone calls me Ade."

"So, you're the boy Billy used to play with in elementary school before he got sick. You played marbles together. What do you want?"

"I want to help you with Billy." Even to me, the words sounded false.

"All of a sudden, after all these years, you want to help Billy? It's a little late. He could've used a friend when he went back to school in the seventh grade, but he didn't find one. So let me ask you again. What do you want?"

Billy was still staring up at me. I couldn't read anything in his stoic expression. His mother was another matter. A slender and fierce-looking woman, she wore Levi's, a blue flannel shirt buttoned to her neck, and high-topped, black leather shoes. Her hair was cut short. Her face, dominated by large black eyes set far back in their sockets, was deeply lined around her mouth and eyes. She stood looking into my face, her arms folded across her chest.

I could not hold her stare. I looked away.

"I'm sorry Mrs. Braithwaite. You're right; I need to talk to Billy about something."

"And this 'something,' it's not about Billy, is it?"

"No, ma'am, it isn't."

She did not speak again; just stared at me tight-lipped.

"Mrs. Braithwaite, I know I wasn't Billy's friend when he needed one. I never knew how mean that was until right this minute. I was just a dumb kid. I guess I'm still pretty dumb. Pardon me for bothering you and Billy."

I turned and started to walk away, my face burning in embarrassment.

"You! Ade!" she said sharply.

I turned back. Something in her eyes had changed. She unfolded her arms and put her hands on her hips.

"No reason to expect you to be any different than anyone else around here. If you're going to give me a hand, let's get to it."

"Yes, ma'am."

I leaned into the car. Billy shrugged and put his hands on my shoulders. His grip was very strong. I put my hands on his muscular arms and pulled him out of the car. He was heavy. I wondered how Mrs. Braithwaite, who couldn't have weighed much over a hundred pounds, managed to do this.

She maneuvered the chair. I lowered Billy into it and stepped back. She got his books out of the car and put them in his lap, then put her right hand on his shoulder and squeezed. He patted her hand as he looked up at her. She walked to the other side of the car and opened the door. She looked at me over the roof.

"Thank you," was all she said, but it seemed to me she was not thanking me for something I had done but for something I might do. Then she got in and closed the door.

I turned and started to push Billy's chair along the walkway.

"Don't push my chair. I get myself around."

"Oh, sorry."

We moved down the walkway side by side.

"So, like Mom said, what do you want?"

"I want to know if you've seen Charlie Merriman lately."

"Lately? How lately?"

"Like over the weekend."

"Nope. But I don't see him very often anyway."

"Billy, I need to talk to Charlie about something really important. Can you find out if he's been around the Village since Friday?"

"Why should I?"

"Can you keep something under your hat?"

"Do I seem to you like someone who yaks a lot?"

"No, no, you don't."

I paused. "Okay, please keep this between us. It's possible that Charlie might be in a lot of trouble."

"I see. And you're not?"

"I'm not in trouble yet. I might be later, but I'm not now. Charlie may be right now. If you see him, could you tell him I need to talk to him?"

Billy thought about it.

"Okay. I'll give him a message if I see him. What should I tell him?"

"Just tell him I have to talk to him about something important. I don't know if he remembers me, but we ran track together when he was a star, and I was just a freshman."

"And how does he find you if he wants to talk to you?"

I stopped walking while he got a pen and opened his notebook. I wrote down my phone number.

"Please tell him if he wants to talk in person; I work at the Union 76 Sunday through Wednesday from six until eleven. I'll be there tonight."

"Okay."

That morning, for the first time, I noticed how different things were for Billy than for the rest of us. When we got to chemistry class, he stayed in his chair. No one, certainly not the teacher, offered to help him up onto one of the stools in front of the high counters equipped with Bunsen burners and sinks. He sat off to the side of the rest of the class, trying to angle his chair so he could see the teacher and the blackboard. When he got his chair in position, he reached behind himself and got a board. He put the board across the armrests on his chair and propped his notebook on it. As I watched him, I realized he must have been doing that kind of thing since the seventh grade, but I had never noticed.

I spent another distracted day in chemistry class. On Friday, I had been worried about the fire on the river bottom. Today I found myself thinking about the challenges Billy Braithwaite faced every day at school, not to mention everywhere else. I also thought about the thoughtful look his mom had given me over the roof of her car.

All morning at school, I heard people talking about the discovery of Sixto's body in the ashes of the House of Three Murders. As the morning wore on, the stories became more fantastic. By second period, Sixto had a gang, and they had been using the house for a hideout. By third period, Sixto had robbed a small casino in Las Vegas, and the mob had followed him to the house, executed him, and burned the house to destroy the evidence. By lunch, Sixto was on the F.B.I.'s "most wanted" list. Several students were going to go to the post office after school to look at his "wanted" poster. The "tales of Sixto" had completely obliterated any talk there might have been about the presidential election coming up the following day.

Judy still refused to talk to Johnny. She kept to herself between classes and looked as distracted as I felt. At noon, her dad picked her up in front of the school. Johnny was not a happy guy.

Johnny went downtown for lunch, but I stayed on campus and ate at the cafeteria. There was a low wall by the auditorium where I liked to sit and read. I went to my locker and got "The Bridge at Andau," a book about the Hungarian Revolution, but I could not concentrate. I finally gave up and thought about how my tidy little world was being turned on its head.

While I was sitting there going over the events for the hundredth time, Charlene Daugherty walked over and sat on the wall next to me.

"I see there are problems with the perfect couple. The homecoming king and queen aren't exactly making moon eyes at each other. In fact, she doesn't seem to want to look at him at all. What's the problem?"

"You'll have to ask her, Charlene."

"Well, I say, 'good for her.' It's about time Johnny got his comeuppance. Big everything hero. Mr. Smooth. I'm glad it happened. That's what he gets for chasing after the rich girl."

"Charlene, I came over to sit on the wall and read, not to get your opinion of Johnny."

"Yeah, well, this isn't your wall, even though you seem to think it is. I see you over here, always reading some book."

"You want this wall? It's yours." I got up and walked away.

Charlene shouted after me. "You and Johnny are just alike. Think you're all special or something."

I kept walking.

After lunch, Benedict McPhearson dropped Judy off in front of the school just in time for afternoon classes. She continued to refuse to talk to Johnny. When the final bell rang, she hurried to the front of the school where her dad was waiting. I saw Johnny standing on the sidewalk looking after them as they drove away. I joined him.

"Hey, buddy. Seems weird not to have football practice."

"Ade, I don't know what to do. I'm going crazy. I love that girl. I want to marry her someday."

"I know, John. I can tell you've got it bad."

"I could take it if she yelled at me, but she won't even look at me! If I stand right in front of her, she just looks at the ground and walks around me."

"I think her dad has laid down the law. She's been told not to have anything to do with you."

"I understand if she can't go out with me or if she's on restriction. But not even talk to me at school?"

"She must be very afraid of her dad."

"I guess so. What do you think he did to scare her so bad? You don't think he hurt her, do you?" His eyes blazed. "I'll kill him if he hurt her!"

"I don't think he'd hurt her. I think it's more likely he told her he has someone watching her at school."

"Like who?"

"Well, I've heard my parents say he's tight with Superintendent Symington. Dad says Symington sucks up to him because he wants to go into politics, and Benedict has money and knows big people. Maybe Benedict told her Symington is reporting to him. And maybe he is."

"I've got an idea. Maybe her dad didn't tell her she couldn't talk to you. Maybe she'll tell *you* what's going on."

"I'll try to talk to her tomorrow."

"Maybe you could call her tonight."

"Not a good idea. If I call out there, her dad might just tell her not to talk to me either. Let it wait until tomorrow."

Johnny seemed to calm down. "Okay. Say, did you talk to Billy?"

"Yeah. He says he hasn't seen Charlie for a while, but he told me he'd tell Charlie I'm looking for him if he sees him."

"You still can't tell me why you think it was Charlie out at the house?"

"Yeah, I think I can. Sorry about the dream thing, but I'd been trying to put a name to that odd run ever since Thursday night. It popped into my head while I was sleeping. Woke me up. Do you remember Charlie ?"

"Sure. The guy who holds the school record for the mile."

"One of his legs is a lot shorter than the other, and when he runs, his left shoulder drops every other step. That's what was tickling my brain about the guy who knocked me down and ran off. It just took me a while to put it together."

"Okay, I see that. So, it must have been him."

"I'm sure it was."

★ ★ ★

It was quiet at work that night, and I did a lot of homework. Charlie Merriman did not come by.

Chapter 10

HORSE

Carlos Caballo, known to everyone in and around Smoke Tree as "Horse," sat in his office at the San Bernardino County Sheriff's Smoke Tree substation. He was the lieutenant in charge of the station. He was sitting with his door closed, thinking about Sixto Morales. Sixto had been a very dangerous man. Even his deputies were afraid of the guy, and they were armed! What he was trying to find out was why Sixto had been in that house when it burned.

His intercom buzzed.

"Yeah?"

"Captain Hardesty for you."

"Thanks. Put him through.

Horse."

"Pete Hardesty here. The autopsy on the burned body you sent us is finished."

"What can you tell me, Captain?"

"First, the fire didn't kill him. He was dead before the fire burned him. There was no smoke in his lungs. A big gun of some kind put a very large hole in him. Maybe a .30-30 or a big handgun. Whatever it was went right through him, and it did some real damage. The pathologist says he died of internal bleeding or maybe sepsis if he survived the bleeding long enough."

"Thanks, Captain. That makes this even more interesting."

Pete Hardesty was the unofficial monitor of murder investigations for the department. Horse had known him for many years. In fact, Pete was a member of the screening board that recommended Horse for hiring. As a Korean War veteran, Horse had already had bonus points added to his score on the hiring exam. Also, it didn't hurt that he had served as an M.P. for a time. The sheriff agreed with the panel's recommendation, and Horse became the first Mexican-American deputy in the department.

After leaving the academy, Horse was assigned to the Smoke Tree substation, an assignment he requested. Since Horse seemed to know everyone in Smoke Tree and up and down the Colorado River in the tristate area, the sheriff thought he would be a great fit. Horse wanted to spend his entire career there. This made him a double minority: a Mexican-American and a deputy who actually *wanted* to be assigned to the Smoke Tree substation. The sheriff quickly promoted him up through the ranks so he could be the officer in charge.

Horse loved Smoke Tree. He also loved the Mojave Desert, a place of extremes. In the summer, the temperature was often over 120; on many winter days, there was frost in the river bottom. Horse didn't mind the summer heat. He didn't mind the cold days either. He found the brisk mornings exhilarating. But even Horse had to admit that the wind that blew relentlessly out of the north from January to March could get irritating, as could the streak of static electricity that leaped from his hand to the knob when he reached to open a door on those dry, winter days.

But best were the times between the extremes. From mid-September until Christmas, and again from April until early June, the Mojave Valley was lovely. Day after day, the sky was such a deep blue it made his heart ache, and on the infrequent occasions when he had to go to the county seat in San Bernardino, he wondered how those trapped under that lead-colored, smog-filled sky could stand to live there.

His intercom buzzed again.

"Yeah."

"Another call for you. Juan Castillo. Castillo Ranch."

"Horse here."

"Hey, Carlos, long time no see. Juan Castillo."

"Juan, good buddy. What can I do you for?"

"One of my guys told me something over the weekend. Said he was on the old road north of the California line on Friday, and he came across an abandoned car. I thought maybe it had something to do with that fire Thursday night, so I went out to look at it."

"What kind of car was it?"

"'50 or '51 Mercury, primer gray. There's a bullet hole through the windshield, and the bullet wiped out the rear-view mirror. There's gasoline and anti-freeze on the ground under the car and lots of blood on the passenger seat. The car is on the Nevada side of the line, but you're closer. Besides, those people in Nevada don't even know we're down here, except at property tax time."

"Are you familiar with the house that burned down?"

"Sure. It's been abandoned for years. That's the House of Three Murders."

"I heard about that place when I was a kid. Is it in Nevada?"

"Nope. California, but just barely."

"Thanks for the call, Juan. I think that car did have something to do with the fire. Please tell your guys to leave it alone. I'll have somebody come and get it."

"Okay.

Come on up and we'll go after some of those big catfish below the dam. They just lay down there all day eating the fish that got ground up by the turbines."

"I might take you up on that, Juan. Thanks."

Horse sat at his desk in the quiet office. So, someone had shot Sixto. Sixto's car had been abandoned north of the fire with one bullet hole in the windshield and maybe a couple more in other places. He got up and walked to the door. He stuck his head out of his office and yelled at the dispatcher.

"Fred, get me the Clark County Sheriff's substation in Boulder City. Transfer the call to me when you get them on the line."

Horse got one of the big pieces of poster paper he kept in his office and took it to his desk. He put an arrow for north in the top right corner. In the middle of the page, he wrote "House of Three Murders/

Sixto Morales" and drew a circle around it. Then he drew an arrow north from there and made a circle he labeled "Sixto's Car."

He thought about the fire scene. The house had been built completely of wood: no plaster, no insulation, just painted wood on the exterior and interior walls. The dried-up lumber had been reduced to ashes. The old house was post and beam construction with the floor two feet above the ground. Sixto's partially burned body had fallen through the burning floor to the ground below, which was why the body wasn't damaged more by the fire.

Horse had smelled the body before he saw it. He was familiar with the barbecued-pork smell of burned human flesh from his time in Korea. He might have been an M.P., but everyone was an eleven bravo when the fighting got hot. He had seen his share.

The intercom buzzed.

"Horse, I've got Clark County Sheriff's substation on the line. A Lieutenant Swanson."

"Hello, Lieutenant. Lieutenant Caballo here, San Bernardino County Sheriff's Department, Smoke Tree substation."

"Good morning. Can I help you?"

"The other night there was a fire in an abandoned house out in the river bottom below Davis Dam. When the fire burned out, we found a body inside. Local bad guy name of Sixto Morales."

"Oh hell, I know Sixto. Had him in jail here a couple of times. Took three of my deputies to hook him up last time."

"That would be Sixto. Anyway, Sixto got charred some in the fire, but the coroner's office tells me he was dead before the fire started. Someone put a hole through him with a big gun of some kind. A while ago, I had a call from a guy who found Sixto's car abandoned on your side of the California/Nevada line."

"How about the house that burned down. Was it in Nevada too?"

"No. The guy who called me about the car says the house is in California."

"Well, the car is closer to your office than mine. Would you be willing to take the lead on this for now?"

"Yeah, until someone tells me otherwise. I'll have the car towed down here."

"Fine with me."

"I wanted to ask you, any reports up your way of a shootout of some kind last week?"

"Not around Boulder City. Didn't hear anything from Vegas either."

"Okay. We'll take this for now. Call me if you hear anything different."

"Got you, Lieutenant."

"Call me Horse. Everyone else does."

"You'll probably never guess that everyone calls me Swanny."

"Talk to you later, Swanny."

Horse hung up and looked at his paper. He drew a slanted line running northwest to southeast between the house circle and the car circle. He labeled one side of the line "California" and the other side "Nevada." Next he drew a wavy line that started at the top of the paper and moved down the paper to intersect the angled line to the right of both the car circle and the house circle. He labeled that line "river." On the right side of the 'river' line, he wrote 'Arizona' in big letters. Near the bottom of the paper, he wrote 'Smoke Tree' and drew a circle around it.

Horse lifted his slender but muscular six-foot frame from his chair and stretched. He opened his door and called to the dispatcher.

"Fred, get me the Mohave County Sheriff's office on the line. Let me know when you have them."

"Yessir. Excuse me, Horse, but why don't you buzz me over the intercom instead of sticking your head out the door?"

"Cause I like to remind myself I can still get up and walk."

He went back inside his office and sat down in front of his chart. If Sixto hadn't been shot in Nevada, it must have happened in Arizona. After all, the road between Arizona and Nevada ran across the top of Davis Dam.

His intercom buzzed.

"Yeah."

"Got Mojave County on the line. Captain Bill Taylor."

Horse picked up.

"Good morning, Captain."

"Morning, Horse. What can I help San Bernardino County with today?"

Horse took Captain Taylor through the story and then asked him if there had been any reports of a shooting up his way the previous week.

"Yeah, we had a strong-arm robbery at a liquor store in Bullhead City, Winslow Liquors."

"I know the place."

"Two suspects came in the store. One of them pulled a .45 and demanded the money. He made the owner lay face-down on the floor. He told the other guy to pick up the money and a case of beer and some other stuff. The guy with the gun told the owner if he got up off the floor before he drove away, he would shoot him. The owner got up anyway after they went out the door. He exchanged gunfire with the fleeing suspect and knocked him partway down. The suspect turned and opened up with the .45. Broke the glass door and knocked some chunks out of the building. Then his accomplice helped him to the passenger side of the car, but before they could leave, the owner shot at the car again and hit the windshield. The suspect returned fire, and then he and the accomplice drove off. The owner got off another shot or two as they drove away – says he heard one round hit the car."

"Just like the Wild West! Well, that sounds like our boy. The big guy was Sixto Morales. When we found his body, we didn't find anyone else, so we don't know who the other guy was."

"Sixto, huh? We sure are familiar with Senor Morales up this way. He's been making trouble around Kingman for years."

"Well, he won't trouble you anymore."

"Horse, I'm embarrassed to tell you how good that makes me feel."

"Did the owner give you a description of the other guy?"

"Yeah, some skinny kid. Thought he might have been an Indian. Kid didn't say much. Owner said he looked real nervous."

"Captain, I know it's your case, but the body ended up on my side of the river. Would you mind if I went up and talked to the store owner?"

"Heck no, I don't mind. I'll call him and let him know the robber was from California, and you're following up from your side of the river. And by the way, Horse, you're gonna love this guy. His name is Lyndon Brooks, and he's one tough sonofagun. He told my deputy he would have let them drive away without a fuss and just made a claim on his insurance, except for one thing."

"What was that?"

"He said when the guy made him lay down on the floor, his hat fell off, and the guy stomped on it. Lyndon said it was his favorite Stetson. Said that's why he got up and shot the guy."

"There's a story to tell at the next cop convention!

I'll pass on anything I get from the guy, and if I figure out who was with him, I'll let you know right away."

When Horse hung up, he wrote 'Winslow Liquors/Lyndon Brooks' on the Arizona side of the river on his map, then drew a circle around it. Now he needed to trace Sixto's movements backward. Horse was sure the whole thing had its roots in Smoke Tree, and it wasn't just because Sixto had lived in town. Examining the area outside the burned house, his deputy had found a railroad fusee. Horse knew it wasn't a highway flare because it had the metal spike in the bottom to stick in a railroad tie. Railroad flares meant Smoke Tree. He was sure if he sent someone out and they looked long enough, they would come up with another fusee or two in the ashes of the house.

Horse picked up the keys to his cruiser and went out his door.

"Fred, call Zack out at the wrecking yard and tell him I want a vehicle towed here. It's a '50 or '51 Mercury. It's north of the house that burned down out in the river bottom. Tell him how to get there."

"Okay, boss. What color is it?"

"Fred, how many '50 or '51 Mercurys are going to be out there this morning? Tell him to get the one with the front window blown out. That should narrow it down. And tell him not to touch anything inside the car."

"Where will you be?"

"I'm headed across the river to talk to a straight-shootin' cowboy.

★ ★ ★

Horse took the road across the Bureau of Reclamation Bridge into Arizona. At the Oatman/Bullhead split, he turned north. He went through miles and miles of mesquite thickets before he emerged into the desert hills. The road stayed in the rolling hills for a few miles before turning west toward Bullhead.

He pushed open the door to Winslow Liquors. The man behind the counter said, "You must be the deputy from Smoke Tree."

"Yes sir, Lieutenant Carlos Caballo."

"Lyndon Brooks. Pleased to make your acquaintance."

"When Captain Taylor called to tell you I was coming, what else did he tell you?"

"You mean about the guy I shot?"

"Yes."

"Said his name was Sixto Morales."

"Did he tell you Sixto was dead?"

"Be surprised if he wasn't. I parked a .357 round right in his brisket."

"And when the captain told you Sixto was dead, did he think you'd have any problem with that?"

"What kind of problem?"

"Well, the guy was fleeing. He was outside the building and in the parking lot. A case could be made that you were no longer in danger. So why shoot him?"

"He waved a gun in my face. He robbed me at gunpoint. He made me lay face-down on the floor, and I thought he was going to shoot me. Then he threatened to kill me if I got up. Hell, I think I did the right thing. I would have shot him sooner, but he took my belly gun out from under the counter. And by the way, I want that gun back. And my money."

"So, did the captain agree with your take on the shooting?"

"Sure! Listen, this was a big guy with a big gun. He was a menace to society. Besides, he was... uh." Lyndon paused.

"Go ahead. Say it. He was what? He was a Mexican?"

"Well, yeah, I guess. That too. There's not a prosecutor in Mohave County that would bring this to trial. And if one did, there's not a judge that wouldn't dismiss the charges. I don't know how you do it across the river in the land of fruits and nuts, but that's how it works over here."

The two stood and stared at each other. Horse was angry, but he knew he had to stay calm if he was going to get any useful information. He changed the subject.

"Okay, let's talk about that big gun. You told Captain Taylor it was a .45. You sure of that?"

"I'm real sure. I've seen enough of them. I served in World War II. When the war was over, I was dumb enough to go into the National Guard and damned if my unit didn't get called up for Korea. Yeah, I've seen lots of .45s. How about you, Lieutenant, you a vet?"

"Yes, I am. I was drafted and served in Korea."

"See any action?"

"Way more than I wanted."

"Me too. Well, always glad to meet a fellow veteran. Sorry about the Mexican crack, but that big guy scared me, and I didn't like it. I was laying on that floor thinking, 'I survived two wars to get shot by some jerk in Bullhead'?"

Lyndon stuck out his hand. After a brief pause, Horse shook it. The two men nodded at each other.

"By the way, your gun is kaput. Sixto died in a fire in an abandoned house across the river. Had his.45 beside him and your .38 in his front pocket. The rounds cooked off in the heat. Blew both guns apart. Your money may have burnt up too, but we're not sure about that. I drove up to ask you about the other guy. Did the other guy have a gun?"

"No, no gun."

"I knew Sixto, the one you shot, and you're right; he was a mean motor scooter. But what can you tell me about the other guy?"

"He was a young guy. Early twenties, maybe. Long, black hair, black eyes. 5'10" or so, real slender. Maybe a hundred and forty pounds, max. Wearing Levi's and a red flannel shirt."

"Captain Taylor said you thought he might be Indian."

"That'd be my guess."

"Any idea which tribe?"

"Not Hualapai. Lots of those around Kingman, where I grew up. Maybe Mojave."

"Can you remember anything about how he acted while this was going on?"

"He was the first one in the door. The big guy was right behind him. They were both drunk. When the skinny one came in, he asked the big guy what kind of candy bar he wanted. I was already looking at the big guy. He was headed back to the cold cases, and I wanted to keep track of him."

"Then what happened?"

"The big guy opened the walk-in door, so he could get into the back of the coolers. I yelled at him to stop, but he went inside anyway. I didn't want to leave the Indian by himself so close to the cash register, so I stayed put. Then the big one came out carrying a case of Lucky Lager. He slammed it down hard on the counter. He told the Indian to get some jerky and some Twinkies. The Indian did what he was told, but he looked a little nervous. That worried me. He put everything on top of the case of beer, and I totaled it all up. That's when the big one pulled out the gun."

"How did the Indian react when Sixto did that?"

"Damned if I know. My attention was all on that .45. I sort of lost track of the other guy. Big and butt-ugly told me to get all the bills out of the register and put them in a paper sack along with the other stuff. I did that. He had me rip the phone cord out of the wall. Then he made me come out from behind the counter and get face down on the floor. That's when he stomped my Stetson."

"Once they had you on the floor and threatened you, did they leave right away?"

"It wasn't more than a few seconds before I heard the door open. I turned my head and peeked that way, and they were outside, walking away. They weren't even looking back. I got up and ran to the office and got my other gun. By the time I got to the door, they were just about to their car. I eased open the door and got off a couple of rounds. One of them knocked the big guy part way down. Things moved real fast after that. He fell to one knee and started shooting as he turned. I ducked back inside the store. He broke the glass in the door and hit the building.

Had a guy come down from Kingman and fix the door on Saturday, but you can still see the holes in the cinder blocks. Must have been shooting hard-ball military rounds cause they penetrated instead of flattening out like hollow points would've.

When he stopped shooting, I looked out the door again. The skinny one was on the passenger side and sliding across the seat to get behind the wheel. The big one was hanging onto the open door. He was drooping a little. I didn't even have to open the door, just stuck my gun through where the glass had been and let go with two more. One of them blew out the windshield. The other one hit metal.

I ducked back before butt-ugly started shooting again. He let off a few more rounds. I heard the car start, and I could hear the tires crunching the gravel. I looked out again, and the car was driving away. I took my time and squeezed off two more. I heard one hit the car."

"Lyndon, not many people would've got up off the floor and did what you did."

"I'd like to claim I was brave, but really I was mad. I told the Arizona deputy I was mad because the guy stepped on my hat, but that's not really the truth. I was mad because he scared me so bad I almost peed my pants right there on the floor. The last time I was that afraid was at Chosin Reservoir."

"Let me ask you something, Lyndon. Do you think the Indian was in on the deal from the get-go? Think about it for a minute before you answer."

Lyndon was silent for a while. His eyes moved around the room, and Horse could tell he was re-living the events. Finally, he spoke.

"I'm not exactly sure, but I can tell you he wasn't mean like the other guy. Now don't get me wrong, he didn't do anything to stop the big one, but when I look back, I think just maybe he got hauled into it by that Sixto guy."

"One more thing, and I'll get out of your day. You gave me a great description of the guy. Much better than most people would've been able to give. But is there anything else you can tell me about him?"

Lyndon was silent again for a few moments. "Come to think of it, there is one thing. When I looked out the door the first time, and they were walking toward the car, there was something funny about the way the Indian moved. I can't quite describe it. It was like his foot hurt or something."

"You mean he was limping?"

"No, not really. Just something odd. I didn't remember it until you asked."

"Thank you, Mr. Brooks. You've been a great help."

Horse took a card out of his pocket and handed it to the man.

"If you think of anything else, please let me know."

"I surely will, Lieutenant. And Lieutenant, sorry again about the remark. I was way out of bounds there. There were Mexican guys in my unit in Korea. They were stand-up guys." He put his hand out, and Horse shook it again. Then Horse touched the brim of his hat with two fingers and turned and left.

★ ★ ★

When he got back to the office, he asked Fred if the Mercury had been towed into town.

"Not yet, Horse."

"When it does, get Allan to dust it for prints. I've got a lead on the other guy. By the way, I just realized Sixto's mother probably doesn't know Sixto is dead."

"Do you want me to send someone out?"

"No, I'd better do it myself."

Horse drove to the County dump just outside the city limits. There was no city dump because there was no city trash pickup. People burned all the trash that could be burned in fifty-gallon drums in their back yards. Every now and then they turned the barrel over and raked out the stuff that wouldn't burn. They took that and any bigger items out to the County dump.

Sixto's mother, Lucinda Morales, lived at the dump in a ramshackle structure built of scrounged cinder blocks and scrap lumber. She had lived there for as long as Horse could remember. Everyone in town referred to her as "Landfill Lucy." Sixto, her only child, had been raised in the shack. Lucinda had once made a living as a prostitute, but those days were long gone. Now she eked out a living of some kind sorting through the trash. It was a town tradition that she had first pick of anything that came in.

Horse stopped at the strange structure. He walked to the ill-fitting door and called her name. There was no answer. He got back in the car and drove into the dump. He found Lucinda picking through a big mound of trash on the side of a hill. She was tossing scraps of metal into a pile. He got out of the car.

"*Buenas dias, Senora* Morales."

"*Hola*, Horse."

"Senora, I'm afraid I have some bad news."

"You mean Sixto?"

"You know already?"

"I mean, it's always Sixto. So how bad is the news?"

"*Siento tener que decirle esto, la Senora Morales, pero Sixto esta muerto.*"

For a moment, Lucinda looked like she would collapse.

"*Yo siempre sabia que esta dia llegaria.*"

As Horse reached out to steady her, she sat down on the trash pile and looked off toward the Black Mountains. For a long time, she did not speak. Tears began to run through the grime on her face, but she made no sound.

"*Como morira?*"

"He was shot during an armed robbery up in Bullhead."

"Who shot him?"

"The guy who owned the liquor store he was robbing."

"From when he was little, he was always in trouble. I tried to tell him things would end bad if he continued. *Es coma hablar à la pared.* I wish I could have stopped him from doing those bad things. And now look what he has come to. *El nino es el padre del hombre.*"

"It sometimes seems so, *Senora*."

"Where is his body?"

"In San Bernardino. He was sent there for an autopsy."

"Then let them keep him. I don't have no money to bury him."

"*Senora* Morales, do you have anyone?"

"No. I had a sister, but she moved off to Flagstaff a long time ago. I don't know where she went after that, but she ain't there no more. But Horse, don't you worry about Lucinda none. She'll be just fine. You just go on your way and leave me be now."

"You sure you don't want to talk about this? The death of a child, any child, is never easy."

"Well, that would be right. Sixto sure wasn't easy. Not from the day he was born."

"How did you come to call him Sixto?"

"I didn't. The hospital did. I wanted to call him 'Six to One'"

"What do you mean?"

"Six to one, like in odds. Horse, you know I was a whore for many years, right?"

"Yes, *Senora*, I knew that. I also know people do what they have to do to get by."

"*Si, pues,* I was real careful when I sold my body. Didn't catch no diseases and didn't never get knocked up, neither. But then something happened. Sixto's daddy came through town. He was a sweet-talkin' man who played guitar for a few weeks down at The Palms. I got to tell you, I fell in love with that man. I did him free every night. One night I was a little drunk and did it without no protection. When I woke up the next morning, I just knew. I thought 'odds 'bout six to one that I'm gonna have a *nino.*'

So, when I went to the Smoke Tree hospital and had the baby, lady there asked me who the father was so she could put it on the paper she was filling out. I told her I didn't know, 'cause the guitar man was long gone, and I never saw him again.

"Then she asked me what I wanted to name him. I told her 'Six to One.' She said there wasn't no such name, and I couldn't name a baby that. I said that's what I wanted, but I was real tired and couldn't argue. She wrote 'Sixto' on her paper. Hell, I was wore out. I didn't know the difference"

She began to cry again. Horse put his hand on her shoulder.

"*Senora, lo siento que tuve que traele estas malas noticias.*"

"*Esta bien*. Part of your job. I'm glad it was you come and told me yourself and not one of your snotty young deputies. You go on back to work now, Horse. *Voy a estar bien.*"

Chapter 11

CHARLIE

Charlie jerked awake. He was shivering so hard he felt like he was bouncing across the ground. The gibbous moon was high overhead, which meant it was well after midnight. The sky was clear. He got up and pulled on his jacket. He was grateful for the flannel lining. At first, his hands were shaking so badly it was difficult to strike a match, but he finally got the kindling started. The resin in the pine cones began to pop as Charlie slowly piled more sticks on top of the kindling. It wasn't long before he had a decent blaze shooting sparks into the night sky. The pinyon smoke was sweet.

Charlie sat cross-legged as close to the fire as he could get without burning himself. As the fire warmed him, he began to doze. Soon he was asleep again. Throughout the night, every time the fire burned low the cold awakened Charlie. When it did, he added sticks to the coals and built up the fire. As soon as it began to warm him, he would fall asleep again. The third time he woke up, snow was falling. The next time he awakened, the night sky was clear.

When the cold dragged him from his exhausted sleep for the last time, he could see streaks of light on the eastern horizon. In the west, where the stars had raced into oblivion, the pale, waning moon was hanging lonely and bereft in the western sky. Charlie was so cold his hands felt like bricks. He piled all the firewood left in his stack on top of the coals and soon had a blaze. He sat before his fire, staring toward the growing light above the Black Mountains.

By the time the sun was fully above the rim, the fire was burning down again. Charlie made the final demanding ascent to the summit of the sacred mountain. He surveyed the huge expanse of desert surrounding him. The storm that had moved through in the early morning hours of Sunday had dropped snow on the Hualapai Mountains to the southeast and the New York mountains to the northwest. To the northeast, he could see Lake Mojave above Davis Dam. Charlie felt dwarfed by the scale of the desert and the power of the natural forces that had shaped and altered the landscape.

He walked back to his dry camp and scattered the dwindling fire before setting out on the next leg of his long journey. Sparks from the fire fled, streaming southward on a freshening wind that had picked up with the rising of the sun.

He realized his sleep the night before hadn't done him much good. The bitter cold had awakened him too many times. But although he was not well-rested, there had been one change for the better. His hunger had disappeared. Although he was physically very tired, he was filled with a strange, nervous energy. He felt the same as he did after he drank too many cups of coffee. His heart was beating fast, and there was a fluttery feeling in his throat. Despite his fatigue, he felt he had to move and move fast. He picked up his water carrier and discovered ice on the surface. He poked through it with a stick and drank deeply. It made his teeth ache. He set off down the mountain to retrace the route he had taken the previous day. When he reached the Three Sisters, he stood among those huge pointed pieces of granite poking into the sky like spearheads abandoned by giants and rested before he walked on. He stopped again halfway down and filled his water carrier. He still felt energetic when he got to the bottom and turned into the west.

He was proud of the distance he had covered the previous two days, especially the thirty miles that had brought him to Avi Kwa'ame. He knew his ancestors had been capable of covering incredible distances on their way to the Pacific coast, and it pleased him to feel he was part of that tradition.

It felt good to be moving again, but soon the nervous energy dissipated. It was not long before he found himself slipping and occasionally stumbling. The fasting, combined with the constant travel over rough ground, was grinding him down. By the time he reached the hot water cistern at the well site, he felt like he was walking through wet cement. His quadriceps had taken a pounding descending the mountain, and his calves kept knotting up

He drank the last of his sweet water and filled the carrier with water from the cistern. He was so tired it was hard to get undressed before getting into the hot water. He stayed in as long as he could stand it before getting out and cooling off. He re-soaked twice, trying to leach the aches from deep in his joints and muscles, but it was obvious his body was cannibalizing itself to come up with the fuel to keep going, and the pain would not relent. Realizing the day was slipping away, he got dressed and started south.

Travelers driving across the desert look at the passing mountain ranges and perceive the ground between the roadway and the distant mountains as level. They also think the mountains are not very far away. They are wrong on both counts. Distances are deceptive on the Mojave. The terrain that looks so flat is actually chopped up and fractured by washes and gullies. Walking across the broken landscape involves constantly scrambling up, down, and sideways. Even though Charlie was moving very slowly, he frequently staggered. Once, he stepped on a loose rock while he was dropping into a small gulley and did not have the strength to recover his balance. When he pitched forward, he had the presence of mind to twist and land on his back while managing to hold the water carrier aloft. He lost half of the water, but at least he didn't break the clay vessel that had belonged to Hera anyai's father.

In the late afternoon, he finally reached the embankment he had to climb to cross the railroad tracks. As he labored up the steep side, he remembered how easily he had climbed up the other side just the day before.

When he reached Klinefelter, the sun had set. He was glad he did not need a fire because he lacked the energy to gather firewood. He drank his fill of the pure, cold water from the gushing spring. As he lay down for the night, he was forced to admit to himself that he could not possibly hike all the way to the maze the following day. He knew, however, that he would have to reach Eagle Pass before sundown to get water.

Chapter 12

AEDEN

Tuesday was Election Day, but I barely noticed. That morning I was in front of the school again when Billy and his mother arrived. Just as the day before, I helped get Billy out of the car and into his chair. Other than "good morning" and "thank you," Mrs. Braithwaite did not speak to me, but she gave me that strange look again before she got in the car and drove away.

Just like the day before, I walked beside Billy as we headed to chemistry class.

"Your mom doesn't talk much, does she?"

"Sometimes she talks a lot. She just doesn't talk to white people much."

"Any luck finding Charlie?"

"No."

"Did you hear anything about him from anybody?"

"No."

"Well, thanks anyway for keeping your ear to the ground. Will you keep trying?"

"Sure, why not?"

We were early for class. Billy established himself in his usual location, and I moved to my spot and sat there as the room slowly filled.

Several of my classmates nodded and spoke to me. Charlene Daugherty gave me a dirty look. No one said anything to Billy.

Judy was one of the last students to class. She did not as much as glance at me. In fact, it was obvious she was trying very hard not to look my way. Johnny came in just as the bell rang. He had a haunted, lost look that worried me. He looked like a guy who was missing sleep and meals.

When class ended, I fell in beside Judy as she walked out the door.

"I want to talk to you for a minute before you leave for lunch."

She didn't say anything – just kept walking.

"Judy, it's important."

She stopped and glared at me. "What's important?"

"Thursday night."

"I thought we fixed that last Friday morning."

"That was before we heard about Sixto."

"That dead guy?"

"That's right, that dead guy. I'll see you after fourth period."

I caught up with Johnny before we went in for second period.

"I talked to Judy. She's going to meet me before she leaves for lunch."

"That's great, Ade. Thanks."

"She is not happy about it. You'd better not be anywhere around. She might get spooked."

"Okay. I'll meet you afterward at my car."

When fourth period ended, I waited outside for Judy.

"Well?" she asked as she headed for the street.

"Walk over here for a minute. I don't want your dad to see us together."

"All right. But I don't have long. He's expecting me."

She followed me to the side of the building. Several people looked at us curiously as they walked by.

"So?"

"What have you told your mom and dad?"

"I went straight to bed after you left on Thursday night. My dad gave me the third degree at breakfast, but I stuck to the story."

"You think he believes you?"

"No, I don't think he does. My mother might, but not him."

"How hard is he pushing you?"

"Hard. From the minute I come down for breakfast. My mother tries to get him to leave me alone, but he ignores her. He keeps it up when we're driving to school and back. He never lets up."

"Do you think he suspects we were at The House of Three Murders?"

"No, that's not it at all! He thinks Johnny and I were doing some kind of sex thing that night. As if I would! Yuck!"

"Be honest with me. Do you think you can just stick to the story?"

She suddenly looked like she was going to cry.

"I don't know. I'm getting tired of denying everything. I think it would almost be better to just tell him what really happened and get it over with."

"Don't think that, Judy. That's the worst thing you could do. Remember the dead guy!"

"Yeah, I remember him. But I didn't do anything wrong. You and Johnny started the fire."

"You'd hang Johnny out to dry to save yourself?"

"You don't fool me, Ade. You don't mean just Johnny. You mean you too, don't you?"

"You're not my girlfriend. Johnny's the one in love with you. All he cares about is protecting you and keeping you out of trouble. But you don't care that much about him, do you?"

"I'm not in love with Johnny. I never said I was. Why should I sacrifice myself to protect him? He's just something to do until I can get out of this ugly town. Just like your girlfriend did."

I looked, really looked, at the girl standing in front of me, her beauty on display in the light of the noonday sun. A light, cool breeze ruffled her blonde hair into a halo around her face and put color in her cheeks. Her blue eyes gazed at me coldly. She was the spoiled daughter of a rich and powerful man. She was a bundle of selfishness with no feelings for anyone other than herself. More clearly than ever, I realized how badly this would turn out for my friend.

I made one last appeal. "Stick with the story, Judy. Just stick with it. Otherwise, we all go down together."

"We'll just see."

She turned and hurried away, the hard heels on her oxblood penny loafers ringing hard on the sidewalk.

Johnny was waiting for me in the parking lot, leaning against his car.

"Did you talk to her?"

"Yes, I did."

"So, what did she say?"

"Let's not talk right here. Let's hit the Jade for lunch again."

As we drove, Johnny peppered me with questions about Judy. How Judy had acted. If she seemed okay. How distressed she was. What she seemed to be thinking.

When we walked into the Jade, Hazel started clapping. "Hey, everybody, football heroes!"

The men sitting at the counter turned and smiled. It brought home to me how much high school football meant to this tiny town. Most of the guys at the counter had probably played for Smoke Tree High, but none of them had ever had a season like we were having. As we walked past, there were a lot of compliments. I noticed most of them were directed toward Johnny. He was the real hero of the season. I was just a guy who got lucky for one play.

We headed for the table in back with Hazel right behind us.

"What a game, boys. What a game."

"You were there?"

"Me and Lee both. He closed up so we could both go to the game. Can you believe it? He never closes up! What a great play, Ade. Changed the whole game."

"Thanks Hazel. It was just luck."

"So, boys, the usual?"

"Just coffee for me," said Johnny.

"A chocolate milkshake and French fries, please."

After she left, Johnny pressed me again for every detail of my conversation with Judy. I withheld the part where she told me she didn't love him. I just couldn't bring myself to include that.

Hazel brought our order. When she left, Johnny dumped sugar and cream into his coffee and sipped at it while I ate my fries.

"So, Judy's dad thinks we were 'doing some sex thing,' huh?"

"That's the way she put it."

"What a laugh. We've never even come close."

"At least it has her dad looking the wrong direction."

"So that's why she's not allowed to see me or even talk to me."

"I'm worried. She's starting to crack. That remark she made about having nothing to do with the fire showed me what she's thinking. I'm afraid she's going to spill the beans."

"Never happen, Ade. You'll see. She would never betray me."

"Okay, if you say so."

All through fifth and sixth periods, I thought about the multiplying complications of the House of Three Murders fire. I was disappointed Billy had not managed to talk to Charlie Merriman. And the conversation with Judy before lunch had been even more troubling. But if I thought the day had been bad so far, I was about to find out things could get worse. When sixth period ended, I put my books in my locker and headed off to practice.

The Smoke Tree Unified School District administration building was on the high school campus, and I passed by it on my way to the gym. Dr. Symington had the big corner office. We rarely saw him on campus during the day, so I was surprised to find him on the sidewalk.

"Mr. Snow, come into my office, please."

"I'm going to be late for football practice if I don't hurry."

"Mr. Snow, I will let Coach Lucas know I was the cause of your tardiness."

He turned and walked toward the administration building. I followed. He led me past his secretary and ushered me into his office.

"Sit down, Mr. Snow. This won't take long."

I sat.

"Mr. Snow, I couldn't help but notice you in conversation with Judy McPhearson before lunch today."

He paused. I didn't say anything. There was a long silence.

"I'd like to know what you were talking about."

He paused again. He looked a little uncomfortable, but not as uncomfortable as I felt with this strange discussion.

"Come now, Mr. Snow. It's not a difficult question. What were you two talking about?"

"Sir, that's between Judy and me."

"Perhaps. But perhaps not. You see, Mr. McPhearson has been in contact with me. It seems he is very concerned about, um, shall we say 'unwanted advances' toward his daughter by your friend Johnny."

"Unwanted advances? She's his girlfriend."

"Apparently, that is no longer the case. Mr. McPhearson is quite adamant that all ties between his daughter and your friend have been severed. So, once again, what were you discussing with the young lady?"

I thought for a moment before saying something I might regret. "Sir, I don't think you have any right to ask me that question."

"Mr. Snow, I've been asked by a concerned parent to intervene in his behalf in this situation whenever his daughter is on school property. The term, Mr. Snow, is 'in loco parentis.' It means ..."

"I know what it means, sir. I'm in my second year of Latin with Mr. Sorrento. Are you telling me that Mr. McPhearson has told you I am not allowed to talk to Judy?"

Dr. Symington's face began to get red.

"I will be the sole judge of the parameters of Mr. McPhearson's request, young man. Now, I am giving you one more opportunity to answer my direct and legitimate question. What were you discussing with Judy McPhearson?"

"I don't think I have to answer that."

Dr. Symington glared at me.

"Young man, you will come to regret your impertinence, I assure you. I will be in contact with your parents. When I get done talking to them, you'll be eager to answer my questions tomorrow. And furthermore, once I report to Mr. McPhearson, I'm sure you will find you will have no more discussions with his daughter."

I was a seventeen-year-old kid. Dr. Symington was the Superintendent of the school district. If he was trying to intimidate me, he was succeeding, but I was determined not to let him know it.

"Sir, you said, 'when I report to Mr. McPhearson.' Are you telling me Mr. McPhearson hired you to spy on us?"

Dr. Symington slammed his fat hands on the desk. I have to admit I jumped.

"That is enough disrespect from you, young man. Leave my office!"

He couldn't have said anything that would have made me happier. As I went through the outer office, I could have sworn I saw a tiny smile on Lettie Thompson's face.

As I jogged toward the gym, I was so badly shaken my legs felt weak. I had never dreamed I would defy Dr. Symington, and even though I believed I was right, I couldn't help feeling I was in serious trouble.

But my bad day wasn't over.

When I walked into the gym, I knew I was late. I couldn't hear any noise from the locker room. But as I hurried past the coaches' office, Coach Lucas opened the door.

"Ade, you want to step in here a minute?"

I followed him into the office. I noticed Johnny was sitting in front of Coach Lucas's desk with his back to me. He started to turn around.

"Just keep facing my desk, Johnny. Don't be looking at Ade."

Coach sat down behind his desk.

"Ade, where were you and Johnny last Thursday night."

For just a moment, I wondered what Johnny had told him. Then I realized Johnny would've stuck to our story as we planned.

"What time Thursday night?"

"Let's say about the time half the town was at the field lighting the homecoming bonfire."

"Johnny and I were over in Arizona. Up by Oatman."

"And what were you doing?"

"We were over at Boundary Cone drinking a six-pack of beer."

"That's what I was afraid of. And that's what Johnny told me. Okay, you boys won't need your pads. Just shorts and helmets and cleats. You're going to be running today."

"How many laps?"

"You're going to run all during practice today, tomorrow, and Thursday. And on Friday, you're riding the team bus to Boulder City, and you're dressing out for the game. But you won't be playing."

"So why dress out then, Coach?"

"I want you to stand on the sideline and feel stupid because of the stupid thing you did on Thursday night.

You know, I just don't understand you two. Three years you boys have played for me. Three years you've worked hard, and both of you have turned into team leaders. The other boys respect you. And as far as I know, you never broke training before. And now this. If I'd known about this on Friday, neither one of you would've played against Sunset Crossing, and we would have lost that game! Of all my players, you two are the last ones I ever thought I'd have to bench for breaking team rules."

"Coach Lucas, can I ask you a question?"

"Speak."

"Who was the rat fink who turned us in?"

He stared at me and didn't reply.

"It was Bobby Quayles, wasn't it?"

He didn't answer. But he didn't have to.

"Now get dressed and get on the field. You've got some running to do."

Once again, Johnny had a T-shirt on under his school shirt. He kept it on and pulled his jersey over it. When we came down the steps and onto the track, Coach waved us over. He had the team form a circle with the three of us in the middle.

"Gentlemen, two of the leaders of this team have let you down. Last Thursday night, they broke training. They were out drinking beer. I will say this much for them: they were man enough to own up to it. If I'd known about this last Friday, they wouldn't have played, but I didn't find out until today.

Today and tomorrow, and Thursday they are going to be running laps all the time the rest of you are practicing. Every time you look up and see them circling the track, remember this is what happens when you break team rules. This is a team, and when you break team rules you hurt the team. And when you hurt the team, you get benched. Doesn't matter if you're third-string or starters like these two. You run until I say you're done, and you ride the pine the next game. The rest of you are going to have to work extra hard this week because we're playing Boulder City without these two.

Johnny. Ade. Start running."

And run we did. We ran until we couldn't run anymore, and then we walked. Coach seemed to have an uncanny sense about just how long we had to walk before we could run again, and when it was time, he sent an assistant coach over to tell us to start running again.

Whenever we walked, we talked. I told Johnny about my strange conversation with Dr. Symington, and we both agreed that Judy wouldn't be talking to either one of us for a while. I asked Johnny what he wanted to do about our Thursday night story. He said we should stick with it, no matter what.

But mostly, we ran. When practice was over, Coach kept us running under the lights until everyone else had showered and gone home. I was so exhausted when we were done that I could hardly get up the concrete steps that led from the field to the gym. Johnny put on his street clothes and left without a shower. The gym seemed creepily quiet while I showered alone.

When I got home, Mom and Dad were finishing dinner.

"You're late," said Mom.

"I know. Coach kept Johnny and me after practice today."

"Your mother had a phone call from Superintendent Symington this afternoon. He told her you got mouthy with him and refused to answer some questions he asked you."

"I didn't answer all his questions, but I don't mouth off to grownups. I've been taught better."

"Well then, one of you is lying."

"It isn't me."

I told them about my session with Dr. Symington. When I got done, neither of them said anything for a minute. Then my dad said, "So this is all about some deal with Johnny and the McPhearsons?"

"Yessir."

"Well, I don't see what right he has to ask you about a talk you had with Johnny's girlfriend. You know, I never liked that pudgy little stuck-up man. And now I like him even less.

Now, why did Coach have you stay late?"

This was the question I had been dreading. I was really stuck. I couldn't tell Mom and Dad I had been drinking because that was a lie.

But I didn't want to tell them where I really had been because I'd promised Johnny we would protect Judy.

"Ade," prompted Dad.

"We broke team rules. We ran laps all through practice and after practice too. We're running tomorrow and Thursday, and we're not playing on Friday night."

"What was this rule you broke?"

I was very careful with my answer.

"Someone told Coach that Johnny and I were out drinking beer last Thursday night."

"And were you?"

"Nossir, we weren't."

"Then why didn't you tell him that?"

"Because I promised Johnny I wouldn't tell where we really were."

"So you're taking this punishment to protect your friend?"

"Yessir. In a way. To keep the promise I made."

"And does this have something to do with Johnny and his girl-friend?"

"Yessir, it does."

"I see. Well, Ade, I suspect you have your reasons. And Johnny has his reasons for taking this punishment and asking you to take it with him. If you can live with the consequences, it's fine with me."

"Thank you, sir, for trusting me."

"But Richard, this is unfair! If you believe he wasn't out drinking, then why should he be punished?"

"Because he made a promise to his friend. And keeping the promise is getting him in trouble. He's willing to stick with his friend. I'm proud of him for that."

They left the table and went in to look for news about the election on television.

★ ★ ★

When I got to work, I had a tiny rush and then nothing. Shortly after the rush died, the phone rang.

"Union '76, Aeden Snow speaking."

"It's me. Good news about the house fire thing."

"I could use some good news."

"My dad knows somebody at the sheriff's office. The word is they did an autopsy on Sixto in San Bernardino. He was dead before the fire started."

"Great! I mean, not great for Sixto, but it sure takes some pressure off of us. We're not murderers anyway."

"Yeah. I'll tell you when my dad told me, it felt like an elephant had climbed off my chest."

"So, how does this affect our story?"

"Not at all. Remember, we came up with this story before we knew about Sixto. Nothing's changed. We still cover for Judy."

"Okay, Johnny."

"Thanks, Ade. See you at school tomorrow."

When Mr. Garrett came to close up, I asked him if he'd heard anything about the election.

"No one really knows yet. They just know it's close. You know, ever since they put out that story about Dewey beating Truman in '48, they've been afraid to stick their necks out. I guess we'll all have to wait and see."

We closed up, and Mr. Garrett made up the deposit. I followed him to the bank as usual. When I got home, my mom and dad were in front of the television. None of the networks was predicting a winner.

Chapter 13

CHARLIE

Charlie came awake in the pre-dawn hours with a terrible headache, so bad it was making him sick. Even at this lower elevation, the temperature was hovering just above freezing. He had to get up and start moving to get warm.

Charlie rolled onto his stomach and got on his hands and knees. As he pushed to his feet, a wave of nausea and dizziness hit him. He dropped back down and began to retch, but there was nothing in his stomach but a few drops of some vile-tasting liquid. He spit it out and thought he was done, but then began to dry heave – spasm after spasm. When he was finally able to stop, he spit repeatedly to get the bitter taste out of his mouth.

He managed to get to his feet, but he was still dizzy. He picked up his jacket and put it on. The gibbous, waning moon had completed three-quarters of its journey and hung above the western horizon. He estimated the time at around five.

There was no point in lying back down. He knew he would not be able to go back to sleep, so he decided to get underway. He had over twenty-five miles to go before he reached Eagle Pass, and his pace was slowing each day. After getting a long drink and topping off his water supply, he headed south. He decided not to cross Highway 95 and the Santa Fe tracks and drop into Paiute wash. Instead, he would cross Highway 66 to the west of where 95 forked to the north.

When he had made his way through the low desert hills and arrived at Highway 66, there were few vehicles on the road, mostly big trucks that came thundering down South Pass or laboring up the hill from Smoke Tree. It still took a while for the right moment to arrive to cross the highway because he was careful not to be night blind before he stepped off the shoulder onto the roadway.

False dawn found him at the northeastern most edge of the Sacramento Mountains. To the west, he could see a small house with a corral, a windmill, and a cottonwood tree. Even though he was far away, he could make out the shapes of a horse and a few cattle in the corral. Charlie stood for a long time in the dim light looking at the small house, thinking how fine it would be to have a place like that of his own. A horse, a few animals, a good well, a big shade tree, and a view of the desert to the north and the river to the east. Who could ask for more? A dog at the house picked up his scent on the breeze and began to bark. He moved on.

Charlie continued to skirt the north edge of the mountains. After a mile or so, he was able to turn south again. He continued steadily, if slowly southward, crossing the many *bajadas* dotted with barrel and cholla cactus. When the sun finally lifted above the Black Mountains, he was grateful. The warmth allowed him to stop for a much-needed rest. He had only gone a few miles since leaving Klinefelter, but it felt like forty. He was tired to the bone. It was a nasty kind of tired he had never felt before. It felt like his body was shutting down and giving up on him. But he still had many miles to go before he could have the dream that would reveal his *sumach a'hot*.

He sat down on a rock covered with desert varnish and faced the rising sun. He wondered if Hera anyai were in his chair in front of his house, feeling the same sun. Charlie wished he were there with the old one. As the sun rose higher, the wind from the north picked up. Little gray birds moved between the creosote and white bursage, their wings thrumming as they darted from plant to plant. He looked at the Mojave Valley spread out below him, tinted with pink by the rising sun. He could see the anchors of his world: Avi Kwa'ame to the north and

Huqueamp Avi to the south. Even though he was weak and weary and sore of foot, Charlie felt at peace for the first time in many days. He lingered longer than he should have to enjoy the feeling.

After an hour of rest, he drank deeply from the clay water carrier and moved on. The sun splayed his shadow onto the side of the *bajada* to his west as he slowly picked his way over the rough ground. Even his shadow looked tired, its head hanging forward as it stumbled onward.

The rest of the day made a mockery of the peace he had felt earlier. Five and a half days with nothing but water had depleted his resources. He had long ago used up his ordinary reserves. His body was breaking down muscle tissue for fuel so he could keep moving. Even though he had soaked in hot water at the cistern the day before, he could smell himself. It was an odor like vinegar and sour laundry mixed together.

The *bajadas* he was crossing were covered with barrel cactus, yucca, cholla cactus, small sagebrush, and broken rock. The Sacramento Mountains, like all mountains in Mojave basin and range country, stood shoulder-deep in the debris of their own destruction. Once towering peaks, the north-south trending ranges in the eastern Mojave had begun to erode on the day of their birth. They had continued to erode for millions and millions of years. The deposits that made up the *bajadas* were unstable piles of rocks and gravel, and Charlie often stumbled and slid before he could regain his balance. His legs quivered with exhaustion. Still, he forced himself onward.

A little after noon, he was forced to move eastward off the side of the mountain. He didn't want to add extra miles to his hike, but he was afraid if he didn't get to level ground, he would fall and injure himself. Fortunately, once he got there and turned south again, it wasn't long before he hit the dirt road in the middle of the broad wash that led to Eagle Pass.

★ ★ ★

It was almost sundown when he entered the twisting pass through the mountains. When he passed some abandoned wood flumes left behind by miners in the early 20th century, he knew he was approaching the spring on Hera anyai's map. Once he reached the base of Eagle Peak, he rested for half an hour. Then he scrambled tiredly up the hillside until he found a tiny seep of water dripping down the side of a slab of granite, right where Hera anyai had shown it on his drawing. He drank the rest of his good water and began the agonizingly slow process of filling his carrier from the slowly dripping seep.

He was so tired he could hardly concentrate on his task. By the time he filled his carrier, it was dark. He moved back down through the pass to lower ground so he could sleep where the temperature would remain above freezing.

Chapter 14

HORSE

On Tuesday morning, Horse drove out to Zack's junk yard. Sixto's car had been dusted for prints the previous afternoon, but Horse wanted to look at it for himself. The tow truck had left it outside the yard. Horse could hear the continuous barking of Zack's dogs inside the fence as he got out of his cruiser.

He walked around the car. A hole in the trunk. A spider-webbed hole high on the front windshield. A hole in the chrome grillwork. Horse felt under the hood for the release and lifted the hood. The engine had been completely cooked. The intense heat had partially melted the spark plug wires. The radiator hoses had burst, and the radiator itself was distended. He dropped the hood and moved to the passenger door.

The front seat was sprinkled with glass shards from the windshield and the rear-view mirror. Sixto had bled heavily. There was dried blood caked on the seat. Fuzzy dice that had hung from the shattered rear-view mirror were stuck in the blood. Horse wondered how a man who had lost that much blood could have made it from where his car was found to the house where he died. "Sixto," he said out loud, "you were one tough *hombre!*"

When he was finished examining the car, he visited with Zack for a few minutes and promised to get him paid for the tow job. He got back in his car and rattled down the dirt road on his way back to the office.

His deputy had found Sixto's prints all over the car. He had also found a lot of prints from someone else. Unless the other person had a record, the prints wouldn't help identify him, but at least they would establish he had been in the car if they ever found him. Horse planned to spend the afternoon visiting the local bars to see if he could get a line on where Sixto had been drinking before the robbery. Maybe he had arrived there with the young Indian man or met him at the bar.

He was downtown at noon having lunch when he remembered all the bars would be closed until eight o'clock that night because of Election Day. Well, if he couldn't go searching through the bars before evening, at least he could vote. He drove to his polling place and cast his ballot. He voted for Kennedy. He thought it was high time his country had a Catholic president!

★ ★ ★

After dinner and a rest, he hit the bars as they began to open. He started with The Boxcar and then moved to The Derail. He had no luck at either. Neither bartender had seen Sixto in over two weeks, and they were both grateful they hadn't. The owner of The Highball was no help either. He had heard that Sixto was dead and didn't look sad about it.

At The Palms, Horse struck pay dirt. The retired Marine sergeant told Horse of his encounter with Sixto the previous Wednesday and explained he had kicked Sixto out for a month.

"Mac, I'm really looking for information about anyone he was with."

"Well, he came in alone, but then he latched onto Charlie Merriman. When I eighty-sixed him, I threw Charlie out too. But afterward, I felt bad about that. It wasn't really fair. Charlie hadn't done anything. In fact, Charlie has never made any trouble in here. I was just so tired of Sixto's crap that I tossed them both."

"Do you remember what time that was?"

"Charlie had been here about an hour before Sixto came in. It wasn't ten minutes before I'd had enough. I thought for a minute Sixto was going to fight me about it. I would say they went out the door about three-thirty."

"We're talking about the Charlie Merriman from the Mojave Village, right?"

"That's the one. Young guy. Drops in for a beer now and then. Never gets drunk, never gets rowdy."

"Do you know where he works?"

"Track crew for the Santa Fe."

"Okay, Mac. Thanks for your help."

"Horse, is it true what I heard? Sixto's dead?"

"Yep."

"Can you tell me how it happened?"

"Liquor store owner up in Bullhead shot him during a holdup. He didn't die on the spot. He made it to an abandoned place across the river and died there."

"Good Lord! I hope Charlie wasn't with him."

"Well, Mac, I hope so too. But it looks like he was."

As Horse walked out, he thought, *so there it is, the Smoke Tree connection. Charlie works for the railroad. He has access to railroad fusees. But unless he walked around with them in his pocket, how'd he get them to the abandoned house?*

Chapter 15

AEDEN

Dad banged on my door in the morning. I was sore and tired. I didn't know how far Johnny and I had run during practice, but it must have been many miles. I wasn't looking forward to doing that again.

When I went into the kitchen, Dad was having his coffee and reading the paper from the day before. He always read the paper from the day before at breakfast. The paper for this morning would not arrive until early afternoon when it came in on the train from Los Angeles. One of the oddities of life in the middle of nowhere.

"Did you find out who won the election?"

"Too close to call. No one knows for sure."

"How late did you and Mom stay up?"

"All the TV stations went off at midnight. I guess we could've turned on the radio, but I was too tired. I went off to bed. I'm wiped out this morning. Not used to being up that late. Now I wish I'd gone to bed earlier. I'll be catching a job mid-morning, and I'll be yawning all day."

I got two tortillas out of the refrigerator. "Well, I'd better get off to school. See you tomorrow sometime?"

"Ade, one thing. The more I thought about Superintendent Symington, the madder I got. Your Mom and I usually leave the running of the school to the school people, but this is different. I'm going to call

and tell him he can't ever question you about a private conversation unless I'm there with you."

"Thanks, Dad. I really appreciate that."

"I don't know what Johnny has dragged you into. I hope it doesn't
come back to bite you on the butt."

I got to school early. I was waiting for Billy and Mrs. Braithwaite
when the old Chevy pulled up in front of the school. I had the back
door open, and the wheelchair on the sidewalk before Mrs. Braithwaite
got out of the car. Billy opened his door, and she started toward him.

"I've got this."

I thought I caught the glimmer of a smile on her face, instantly
suppressed.

"This is getting to be a regular thing with you."

"Making up for lost time."

I helped Billy out of the car as his mom maneuvered the chair so
I could ease him into it. Mrs. Braithwaite got Billy's books out of the
car and put them on his lap. Then, just as she had done the day before,
she squeezed his shoulder. He patted her hand and smiled up at her. She
walked around the car, but before she got in, she gave me one of those
direct stares.

"Thanks for your help, Ade."

"You're welcome, Ma'am."

I walked along beside Billy as he wheeled himself to class. I opened
the door for him, and he rolled to his usual spot. We were the only people in the classroom.

"Any luck with finding Charlie?"

"No. But I did talk to some people who saw him last Saturday
morning. One told me he saw Charlie with one of the old ones. The
other one said he saw him leaving the Village. The guy said hello, but
Charlie didn't answer. Just kept walking toward the highway. As far as I
can tell, no one's seen him since."

"Does Charlie have family in the Village?"

"The whole Village is his family."

"I mean family he lives with, in a house."

"He lives with his mom."

"Do you think I could come out to the Village and talk to her?"

"You could come out, but she won't talk to you."

"How about this 'old one,' could I talk to him?"

"I don't think so."

"Thanks, Billy. Thanks for asking around."

The other students began arriving. Once again, several nodded and spoke to me. No one said anything to Billy. It was as if he weren't there.

I was in history class third period when Superintendent Symington's voice came over the intercom.

"Your attention, please. At 12:47 p.m. eastern standard time, Vice-President Richard M. Nixon conceded the election. The next president of the United States will be John Fitzgerald Kennedy. That is all."

He did not sound happy.

Mr. Miller began to explain how the Electoral College worked. I could see eyes glazing over. When he got done with his diagram, he explained it was possible for someone to win the popular vote and still lose the election. That woke everyone up. Students who hadn't cared about the election five minutes before were suddenly outraged. But regardless of how the popular vote came out, we had a new president.

During the campaign, Nixon and Kennedy had tried to outdo each other as cold warriors, each trying to trump the other on how tough he would be on Russia and on Communism anywhere in the world. Kennedy would say in his inauguration speech, "We will pay any price, bear any burden, meet any hardship, support any friend, oppose any foe, in order to assure the survival and the success of liberty."

As we sat in our high school class that November morning, we had no way of knowing the price many of us would pay, nor did we have any foreshadowing of the burden some of us would bear for the rest of our lives because of what was coming. Some would manage to shoulder that load. Others, through no fault of their own, would not. A piece of the prelude to our coming national nightmare had just snapped into place.

★ ★ ★

At noon, Johnny and I met in the parking lot. As we drove downtown, I gave him a rundown of my parents' reaction to getting in trouble with Coach Lucas. He laughed when I told him about my dad's plan to call

Superintendent Symington. It was the first time I had heard him laugh since Thursday night.

"Here's the part I'm worried about. What did they think about our beer-drinking story?"

"I told them we really hadn't done that."

"Uh-oh. Didn't they want to know where we really were that night?"

I told them I couldn't say. I told them I had promised you I wouldn't tell anyone what we were really doing that night."

Johnny let out a low whistle. "And they were okay with that?"

"Mom wasn't. Not really. But Dad said it was a good thing I was keeping my promise, even though it meant I would be in trouble."

"Thank God for your dad!"

"What about you? What did your dad think?"

"He was out when I got home last night, and he wasn't back yet when I left for school this morning. I'll tell him when I see him, but I don't think he'll care much about it."

When we got downtown, we went to Lulu's. The place was packed, as usual. It was the regular hangout for the high school kids at lunch and after school. Lulus had a great jukebox with all the latest hits and the best pies in town. All the booths were full, and so were all the stools at the counter. That left the tiny table next to the back door.

As soon as we sat down, we were surrounded by guys from the team. We had to tell our beer-drinking story a few times before everyone had a chance to hear it. Estaro Munoz summed up the team reaction best.

"Man, I never thought you two would be busted for breaking training. Wow! Mr. Pure as the Driven Snow and Mr. Team Leader! Well, Ade, just means more carries and more glory for me. I'll bet Bobby Quayles is happy."

"He should be. He's the guy who turned us in."

"C'mon," said Sammy West, one of our defensive ends, "no lie?"

"I asked Coach if it was Quayles. You know Coach – he won't lie if you ask him a straight-up question."

"What'd he say?"

"He didn't say anything. Just stared at me."

"Hot damn! It was Quayles. What a fink! Well, he'd better hope this doesn't cost us the game. It'll be a long walk back from Boulder City, 'cause Seve won't let him on the bus if he screws this up!"

Johnny was so happy everybody was buying the story that he sprang for butterscotch pie for dessert for both of us. On the way back to school, he thanked me again for talking to Judy on Tuesday.

"Well, you can be sure I won't be talking to her again. Once Symington reported to her dad, I'm sure I went right onto the forbidden list with you.

So, what are you thinking?"

"I don't know what to think. I know her dad is putting the screws to her. I know he's got Symington watching her at school. But I keep thinking about what I'd do if it was the other way around. I mean, I'd manage to talk to her somehow, you know? Let her know that I was stuck, but I still loved her. But she not only won't talk to me – she never even gives me a smile or anything. I don't know what's going on in that pretty head."

I still didn't think Johnny could bear to hear what she had told me about not caring about him. He was already lower than a snake's belly. I didn't want to make it worse, so I changed the subject.

"The Smoke Tree Weekly will be out. Might be interesting to see what kind of story they write."

"Maybe. By the way, how are you doing? You've been worrying about my girl troubles, but what about yours?"

"When I called Linda's mom on Friday, she told me Linda had met a guy at college and was getting serious about him."

"That was quick! She's only been up there a couple of months."

"Guess I wasn't that hard to replace."

"She isn't either. Find yourself a new one. There's lots of girls in this school would like to go out with you."

"Sure. I could say the same to you."

"Right. I see what you mean."

"By the way, Charlene Daugherty told me she thinks Judy's dumping you for good, and she's glad. Said you had it coming. Said you and I both were stuck up."

"Who cares what she thinks?"

At practice that afternoon, we were both on the track running endless circles again. We didn't talk much. If it's possible for someone to run without seeing anything, Johnny was doing it. He was lost inside himself.

At least Coach didn't make us stay after practice and run some more. As soon as we were done, Johnny picked up his stuff and left without showering again. Nobody but Judy and I knew he'd been burned.

When I got home, Dad was out. Mom told me he'd made the call to the superintendent. She said Dr. Symington was pretty unhappy.

"Well, whatever he said, it worked. Symington didn't bother me today."

I finished dinner, gathered up my books, and went to work. I called Johnny and gave him the update about my dad calling Symington. He was impressed.

"I have to admit, I wasn't sure he would do that. I don't think my old man would do that for me."

"You know, Johnny, I don't know much about your dad. We've been friends a long time, but as long as I've been coming to your house, your dad's never said much to me."

"Join the club, Ade. He doesn't say much to me either. He has most of his conversations with Mr. Jack Daniels. I never saw a man who could drink so much and still be sober."

When I followed Mr. Garrett to the bank that night to drop the deposit, I was running on empty. I was glad I wouldn't have to work again until Sunday night. When I got home, Mom was up watching Martin Black's Night Owl Club out of Las Vegas. As usual, he was interviewing somebody I'd never heard of. Probably one of the lounge acts. I went down the hall and fell in bed.

Chapter 16

HORSE

When Horse got to the office on Wednesday morning, he assigned Stuart Atkins the task of going out to the fire scene to look for remains of fusees.

"I know it's dirty work, Stu, but you were on the scene with me the morning of the fire. You already know your way around out there. Call a few of the fire department volunteers and see if you can get one of them to go out with you. They might have some experience with finding where the fire originally ignited. And by the way, pick up that fusee you saw out behind that corral and bring it back too."

Horse got in his cruiser and drove downtown to the Santa Fe Depot. He walked into the office and told one of the clerks he wanted to see the Trainmaster. The clerk went to an open door and yelled, "Emma, Sheriff Caballo to see Mr. Langford." Horse could hear Emma when she called Langford on the intercom. She told the clerk to have Horse come in.

Emma White was Trainmaster Langford's secretary. Everyone in Smoke Tree knew her, and she knew everything about everyone who worked on the line. That included demerit information. Whenever a crew member did something wrong, he got demerits. Get enough demerits and he got "fired." Getting fired wasn't as serious as it sounded.

Almost everyone got fired at some time or another, especially if there was a derailment and the Santa Fe needed someone to blame. That's why most trainmen carried job insurance. The insurance paid a percentage of their regular wage while they were off work. When they had been off for a few weeks, they were re-hired.

"Hello, Horse."

"'Lo, Emma."

"Is this something I could help you with," she said a little too eagerly.

"No, I'd better talk to Mike about this one."

"All right, go on through."

When Horse walked in, Mike Langford stood up and shook his hand. Mike was a big man and a heavy one. Every day he wore a brown suit, a red tie, and a snap-brim hat to work. He never took the hat off, just as he rarely took the unlit cigar out of his mouth. As Trainmaster, he controlled the working lives of a lot of people in Smoke Tree. He had a reputation as a fair man but a hard one, and it made for a lonely life in a small town. He had no friends that Horse knew of.

The biggest sin on the Santa Fe was coming to work drunk or, even worse, drinking on the job. Mike had a keen nose. He was often on the platform when crews got on or off the trains, and if he smelled alcohol on a trainman's breath, the man was in serious trouble.

"What's this about, Horse?"

"Something very serious."

"Would you mind closing my door?"

Horse closed it.

"Have a seat and lean in close and keep your voice down. They don't call Emma out there the semaphore of the Santa Fe for nothing. If she hears you, the story will be out of the building before you are."

"Mike, do you have an employee named Charlie Merriman?"

"Yeah. He works track maintenance."

"Is he working today?"

"I don't know. But I do know there are too many ears in this building, and not just Emma's. I don't dare do this one on the phone, so I'm going to take a walk over to maintenance and talk to Manuel Cardenas.

I'll meet you out in the park by the cannon in about twenty minutes. If Charlie's out on the line, Manuel will know where."

He got up and escorted Horse to the door. When he opened it, he said, "Thanks, Horse, for coming by and letting me know about this. We appreciate it when the Sheriff's Department helps us with vagrants around the tracks."

The two men shook hands again. Horse nodded to Emma as he went through her office.

Horse left the depot and walked into the park. The Bermuda grass, dormant for the winter, was brown and stiff beneath his boots. He walked to the center of the park where the American Legion had put a World War I field gun on a raised cement slab. There was an iron railing around the gun and a small bench beside the fence. Horse sat down. There was a weak sun in a winter sky filled with high, white clouds.

Horse remembered Friday would be Veterans Day. The American Legion always held an event at the cannon. In alternate years, the Sheriff's Department provided a color guard for the observance, but it was the Smoke Tree Police Department's turn this year. Veterans and their spouses from World War II and Korea would sit in folding chairs, along with the older men who had served in World War I and one from the Spanish-American War. The Post Commander would read the names of those who had died the previous year. After each name of a departed veteran, there would be a brief silence, and then the adjutant would call out, "No response." Afterward, the women from the Auxiliary would lay a wreath in front of the cannon, and a trumpet player from the high school band would play taps.

Horse sat on the bench and thought about the people he had served with in Korea. He thought of friendships formed and comrades lost. He thought of bugles echoing off snow-topped hills above long valleys in a bitterly cold and hostile place far, far away from the Colorado River Valley he loved. He thought about a veteran who had seen so much carnage in two wars he could shoot a man in the back and worry more about replacing the glass in his door than the life he had taken. A man who had thought he would never have a gun pointed at him with malicious intent again. A man who was so incensed when it happened, he would only admit his fear, and his anger at that fear, to a fellow veteran, choosing instead to tell an Arizona deputy he had killed the man for stepping on his Stetson. But he was also a man who knew, as he pulled back the hammer on a .357 and took aim with a steady hand, that he could shoot a fleeing robber and never be charged in Mohave County, Arizona because the man was a Mexican.

Horse was still lost in thought when Mike sat down on the bench beside him.

"Manuel tells me Charlie's crew is working near Yucca Flats, but Charlie's not with them. Charlie's on vacation. He's not due back until Monday. Care to tell me what this is about?"

Horse told him about the robbery and the shooting in Bullhead and Sixto's death, and the fire that followed. He explained Charlie's name had come up because he'd been seen with Sixto at the Palms the afternoon before the robbery and because of the description given by the liquor store owner.

When he was finished, Mike said, "That doesn't sound like the Charlie we know. He's a very likable young guy, a hard worker who's never in trouble. He's conscientious and reliable."

"That could be, Mike, but it sounds like he was with Sixto."

"Then Morales dragged him into this somehow. I can't believe Charlie Merriman would go into a liquor store intending to rob it."

"That's why I need to find him. And Mike, I need to find him outside the Village. I can't arrest him there. My department has no jurisdiction on reservation land."

"Yeah, Manuel told me Charlie lives in the Village with his mom."

"No dad?"

"Killed in World War Two."

"Well, I've got to find him to sort this out. Will you let me know if you hear anything about his whereabouts?"

"Certainly."

"Thanks. And Mike, keep this under your hat."

"Never take it off."

The two men got up and shook hands.

Horse got in his cruiser and returned to the office. When he got there, he wrote up a description to go with the name Charlie Merriman and gave it to Fred.

"Put this out to the units on patrol. I want this guy picked up and brought in for questioning. He's a suspect in the robbery up in Bullhead. And send a deputy to the high school to find a yearbook picture. Somebody will know what year Charlie graduated. Tell the guys to approach him with caution, but tell them I don't think he's armed."

"Is Mohave County going to want to talk to this guy?"

"Yeah, but let's keep this on our side of the river for now. I don't want to talk to them until I've had a chance to question him."

"Okay, Lieutenant."

"And ask everybody if they know anything about Merriman's mother. I'm not sure I want to spook him by talking to her yet, but I'd like to know where she works."

"Got it."

Horse went in his office and got his poster board. On the diagram, he wrote, "Mojave Village – Charlie Merriman" just north of Smoke Tree.

Chapter 17

CHARLIE

Charlie moved off to the southeast on Thursday morning as he left Eagle Pass behind. He was amazed at how late he had slept on the cold, hard ground just east of the pass. The sun had been well above the horizon before the drone of a small plane pulled him from his dreamless sleep. As he walked in the chilled morning air, he took an inventory of his body. The nausea he had been experiencing had passed, as had the tendency to stumble and lose his balance. Clearly, his body was adjusting to burning muscle for fuel. Also gone was the terrible reek from his sweat of the day before.

All those symptoms had been replaced by a new, major problem: a deep and profound ache in every joint of his body. His hips, knees, shoulders, and neck ached, as did his hands, fingers, feet, and toes. Even his jaw and teeth hurt. "This must be what it's like," he thought, "to be as ancient as Hera anyai and have arthritis." He remembered the old one's shuffling and tentative gait as they had walked to the river together on Saturday morning and his remark about his bones. He wondered what the old one would think if he realized Charlie was now moving the same way. But at least he was moving. He was confident he would reach the maze and then the river before sunset.

As he traveled beneath a weak sun and a winter sky laced with high clouds, he kept moving steadily to the south, even though his path kept him climbing in and out of drainage after drainage that moved from west to east toward the river. His plan was to keep well away from both Smoke Tree and the Smoke Tree Airport. Hera anyai had predicted it would not take long for Horse to determine his identity and come looking for Charlie. It was best to stay out of sight as much as possible. Traveling unseen was not difficult up here on the southwest edge of the Sacramentos, where there were no roads, but at some point, he was going to have to cross two highways: first 95 to get to the maze and then 66 to get to the river.

Still, he had all day and enough water to get him to the river, so, painful as each individual step was, he began to enjoy the journey. Because he was moving so slowly, creeping along really, life revealed itself all around him. There were whip-tail lizards in the gravelly washes, even occasional chuckwallas on the faces of the hills, and now and then a horned toad. A small group of little gray birds took an interest in him and followed him for over a mile, flitting from bush to bush ahead of him as he walked.

At the bottom of one steep hillside, he found a badger den dug into the rock-filled clay. The tracks of the badger were all around the entrance, but there was no way of telling whether the badger was inside. Nothing interfered with badgers: not hawks, not golden eagles, and certainly not foxes or coyotes. One of the "below-ground people," Hera anyai would say.

Because of the frequent stops to rest, Charlie didn't reach the very southern edge of the Sacramento Mountains until around two in the afternoon. Just beyond the terminus of the higher ground, Highway 95 turned west from its straight southward course and began to wind through low hills. Charlie found a large wash that was cut through by the highway on one of the curves. The wash was filled with desert willow and even a few smoke trees. As he lay on his belly beside the biggest willow he could find close to the road, he listened for any sound of an approaching vehicle. As he listened, he could hear bees working busily all around, but they ignored him.

Once he had managed to cross 95 without being seen, he followed the wash to the southeast. When he was completely out of sight of the highway, he turned toward the maze.

★ ★ ★

The sun was at his back and near the western horizon when he arrived at the sacred place. He stood above the forty acres of barren hillside with its rows and rows of stones forming twisting, complicated, elliptical pathways. He tried to estimate where the figure of Mastamho had once stood in profile, holding the body of the slain sea serpent that had threatened the Aha Macav in First Times.

Charlie entered the maze and moved carefully and respectfully among the stones until he came to the center. To the southeast lay Huqueamp Avi, where the battle had been fought. From what Hera anyai had told him, Charlie realized the figure must have stood at the southeastern edge of the maze to deny the ones who were not allowed to enter the spirit world access to the Spirit River that led to Huqueamp Avi, the gateway to that world. In his mind, he drew a line from that point across the railroad tracks and Highway 66 to the river's edge. That must have been where the tail of the serpent and the feet of Mastamho had touched the river.

Charlie was very tired and very hungry. His water carrier was almost empty. He wanted to sit down and rest, but Hera anyai had told him he had to submerge himself in the waters of the Colorado at sundown before the vigil would be complete and he would be ready for his dream.

He crossed the railroad tracks with their strong smell of creosote-coated ties and dropped off the right-of-way into a curving, sandy wash. The wash took him to Highway 66. Once again, he had to wait a long time for an opportunity to cross. He knew he would not be able to avoid being seen, but he hoped he was far enough from Smoke Tree that it wouldn't matter. He noticed many startled, white faces turned toward him as the cars passed. Once he was on the east side of the highway, he slid down a steep embankment that dropped him almost at the edge of the river.

As Hera anyai had explained, there was a heavy growth of tamarisk bordering the river. He made his way through the thick stand. On the other side, a white, sandy beach stretched between two promontories. As he stood on the white sand and looked back toward the highway, he realized he was indeed shielded from view by the tamarisk. He could hear the steady hum of traffic on 66 but not see it.

The western sky was blanketed with red, and bats were appearing over the river by the time Charlie took off his clothes and piled them on the beach. At the river's edge he got down on all fours for a long drink. Then he walked into the fast-moving current. The shock of the icy water took his breath away. He submerged himself completely, his heart racing in his chest. In the few seconds, he was underwater, he was carried thirty feet from where he had walked into the river. He got out, walked back to his clothes, and dressed. A cold wind was kicking up out of the north.

By a half-hour after sundown, the wind was blowing steadily at what he estimated to be thirty miles an hour, with harder gusts. As he sat shivering in the twilight air, Charlie looked down the river toward Huqueamp Avi and reviewed the creation story Hera anyai had chanted for him. He had marveled at the prodigious memory of the old one as he sang the long and complicated tale, but he hadn't understood quite how amazing Hera anyai's memory was until the grandfather repeated word for word the tale Charlie had told him. Charlie did not think he could have repeated his own story in such accurate detail. It made him wonder why Hera anyai thought Charlie could be one of those with the long memory.

He suddenly began to feel sick. He crawled into the tamarisk thicket. In the space of a few minutes, he went from being merely uncomfortable to being very ill. He began to hallucinate. His fast, coupled with the stress of endless hiking, was affecting his mind. Several times he thought he heard drumming and voices chanting. He became convinced the headlights of the 66 traffic were spirits flashing through the air above the tamarisk and that the gusting wind was the moaning of lost souls.

The ground beneath the tamarisk thicket was covered with dusty gray-green leaves. He lay down on his side and covered himself as best he could with his Levi jacket. Soon he was asleep.

★ ★ ★

The nausea was back, and it was worse. Even as he awoke, he was rolling onto his hands and knees and scrambling away from his sleeping spot, tossing his jacket aside. His stomach contracted relentlessly. He gagged so hard, it felt as though his eyes were hemorrhaging. Nothing came up except a thin trickle of water and something that had the iron taste of blood. It was too dark to see what it was.

When the spasms stopped, he retrieved the jacket and buttoned it all the way to his chin. He crawled out of the thicket and started walking up and down the beach to warm himself. The third-quarter moon was just above the horizon, so he knew it was about an hour after midnight.

Charlie tried to recall any shred of a dream. He could not. He was bitterly disappointed. Had he gone through all the agony of the last few days for nothing? Was Hera anyai just a nearly-blind old man dreaming of things that once were or maybe had never been? He did not know. He walked to the river's edge and tried to rinse the terrible taste from his mouth, then sat listening to the rush and swirl of the current. He could hear no traffic passing on 66. It was as if he were all alone in the world with his troubling doubts.

Disheartened, he walked to the edge of the tamarisk thicket and crawled to his sleeping spot. He lay down on his side and pulled his knees up against his chest. He despaired of ever finding his *sumach a' hot* if there even was such a thing. He closed his eyes .... And dreamed a strange and frightening dream: a dream about an older Charlie who was both him and not him at the same time.

★ ★ ★

The moon was farther above the horizon when he awoke. It was putting out enough light for him to begin his journey home. He had made his sacrifice and had his dream. He no longer cared whether he was seen or not. He set off by the most direct route, paralleling Highway 66, thinking about his dream.

Charlie had once read that some people dreamed in color and others dreamed in black and white. But parts of his dream had been in color, and parts had been black and white. Not only that, his dream had shifted from one to the other and back again at unpredictable intervals. It had also moved seamlessly from silence to sound without warning. In the parts of the dream that were in color, the colors did not look real. At times they were the bright, neon colors of Las Vegas; at other times, pastels. Some parts of the dream were oppressively, eerily silent. Some parts were unbearably loud.

As he walked beneath the waning moon, he began to understand that at times he had been watching an older Charlie, sometimes from beside him and at other times from far above him. But strangest of all, sometimes he had been inside that older Charlie, experiencing the world with that Charlie's senses and aware of what that older Charlie was feeling. That older Charlie was deadly.

He traveled toward home like a sleepwalker. After struggling for over an hour to make sense of his dream, he realized the events had not been in chronological order. Once he understood that, he bent his efforts to creating two different sequences. The first sequence was the dream in the order in which he had dreamed it. Disjointed as that version was, he knew Hera anyai would want to hear the dream exactly as it had unfolded. He was halfway to Smoke Tree before he had assembled that version of his *sumach a' hot* dream.

The second task was to put the dream into linear form — to reorder the story so that it moved chronologically from event to event. He was back in Smoke Tree before he was finished with the second task. When he was done, he realized he could recount both versions, detail by exacting detail. Perhaps, he thought, that was why Hera anyai thought Charlie could become one of those with the long memory.

As he neared home, the stars streaked down to their deaths on the western horizon, and faint light began to appear above the Black Mountains. Charlie walked through the deserted streets of town. He was not tired. He was not sore. He was not hungry. He was not sick. But he was somber and sad.

★ ★ ★

In its linear form, this is the dream Charlie Merriman dreamed beside the Colorado River under a third-quarter moon inside a tamarisk thicket on a cold, clear, desert night in November of 1960.

The dream begins in strange, neon colors. There is no sound. Charlie-who-is-dreaming sees a figure he somehow knows to be a different version of himself from high above. Charlie-in-the dream is dressed in a uniform of flat, drab green that stands in contrast to the neon grass he is lying in. He is wearing a helmet. There is a black rifle on the ground in front of him. The grass is even taller than the cattail reeds along the Colorado. It is obscenely, sickeningly, yellowish-green, and the wind is blowing ripples across it like plains winds blowing though an Iowa cornfield. The grass fills a clearing surrounded on all sides by densely-leafed, fantastically-green trees.

As the grass ripples, Charlie-who-is-dreaming can see other men in uniforms and helmets. They are scattered throughout the clearing. Most of the men have black rifles like Charlie-in-the dream, but some have short-barreled weapons that look like single-barreled, cartoon shotguns. There are two men with a machine gun mounted on a tripod.

Charlie-who-is-dreaming also sees that some of the men are in unnatural positions with their limbs akimbo. He realizes these men are dead. The knowledge fills him with sorrow and trepidation.

The colors shift to pastels, and Charlie-who-is-dreaming is lying next to Charlie-in-the-dream. There are sergeant's stripes on that Charlie's sleeves and a dark patch shaped like the upside-down head of a spear. There is a diagonal line across the patch, and in the upper right corner is the silhouette of a horse's head.

Charlie-in-the-dream has his face turned toward Charlie-who-is-dreaming, but it is obvious he does not see him, and is, in fact, looking through him toward something to his right. Charlie-who-is-dreaming turns his head and looks that direction. The wind pushes the pastel grass aside, and he sees two men lying flat on the ground. One has a large, boxy object with an antenna sticking out of it strapped to his back. The other man is holding a handset hooked to the box by a flexible cord. He seems to be screaming into the handset, but since there is no sound, Charlie-who-is-dreaming cannot understand what he is saying.

And at that moment, the dream goes to full, blaring sound, and the color gives way to black and white. High-velocity bullets rip through the tall grass. They sound like angry yellow jackets moving at supersonic speed, and they are coming from two directions. Charlie-who-is-dreaming is very afraid and presses himself to the earth. He can hear the machine gun on the tripod hammering. He hears only sporadic fire from the men in the grass with the rifles.

The dream returns to neon color. Charlie-who-is-dreaming is staring at the ground beside him. There is a grotesque, luridly colored spider bigger than a saucer scurrying toward him. He scrambles backward. There is a huge explosion. Charlie-who-is-dreaming sees the man with the boxy radio lifted into the air and slammed back to earth. Dirt and grass fill the air. The man who had been screaming into the radio is on his back. He is staring into the impossibly blue sky above the clearing. He does not move as the dirt and grass falls on his face and body and all around him. He is no longer holding the handset.

The dream goes silent and reverts to black and white. Charlie-in-the-dream is crawling toward the staring soldier, and Charlie-who-is-dreaming is inside of him. It is as hot and humid as the Mojave when a sudden monsoon cloudburst falls on a hundred-and-twenty-degree day and the water is vaporized and sucked back into the air. His body is soaked with sweat. He can smell his own rank odor. He is exhausted. He has cuts on his hands from the strange grass. He is very thirsty. He can smell gunpowder and cordite. His ears are roaring as if he has heard a dynamite explosion in a mine shaft. He reaches the soldier staring at the sky, and puts his fingers on his neck. There is a pulse. The man's lips are moving, but no sound is coming out. He crawls to the other man.

And the dream goes to neon color with full sound, and Charlie-who-is-dreaming is suddenly standing outside Charlie-in-the-dream again and staring in horror at the man who was slammed to earth. The left side of the man's face and his left arm and shoulder are gone. Neon-red blood is pumping out of his neck in thick pulses. Charlie-who-is-dreaming remains standing because he understands he is now just an observer. Charlie-in-the-dream continues to crawl to the man who was slammed to the earth. By the time he gets there, the man is no longer moving. His uniform is soaked in neon blood. There is no longer blood pulsing from his neck. He has bled out.

The sound is gone. The dream is in black and white. Charlie-in-the-dream picks up the handset attached to the radio and begins talking.

And suddenly, Charlie-who-is-dreaming is far above the clearing. The trees and the grass and the sky are pastels. In the distance, he sees a line of flying objects approaching. In their pastel colors, they look like green dragonflies. Sound returns. Charlie-who-is-dreaming hears the deep, heavy, thumping sound of blades beating the air. The ships come in low and fast over the canopy and turn and cut in a straight line across the clearing. He hears the sound of machinegun fire and sees lines of tracers from the open doors of the helicopters slicing into the tree lines on two sides of the clearing.

And he is on the ground again. The dream is once again silent and black and white. He is beside Charlie-in-the-dream. Charlie-in-the-dream is no longer talking on the radio. He has the man who was staring at the sky over his right shoulder and is carrying him in a shambling, crouching run. His rifle is slung over his left shoulder.

And the pastel colors return, and he is inside that other Charlie again and feels again the terrible, oppressive heat as he struggles to balance the awkward weight of the man he and Charlie-in-the-dream are carrying. He smells the blood, urine, and feces of the man and hears his moans of pain every time their right foot strikes the ground.

And he is outside Charlie-in-the dream but beside him now as that other Charlie eases the wounded man to the ground and takes something that looks like a soda can off a canvas strap hooked to his wide belt and pulls something off the can and tosses it away.

And Charlie-who-is-dreaming is above the clearing again in soundless neon and sees royal blue smoke drifting toward the sun, and one of the helicopters, this one with a red cross on the side, glides down over the blue smoke and settles to the ground.

And in silent black and white, Charlie-who-is-dreaming sees soldiers loading the wounded into the helicopter and then backing away.

And the sound comes back, and the helicopter is straining to rise but seems too heavy to leave the ground, and an unwounded soldier is standing on a metal rail hooked to the bottom of the ship, clinging to the door and refusing to get off. Charlie-in-the-dream runs over and slams the butt of his black rifle into the man's back, and the man lets go and falls to the ground, and his helmet spins away. The helicopter slowly begins to gain altitude.

And Charlie-who-is-dreaming is far above the clearing again. In neon color, the machine gunners in the side doors of the helicopters above are still pouring fire into the impossibly-green trees, but now Charlie hears a much heavier machine gun that cycles at a slower rate firing from the tree line, and tracers are coming the other way and slamming with sickening concussions into the ship bearing the wounded. Rounds strike the rear rotor and the engine, and the whole craft begins to slowly rotate, and Charlie-who-is-dreaming watches in horror as the ship tilts sideways, black smoke pouring from the engine that is now shrieking with a high-pitched, grinding whine. The helicopter falls back to the earth and erupts in a ball of flame.

And dreaming Charlie is back inside Charlie-in-the-dream and feeling the heat from the burning helicopter and he and Charlie-in-the dream scream together in sorrow and rage and move off at a low run through the obscenely green grass toward the impossibly-green trees where the heavy machine gun is firing. And Charlie wakes, shaken, trembling, confused and disoriented in the cold November desert night.

★ ★ ★

By the time the sun was above the horizon, Charlie was back in the Village. As he walked past the tiny, pre-fabricated cottages, he understood he had changed in some fundamental way and would never be the same as he had been less than a week ago. He found Hera anyai sitting on the metal folding chair in front of his cottage. The old one called to him as he approached.

"Greetings, Herow heilhevow. I see you have come to return my water carrier. Come into my house. I have food for you. After you have eaten, you and I will walk to the river. You must tell me of your trial and of your dream."

Charlie followed the grandfather into the house. He smelled cinnamon. When they walked into the tiny kitchen, Charlie saw *pinole* in a black skillet on the small stove. The flame under the skillet was on very low. Hera anyai turned off the heat and stirred condensed milk into the mixture.

Charlie sat at the little table and slowly ate small spoonfuls of the toasted cornmeal flavored with cinnamon and brown sugar. The texture of the *pinole* felt good in his mouth. Strangely, he had little appetite, but out of courtesy, he finished the bowl the old one had put in front of him. He took the empty bowl to the sink and rinsed it clean.

"Herow heilhevow, I spoke with your mother the morning you left. She understands where you went and why. I have talked to her twice while you were gone, and she is not worried. She is pleased you are following the old ways."

"Thank you, Hera anyai, for putting her mind at rest."

The two men, one very old, one very young but weary, made their way to the river and sat. The grandfather tilted his face up to the rising sun. The river flowed past in front of them, making the swirling and gurgling noises a fast-moving river makes. Across the river, someone was burning the stubble off an agricultural field. The smoke rose straight up into a windless, blue sky and slowly changed the sun from yellow to orange. The old one spoke.

"Herow heilhevow, this fine day stretches before us as a blessing. It is a good day to hear of an important matter. Tell me of your journey and your dream."

And Charlie did. He told Hera anyai everything that had happened since the Saturday before when they had parted. He spared no detail. Then he told him of his dream. He told both versions: the disjointed, confusing dream exactly as it had flashed through his mind and the re-ordered version he had created to bring order to the dream-world chaos.

Then he told the old one of his final walk. How he had no longer been tired or hungry or sick. How he had walked under the waning moon without seeing the ground beneath his feet but without ever stumbling as he worked through the dream and its reconstruction. He told him everything up until the grandfather had greeted him.

When Charlie was finished, the sun was overhead. He stood and stretched. He walked to the river's edge and drank long and deep. He returned and sat at the old one's side.

"You have done well. Your ancestors would be proud of you. Proud because you have followed their ways without complaint or faltering.

Herow heilhevow, as you can clearly see, your dream reveals you are to be a warrior. Your ancestors were fierce warriors who defended our river bottom homeland from outside invaders. And your father before you was a warrior. You were only two years old when he left for the islands in the Pacific Ocean, never to return. Your mother has never shown you because she is angry he gave his life in a white man's war, but she has a box. Inside the box is a ribbon. The ribbon is attached to a silver star. Attached to the star is an oak leaf cluster. It is the second-highest honor shown to a soldier by the Army of the United States. Many in the Village have said that had your father been a white man, the medal would have been the very highest that can be given.

Perhaps this place you dreamed, a place I myself have never heard of, with the tallest, strange grass and the greenest trees, is like a place where your father once fought in the islands of the far Pacific Ocean. Perhaps he passed this knowledge to you from the spirit world while you were dreaming. I do not know, but it is possible, for dreams are mysterious and wonderful things. We do not know how they come to us. We only know we must struggle to understand what they reveal to us about our path forward with our special gift.

But your dream also explains that you are invisible to the world outside this village. That is why, in part of the dream, you are only watching Charlie-in-the-Dream. And in truth, that is so. Only people in this village see you. The white people look at you, but they do not see you. Your dream reveals that they will be forced to see you and reckon with you. The stripes on your uniform show you are to be a leader like your father before you, who also wore such stripes and led men who were not Pipa Aha Macav. As your dream revealed this, you, Charlie-who-was-dreaming, became one with Charlie-in-the-dream, and at the end of the dream, Charlie-who-was-dreaming and Charlie-in-the-dream were one, and you moved off together to find the people who had destroyed the helicopter trying to bear away the wounded.

The patch you saw on Charlie-in-the-dream's uniform is the patch of the pony soldiers. Those are the soldiers who were with Custer at the Little Big Horn. Custer cast away the men of the Crow Nation who were with him and ignored their advice. He and his men paid a heavy price for his prideful stupidity.

Your dream came to you jumbled together to test your ability to make sense of it. And you have made sense of it. And you are able to remember the dream, both as it occurred and as you have put the events in order. Herow heilhevow, it is no easy task to hold both versions in your head, but you have done it, and if I asked you to recount both versions again, I am sure you could do it. You show great promise. You may indeed be one with the long memory, and beyond that, you may be one of the deep thinkers who can look into mysteries and coax out their meanings.

So, now you have dreamed your dream and are back with us. While you know you will someday go forth to this place, we do not yet know the name of and do what your destiny demands you to do in that place; I hope you can return to us when you are done. The Pipa Aha Macav will have need of you when you return, just as they will need the other boy, the one who cannot walk."

Hera anyai's words filled Charlie with sorrow. He did not feel like a warrior, and he had no wish to be one. But because of his dream and the grandfather's words, he had no choice.

"Herow heilhevow, you know that I am of the Hipa."

"Yes, Hera anyai, I know the clan name you carry, even though it is not part of your spoken name."

"And you, Herow heilhevow, are the silent carrier of your own clan name. Only you can save the clan name by passing it on to your daughters so that it becomes part of their names. And only you can pass the clan name to your sons so they can, in turn, become the silent carriers of the name and hand it on to their daughters to use in their names and to their sons to carry silently on and on forever and ever and until time ends for Pipa Aha Macav.

You know our white names are not from marriage. Those names were forced on us by the white people. If we refused to take them, we could not be registered as members of our own tribe.

Clan is everything to the Pipa Aha Macav. The clan names tie us to our beginnings and to our dreams. Mutavilya, The Creator, gave our people these names. But our numbers are dwindling. Two of the clan names have died out and can never be reborn. Five more clan names tremble on the edge of extinction. Your clan name, too, is in danger,

Herow heilhevow. That is why you must return to us and make a family. Do not let your clan name die!"

"I will not, Hera anyai."

"I have been told by a friend who knows a man who knows another man that Horse has already learned of you, just as I feared he would. He has been to your place of work to ask about you. His deputies have been told to watch for you. I smile to think of you walking unseen through Smoke Tree this morning.

Now that you have had the dream that has revealed your *sumach a' hot* and have allowed me to help you understand its meaning, you have little need of advice from me. You are a man. So I ask you, Herow heilhevow, as one man to another, what will you do now that you know Horse is looking for you?"

"I have nothing to hide, Grandfather, and nothing to be ashamed of. I became entangled in the wrong world, and now I must un-tie the knot that binds me. I will go to Horse. He will not have to seek me. I do not wish to be found by those who look for me. I will present myself and tell my story. On the way to do that, I will stop at my mother's work and tell her all so that she will understand.

After I tell Horse my story, whatever happens, will happen as it must. I am no longer afraid of being locked away forever in some white man's prison because now I know my destiny will carry me elsewhere."

Chapter 18

AEDEN

On Thursday morning, I met Billy and his mother in front of the school. Once again, I helped her get him into his chair, and once again, she thanked me. Once again, I walked beside him to class, and as before, we were the first ones there. Once again, we talked in the empty classroom.

"So, did you see Charlie?"

"No."

"Did you talk to the old man who was seen with him?"

"Yes. I talked to him yesterday. I asked him if he would talk to you. He said 'no.'"

"That's it. Just 'no'?"

"Just 'no.' I also asked him if I could tell you his name. He said it didn't matter because he isn't going to talk to you anyway. His name is Webster Charles."

"Can you tell me anything about him?"

"He is the oldest man in the Village. He is also the most respected elder. If he says he won't talk to you, he means it. There is no point in asking again."

"Didn't he even ask why I wanted to talk to him?"

"I'm sure he already knows."

"How?"

"The way he knows everything."

I talked with Johnny between first and second periods and explained what Billy had told me.

"Any change with Judy?" I asked him.

"I thought you'd noticed. Now she won't look at either one of us."

"But there is a difference."

"What's that?"

"You care."

Johnny gave me a quizzical look. "Let's go downtown for lunch today. Renee's this time. There's a Smoke Tree Weekly rack there. We can pick up the paper and see what it says about the fire."

At noon, we each got a copy of the paper to read with our greasy burgers. The reporter had done a good job writing the story. She had interviewed Horse. Horse had detailed a liquor store robbery in Bullhead. He explained Sixto Morales and an unnamed accomplice had held up the store, and Sixto had been shot and later died in a house on the California side. Authorities in Mohave County had asked for help in identifying the accomplice. Horse said an investigation was underway.

Horse had given very little information about the fire at the house where Sixto had died. He said he didn't know for sure who had started the fire or why. The reporter concluded the story with a final quote from Horse. "If you and your partner had committed a robbery and hid out in the middle of nowhere and your partner had died from his wound, why would you set the house on fire? I mean, could there be a faster way to bring people to the house than to burn it down? If not for the fire, that body could have laid out there for years before anybody found it. There's a lot we don't know yet about this story."

We both read the story several times, but neither of us said much about it on the way back to school. I think we were trying to determine what this meant for us. Johnny was worried about what it meant for Judy, while I was more concerned about what it meant for Charlie Merriman.

That afternoon at practice, while we ran endless circles around the football field, we talked about the story. We had discovered if we didn't run too fast we could talk, and nobody seemed to yell at us as long as we kept moving. After reading the story, we were sure that no one had any idea we had been at the house. Johnny wanted to keep it that way for Judy's sake. I didn't think Judy was worth protecting, but I had made my friend a promise.

After we had exhausted the subject of the newspaper story, Johnny started in about Judy again. He talked about how lucky he was to have her as his girlfriend. As he ran and talked about how much she meant to him and how much he loved her, tears began to stream down his face. I was said for him, but I was also embarrassed for him in an odd sort of way. I was glad none of the other players knew what was happening.

Suddenly, he stopped running.

"I've got an idea. We'll have one of the girls talk to Judy for me. Her dad won't be suspicious, and Symington won't pay any attention. Who can we get to do it?"

"Johnny, don't you know she has no friends? Not one?"

"That's not fair! Why aren't they friendly?"

"Man, you're really in love. Don't you see it? Lots of girls have tried to make friends. Judy won't have anything to do with them."

"Well, maybe one will try to talk to her if I ask. How about Mindy? Mindy seems to like me. Maybe she'll do me a favor."

"Like you? Good God, Johnny, that girl's been stuck on you for the last year. Why do you think she doesn't go out with anyone else?"

"She doesn't? I didn't notice."

"Yeah, well, there are a lot of things you don't notice lately. Mindy would do almost anything you asked her to, but carrying love messages to the girl who's beating her time isn't one of them."

"What about Linda? Linda was always her friend. Maybe she'd call Judy if you asked her."

"Linda stood me up for the Homecoming dance. She doesn't answer my letters. Linda dumped me and didn't even call to let me know. I had to hear it from her mother, for Christ's sake."

"I know, I know, but you could try. She might do it!"

One of the assistant coaches came trotting over.

"What are you two doing walking? Coach Lucas says to get moving again. Now!"

We started running again. The dirt track was as hard as brick beneath my feet. The cold wind was driving hard out of the north, blowing straight into our faces as we came into the last curve each lap. I was freezing because I was soaked with sweat. I picked up the pace to get warm. We ran a few laps in silence, our breath steaming in the cold air.

"Ade, please, this is so important to me!"

"I'll try, but I don't know what she'll say."

"I knew you'd come through!"

"If she'll agree to do it, what do you want her to say to Judy?"

"Have her tell Judy I know this is not her fault. That I know it's her old man. That I'm not mad at her and I understand. And here's the most important part, Ade. Have her tell Judy we can wait until she's eighteen and her dad can't control her anymore. Then we can get back together. Have her tell Judy I can wait and not bother her if I just know she still loves me. And tell her I'll stop parking in front of her house at night. I know it makes her dad crazy, 'cause he's called the cops on me twice."

"Jesus, Johnny, you've been parking in front of her house?"

"Yeah, I can't help it. I miss her so much. I just want to be close to her."

He stopped talking for a while as we ran on.

"So, when can you do it?"

"I'll try tonight. But I can't guarantee anything. The only way I can get in touch with her is to call her dorm. She may not even come to the phone. But I'll try."

"Thanks, Ade. Really. I feel better now. At least we're doing something."

Practice ended. Coach sent the rest of the guys in before us. He told them to take their cleats off and meet him in the gym for a team meeting. As he walked by he told us we weren't to come to the meeting.

"You two are still in trouble. You're not going to be playing, so there's no reason for you to be distracting everyone by coming to this meeting."

Johnny and I went into the locker room. There were football shoes scattered everywhere. Johnny pulled off his helmet, cleats, jersey and shorts and shoved them in his locker. He put on his street clothes.

"Call me, Ade. Whether she agrees to help or not. Call me and let me know."

"Okay, Johnny. I'm going home for dinner first, then I'll call her."

I went into the shower. The sound of the splashing water echoed off the tile walls. It was a lonely sound. I got out of there quickly.

As I was walking down the hall toward the exit, the doors to the gym opened, and the guys spilled out into the hallway. Bobby Quayles reached out and grabbed my arm as I went by.

"I'm sorry about this, Ade. I didn't know you guys would get benched for the whole game. I just wanted to start."

"Bobby, if you don't get your hand off me, I'll break your fingers." He stepped back, and I went out to my car.

★ ★ ★

After dinner, I drove downtown to the payphone by the bus station. It was cold, and I shivered inside the booth under the weak light as I got the operator and charged the call to our home number. My mom was going to have a fit when she got the phone bill for November.

The girl who answered the phone said she'd see if Linda was in her room. I told her to be sure and tell Linda it was Aeden calling. She repeated the name to be sure she had it right, then put the phone down. I heard her footsteps echo as she walked away.

A few minutes passed. I was worrying about the cost of the call when I heard footsteps coming back. I was pretty sure it was the girl coming back to tell me Linda wasn't in or didn't want to talk to me.

"Hello, Ade."

My heart gave a little lurch. This was the girl I had been missing more than I cared to admit.

"Hello, Linda."

"Ade, I'm glad you called. I wanted to apologize for last weekend. What I did was thoughtless."

"I was thinking more along the lines of 'mean.'"

"I'm sorry. Really."

"Okay, apology accepted. But that's not why I'm calling. I'm calling for Johnny."

"Johnny Quentin? What does he want?"

"Johnny wants you to do something for him."

She hesitated.

"Well, sure, I will if I can."

I gave her a very abbreviated version of why Judy was not talking to Johnny and why she wasn't talking to me either. I left out everything about the fire and the other events of Thursday night.

When I got done, she seemed a little puzzled.

"Sounds like a little lovers' spat to me, Ade. She really won't talk to him at all?"

"No, and as I said, her dad won't let her."

"Well, why doesn't he just talk to her at school?"

I explained about Mr. McPhearson bringing Judy to school and picking her up at lunch and after school. I told her about Dr. Symington watching all of us for Mr. McPhearson.

"Ade, there's got to be more to the story than this. What are you leaving out?"

"Maybe Judy will tell you the rest. That's up to her. Look, I told Johnny I would ask, so I'm asking. Will you do it?"

"Okay, but not tonight. It's getting late. I'll call her tomorrow afternoon if you think she'll be home."

"Oh, she'll be home all right. She's not allowed to go out."

"Okay, tell me what I'm supposed to say to her."

I went through the message. Linda agreed to pass it on.

"We've got a game tomorrow night in Boulder City. I'll call you after it's over. Johnny will want to know what Judy said, and he won't leave me alone until he finds out."

"All right. I'll be here. Goodbye Ade. It's good to hear your voice."

"Good night, Linda. Talk to you tomorrow."

I broke the connection and then dropped a dime in the slot and dialed Johnny's number.

"She'll do it."

"That's great. When?"

"She said it was too late tonight. She's going to call her tomorrow night. I told her I would call her after the game to see what Judy said."

"Thanks, Ade. You're the greatest."

"Go to bed, Johnny. And don't be parking in front of Judy's house tonight, okay?"

"Okay."

I got in the car and turned on the radio. Paul Anka was partway through "Puppy Love." I turned it off.

On the way home, I thought about the conversation with Linda. It was interesting. First, she came to the phone. Second, she apologized. Third, she said it was good to hear my voice. And last, she was going to be in the dorm on a Friday night. Something wasn't working out in Santa Barbara.

Chapter 19

HORSE

Horse held a brief staff meeting early Thursday morning.

"Thanks for coming in a little early. I wanted to catch both shifts before I go off to talk to the Smoke Tree P.D. I want to give everybody a quick summary of everything we know about this case."

Duane Lambert, a new hire just arrived in Smoke Tree, raised his hand.

"Lieutenant, I don't understand this. The robbery was in Arizona. The car was found in Nevada. The only part of this case that happened in California is the abandoned house fire, and that's the least important part. So, why's the Smoke Tree substation handling this?"

"Deputy, things work a little different here in the tri-state area. Criminals wander all over the state lines. Because of that, we have to cooperate with Arizona and Nevada. In the case of the car, Nevada isn't even aware of the road where the car was found, so it's a minor matter to them.

I'll grant you the robbery was in Arizona, but everything we have learned shows both the guys involved were from Smoke Tree. We still strongly suspect the second individual was the young Mojave man, Charlie Merriman. This morning you've all got a copy of the photo from the Smoke Tree High School yearbook, 1958. He probably looks pretty much the same now. We know he lives in the Village with his mother, Cordelia. Anybody come up with a line on her?"

Allan raised his hand. "Lieutenant, I was told she works at the Travel Lodge as a maid."

"Thank you, Allan. I'll have to decide whether to talk to her. I don't want to spook her and have her hide Charlie out in the Village. We have no jurisdiction there, and we'd have to contact the B.I.A. for help. They cooperate, but you know how long it takes to get them to move.

In the meantime, keep an eye out for Charlie Merriman. From what I've learned from talking to the guy who shot Sixto, I don't think Charlie's dangerous. It may just have been wrong place, wrong time. But be careful anyway.

Well, that's all.

Deputy Atkins, step into my office a minute before you go."

"Yes, sir."

Horse sat on the edge of his desk and motioned Stuart to a chair.

"Tell me what you found at the burned house."

"Well, sir, I got one of the fire guys, Mark Evans, to go out there with me. I'm glad I took him along. The whole mess looked the same to me, but Mark could tell somehow where the fire had started. It was near the front of the house. We found the flare there. There wasn't much of it left — just the spike. I picked up the flare out by the corral too. Both of them are in a paper bag on Fred's desk."

"Thanks, Stuart. Good work!"

Horse got in his cruiser and drove downtown to the Smoke Tree Police Department. Chief Rettenmeir had the officers coming off night shift and the officers going on the day shift in the squad room. When Horse walked in, the room got quiet. One of the officers said, "Well if it isn't our favorite Mexican with a badge."

"Nichols, if you work really hard, you might someday be half the lawman this man is," said the chief. "Show some respect! Lieutenant Caballo is here to ask for our help on a case."

Horse took them through the information he had on Charlie. He distributed pictures and asked the officers to keep an eye out for him around town.

Officer Nichols spoke again. "Lieutenant, I heard you talked to the guy who shot Sixto."

"That's right."

"I was just wondering if both departments could take up a collection and buy him something nice. He just cut the Smoke Tree crime rate in half by killing that creep."

Everybody laughed. Everybody but Horse.

"Officer Nichols, I am as happy as you are to have Sixto out of circulation. But I'm not happy he's dead. I'd settle for having him back in prison. I don't think the death of anyone, even someone like Sixto is a cause for celebration."

"Come on, Lieutenant. The guy was a walking nightmare."

"Maybe so, but I wonder how any of us would've turned out if we'd been raised at a dump in a shack made of discarded junk."

There was silence for a moment. Then one of the patrolmen broke the tension.

"Lieutenant, I guess you've never seen my mom's house."

This time, Horse laughed along with everyone else.

"Well, thanks for your help, Chief Rettenmeir. And remember, officers, we don't think Charlie's dangerous, but you never know. Call for help if you come across him. I don't want anyone getting hurt, not even Charlie."

When Horse got back to his office, he filled in times for the events on his poster board drawing. When he was done, he was very conscious of the gap of almost six hours between the time Sixto and Charlie were kicked out of the Palms and the time of the robbery. Lyndon Brooks had told him both men were pretty much in the bag when they came into his store, but from what Mac had told him, they hadn't had much to drink at the Palms. Horse had already checked the bars in town to see if Sixto and Charlie had been there on Wednesday, and they hadn't.

He didn't think Sixto was the kind of guy who bought a bottle and went off and drank with just one other guy. But just to cover all the bases, Horse spent an hour checking the local liquor stores. None of the clerks had seen Sixto and Charlie, or Sixto alone, and like the bartenders, they hated to see Sixto come into their place and would remember if he had.

That left only two drinking spots close to Smoke Tree: one down in Topock and one up in Oatman. "If I wanted to go somewhere and get drunk," Horse thought, "and not worry about getting a D.W.I. on the way home, where would I go? Not Topock. Always a chance of a highway patrolman pulling me over on 66. But Oatman? Not an officer of the law within miles!"

Forty minutes later, he was talking to Maggie McKellep at the Oatman Hotel. After explaining why he was poking around in Arizona, he got down to business.

"Maggie, was Sixto Morales in your bar a week ago Wednesday?"

"Unfortunately. I can't tell you how much I hate seeing that animal come through my door. He is nothing but trouble every time he comes in."

"Well, he won't be in anymore. Somebody shot him over in Bullhead. He's dead."

"I'll try to feel bad about that."

"Did he come in alone?"

"No, there was an Indian with him."

"Can you describe him?"

"I can do better than that, Lieutenant. I can tell you his name. I carded him because he looked too young to drink. His name is Charlie Merriman."

"How did he act while he was in here?"

"Like he'd rather land face down in a cholla patch. I could tell he didn't like being with Sixto."

"How was he otherwise?"

"What do you mean?"

"Was he loud, obnoxious?"

"Oh no, quiet. Called me 'ma'am,' kept his voice down. Drank his drinks and kept his mouth shut."

"What time did they leave?"

"They ran out of money about nine. Sixto tried to start a tab, but I wouldn't give him credit. He swore at me for a while and then left."

"Thanks, Maggie."

"You're welcome.

Say, you're married, aren't you, Lieutenant?"

"Yes, I am."

"Why don't you bring the wife up some Friday night? There's a real nice dance here on Friday nights. Lots of married folks come. We've got a real good country, and western band comes over from Kingman."

"Thanks for the offer, Maggie, but every time I'm up here, I see about ten people whose faces are on circulars in my drawer. If federal agents ever came by, you'd lose half your clientele."

He picked up his hat, waved politely, and went out the door.

★ ★ ★

Back in his office, he added "Oatman" to his drawing and put the approximate time Sixto and Charlie had arrived there on the poster board. Now he was positive Charlie was the second guy at the liquor store, and he knew when they printed Charlie, they'd have a match to the prints all over the inside of Sixto's car.

All during the drive back to town, he had been debating with himself about going to talk to Charlie's mom. He didn't want Charlie to know they were looking for him, but he was also worried for Charlie. Horse didn't think the young man was a criminal. Nothing Horse had heard about him pointed that direction, and Charlie had never been in any kind of trouble with the law. Horse was afraid Charlie could get hurt if the wrong guy found him. Smoke Tree police officers had a well-deserved reputation as head-knockers. Especially when it came to Indians and Mexicans. The force was lily-white and made up mostly of rejects from big-city departments – many forced out because of excessive violence or suspected corruption beefs.

He made a mental list of pros and cons. In the end, he decided it would be best to talk to her. He knew the maids' shifts at the motels began at seven a.m. so they could begin cleaning rooms as travelers checked out. They got a half hour for lunch and clocked out at 3:30. Horse wanted to talk to her right after she left work. No point in embarrassing her in front of her employer.

He parked across the street from the motel. A few minutes after 3:30, a heavy-set woman with long, black hair came out of the maids' supply room. She was wearing a blue nylon dress and carrying a large purse. She very slowly stopped in front of a pre-war Desoto parked half a block up the street. She was digging her keys out of her bag when Horse parked nose-to-nose to her car and got out. She didn't look surprised to see him.

"Mrs. Merriman?"

"Yes."

"I'm Lieutenant Caballo from the sheriff's department."

"I know who you are."

"I want to talk to you about your son, Charlie. It's important. He's wanted for questioning about something that happened over in Arizona, and I'd like to pick him up before one of these bust-head Smoke Tree cops finds him. Could I buy you a cup of coffee and a piece of pie at Lulu's?"

She stood for a moment with her keys in her left hand, her right arm holding her big purse defensively against her chest.

"All right."

"I'm gonna walk down there and get a booth. You drive there and park and come in and join me. How's that?"

"Okay."

"Mrs. Merriman, I'm counting on you to show up. I know you don't have to come. You're not in any kind of trouble. Heck, you could just drive back to the Village, and there'd be nothing I could do about it."

"Horse, I know you. I remember when you played basketball for Smoke Tree High. Everybody on this side of the river knows you. Walk on down there, and I'll be along."

Horse walked the three blocks to Lulu's. He hoped showing trust and courtesy to Mrs. Merriman would make her more cooperative. When he went inside, there were high school kids in two of the booths. They were drinking cokes, the least expensive thing they could order. "Tequila" was playing on the jukebox, but not too loud. Lulu didn't mind the rock and roll that brought the student crowd in, but she kept the volume down.

Horse walked to the rear booth.

Lulu came over.

"Hello, Lieutenant."

"Hi, Lulu. I'm expecting someone. Just coffee for me now, and we'll order when she gets here." He moved to the back booth.

Lulu brought him his coffee. He noticed the kids sneaking glances at him as he drank his coffee, but they soon lost interest. The jukebox went silent, and one of the boys went over and dropped in some coins.

"Tequila" played four more times. Horse was beginning to think he had made an error in judgment, and Mrs. Merriman had headed to the Village to warn Charlie. He was reaching for his wallet when she came in the door, her eyes searching for him. He stood up, and she joined him at the booth.

"Please, Mrs. Merriman, sit down."

She slid into the booth. She reached in her purse and pulled out a pair of glasses with cheap frames. She put them on and studied him intently, her black eyes unblinking, her broad face completely without guile.

"Lulu makes wonderful pie, Mrs. Merriman. Please let me get you a piece and a cup of coffee."

"Thank you."

Lulu returned to the booth and recited the day's pie menu. Mrs. Merriman had her repeat the list and then ordered lemon meringue. Horse got his usual: coconut cream.

They did not speak until Lulu brought their pie, along with coffee for Mrs. Merriman.

"Mrs. Merriman, have you seen your son?"

She looked at the big Timex watch on her wrist.

"Horse, would you mind if I had my pie and coffee before we talk? I'm very tired. I've had a long day."

"No, ma'am. That's just fine. You go ahead."

She ate her pie in delicate bites, putting her fork down after each one. She finished her coffee, and Lulu brought her a refill. When her plate was empty, she said, "Now, what was your question?"

"Have you seen your son?"

"I saw Charlie this afternoon. He came by my work."

"Mrs. Merriman, have you read this week's Smoke Tree paper?"

"No. That paper never writes anything about the Mojave, so why should I read it? I read the San Bernardino Sun or the Los Angeles Times when people leave it in their rooms."

"Do you know about the death of Sixto Morales?"

"Yes, I've heard about that."

"Do you know about the old house that burned down up the river?"

"Yes."

"Where did you hear about those things?"

"Charlie told me."

"Mrs. Merriman, did he tell you he was at those places?"

"It's up to Charlie to tell you that."

"Mrs. Merriman, it's very important that you tell me what Charlie told you. Please, will you do that?"

She looked at her watch again.

"No."

"Why not?"

"Because Charlie is going to tell you. I might tell you wrong."

"You mean when I find him."

"That's right."

"Mrs. Merriman, I need your help here. Can you give me any idea where I might find Charlie?"

She looked at her watch one more time.

"Sure. At your station."

"My station?"

"That's where Charlie was headed after he talked to me. He should be almost there by now."

"Is he driving?"

"No, Charlie doesn't have a car."

"Mrs. Merriman, if he's on foot, one of the Smoke Tree officers might pick him up." He started to get up. Mrs. Merriman put her hand on his hand.

"Finish your pie, Lieutenant Caballo. You've hardly eaten a bite. The Smoke Tree Police drive up and down Broadway. They don't drive the back alleys, and they don't drive out into the desert. Might get their shiny cars stuck in the sand.

By the time you finish your pie and drive out to the station, he'll be there. Give him a few more minutes. It's real important to Charlie to turn himself in and not get picked up."

Horse relaxed and started to finish his pie.

"What do you think about all this, Mrs. Merriman? This situation Charlie's involved in?"

"I think he had bad luck. But Mojaves in Smoke Tree always have bad luck. You listen to me, Horse." She turned that unblinking stare on him again. "My son is a good man. Just like his father was. Never been in any kind of trouble. Never missed school. Always got good grades, even though he got teased about that by the other boys in the Village. Has never missed a day's work since he went with the Santa Fe. Helps me buy our food and put gas in my car. Saves the rest.

Whatever happened, he may have seen it, but he didn't make it happen." She picked up her big purse and slid out of the booth.

"No, no, don't get up! Take your time. He's going to be there waiting for you. I guarantee it. If my Charlie says he will do something, it will be so."

She walked out the door.

Horse had to smile at the way she had played him, stalling for time while Charlie headed to the station to turn himself in. He hoped she was right about the Smoke Tree officers not being able to spot him.

He finished his pie and got one more refill on his coffee. Then he left three dollars on the table and walked to his cruiser.

When he walked in the station door, Fred said, "Horse, you won't believe who's in your office."

"Charlie Merriman."

"How did you know?"

"Just part of the mystique, Fred. Did you arrest him?"

"Nossir. I thought you just wanted to talk to him."

"You did good!" Horse leaned in close. "This is a tricky area. This man has come in on his own. As long as he is here willingly, this is not a custodial questioning until or unless we arrest him. I'm going to see if he's willing to talk. If he's volunteering to talk, we don't have to tell him he can get a lawyer. Either way, be ready to book him as an accessory to robbery when I get done. And Fred, if anyone calls, I'm not here. This might take a while."

When Horse walked into his office, Charlie was sitting in front of his desk. He got to his feet.

"Sit down, Charlie. I'm Lieutenant Caballo. I want to talk to you about Wednesday night a week ago. I'm going to get a tape recorder out of my desk and turn it on. Give me a minute to set it up."

"Okay."

Horse set up the Wollensak reel-to-reel and plugged in the microphone.

"This is Lieutenant Carlos Caballo of the Smoke Tree substation of the San Bernardino County Sheriff's Department. I am conducting this interview at approximately four o'clock in the afternoon on Thursday, November 10, 1960, in my office. I am going to interview Charlie Merriman, also of Smoke Tree. He has agreed to talk to me.

Mr. Merriman, is that correct? Did you come here voluntarily to talk to me?"

"Yessir."

"And you are aware this interview is being recorded."

"Yes."

"So, tell me about last Wednesday."

"Beginning when?"

"How about when you walked into the Palms?"

Charlie gave a very detailed narrative about everything that happened up until the time Sixto died in the abandoned house, and someone set it on fire. Horse did not interrupt him. When Charlie was finished, Horse asked him if he had anything to add.

"Nossir."

"Okay, I've got some questions. When you went into that liquor store with Sixto, did you intend to rob the place?"

"Nossir."

"Did you know Sixto intended to rob the place?"

"Nossir. I didn't even know he had a gun. When I was tied up on the floor that night, I ran through the whole thing in my head. When we were walking to the store, Sixto told me he was going back to the car because he'd dropped some money on the floor. I think that's when he got the gun and stuck it in his pants underneath his shirt. I never saw it until he pulled it in the store."

"When he pulled the gun and pointed it at the man in the store, did you do anything to stop him?"

"No."

"Why not?"

"He had a gun."

"When Sixto got shot, why did you drive the car for him?"

"He was pointing that big gun at me. Told me he'd shoot me if I didn't."

"Did you really think he would shoot you?"

"I was sure of it."

"When you were helping Sixto down the road to the old house, why didn't you try to get away?"

"He would've shot me."

"Why did Sixto tie you up when you got to the old house?"

"Because he knew I wanted to get away from him, and he was afraid I'd turn him in if I did."

"Would you have?"

"I don't know. Probably. I never had a chance to find out."

"You told me you had just finished sawing through the cord that tied your hands to your feet when you heard a car drive up."

"That's right."

"And then you could hear people outside talking?"

"Yessir."

"Did you recognize the voices?"

"No, and I couldn't tell what they were saying."

"Tell me what you can remember about the voices. How many people do you think there were?"

"I could hear two guys and a woman. I don't know if there were other people."

"Tell me again what happened next."

"I got my hands out from behind my back."

"If I tied your hands behind you, could you do that again?"

"I could, but I wouldn't like to. It hurt to do it."

"Then what happened?"

"I started trying to cut the cord tying my feet together. I didn't want to be tied up and helpless if someone came in there. Then I heard a scratching sound, and I could see a red light under the door."

"What did you think that was?"

"I knew someone had lit a fusee."

"Why do you think they did that?"

"I don't know, sir. By that time, I was almost through the cord. I heard footsteps coming toward the door to the room where Sixto and I were. I finally cut through the rope and ran out the door."

"Then what?"

"I ran straight back toward the mesquite thicket and crawled into it. Scratched myself up pretty good, hands and face both. At first, I thought I was okay, but then I realized someone had followed me out. Someone who was carrying a fusee. I could tell they were swinging it back and forth, trying to see me, so I held real still. Then the fusee burned out.

That's when I heard another sound and smelled smoke. At first, I thought it was from the fusee, but then I realized it was wood smoke."

"You can tell the difference?"

"I work on the railroad, Lieutenant. I've smelled lots of those fusees. This was wood smoke."

"Okay, what did you do?"

"I thought they were trying to burn me out of the thicket for some reason, so I turned around and crawled back out. I figured nothing could be worse than getting burned up. When I crawled out, I saw the house was on fire, and a big chinaberry tree behind the house was burning too. The guy who had been looking for me had his back to me. He was turned around looking at the fire."

"Did you recognize him?"

"No, sir. Just some guy in a T-shirt."

"Young or old?"

"No idea. Why is it so important who these people were? They burned down the house, but who cares? Sixto was already dead."

"That's your story. The autopsy showed he was dead before the fire burned the house, so that's a point in your favor. But that doesn't prove you had nothing to do with his death. A prosecutor could claim you choked him and burned the house down yourself to cover your crime."

"That's crazy."

"You think so. Others may not. So, what did you do next?"

"The fire was so loud I could sneak up right behind him. He never heard me coming. My hands were still tied in front of me, so I raised my arms and slammed my fists down on his back as hard as I could. He went down, and I ran off around the corner of the house."

"Did you see anyone?"

"I saw a car. I didn't see any people. As soon as I saw it, I cut through the mesquites on the north side of the house. When I got far enough in that no one could see me, I went west. I kept going until I could climb up out of the river bottom onto a little hill. I sat on that hill and watched the fire and the lights of the cars coming and going. The fire burned for a long time. It burned so long I fell asleep on top of the hill while it was still burning."

"Let's go back to the car. What can you remember about it?"

"It was a dark color. A Ford coupe – 1950 or so. It was very shiny."

"Are you sure about the color? Colors can be hard to identify at night."

"I could see it pretty well. There was a lot of light from the fire and the full moon."

"Anything else?"

"Yes. It had flames along the side and on the hood."

"What did you do in the morning?"

"I went down to look at the fire. I didn't have trouble getting through the mesquites – they were all burned. I was looking at what was left of the house when I saw the dust plume your deputy's car was raising. I didn't think I had time to get out of there before he showed up, so I climbed up in one of those big salt cedars along the driveway."

Horse had to smile. "I'll be darned. How long were you up there?"

"Most of the morning until you and the other deputy left."

"So, you saw them haul Sixto's body away?"

"Yessir, I did. It didn't bother me. I knew he was dead before the fire ever started. I'll never forget that sound that came out of him when he died."

"Thank you, Charlie." He opened the door to his office.

"Fred, come in here. Book Charlie as an accessory to robbery. Print him too. Then put him in the holding cell."

"Will do, Lieutenant."

Horse turned to Charlie. "Charlie, I'm arresting you. You're going to be in custody. If we have to ask you any more questions, you can have a lawyer."

"Don't want one. I've told you the truth."

Fred led Charlie out of the office. Horse picked up the phone and called the Mohave County Sheriff's station.

"Lieutenant Caballo from the San Bernardino County Sheriff's Department for Captain Taylor. Even if he's busy, he'll want to hear this."

The line went dead for a moment.

"Afternoon, Horse. What have you got?"

"We've got the guy who was with Sixto at the liquor store. We're booking him right now for accessory to robbery."

"You know we're going to want him."

"Yes. Can you send me a demand by teletype?"

"Sure can."

"As soon as I get it, we'll get a California Governor's warrant. Once we've got that, we'll ask for a probable cause hearing for extradition to prove to Superior Court Judge Sherman over here that the suspect is not being falsely accused. If the judge agrees, you come and pick him up."

"When do you think you'll have the hearing?"

"Could be next Tuesday if we're lucky."

"Do you want me to come down for the hearing?"

"Won't be necessary. The suspect has made a statement, and I will play it in court and testify. Shouldn't be any problem."

"Horse, that's some real good cop work! Thanks for all your help. Did talking to Lyndon put you on the right track?"

"He pointed us the right direction. Maggie, up at the Oatman Hotel, gave me everything else I needed."

"Oatman? Jesus, Horse, Mohave County's going to have to put you on the payroll."

"Glad to help. I'll call you again after the hearing."

Chapter 20

AEDEN

On Friday morning, I was on the sidewalk, waiting for the Braithwaites to arrive. There was frost on the ground. Across the street from the school, a man was burning a big pile of fruitless mulberry leaves. I could smell the smoke twisting in the wind. Mrs. Braithwaite drove up, and we conducted what was becoming a choreographed routine.

When Billy was in his chair, and they had completed their usual shoulder and hand squeeze, she turned to me.

"Ade, you won't have to meet us out here anymore."

"Why not?"

"Because I know what you want to know."

"You do?"

"Billy told me you've been trying to find Charlie Merriman. You can stop trying. Charlie is in jail."

My mind went into overdrive, sorting possibilities. None of them were good.

"Where did they find him?"

"They didn't. He turned himself in yesterday afternoon."

"Uh oh."

"Billy said you thought Charlie was in trouble. Now I know why."

"How did you find out about all this?"

"I'm the only woman on the tribal council. Mrs. Merriman came to our house to talk to me because she's not comfortable talking to the men."

"What did she tell you?"

"Everything Charlie told Lieutenant Caballo."

"What's he being charged with?"

"Accessory to armed robbery."

"Good Lord, that's serious. Mrs. Braithwaite, can I ask you something else?"

"You don't have to. The answer is "no," your name didn't come up. So, if you still want to talk to Charlie, they will probably let you visit him at the Sheriff's office. They're holding him there, but I don't think you're going to go see him, are you?"

"No, ma'am. I don't think that would be a good idea right now."

"But it might be sometime soon?"

"Yes, ma'am, it might."

"Now that you know what you need to know, we probably won't be seeing you in the mornings."

"If you don't mind, I'd like to keep doing this. It's sort of getting to be part of my day."

She nodded, then walked around the car.

I walked alongside Billy as he wheeled himself to Chemistry class. As usual, we were the first ones there. After he had situated his books on his shelf, Billy had a question for me.

"When you asked me to take Charlie a message, you told me he was in trouble. And you told me you weren't in trouble, but you might be later."

"That's right."

"So, are you in trouble now?"

"I don't know, Billy. Maybe not yet. It depends on what Charlie tells the Sheriff."

"Is this about the house that burned down?"

"It is."

"And you know something about that?"

"You could say that."

"What are you going to do?"

"I don't know. I really don't. Are you or your mom going to say anything about this to anyone?"

"Hey, Ade, do we look like people who yak a lot?"

I had to smile. It was the last smile I would have that morning.

I have no idea what we did in Chemistry that day. I sat in the class-room, trying to figure out what might happen next. No matter how I turned it around in my head, it didn't get any better.

I caught up with Johnny when he came out the door.

"Let's talk. Something big has happened."

Outside, I got right to it.

"Charlie Merriman is in jail."

"Oh no!"

"According to Billy's mom, he turned himself in. They're holding him at the Smoke Tree substation. He's being charged with accessory to armed robbery."

"What happens next?"

"I don't know how any of that stuff works, and I don't know any-one we could ask."

"Me neither. Do you think they know about us?"

"I don't think so. But maybe I did something dumb when I asked Billy to get a message to Charlie. Now that Charlie's in jail, Billy and his mom know I know something."

"Will they tell anyone?"

"No."

"How do you know?"

"I just know."

"Like you knew about Charlie because of the dream? What do we do now?"

"Up to you, Johnny."

"I'd like to wait and hear what Judy tells Linda tonight before I decide anything."

I stayed at school for lunch. Bad choice. It was Friday: soggy fish sticks and stewed tomatoes. However, we did get a big, peanut butter cookie, so it wasn't a complete bust.

After lunch, I retreated to my wall to think things through again. Charlene Daugherty, Janice Minton, and Karen Patterson walked by. Charlene looked at me and said something behind her hand. They giggled.

A while later, Billy rolled down the sidewalk. He stopped and tried to wheel his chair over the uneven grass strip separating the sidewalk from my wall. I got down and walked over.

"Okay if I help?"

"Appreciate it."

I pushed him up the incline and turned his chair, so the back was against the wall. I hopped back up.

"So, you know about the robbery in Bullhead?"

"Yes. Read it in the paper yesterday."

"I guess Charlie is the 'unknown accomplice'."

"Looks like it."

"Doesn't sound like him."

"Sure doesn't."

We both stared across the faculty parking lot at the gym.

"And Sixto Morales died in the house that burned down."

"That's right."

"And Charlie burned the house down?"

"No, he didn't."

"But he was there."

"Yes."

"And you were too?"

"Uh-huh."

"Was anybody else there?"

"I guess Sixto."

"You guess? You didn't see him?"

"Nope."

Above us, the sky was deep blue. Contrails from a big, four-engine jet, probably a B-52, were drifting across the sky. The bomber was out of sight before the sound reached us.

"Other than Sixto, Charlie, and you, was there anybody else there?"

"Yes."

"If they accuse Charlie of burning down the house, what will you do?"

"I'm not sure yet."

We sat there for the rest of the lunch period without speaking again. When the five-minute bell rang, I pushed Billy's chair down to the sidewalk and walked beside him as he headed for class.

★ ★ ★

After school, we got on the bus for the ride to Boulder City. Coach told Johnny and me he wanted us in front in the seat next to his. This meant we couldn't talk about the latest development, which was fine by me. I had been thinking about it through all my afternoon classes, and it was making my head hurt.

When we passed Arrowhead Junction, I looked for Mr. Stanton but didn't see him. The junked-out, rusty cars deteriorating in the desert behind the station made the place look deserted and lonely. To the west, I could see the Piute range: to the east, Spirit Mountain. I wished I were at either one of those places.

Farther up the road, we stopped in Searchlight, an old, nearly abandoned mining town, to use the restroom at the dingy casino. In Boulder City, we had our pre-game meal in a banquet room at a restaurant. We had our choice of chicken-fried steak or chicken-fried steak.

At kick-off, the temperature was in the low forties, and the strong north wind was providing extra chill. It was not a good night to sit on the bench and freeze but sit on the bench we did. At least for the first half.

It should have been an easy game for Smoke Tree, but it didn't turn out that way. Our defense was as good as ever, but the offense kept going three and out. Without Johnny to energize the team, everyone was flat. Billy Quayles had been campaigning for more playing time all season, and I was seeing why he hadn't been getting it. He was terrible. He had no poise. He was afraid of getting hit. He couldn't, or wouldn't, run. In his haste to get rid of the ball, he over-threw or under-threw pass after pass. Then he yelled at the receivers. His ball-handling skills were awful. When he faked a handoff, he didn't fool anyone.

My replacement at right halfback, Eldon Richards, was game but inexperienced. He was also slow. That left a lot of pressure on Estaro Munoz. He was a good back, and he should have been having a good night against the Boulder City defense, but the timing between him and

Quayles wasn't working, and they muffed the handoff and fumbled the ball twice.

My replacement at right side defensive corner, Jason Riles, had one important thing to remember. Boulder City ran a trick play where the tight end fell down on purpose when it looked like he was trying to block for a sweep. When the corner committed to the running play, he would get up and go out for a pass from the halfback.

Boulder City tried it in the first quarter, but Jason did what he was supposed to and batted the pass away. But when they ran the play early in the second quarter, Jason bit, dropped his pass coverage and took off after the halfback. The back pulled up and threw a strike to the end, running free down the field. Extra point – seven nothing.

Next series, Quayles got intercepted. He was the only guy who could've stopped the cornerback who picked him off, but his attempt at a tackle was so feeble I thought Coach was going to eat his clipboard. Extra point – fourteen nothing.

Boulder City began to realize they could win the game. After the kickoff, we went three and out again. We had not made a single first down in the entire half, and our defensive unit was exhausted. Boulder ran what looked like the trick play again, and Jason was so snake bit he watched the end who had fallen down so long that the halfback ran right past him. Twenty-one nothing at halftime.

Throughout the second quarter, Superintendent Symington, who was always on the sideline, began to try to argue with Coach Lucas. This was nothing new. Dr. Symington considered himself an expert on the game. During every game, he made suggestions that Coach ignored. But by the time we were down fourteen nothing, he was right on Coach's heels, sometimes even tugging on his windbreaker to get his attention. During several of these conversations, he pointed at Johnny and me on the end of the bench.

In the locker room, there were lots of angry words and lots of frustration. At one point, I thought Seve was going to stuff Billy Quayles into a locker. After a few minutes, the room began to quiet. The team was suddenly aware that there were no coaches in the room. The chalkboard Coach Lucas always set up so he could diagram second-half adjustments sat on its tripod.

Dr. Symington came in. "Gentlemen, I will be assuming the coaching duties for the rest of the game."

Someone yelled, "Where's Coach?"

"I have relieved him of his coaching duties for the remainder of the season."

Deke spoke up. "So, where are Coach Lewis and Coach Bernardo?"

"The assistant coaches have chosen to side with Coach Lucas. I have relieved them as well, although I am sure they will re-consider before our next game. Coach Lucas, however, will not be coaching again this year."

Johnny was suddenly interested.

"Sided with Coach about what?"

"About strategy. About leaving you and Aeden on the bench. You and Aeden will be starting the second half."

There was silence for a moment.

Then Johnny stood up. "I won't play."

I stood up. "I won't either."

Dr. Symington was dumbfounded.

"You two will let this team surrender its undefeated season?"

"Coach Lucas benched Ade and me because we broke team rules. As far as I'm concerned, we are out of the game until Coach Lucas says otherwise. What do you think, Ade?"

"Johnny's right. I'm not playing for you, and I think a lot of the other guys won't either."

"Got that right," said Seve. Although no one else spoke up, there were nods of agreement. Nobody wanted to disagree with Seve.

Dr. Symington glared at us. Then he shook his head.

Seve said, "Get Coach Lucas back in here."

"Coach Lucas and his assistants are on their way back to Smoke Tree in Coach Bernardo's car."

Johnny thought for a moment.

"Dr. Symington, go outside while we decide this."

"I will not!"

"Okay, then tell the officials Smoke Tree forfeits."

"All right. All right. But we have only five minutes before the second half begins."

"You're a big talker. Buy us a few more minutes. Make up something. We'll meet you out there."

Dr. Symington went out the door in a hurry.

"Here's what we're going to do. Seve, you move to right halfback. Sammy will replace you at end. Sammy, you're going to have to play offense and defense both."

"I'm ready."

"All right. Almost every play in the second half will be a running play. We are going to pound on these guys until we beat them. The offense may go three-and-out once or twice while Seve gets the hang of this, so the defense is going to have to be extra tough.

Seve, you know these plays, but now you're going to carry the ball. You'll be the 'two' back. We're going to keep this really simple. No crossbucks, no counters. If pin-head here calls,'22 dive,' you carry the ball to the right of the center. If he says,'22 blast,' you take it to the right of the guard. '22 slant' and you take it to the right of the tackle. Dive, blast, slant. Middle, right, farther right. If he calls either of the other backs, you get to the left side of the field after he hands off and knock somebody down. But almost all the plays will be to the right.

Only one other call. If he says '27 sweep,' he's going to pitch you the ball, and you're going to follow Deke and Estaro around the left end. Okay?"

"Sure, I can do it."

"Estaro and Eldon, you two are going to alternate every play at left half. Every time you go in, you take the play in with you. When you come out, I will be standing beside Symington. Come straight to me. I will give you the next play. If Symington says anything, ignore him. Listen only to me."

"Bobby!"

"Yes, Johnny."

"On second and very short, I'm going to let you pass now and then to keep the linebackers honest. Only quick look-ins to the tight ends. Nothing long."

"But ..."

"But nothing. Call anything other than what I send in, and Seve will pound your sorry butt into the ground.

Defense, when you come off the field, meet with Ade behind the bench. He's the defensive coach. Everyone clear on what will happen?"

There were nods and 'okays.'

"One last thing." He paused. "Let's win this game so Coach Lucas can get to the play-offs. Kick-off team on the field. Let's go!"

It was a grim Smoke Tree team that went out the door. Johnny and I were the last two out. Dr. Symington was waiting for us on the sideline.

During the kick-off and the first series of downs, Johnny explained to him how it would work. Of course, he objected and got red in the face.

"I'll be right beside you, Dr. Symington. From the stands, it will look like you're coaching the team."

In the second half, it took the offense a while to get in gear. We went three and out on our first two possessions, but both times our defense held and we got the ball back. Then the system began to work, and our defense was not on the field all the time. Looking back, I'm sure Coach Lucas would've made some kind of similar change at halftime, but he never had the chance because Symington panicked. We were aided by two things. Boulder City was a terrible team, and the guys were determined to get Coach Lucas to the playoffs.

Seve was magnificent. He never fumbled or stumbled. He had power and speed. He dragged players all over the field, and when he got past the linebackers, he ran over the defensive backs. By the end of the third quarter, it was 7-21.

Every time the defense came off the field to meet with me, they had more confidence. I made only a few simple adjustments, but mostly I was just a cheerleader. As the game went on, I had more and more to cheer about.

By the fourth quarter, it was all Smoke Tree. We were too big and too strong, and even Quayles could run the simplified offense. On second and short, Johnny sent in a pass play, and Quayles hit Sammy for a big gain on a quick look-in. That opened up the run, and Seve scored on the 27-sweep on the next play. 14-21. The defense shut down Boulder City's offense for the rest of the game. Sammy caught a couple more passes, and Seve kept pounding for three more scores. We won the game 35-21.

Dr. Symington didn't know whether to be happy or mad, but in the end, happy won out. We were in the playoffs. He went around congratulating everybody, then strutted off toward the bleachers.

Principal Flowers rode home on the bus with us. I think Dr. Symington was afraid to. Johnny talked the principal into stopping at the same restaurant where we had the team meal and buying pie and ice cream for everyone.

When the team got off the bus, Johnny and I headed for the phone booth at the Terrible Herbst station next door. I called Linda. One of the girls answered and went to get her.

"Hello, Ade."

"Hi, Linda. Johnny's with me. Did you call Judy?"

"Yes, I did. I talked to her for quite a while."

Johnny was waiting outside the phone booth. He had his hands spread, palms up, and his eyebrows raised. I gave him the "thumbs up" sign. A big smile spread across his face.

"Did you deliver his message?"

There was silence.

"Linda?"

"Yes, Ade, I did."

"All of it?"

"All of it."

"So, what did she say?"

"I'm embarrassed to tell you."

"Go ahead, tell me anyway."

"Ade, Judy laughed! Said the thing about him waiting until she was eighteen was the funniest thing she'd ever heard. Said she didn't love him, never had, and never would. Said to tell him to stop staring at her all the time and to stop parking outside her house because it's creepy and she doesn't like it."

"That's not good."

"I know. Is he really, really stuck on her?"

"Yeah. Did she tell you why she wasn't allowed to see Johnny anymore?"

"She told me her dad thinks she went all the way with Johnny the night she came home late. That's why he's so desperate to keep them apart."

"Well, that didn't happen. Did she tell you the real reason we were late?"

"She said the three of you had been out of town, and you and Johnny had done something stupid. She was tired of denying it and was going to tell her dad what really happened. But then he promised to get her something really extra special if she agreed never to go out with Johnny again. She realized if she ever told her dad what really happened, he wouldn't give her the special thing."

"And what is this 'special thing'? Does she know?"

"No. She thinks it something very expensive, so she promised not to date Johnny ever again or even talk to him or anything."

"Good Lord. This is going to be a knife in his heart. I don't even want to tell him."

"I'll do it. Maybe I can let him down a little easier than you would."

I wasn't going to turn down that offer.

"Okay, I'll put him on."

I opened the door.

"What'd she say?"

"It's not good, buddy. Linda will tell you about it."

I handed him the phone. I pulled the door shut and stepped away to give him his privacy. They talked for over ten minutes. Then Johnny opened the door and walked out without hanging up the phone. As he walked by me, he said, "She wants to talk to you." He sounded like he was a hundred years old. His mouth was a tight, bitter line. The look on his face was positively murderous.

I went in and picked up the phone.

"Hi."

"That was terrible."

"Well, thanks for calling Judy for him. And thanks for telling Johnny what she said."

"Ade, before you go, I've got a question. Am I going to see you at Thanksgiving?"

"It's a small town, Linda."

"Ade, please don't make this harder than it already is. You know what I mean."

"Sorry to be a jerk. Sure, I'll see you at Thanksgiving."

"Thanks, Ade. I'm looking forward to it. Hey, I almost forgot. Did Smoke Tree win the game?"

"Yes, we did."

"How did you do?"

"I didn't play."

"Why not? Are you hurt?"

"No, coach benched Johnny and me."

"For what?"

"I'll tell you at Thanksgiving. This phone call is costing a fortune. My mom's going to have a cow when she sees the bill."

"Okay. Good night."

When I walked past the bus, it was empty except for the driver and Johnny. Even though it was bitterly cold outside, I didn't feel like going into the restaurant, and I wanted to give Johnny some time to himself. He had a lot to absorb. I walked out behind the buildings and up a low hill dotted with creosote. Once I got away from the lights, there were a million stars in a deep black sky. I sat down on a rock, stared up at the stars, and tried to figure out how all of this was going to turn out.

I was late getting back to the bus. Principal Flowers was scanning the parking lot for me. I took my seat beside Johnny. He nodded. As soon as the bus pulled out of the parking lot, Johnny turned his head and stared out into the blackness.

When the bus reached Railroad Pass and turned south on U.S. 95, the team wanted the driver to turn on the radio and tune it to KOMA in Oklahoma City. The driver asked Mr. Flowers if it would be all right, and he said yes. We drove down a deserted highway in the middle of the Mojave Desert, listening to rock and roll from a station in Oklahoma.

Elvis Presley sang "Are You Lonesome Tonight" and "It's Now or Never." Mark Denny whined, "Teen Angel," even though there were cries of "turn that crap off." The team was much happier with Roy Orbison's "Only the Lonely" and Bobby Rydell with "Wild One." Then "Stagger Lee" came on, and the guys started screaming out the lyrics.

After we stopped in Searchlight, Principal Flowers declared he'd had all the rock and roll he could stand. The radio went off.

By the time we got to Arrowhead Junction, most of the team was asleep. As we approached the old station, I saw a faint yellow light seeping out of the window at the back of Mr. Stanton's living quarters. I thought maybe he was sitting in his kitchen listening to 'Lucky Lager Dance Time' on KOB Albuquerque. I was pretty sure he wasn't listening to rock and roll.

★ ★ ★

When Boulder City kicked off to Smoke Tree in a small-town football game in the middle of the Mojave Desert, it was nine o'clock on Saturday morning in Saigon. A coup against President Diem of South Vietnam had been underway for twelve hours. The coup would fail. Harsh repression would follow. More than 50,000 South Vietnamese would be put in prison at hard labor. Thousands more would flee to North Vietnam. Many of them would return as members of the National Liberation Front. Americans would come to know them as the Viet Cong.

Chapter 21

CHARLIE

Charlie woke up in jail early Friday morning. The cell next to his was empty, and it was very quiet in his part of the building. His bed was a metal shelf bolted to the wall and supported by chains. There was a thin mattress, a small pillow, and a wool blanket. All in all, it was more comfortable and much warmer than the places he had been sleeping the last few nights. He was so comfortable he shifted his position, pulled the blanket up to his chin, and went back to sleep.

Later in the morning, he woke up when he heard Fred call his name. He sat up and put his feet on the floor.

"Your breakfast is on its way. One of the deputies picked it up at Lulu's."

Fred tossed a tiny towel and a bar of soap the size of a postage stamp through the bars. When Charlie stood up to move to the sink, his Levi's almost fell off. Fred had taken Charlie's belt and shoelaces before putting him in the cell. He had lost so much weight during his ordeal he had to hold his pants up with one hand to keep them from sliding over his hips.

Not long after Charlie finished washing up, Fred came down the hallway. When he slid breakfast under the bars, Charlie realized his appetite was back. The pancakes and scrambled eggs were great, and the big cup of black coffee couldn't have tasted better.

He sat quietly in his cell all morning. He didn't mind the solitude, and his body needed the rest. After being booked the afternoon before, Charlie had gone to sleep. In spite of having slept over thirteen hours, he nodded off twice after breakfast. Each time he woke up, he felt better.

He was surprised to find he didn't mind being in jail. First, he appreciated having the time to think back over the events that had led him to this place. When he did, he found he no longer felt sorry for himself. Everything had happened as it had to happen to lead to the dream that revealed his *sumach a 'hot*.

Second, because of his powerful dream, he knew his stay in jail was temporary. Even if he were convicted, he wouldn't worry. He had once heard the foreman of his track crew tell about a friend who was convicted of a crime. The foreman said the judge gave the man a choice: go to jail or join the Army. The foreman said his friend chose to go to jail. Since Charlie's destiny was to be a warrior, he would take the Army.

Lunch was from Lulu's again. A big cheeseburger and fries and a coke. It tasted just as good as the breakfast. After lunch, he took another nap. When he woke up, he ran through both versions of the dream over and over. He wanted to be sure he retained every detail.

★ ★ ★

Late in the afternoon, the door at the end of the hallway opened, and Fred and another deputy came down to his cell.

"Charlie, your mom has come to visit you. Horse says you two can talk in his office, but I'm going to have to cuff you."

"Why? I won't try to run off. I turned myself in, didn't I?"

"Count your blessings. I've never known Horse to do anything like this for a prisoner. Ever. He told me your mother is a great lady, and he didn't want her to see you in a cell. So come over here and turn around."

When Charlie complied, the deputy reached through the bars and cuffed him. Then Fred opened the cell door. When they led him into Horse's office, his mom was already sitting there. He noticed they hadn't let her keep the big purse she always carried. The deputy guided him down onto the chair facing hers. It was uncomfortable balancing on the front edge of the chair with his hands cuffed behind him.

"Hello, Son."

"Hi, Mom. Thanks for coming."

"Are they treating you all right in here?"

"Just fine, Mom. I've been catching up on sleeping and eating. How about you? How are you doing?"

"It hurts my heart to see you here, Charlie. And I miss you."

"What are people saying in the Village?"

"I talked to Betty Braithwaite yesterday, and she got the tribal elders together. Webster Charles told the others what they needed to know. The elders have put a stop to any gossip."

"Webster Charles has been very kind to me."

"He is very proud of you, Charlie. He told the elders that of all the young men, you understand the ways of the Pipa Aha Macav the best."

"Are you worried, Mom?"

"I don't like this. I don't care about what happened to Sixto Morales. I don't care about any fire. I am worried about you being in jail, but even more I am worried about your *sumach a 'hot*. I lost your father in a white man's war. I don't want to lose you too."

When she finished talking, Charlie could see the shine of tears in her black eyes. He knew there was nothing he could say that would assure his mother he would be all right when he went off to fulfill his destiny.

Neither one of them spoke for a while.

"Mom, has Horse told you what will happen next?"

"Yes. Arizona wants you to stand trial. There will be a hearing before a judge in Smoke Tree. Horse says it is not a trial. The judge will decide whether you were the person who was with Sixto when he robbed the store. If he believes you were, you will be sent to Kingman for a trial."

"I told Horse everything that happened. He made a recording of it. I will be sent to Kingman for trial, I am sure."

"Yes, it seems so."

"And Mom, don't you be driving that Desoto up the hill to see me. It might not make it. I will be just fine. I know I will be set free after the trial. I know it because of my dream."

"I believe what you say. Dreams tell us true."

Fred leaned in through the doorway.

"Time's up, Mrs. Merriman."

"I will be back to see you tomorrow and the next day. And Charlie, one more thing. Do you want a lawyer?"

"Waste of money, Mom. Money we don't have. I'm not going to deny anything I told Horse."

She nodded. "Goodbye, my son."

"Goodbye, Mom. It was good to see you. And please, thank Mrs. Braithwaite and Webster Charles."

After his mom left, they took Charlie back to his cell.

★ ★ ★

At about five o'clock that evening, he heard a car blast out of the parking lot. Other than that, it was quiet at the substation until Sunday night. He had a long time to sit and think about his future.

Chapter 22

HORSE

On Friday morning, Judge Sherman told Horse he would conduct an extradition hearing the following Tuesday if the Governor's warrant was produced by Monday. Horse spent all day Friday getting the paperwork together. The demand for extradition had been sent from Mohave County to his office and also to the San Bernardino County Sheriff's Department. Horse talked with the undersheriff about the situation. The Undersheriff made a few calls himself, then called Horse back late in the afternoon.

"Horse, the D.A. is talking to the Attorney General's office right now. The warrant will be in your office on Monday. I will see to it personally. Have you scheduled the evidentiary hearing?"

"Yes, sir. The matter will be heard by Judge Sherman on Tuesday afternoon."

"Then that's everything. By the way, I had a call from Captain Taylor. He was very complimentary about your work on this case. I asked him to put his comments in writing and send them to Sheriff Bland. He agreed to do that."

"That was good of him."

"Well, he was impressed. I am too. You put this all together very quickly. How good do you think the case is against this Merriman guy?"

THE HOUSE OF THREE MURDERS

"It's a lead pipe cinch as far as the hearing is concerned. I'm sure he'll be extradited. But the case itself is something different. I think Merriman got pulled into this against his will. He may not have been an innocent bystander, but apparently, he was a powerless one."

"Horse, let them sort that out over in Mohave County. You've done your part. The rest is up to them."

When Horse hung up, he sat and thought for a while. He had an uneasy feeling. He appreciated the kind words Captain Taylor had said on his behalf, and it was very thoughtful of the Undersheriff to ask him to put the remarks in writing. But Horse didn't really need any more letters of commendation. He had a file full already. And it was not as if he were looking for a promotion. Sub-station commander was a lieutenant's slot, and the only job he wanted was Smoke Tree Substation Commander.

He was worried about Charlie Merriman. When he interviewed Lyndon Brooks, it gave him a disturbing glimpse into the attitudes toward Indians and Mexicans over in Mohave County.

Up to this point, he hadn't worried a lot about the fire at the House of Three Murders. He wasn't even sure if anyone owned the place. It may have gone back to the county for back taxes. There might, however, be some question about whether Charlie had started the fire to cover the death of Sixto. He had no idea what the county prosecutor would think about Lyndon's story. He would have to put him on the stand to establish Charlie's identity, but when he did the pre-trial interview, would he ask him any probing questions about Charlie's attitude and not just his presence? And if Lyndon hinted Charlie may have been surprised by Sixto's actions, would he pass that information on to Charlie's assigned attorney? If Charlie even had an attorney?

Probably not. If the Assistant District Attorney decided to prosecute Charlie, he certainly wouldn't want to do anything to harm his own case. Charlie knew the man wanted to run for District Attorney. He didn't like to lose cases. And even though A.D.A.s are supposed to pass along exculpatory evidence to the defense, Horse had been around long enough to know that passing along physical evidence was one thing; reports of impressions and speculations about motive were something else entirely.

Therefore, the question of who burned down the house could have a major impact on Charlie Merriman's chances to avoid a stretch in state prison. It was important to track down the owner of the dark-colored Ford with flames on the hood. While he was thinking about the best way to accomplish that, his intercom buzzed.

"Yes, Fred."

"Shooting at Vidal Junction, Horse. At the agricultural inspection station. One of the inspectors thought a guy coming in from Arizona was acting a little nervous and had him pull over and get out of the car. He told the driver to open his trunk. The guy shot him instead, then jumped in and drove off in our direction. The station called the Highway Patrol, but the officer assigned to that area was between Desert Center and Vidal when he got the call. By the time the officer got on 95, he found the car abandoned. Ran out of gas or broke down. The shooter may be on foot in the desert."

Horse picked up his hat and went into the outer office.

"I'm on my way. Call Jim Harkness and Andy Chesney. Have them get their horses and meet me out there."

"Yes, sir, I'm on it."

"And Fred, Chesney has a double trailer. Have him go by my house and get my horse and tack too. My horse is in the corral. The tack room is open. Have him tell Esperanza I need my deer rifle, the .30-40 Krag with the scope, and my hunting boots. Have him tell her I may be gone for quite a while on this one. Got all that?"

"Yes, sir."

Horse got his jacket and went out the door. He headed for his cruiser at a run. His search for the car with the flames on it would have to wait. "It would be nice," he thought, "if I could deal with one thing at a time. But that's not the way this job works." By the time he passed the Smoke Tree airport, he was going over ninety.

★ ★ ★

That was the beginning of a two-day, two-night odyssey. Horse and his deputies tracked and apprehended the man who shot the agricultural inspector. The man, who was from Parker, had also killed his wife. Her body was in the trunk of the abandoned car. After turning the suspect over to the Arizona authorities, Horse was glad to be heading home by Sunday night.

Horse got back to Smoke Tree in the early hours of Monday morning. Esperanza woke up when he came in the door. His dinner was in the refrigerator. She warmed it while he took care of his horse and put it away. She sat with him as he ate his dinner. Horse told her everything that had happened. When he was done, she hugged him and kissed his face. "I'm so glad you weren't hurt. I always get nervous when you go off on one of these searches."

After a shower, he fell into bed. Esperanza scooted up against him and turned out the light. Just before he fell asleep, he thought again about finding the dark-colored Ford with the flames on the hood.

Chapter 23

AEDEN

I awoke before dawn on Saturday. My guns, hunting vest, and sleeping bag were on the floor by my bed. I put on my hunting boots, got my jacket, and carried everything down the hall. When I walked into the kitchen, I was surprised to find my dad drinking coffee and reading the previous day's paper.

"You're up early."

"I'm slept out. Went to bed at eight last night. You headed for the mountains again?"

"Yessir."

"Been spending a lot of time up there this fall."

"Yessir. I like it there."

"Me too."

"Why don't you come up?"

"I'd like to, but I'm marked up. Probably be out before evening. Say, did the team win at Boulder City?"

"Yes. But it was a strange game."

"Did you and Johnny really sit on the bench?"

"Not in the second half. But we didn't play either."

"Care to explain that?"

I told Dad everything that had happened in the game. When I got to the part about Superintended Symington relieving Coach Lucas, he started shaking his head. When I finished, he sat silently for a while.

"I can't believe this. He fired the guy who has been Smoke Tree football for ten years?"

"He did."

"And the assistants, too?"

"I'm not really sure about that. He said they sided with Coach Lucas and had left the game. I don't know whether he fired them or they walked out with Coach."

"Okay, Ade. You go ahead on to Lee's place. I've got to think about this."

I took my guns, vest, and sleeping bag out to the car. I brought in the food box and loaded it up. It put my schoolwork on top. By the time I was ready to go, Dad had filled a big Stanley thermos with coffee and put a sausage sandwich in a bag for me. I could see the gray of morning twilight outside the kitchen window.

"Thanks for the food and coffee, Dad. I'm off."

"Okay. Safe trip."

Because of my late start, I didn't stop at Arrowhead Junction to see Mr. Stanton.

★ ★ ★

It turned out to be a beautiful weekend. The unusual cold snap was gone. The temperature was in the 60s and 70s both days. On Saturday, I walked out of Carruthers Canyon and turned in behind the north side of the Pinto Mountains. I kept going until I reached Bathtub Springs. On the way, I crossed over the abandoned roadbed of the Nevada Southern Railway. It had eroded away to a faint trace on the side of the mountain.

I mostly walked but managed to hunt a little bit. When I got back to the adobe, I fried a rabbit on the wood-burning stove, then did homework by the light of the oil lamp before turning in.

I was up early in the morning making coffee when Lee Hoskins pulled up in his battered Willy's pickup. Four-wheel-drive vehicles were extremely rare in those days, and Lee had one of the only ones in town. The utilitarian truck had the reliable jeep four-banger and was a great vehicle unless you were in a hurry. On the highway, the transmission whined, and the thing wouldn't go as fast as my old Plymouth, but on bad desert roads and places where there were no roads at all, it was perfect.

When Lee walked in, he said, "Just in time for breakfast!"

"Yessir. Fixing pancakes. Got plenty for both of us."

"I'll make the syrup while you cook the flapjacks."

After breakfast, we got in Lee's truck and drove over to the Keystones to hunt. I hadn't been over there all season, and from the look of last year's bleached shotgun shell casings on the ground, neither had many other people. While we were there, I shot and cleaned two rabbits to take to Mr. Stanton.

I had hunted with Lee many times. I could hunt with him all day and never get a word of conversation out of him, but somehow, I understood he enjoyed my company.

Back at the adobe, I loaded up my car.

"You staying up, Mr. Hoskins?"

"Yeah. I'll go back early in the morning. I'm not due out until noon tomorrow.

You still working at that gas station?"

"I am. That's why I've got to get down the hill. I'm due at work at six, and I want to stop and leave these rabbits for Mr. Stanton."

"That's thoughtful of you, Ade. You've really taken a shine to that old man.

Give my best to your mom and pop."

"I will. Thanks for hunting with me."

"Always a pleasure, Ade."

The drive from Carruthers Canyon through the Lanfair Valley to Goffs was beautiful. A light breeze from the north was ruffling the creosote bushes and blowing the smell of sage in the window. The sky was a heartbreaking blue, and the air was pure and clear. The coyote gourds on the shoulder of the road were turning yellow on their vines. I wished I could turn around and go back and stay for a week, but I always felt that way. It was like being homesick for a place that wasn't really my home.

It was three o'clock by the time I got to Arrowhead Junction. When I pulled into the station, Mr. Stanton was puttering around the pumps. His face split into a smile when he saw me.

"Howdy, Ade. Thought I saw you goin' by yesttidy morning."

"Afternoon, Mr. Stanton. I just stopped to leave you a couple of rabbits."

I got out of the car and handed the rabbits to Mr. Stanton.

"Well, lookee there. Cleaned and ready to cook. My, those will be tasty! Tell you what, I'll trade you a grape soda and a candy bar for them rabbits."

"Thank you, Mr. Stanton."

"Don't thank me. Nossir. I'm gettin' the better of the deal. Two rabbits'll feed me for three days. Come on up the porch and sit a spell."

I followed him up the steps. He disappeared into his living quarters. When he came back he had a cold bottle of Nehi grape and a Milky Way. We sat on the metal chairs and looked out over the desert landscape.

"Saw the school bus go by on Friday. Expect that was you boys off to Boulder City."

"You don't miss much, Mr. Stanton."

"Not a lot to see out here, so I see it all. How'd the game come out?"

"Smoke Tree won."

"That's good. That's real good.

Say, how's your friend Johnny making out with his young lady?"

"Not well. I'm afraid she's broken his heart."

"I'm sorry to hear that. Yes, I am. Right sorry. That kind of thing can really hurt a young man."

"Well, it's hurt Johnny bad."

"Happened to me when I was not much older'n him. Had me a girl. Fine girl. Thought I was going to marry her. Then she up and run off with a farming equipment salesman. Think that's why I never married." He laughed. "Just as well though. Don't think I'd a ever found a missus would live out here with me. I surely don't."

"How did you get over her?"

"Don't rightly think I ever did. First World War come, and I joined up. Went off overseas. Saw Belgium and France. Mostly the mud in them two places. Tell you about it someday."

"I'd like to hear it. Mr. Stanton, do you ever miss Oklahoma?"

"Not anymore. I did when I first come here. Missed it somethin' terrible. I was used to considerable more green in my surroundings. Big fields of wheat and so on.

But then a funny thing happened. This old desert just burrowed into my heart somehow, and now it's home. Wouldn't want to live no-wheres else."

"You told me your brother and his wife went on to the coast. Did you ever go and see the ocean?"

"No, no, never did. Thought I would someday, but just never got around to it. Would have to close up the station, you see. Surprising how busy a man can get hisself doing not much.

You know, one time a feller came by here and talked to me for quite a spell. He was a geologist, he said. Was with them people that drilled for oil a ways down the road and hit all that hot water. Anyways, he told me this whole place was a ocean at one time. I told him that was hard for me to picture. He said that down there by Cadiz, there's fossils of sea creatures that lived millions of years ago. Called them tri-some-thing or others.

Anyways, after he left, I thought about it for a long time. Decided I'd already been to the ocean. Just one that don't have no water. So all this sand out here in the wash is just one big old beach." He laughed again.

I got up. "Thanks for the soda and the Milky Way, Mr. Stanton"

"And thank you for them bunnies. I appreciate it. And my regards to Johnny. Tell him not to let this put him off women like it did me. I sure hope his heart heals up."

"Me too, sir."

★ ★ ★

At home, I unloaded the car, cleaned my guns, showered, and dressed for work. When I went into the kitchen, mom had fried chicken, mashed potatoes, gravy, and a bowl of succotash on the table along with a pitch-er of iced tea. I sat down. Mom sat down at the end of the table.

"Help yourself, Ade."

"Where's Dad?"

"He didn't catch a job until late yesterday afternoon. He'll be back tomorrow.

Ade, what did you two talk about yesterday morning?"

"The Boulder City game. Why?"

"Whatever it was, your father had a bee in his bonnet all day yesterday. He made a lot of phone calls, then drove off to meet with some people. Only came back in time to leave for work. Even missed his lunch! Your father never misses lunch."

I thanked mom for dinner and went to work.

The usual slowdown hit at 7:30. I got out my books and went to work on my essay for English class. Around a quarter after eight, the phone rang.

"Union '76, Aeden speaking."

"Your daddy's been a busy man."

"Hello, Johnny. What do you mean? I haven't talked to him since yesterday morning."

"Then you're the only person he hasn't talked to. He called my dad yesterday, then came by and picked him up. The two of them went off to see Mr. Baldwin."

"The school board president?"

"Yeah. There's going to be a special meeting of the school board tomorrow night."

"About Coach?"

"Yep. My dad says I should be there. I think you should too. The Board is going to want to know what happened. My dad doesn't think we should let Symington tell the whole story."

"But I've got to work tomorrow night. So do you."

"Talk to your boss. I talked to mine. He's going to let me have the night off. Man, Smoke Tree is buzzing. People are mad at Symington. Be a lot of people there."

"Okay, I'll ask Mr. Garrett. Maybe he'll let me."

"I hope so."

I was glad to hear some enthusiasm about something in Johnny's voice, but it was suddenly quiet on the other end of the phone.

"Johnny, how are you doing?"

"Not so good. I'm not going to get over this for a long time."

"I wish you had come with me to Lee's Camp."

"I just needed some time to think on my own. To try to work this out in my head. I've never been blindsided like this before. I've been so stupid."

"So, what did you do?"

"I went fishing."

"Catch anything?"

"No. I wasn't really trying. But I did get to think a lot."

"What did you decide?"

"Other than the fact that I'm an idiot? I don't really know. I'll let you know if I ever figure it out. See you at school tomorrow."

When Mr. Garrett came by to help me close up, I asked about the possibility of getting Monday night off."

"It's already been arranged. Doug is going to cover for you."

"You've already heard about the meeting?"

"Everyone in Smoke Tree has heard about it. Dr. Symington has poked the hornet's nest. Coach Lucas is very popular in Smoke Tree."

When I got home, Mom was up reading a book. I went to Dad's office and typed the essay I had written. When I was finished, I went down the hall and said good night, then climbed into bed. Before I fell asleep, I thought about driving by the lonely phone booth on Lanfair Road earlier in the day and how much things had changed since I had driven by a week ago.

Chapter 24

CHARLIE

Charlie jolted awake in the pre-dawn hours inside his cell. His body was bathed in sweat, and he could smell his own rank odor. He had been dreaming the dream again, just as he had also dreamed it on Friday and Saturday night, but for some reason, last night it had been especially vivid. And something strange was happening. Last night he had been aware that he was dreaming while he dreamed. That meant there were had been three Charlies: the Charlie who was dreaming, the Charlie *in* the dream, and another present-day Charlie who was aware he was dreaming about the Charlie who was dreaming about the Charlie in the dream. It was getting confusing.

He sat up with his feet on the floor and wondered if he was losing his mind. Perhaps, he thought, his efforts to recreate and reorder his *sumach a 'hot* dream in exact detail was making it haunt him in his sleep.

He stood up and began to pace the tiny cell. Six steps from the bars to the back wall. Four steps from one side of the cell to the other. Repeat. Repeat. Repeat. A half-hour later, he stopped pacing, dropped to the floor, and did push-ups until he couldn't do anymore. Then he did sit-ups. He sat on his metal bed for a few minutes and then started again: One-half hour of pacing, then push-ups, then sit-ups. After three days of catching up on meals and sleep, Charlie was restless. He longed to be outside.

After breakfast, he heard the hallway door open, and Horse and Fred came to the cell. Fred unlocked the door. After Horse was inside, Fred closed the door and locked it.

"Do you want me to stay here, Lieutenant?"

"No. I'll holler when I'm done."

Fred went out the door at the end of the hall.

"How are you making out in here?"

"Fine, sir. Food is real good. I'm all caught up on my rest."

"Good. Charlie, you've been booked now. So if I ask you any questions you don't want to answer without a lawyer, just say so, and we'll get someone in here."

"No, sir. I don't need a lawyer. You've been straight with me. And thank you for letting me meet with my mother in your office when she came. Fred told me that's never been done before. I appreciate the kindness."

"You're welcome. I think your mother is a fine lady and a clever one who's always looking out for you. The day I went to talk with her, she managed to stall me long enough for you to walk out here. I never knew anyone could take that long to eat one slice of pie."

Charlie smiled. "Yeah. She told me about that."

"So, Charlie, this is not in the form of a question, and you don't have to respond in any way, but I don't think you'll be surprised to hear the prints all over the inside of Sixto's cars match the ones we took from you when you were booked."

"I'm not surprised."

"I came to tell you what's going to happen next. I know the hardest thing for someone who's never been in trouble with the law is sitting in here wondering what's happening.

There's going to be a hearing in front of Judge Sherman tomorrow afternoon. A governor's warrant, which is a response to a request for extradition from Arizona, will be arriving today. I will present it to the judge at the hearing."

"I understand. My mother told me some of this."

"The purpose of the hearing is to establish Arizona is requesting the extradition of the right guy. It is not a trial. You don't have to say anything, and you will not enter a plea."

"Okay."

"I will testify under oath about what I know. I interviewed the guy who shot Sixto. He gave me a description of Sixto's accomplice. I will point out that I believe it was you. I will then play the recording of our interview. I will also tell the judge that you presented yourself at the station voluntarily.

When I'm finished and have answered any questions the judge may have, he will decide if there is enough evidence to assume you are the person Arizona wants."

"Okay."

"You can have a lawyer present at the hearing if you want to. If you can't afford one, I can have the court appoint one today to be there with you tomorrow."

"I don't need one."

"That may not be a wise decision, Charlie."

"It may not, Lieutenant Caballo, but that's what I want."

"All right. You will have to repeat that for the judge so he can note the offer was made and declined."

"Okay."

"If the judge decides you're the right guy, I'll bring you back here and call the Mohave County Sheriff's office. They'll send someone down from Kingman to pick you up.

"Okay."

Horse paused and looked at Charlie for a long time.

"You puzzle me, Charlie. Most people in your situation would be very upset. You don't seem to be. Why not?"

"I'm just not."

"Do you know something I don't know?"

"Yes."

"I can't imagine what it is. You're really painting yourself into a corner here."

Horse looked around the cell, then turned to Charlie again.

"Do you like this cell?"

"Not really."

"Well, this is like a room at the Desert Inn in Las Vegas compared to what the accommodations will be like if you're convicted and go to state prison. I don't think you can imagine how depressing it will be. It's never quiet. Cell doors slamming shut, people screaming, inmates banging on the bars, crazy people moaning in the night.

And you won't be alone in a cell there. God knows what kind of evil men will be in there with you. It will be like living in the bear exhibit at the zoo. If you're convicted, they're going to send you to Florence. You'll be in the general population with some vicious, scary men. Can you cope with that?"

"I won't have to."

"Why not?"

"'I'm not going to prison."

"How do you know?"

"I just know."

"Well, I suppose you might get lucky, but that Assistant District Attorney is very ambitious. If he files a case against you, he's gonna try to nail your hide to the barn door."

"I'm not going to prison."

Horse sighed in exasperation.

"Okay. I tried to warn you. I'm afraid the system is going to eat you alive. I'm going to ask you another question, Charlie. And once again, you don't have to answer. When I interviewed you on Thursday, you told me all about what happened up until you saw me at the burned-out house. What happened after that?"

"What do you mean?"

"Well, where did you go?"

"I came home."

"How did you get there?"

"I walked."

"Then what?"

"Then I did some other stuff."

"What other stuff? You got back to the Village on Friday, but you didn't turn yourself in until the following Thursday. Why?"

"There were things I had to do."

"What things?"

"Can't tell you."

"Can't or won't?"

"Both."

"Okay, let me put it another way. Is whatever you did during that time the reason you're so sure you're not going to prison?"

"I can tell you that much. Yes, it is."

Horse walked to the cell door.

"Hey, Fred, come open the door."

While Horse waited for Fred, he stood staring down at Charlie.

"I sure hope you know what you're doing."

Fred came down the hall, let Horse out, and locked the cell.

After Horse was gone, Charlie stood up and began pacing. He knew Horse had tried to help him. He also knew he didn't need Horse's help. He had doubted Hera anyai once when he woke up on Wednesday night without having had his important dream. But then he went back to sleep, and something mysterious and significant happened. He would never doubt Hera anyai again. He was not going to prison.

Chapter 25

AEDEN

On Monday morning, I met Billy and Mrs. Braithwaite at the curb. After we got Billy in his chair, I asked his mother if she knew anything else about Charlie Merriman's situation.

"I talked to his mother yesterday. There's going to be a hearing on Tuesday."

"What kind of hearing?"

"About extradition to Arizona. They want to try him as an accessory to the robbery at the liquor store in Bullhead."

"How about the fire at the house?"

"Lieutenant Caballo told Mrs. Merriman the Arizona authorities may try to claim Charlie set the house on fire to conceal Sixto's death."

"Uh oh."

"Yes, 'uh oh.' So, are you ready to tell what you know about that?"

"I think so. Somebody else will have to be ready to do that too before I can. But I promise I'll tell Horse what I know about the fire before Charlie goes to trial."

"No matter what this 'other person' may say?"

"I'm sure the other person will agree. Things have changed since the first time I talked to you."

Billy had followed the conversation intently, turning his head back and forth between his mother and me.

"Mom, I'd better get started to class."

"You go ahead, Billy. I want to talk to Ade about something else for a minute."

Billy nodded and rolled off toward class. As I watched him leave, I noticed students in front of the science building looking toward us. I also noticed Vice-Principal Fertig looking our way.

"Ade, do you mind being late to class just this once?"

"No, ma'am."

"There's something I want to talk to you about while Billy's not here."

"Okay."

"Have you given any thought to where you're going to go to college?"

"Who says I'm going to college?"

"Well, you're in all the college-prep classes with Billy."

"That's only because all my friends are in them. Also, Mr. Sorrento keeps telling me I have to take those classes, and he's my favorite teacher."

"If you're not going to college, what are you going to do?"

"Work on the Santa Fe, I guess. I think my dad can get me on. They're the best paying jobs in town. Heck, my dad makes more than twice what a teacher makes."

"And you want to do that for the rest of your life? Ride trains back and forth to Barstow?"

I hesitated. "I never thought about it that way. Riding back and forth to Barstow for the rest of my life, I mean."

"Aeden, there's nothing wrong with railroad jobs, at least if you're white. They pay well. I just thought you might want something more."

"Like what?"

"I don't know. That's what you find out in college. If it turns out you don't want anything else, you could come back and work for the Santa Fe."

"But isn't college expensive? I mean, my ex-girlfriend is in college, and it's costing her dad a lot of money."

"Well, Dr. Bergstrom can afford it."

"How did you know I was talking about Linda Bergstrom?"

"I know a lot about what goes on at this school. You think Billy just sits in his wheelchair with his eyes closed and his fingers in his ears?

He may be just a Mojave to your friends, but he's grown up with all of you. He pays attention."

Just then, the bell for first period rang. When I looked down the walk, I realized all the students were inside. Only Vice-Principal Fertig remained.

"I'd better get going, Mrs. Braithwaite."

"You're already late. One more minute, Aeden. I've been working on a scholarship for Billy at Central Coast College."

"Where's that?"

"In Cambria, about halfway between Santa Barbara and San Francisco. There are funds for Indian students who show promise."

"That lets me out."

"You have certain assets, Aeden. You're a good football player. You're a track star and the fastest kid in the school. In fact, Billy says you're the fastest kid on the desert."

"Well, that's not saying much. There's guys on the coast who can run right past me."

She went right on as if I hadn't spoken. "Your grades are good. Billy says you're near the top of the class. You could easily get an athletic scholarship to a mid-size college. Don't you know that?"

"Never thought about it."

"Then start thinking about it."

"Mrs. Braithwaite, I don't mean to be rude, but why do you care? I'm just some white kid who didn't help Billy when he needed a friend."

"Billy's going to need help in college. Help getting to school and back. Help getting around the campus. Help because he's homesick. A lot of help. You don't know how hard it is for Mojaves to leave this valley."

"I see."

"I know the people at Central Coast. I mentioned your name and qualifications as someone who might come to the school with Billy. They're interested in you. Tell me you'll at least consider it."

"Okay, I will. Thank you, Mrs. Braithwaite."

I turned and walked toward the science building, my head spinning. Vice-Principal Fertig met me halfway.

"Mr. Snow, is there some reason everybody but you is in class?"

"Sorry, sir. I was talking about college with Mrs. Braithwaite, and I lost track of the time."

"Sure. You were talking college with a Mojave woman, and you lost track of time. Well, maybe detention will help you remember in the future."

"I have football practice after school."

"You're just going to have to miss some of it. Now get yourself to class, and I'll see you in the library for detention."

When I walked into Chemistry, everyone but Billy turned to look. Mr. Shaver looked like he was going to say something, but he didn't.

After class, Johnny walked out with me. "Why were you late?"

"Talking to Billy's mom."

"About Charlie?"

"Yeah, and some other things. She seems to think I should go to college. And by the way, I got busted by Fertig. He gave me detention, so I'm going to miss part of practice."

"I'm going to miss all of it. Unless Coach Lucas is back."

All morning long, the campus buzzed with talk about Coach Lucas and Superintendent Symington. It seemed like every kid in school had heard about the emergency school board meeting.

Just before school let out for lunch, Principal Flowers came on the P.A. system.

"Your attention, please. I have just been notified that Smoke Tree High School has been accepted in the C.I.F. small-schools division play-offs. Smoke Tree will travel to Riverside this Friday to play the Jensen Academy. Congratulations to the team."

After class, Johnny and I walked to the parking lot to go downtown for lunch. That's when we saw it.

It was candy-apple red, the same color as the Cadillac Eldorado parked next to it. It was a 1962 Corvette convertible, the one with the re-designed rear end and bulls eye taillights. Benedict McPhearson was leaning against the car. He waved to us and smiled. The hand he waved held the keys to the car.

While I was wondering why Benedict would wave at us, I heard a piercing shriek behind us. I turned in time to see Judy running toward Benedict and the Corvette.

"Is this my surprise, Daddy?"

"Yes, sweetheart, this is it."

"Oh, Daddy, I love it. I just love it. It's gorgeous! It's beautiful! When can I drive it?"

"Right now, honey. Take it to lunch. Just remember our deal."

As he turned to walk to the Eldorado where Mrs. McPhearson waited, he pointed his index finger at Johnny and cocked his thumb as if to say, 'there boy, compete with that.' Mrs. McPhearson scooted out from behind the wheel as he got in. They drove away.

Judy walked all around the new car. While she examined it, other students began to gather. She ignored them. Finally, she got into the car and started it up. The dual exhaust gave off a throaty rumble. She revved the engine a few times, then put the car in gear and let out the clutch. The car stalled and lurched to a stop. She started the car again but gave it too much throttle as she let out the clutch. The back end fishtailed and sent loose gravel from the edge of the road pinging against several cars in the lot before the Corvette stalled again. On the third try, she managed to drive away.

We got in Johnny's car and drove to Renee's for lunch. We got our burgers and fries and sat at one of the picnic tables at the rear of the lot. As we ate, starlings walked around us, hoping for a French fry or some burger. Johnny threw them all his fries. Instantly, twenty or thirty more showed up and began to fight over the food.

"Now we know what she traded me for."

"I take it we're not protecting Judy anymore."

"Hardly."

"Then we'd better talk to Horse. Mrs. Braithwaite says it looks like they're going to try to send Charlie to Arizona to go on trial."

"That's bad news."

"Yeah. Mrs. Braithwaite also says Horse is afraid Arizona may claim Charlie set the fire to cover Sixto's death."

"How soon will the trial be?"

"I don't know."

"Well, what do you say you and I run out there at lunch tomorrow and talk to the Lieutenant?"

"Let's do that."

Later, I saw Johnny and Seve talking to guys on the team between classes.

After school, I reported to Fertig in the library. When my detention was over, I headed for the gym. I went around the side of the building and looked out at the field. There was no one there. The back door was locked. I went around front, and that door was looked, too.

In the parking lot, Johnny was sitting on the hood of his car.

"Short practice today?"

"Yeah. Only six guys showed up and dressed out, none of them starters. They went out on the field and talked to Symington. He walked off and left them there. He didn't look real happy."

"Where were you when this was going on?"

"Sitting on the railing behind the gym. Symington didn't even say 'hi' when he stomped past."

"Downright un-neighborly."

"Downright."

"So, see you at the meeting at seven."

"Yep. Be there or be square."

When I got home, Mom was cooking dinner. Dad was in his office. I knocked on the open door as I walked in.

"Dad, I want to talk to you about the other night."

"Which other night would that be?"

"The one when Johnny and I weren't out drinking beer."

"Oh, that one. Well, come on, we'd better go down to the kitchen so your mom can be a part of this. She's been worried."

While Mom moved around the kitchen fixing dinner, Dad and I stood around, trying to stay out of her way while I explained what had happened at the House of Three Murders. By the time I was finished, Mom had dinner on the table. There was not a lot of talk during the meal.

When Dad was finished, he pushed his plate away and complimented Mom on a fine dinner. She got up and got him a cup of coffee.

"So, this Charlie Merriman is in jail?"

"That's right, sir."

"And it sounds like he may be in a lot of trouble."

"Sounds like it."

"So, what are you going to do?"

"Johnny and I are going to go talk to Horse tomorrow at lunch and explain what happened."

"Well, I'm pretty sure he won't throw you in the hoosegow. I doubt anyone cares about that old house."

"I hope not."

"And Johnny's decided not to protect the McPhearson girl anymore?"

"That's right."

"Good. Good on both of you. I'm glad you've decided to do the right thing.

Now, I'm going to get a shower and get ready for a school board meeting. Are you coming with me, Denise?"

"No, I think I'll stay home and read."

"How about you, Ade, want to ride to the meeting with your old man?"

"Yes sir!"

★ ★ ★

The Smoke Tree Unified School District held its board meetings in an auditorium at city hall, the same auditorium used for city council meetings. The five board members sat on a raised dais. The audience sat on folding chairs set up in front of the stage.

While Smoke Tree city council meetings were poorly attended, it was rare to have anyone at all at a school board meeting unless teacher salaries were being discussed. But on Monday night, November 14, 1960, there was a packed house. Extra folding chairs had been brought in. It looked like they were all taken when Dad and I showed up. There were people who couldn't find seats standing in the rear and on both sides of the auditorium.

When we walked in, School Board President Dennis Baldwin stood up and waved Dad forward.

"Come with me, Ade."

I went with him to the front of the stage. Mr. Baldwin came forward to meet us. A long-time engineer on the Santa Fe, Dennis Baldwin was in his late fifties. He wore his hair in a flattop, the white hair gleaming with pomade and allowing his pink scalp to show through. Mr. Baldwin was well over six feet tall, and his shoulders and chest were so thick they strained the seams of his snap-button cowboy shirt, but his stomach was flat and solid. His sole concession to formality was a western tie that looked like a piece of string draped around his huge neck. He stuck out his hand to shake with Dad. His blunt-tipped fingers were the size of cigars.

"Hello, Dick. The four empty chairs in the front row are for you and Ade and Johnny, and Will Quentin. I may want to call on the boys before the night is over." When we turned to walk to our seats, the audience applauded. My dad broke into a grin. I realized he had organized this entire show.

Before we sat down, I saw Johnny and his dad come in the door. Mr. Baldwin gestured them forward too. They came down front and joined us. Coach Lucas, Coach Bernardo, and Coach Lewis were seated in the same row. They stood up and shook hands with my dad and Johnny's dad.

"Some show, Dick."

"Should be interesting."

The board members, who had been walking around the stage talking to one another, took their seats. Superintendent Symington was seated at the left end of the table. His secretary, Lettie, sat at the other end of the table with a steno pad open.

At seven o'clock, Mr. Baldwin said, "Please rise and join us in the pledge of allegiance."

When the pledge was over, and everyone was seated, Mr. Baldwin banged the gavel and said, "This meeting will come to order."

"I object," said Superintendent Symington.

"You object to the meeting coming to order?"

"I object to this meeting. This is an illegal meeting. You cannot call an illegal meeting to order. Therefore, I object."

"And why do you think it's illegal?"

"This is not a regularly scheduled meeting. In order to have an emergency meeting, you must give forty-eight hours' notice."

"All right. I informed every board member of this meeting on Saturday afternoon between three and five o'clock. More than forty-eight hours have passed since then."

"But the two days required must be working days. Therefore, this meeting cannot be held before Wednesday."

"Dr. Symington, I work for the Santa Fe. So do every one of my fellow board members, including Mrs. Fiske, who works as a dispatcher. Every day is a working day on the railroad. Trains don't stop running because it's Saturday or even the Sabbath. Saturday and Sunday are working days in a railroad town."

Color began to rise on Dr. Symington's neck. "I object. You are violating, if not the letter, then the spirit of the law."

"Look at the room in front of us. I have never seen this many people at a board meeting, and neither have you. There is plenty of spirit here."

The audience cheered and whistled.

Mr. Baldwin rapped his gravel again.

"Now, now. Let's not have too much carryin' on. You'll make the Board nervous. We're not used to an audience. We're here to talk about the firing of Coach Lucas and his assistant coaches at halftime during the football game in Boulder City last Friday night."

"I object."

Mr. Baldwin sighed loudly. "Now what?"

"Mr. President, this is a personnel matter. It cannot be heard in open session. You must adjourn this meeting to executive session and clear the room. You can discuss the matter and then let the audience back in to hear your decision."

The crowd exploded in boos and jeers.

Mr. Baldwin let the shouting go on for almost a minute before he banged his gavel.

"Order," he said in his calm, deep voice. "This meeting will come to order!"

The audience grew quiet.

Coach Lucas stood up.

"The Board recognizes Coach Dean Lucas."

"I object!"

"What is it this time?"

"This is not the time for public comment. You will have to open a public hearing before Coach Lucas can speak."

"Coach Lucas is not the public. He's an employee of the district."

Dr. Symington was growing more and more exasperated. "If he is rising to speak as an employee, then he cannot speak about his situation until you adjourn to executive session."

Coach Lucas was still on his feet. His voice boomed out over the room. "I waive my right to have my personnel matter heard in executive session."

Coach Lewis stood up.

"I waive my right to have my personnel matter heard in executive session."

Coach Bernardo stood up and said the same thing.

Dr. Symington came out of his seat.

"These men cannot waive that right."

"Dr. Symington, you cannot, on your own authority, terminate our coaching contracts either, but you did," said Coach Lucas.

The crowd cheered. Mr. Baldwin let the noise continue again, then rapped his gavel.

"Coach Lucas, Coach Lewis, Coach Bernardo, I officially recognize your voluntary waiver of your rights to an executive session for this personnel matter."

Dr. Symington was still on his feet. His voice was taking on a strained quality.

"I must repeat my objections. One, this meeting is illegal; two, even if this meeting were legal, this matter would have to be heard ...."

Mr. Baldwin banged his gavel again, harder this time.

"Dr. Symington, you are out of order. If you keep interrupting me, the next adjournment to executive session will be to discuss *your* contract."

Dr. Symington's face was in transition from scarlet to near purple.

"You cannot threaten my contract in open session."

Mr. Baldwin stared at Dr. Symington. The room grew silent, so silent I could hear the sound of the second hand on the electric clock jerking around its circle. Dr. Symington seemed to suddenly realize he was standing. He sat down.

"Dr. Symington, ever since we hired you, you have bullied this board. You ignore our requests to put things on the agenda because you don't want to talk about them. You lecture us about the California Education Code as if most of us have not been dealing with the code for many years. You treat us like rubes and hicks. You speak to us sarcastically and sometimes with open contempt during meetings. You seem to think you run this board."

He turned his gavel so he held the round head. It disappeared inside his huge fist. He sighted down the handle at Dr. Symington.

"I'm here to tell you that is going to stop. You are going to sit there and be quiet unless I call on you to speak. Have you got that?"

"Mr. Baldwin, I ..."

"Have you got that? Because if you don't, I will have you removed from the room and continue this meeting without you."

"Mr. Baldwin, we do not have a sergeant-at-arms. Who will remove me?"

A huge smile split Mr. Baldwin's face. He said "Do I have any volunteers?"

Hands shot into the air. "That should answer your question."

In that instant, I almost felt sorry for the superintendent. He was, after all, a sophisticated, well-educated intellectual who had worked hard to recruit good teachers and improve the academic performance of the district. He could probably have continued his dominance over the board indefinitely if he had not made the fatal error of firing a beloved football coach and angering the town. But then I remembered how he had treated me in his office, and I wasn't sorry for him anymore.

"Now I have a question for you, Dr. Symington. Under what authority did you relieve Coach Lucas of his coaching duties?"

"I felt I had a responsibility to protect the interests of the district."

"Protect the district from what?"

"From the incompetence I observed."

"Let me be clear. You're talking about Coach Lucas's ability as a football coach. Not some other issue that we're not aware of?"

Dr. Symington seemed to be regaining his composure.

"That's right, Mr. President."

"But wasn't his team undefeated this season?"

"Yes. But it was headed for a completely unnecessary defeat. A golden opportunity for an unblemished regular season was about to be lost. I exercised my best judgment and intervened to prevent that from happening."

"And how did he show this great lack of ability?"

"He was causing us to lose the game."

"But we hadn't lost it. It was only halftime."

"We were well on the way. If changes had not been made, we would have lost."

"Let me be sure we understand. You fired him because you thought Smoke Tree was going to lose a game we hadn't yet lost."

"I've already made that clear."

"Dr. Symington, answer the question. I want your answer in the minutes of this meeting."

"Yes, I relieved Coach Lucas because we were going to lose the game."

"Dr. Symington, by that standard, half the football coaches in San Bernardino County should have been fired at halftime last Friday night."

There was laughter from the crowd.

"Half the coaches in the county weren't throwing away games they could easily have won. And half the coaches in the county weren't threatening a perfect season for no good reason."

"I see. And, in your opinion, how was Coach Lucas 'throwing away' this game?"

"He had two of his best players sitting on the bench, and he refused to allow them to play."

"Coach Lucas, since you have waived your right to executive session, can you tell us why the two players Dr. Symington is talking about were on the bench? And before you answer, I want to make it clear that we are not questioning your authority there. We just want to know why you did it."

"They were benched for violating a team rule. It was a serious violation, and because of it, they ran laps for punishment all during every practice last week."

"Dr. Symington, does that square with what you know?"

"Yes. And in my professional view, sitting out the first half would have been more than sufficient punishment. Any reasonable adult would agree. But when I told Coach Lucas this at halftime, he let me know he was not going to let the boys play in the second half. I objected and ordered him to put them in the game. When he made it clear he would defy the direct order of the district's highest administrative official, I relieved him of his coaching duties."

"What about his assistants? Why didn't they coach the rest of the game?"

"They took Coach Lucas's side in the discussion, so I had no choice but to relieve them."

"Then what happened?"

"The team rose to the challenge and soldiered on without the regular coaches. Their effort, I am delighted to say, ended in victory."

"So, you coached the team in the second half."

"In a manner of speaking."

"'In a manner of speaking'? What does that mean?"

"I acted as a stabilizing presence on the sideline and provided the legally required adult supervision of the team."

"So, who actually coached the team."

"Well, … it was a group effort."

"The team coached itself? You're ducking my questions here, so let me ask this a different way. Who told the offense what plays to run and who coached the defense?"

"That would be Johnny Quentin and Aeden Snow."

"The two lads who had been benched for violating a team rule?"

"That's right. Improperly benched, as I have previously stated."

"Dr. Symington, if you fired Coach Lucas for refusing to put these boys in the game, why didn't you put them on the field in the second half?"

"They refused to play."

"What reason did they give for refusing?"

"They said Coach Lucas had benched them, and he was the only one who could tell them they could play."

"So, they were loyal to their coach?"

"That's one way to look at it. I saw it as insolence. I might add that I had already had one incident of willful defiance from Aeden Snow in another context earlier that week."

"But in spite of this 'insolence,' you let them coach from the sideline?"

"I had no choice. Johnny Quentin and Aeden Snow had encouraged the rest of the team to defy me, as had Seve Zavala."

"Dr. Symington, have you ever coached football?"

"Well, no, not exactly. I am a student of the game."

"Aren't we all," he said drily.

The crowd laughed.

"All right. We've heard from you and from Coach Lucas. Now let's hear from someone else."

Mr. Snow, Mr. Quentin, we'd like to have your boys talk to the board. Do we have your consent on that?"

My dad and Mr. Quentin nodded.

"Boys, please stand so everyone can hear you.

Johnny, Aeden, you were actually coaching?"

Johnny looked at me. I pointed at him.

"In a way, Mr. Baldwin. We came up with a simple plan."

"And what was this plan?"

"We moved Seve Zavala to right halfback and pounded away at them. After a while, he wore them out. Heck, tackling Seve would wear anyone out."

There was laughter from the crowd.

"And where did you get this idea?"

"When we came in the locker room at halftime, I noticed Coach Lucas had the chalkboard on the easel. I knew he was going to make some changes for the second half. I just thought about what changes he might have been thinking about."

"So you made up new plays for Seve?"

"No, sir. Same plays. Just a different guy in the backfield, but a guy who's been blocking for those plays for three years."

"And how did your replacement at quarterback know which plays to run?"

"We shuttled two guys at left half – Estaro Munoz and Eldon Richards. They took in the plays."

"And what did you do, Aeden?"

"Mostly tried to keep the guys fired up, sir. Also, I watched the Boulder City offense for giveaways and told the defense about them."

"What are giveaways?"

"Well, like their left halfback. If he was going to carry the ball, he would turn his head toward the quarterback just before the snap. And their left end changed his stance slightly if he was going to go out for a pass instead of block. Stuff like that."

"Interesting. You boys ever considered careers in coaching?"

There were chuckles from the audience.

"All right. Thank you, boys. You can sit down.

Coach Lucas, would you be willing to answer another question for the board?"

"Certainly."

"In spite of the fact that you were, illegally in my opinion, fired from your position, would you be willing to continue coaching these boys for the rest of the season?"

"I would be glad to."

"How about you, Coach Bernardo, and you, Coach Lewis?"

"I would. As long as Coach Lucas is coming back."

"Me too."

"All right, can I have a motion from the board to re-hire Coaches Lucas, Bernardo, and Lewis for the rest of the season?"

"So moved," said Don Erikson.

Sharon Fiske seconded the motion.

"Any discussion?"

For the next ten minutes, members of the board took turns lauding Coach Lucas and his assistants for their work at Smoke Tree High. When everyone had finished, Mr. Baldwin called for the vote. It was unanimous.

"Motion carries. Welcome back to the game, gentlemen."

"I object," said Dr. Symington.

"And I object to your objection. This meeting is adjourned."

He banged the gavel. There was sustained applause. Dr. Symington stalked from the room. People moved toward the stage to congratulate the board.

Chapter 26

HORSE

When Esperanza shook Horse awake at seven on Monday morning, he reluctantly rolled out of bed and planted his feet on the floor.

"Come on, cowboy. Up and at 'em! Breakfast is on the table."

When Horse got to the station, he called the Undersheriff to make sure the warrant was on its way.

"It's with the mail on the Super Chief. Should be in your post office box before noon."

Horse spent much of the morning preparing his presentation for the extradition hearing. After lunch, he headed to the post office and picked up the warrant from the department post office box. When he got back to the substation, he called the judge's office and let the clerk know the warrant was in.

"Hold on a minute, Horse. The Judge is in a really boring trial. I'll walk in and whisper in his ear. Probably have to wake him up."

Horse held the phone, listening to the receding footsteps ringing on the hardwood floors of the old building. After a few minutes, the clerk returned to the phone.

"He told me to schedule the hearing for two o'clock tomorrow afternoon."

"Thanks. I'll bring the governor's warrant by right now."

When the clerk hung up, Horse's thoughts returned to finding the Ford with the flames on the hood. He thought a car like that wouldn't be too hard to track down in a small town, but he was reluctant to involve the most obvious source of information: the Smoke Tree Police Department. If the fire had been some kind of stupid accident, he didn't want to make a big issue of it. After all, it was an abandoned house that had been sitting empty and neglected for years. He decided he would rely on his own resources to find the car's owner.

Horse took the warrant to his cruiser and headed downtown to the courtroom at city hall. As he was driving the section of 66 paralleling the railroad tracks, a red Corvette flashed past in the opposite direction doing at least sixty in a thirty-five zone. He turned on his lights and siren and made a U-turn.

By the time he caught up with the car, it was turning into the heights. He followed it with his lights flashing, but it didn't pull over. Horse wasn't overly concerned because he knew this was the only road in and out of the heights. The car didn't stop until it reached the end of the road and turned into the flagstone driveway at the McPhearson house.

Horse killed the siren but left his lights flashing as he got out of the cruiser. The driver, who he now realized was the McPhearson girl, got out of the car and headed for the house as he approached.

"Hey."

She kept walking.

"I'm talking to you, young lady! Stop right there!"

She had one foot on the bottom step before she turned to face him. As he walked toward her, he said, "Didn't you see the lights and hear the siren?"

"Oh, I'm sorry. I must have been listening to the radio."

"Give me your license and registration, please."

"I don't understand."

"You do have a license, right?"

"Oh, yes."

"And the car is registered, isn't it?"

"I guess so."

"Then give me your driver's license and get the registration out of the car."

"What for?"

"Speeding."

"How fast was I going, officer?"

Benedict McPhearson, who had opened the door during this conversation, walked onto the porch.

"Yes, officer, how fast was my daughter going?"

"At least sixty, sir."

"At least? You mean you didn't clock her?"

"I was going the other way when she sped past me."

"So, did you clock her when you caught up with her?"

"No. She was doing the speed limit by the time I got to her."

"Then we won't be writing a ticket today, will we?"

"Excuse me?"

"Since you didn't clock her, you can't write her a ticket. Isn't that right?"

"Not exactly. If you want to make this difficult, I can cite her for reckless endangerment. I don't need an exact speed for that. Of course, that's a much more serious offense than speeding and will probably lead to the loss of her license."

Benedict hesitated. "I don't think that will be necessary. Judy, give the officer your driver's license. And get the registration. It's in the glove compartment."

Judy got her license out of her purse and handed it to Horse.

While she went to the car to get the registration, Benedict said, "I didn't know sheriff's deputies could write tickets."

"Any sworn law enforcement officer can issue a traffic ticket."

"I see."

Judy came back with the registration and handed it to Horse.

"Young lady, have you ever had a ticket before?"

Realizing that her father had backed down from a confrontation, Judy changed her tactics.

"Oh no, sir. Never."

"And how long have you had your license?"

"For over a year now."

"And how long have you had the new car?"

"I just got it today."

"Well, Judy, I'm going to let you go with a warning this time, but I'll be watching for you, and so will my deputies. I know it's tempting to drive fast in a fast car, but resist that temptation. Keep it to the speed limit. Understood?"

"Certainly, officer. Thank you very much."

"One more thing before you go in the house. You go to Smoke Tree High, don't you?"

"Yes."

"I'm looking for the owner of a particular car. Are you familiar with an older Ford coupe, painted black or dark blue, with flames on the hood and fenders?"

"Sure. It belongs to Johnny Quentin."

"And how are you acquainted with the young man?"

"He used to date my daughter, Lieutenant. I no longer permit her to associate with him," said Benedict.

"Isn't he the young man who quarterbacks the football team?"

"That's right."

"Well, he shouldn't be hard to find. Thanks very much for your assistance."

Horse touched his fingers to his hat and headed to his cruiser.

As Horse drove away, he was pretty sure he now knew the owner of the female voice Charlie had heard the night of the fire.

Horse drove downtown and delivered the warrant for the next day's hearing to the clerk of the court, then returned to the substation. When he went in, he stopped to talk to Fred.

"Fred, what do you know about a young man named Johnny Quentin?"

"I know he's one heck of a quarterback!"

"Have you ever heard about him being in any trouble around town?"

"Never."

"Do you know who he pals around with?"

"Sure. His buddy lives just up the street from me. Kid named Aeden Snow."

"Does he play football too?"

"Yes. Halfback."

"I think I'll head over to practice and see if I can find these two."

"I don't think there's practice today."

"Don't they have a playoff game this week?"

"You mean you haven't heard about what happened Friday night in Boulder City?"

"Fred, I spent Friday night sleeping on a desert hillside in the foothills of the Chemehuevi Mountains. I spent Saturday night further up the range. Not a lot of football news out that way."

"Sorry. Anyway, the district superintendent fired the football coach at halftime."

Horse let out a whistle. "He fired Dean Lucas?"

"That's right. And both of his assistants."

"Wait a minute. Wasn't the team undefeated?"

"Yes, sir. Still is."

"So, who coached the second half?"

"The way I heard it at the barbershop on Saturday afternoon, it was the two young men you're asking about."

"You mean they played and coached both?"

"Just coached. Coach Lucas had benched both of them."

"This is getting confusing. Just answer me this. Who's going to coach the team in the playoffs?"

"There's a school board meeting tonight to decide that. Seven o'clock in the city hall auditorium."

"You think this Johnny Quentin and Aeden Snow will be there?"

"For sure."

"One more question, Fred. What kind of car does Johnny Quentin drive?"

"'50 Ford coupe, midnight blue, flames on the hood and fenders, almost- illegal glass packs."

* * *

When Horse got home for supper, he told Esperanza he had to go back out that evening. He explained everything that had happened that day and told her why he was going to the school board meeting.

"Aren't you leaving something out, Lieutenant?"

"Like what?"

"Like how pretty the McPhearson girl is."

"You know her?"

"I've seen her around town. She's very beautiful. Is that why you let her off with just a warning?"

"No, at least I don't think so. No, I thought if I let the girl slide on the ticket, I might get an answer to an important question I had."

"And did you?"

"Yes. Charlie Merriman saw a Ford coupe the night of the fire. A Ford Coupe with flames on the hood and fenders. When I asked the McPhearson girl if she knew anyone at the high school with a car like that, she said Johnny Quentin."

"Very clever, Lieutenant."

"When I got to the office, I asked Fred if he knew anything about Johnny Quentin. Turns out Johnny's best friend Aeden Snow lives just up the street from Fred, and Johnny drives that car past Fred's house all the time. Apparently, the three voices Charlie heard outside the House of Three Murders were Johnny Quentin, Aeden Snow, and Judy McPhearson."

After he had dinner and Esperanza's perfect flan and coffee, Horse drove to the meeting. He parked his cruiser with the Smoke Tree Police Department cars and walked to the meeting. Still in uniform, he eased into the back of the room.

When the meeting ended, Horse waited as the room slowly emptied out. Finally, he saw Richard Snow and his son Aeden walking toward him. They were followed by Johnny Quentin and his dad. Richard saw Horse and headed directly for him.

"Evenin' Horse."

"Evenin' Mr. Snow."

"Horse, my son and Johnny Quentin were planning to come and see you tomorrow at noon. If you've got a minute, maybe they could talk to you tonight."

"I've got plenty of time, and I'd like to talk to them. But let's not attract a lot of attention. I'm going to drive out to the Smoke Tree Truck Stop. If you'd follow me out there, we could get a booth and have a talk. Not many locals out that way, especially at this time of the evening."

Horse was already in the back booth when the Snows and Quentins walked in. He stood up, and they slid in, a boy and his father on each side. Horse brought a chair to the end of the table and sat down.

The waitress came over.

"Hello, Sharon. Please give these gentlemen today's pie selection. County of San Bernardino is paying. And could you make sure that booth next to us stays empty?"

Sharon recited the pie list, took their orders, and returned with pie and coffee for the men and pie and milk for the boys. Horse waited until everyone had a few bites and a sip or two of coffee. He wanted the boys to feel comfortable and unthreatened before he started.

"First off, Mr. Snow, Mr. Quentin, your boys are juveniles. That means I need your permission before I ask them questions. Also, I need to tell you that if I ask them anything you don't think they should answer, you can just tell them not to answer, and I'll drop it. So, do I have your permission to talk to them?"

"Sure."

"Likewise."

"Thank you both. The first question is the most important one and the one you might not want them to answer. And if they don't answer that one, then there's no point in asking any other ones. We'll just finish our pie and go on home. Johnny, Aeden, were you boys at the House of Three Murders the night of the fire?"

Aeden looked at his dad for permission. Johnny looked at his. Both men nodded.

"We not only were there, Lieutenant, we started the fire."

"I started the fire," said Johnny. "Ade was going after someone we heard running through the back of the house."

"Was the McPhearson girl with you?"

"Yes, sir, she was."

"Did you start the fire on purpose?"

"No, sir. We went to look at the old house because of the legend and all, but when we got there, my flashlight batteries were dead. I got some fusees out of my trunk, and we went in the house. I lit one. It dripped hot stuff on me, and I threw it away. That's how the fire started."

"Ade, did you catch the person you went after?"

"No. I followed him to the mesquite thicket behind the corral, but I didn't go in there after him. Then my flare went out, and when it did, I heard the fire behind me. It was already coming out through the roof, and it caught a big chinaberry tree on fire. I started toward it, but I knew we couldn't put it out. While I was standing there, someone hit me from behind and knocked me down. By the time I got back up, he was tearing around the corner of the house. I never saw his face."

"So, you don't know who it was?"

"I didn't at first, but I thought there was something familiar about him. It came to me a few days later. It was Charlie Merriman."

"And you know that because?"

"Because of the way he runs. He has a funny stride because one of his legs is shorter than the other. That and the skinny build and the long black hair."

"Did you boys know Sixto Morales was dead in that house when you walked in?"

"No sir, we did not," said Johnny."

"Did you ever see his body?"

"No, sir, we did not," said Ade.

"Okay, I'm sure there's more, but here's another important question. Do you boys know that Charlie Merriman is in the substation jail?"

"Yes, sir, we do."

"Do you know what he may be charged with?"

"Yes, sir. Accessory to armed robbery."

"Right. A robbery where someone was shot and later died. How do you know about him being in jail?"

"I've been talking to Mrs. Braithwaite. She's good friends with Charlie's mom."

Horse sat quietly for a few moments.

"Now I have a question, sir. How much trouble am I in?"

"Not much, Johnny, in my opinion. I don't know for sure who owned that old house, but I'd almost bet it went back to the county years ago for back taxes. I guess you were trespassing, but if you didn't start the fire on purpose, that rules out vandalism."

"That's a relief," said Johnny's dad.

"One more thing. Did you boys see the story in the paper about the robbery and the fire?"

"Yes, sir."

"Do you mind telling me why you didn't come to see me when you read that story?"

"That was my fault. I talked Ade into agreeing with me that we would protect Judy. She was afraid her dad would find out we weren't where we were supposed to be. We drove away after the fire started, but we stopped at the top of Paiute wash to see how big it was. That's when we heard sirens coming, so we pulled way off the road. We waited for all the cars to go by before we drove back to town. So, it was almost midnight when we got her home that night. She was supposed to be home at ten."

"You said she was afraid her dad would find out you weren't where you were supposed to be. Where were you supposed to be?"

"At the homecoming bonfire that night."

"What did she tell her dad about why she was so late?"

"She didn't," said Ade. "I did. I took her to the door because Johnny had been burned real bad and couldn't wear his T-shirt. Her dad came out the door, and I told him we were late because Johnny got sick after the bonfire."

"Wait a minute. I thought Johnny burned his hand. So why wasn't he wearing his shirt?"

"No sir, I didn't burn my hand. When we heard the steps in the back of the house, Judy got scared. She turned around and ran into me. I held the fusee over my head so it wouldn't get on her. The stuff dripped on my chest. That's when I threw it away."

"Why didn't you just go get it and toss it outside?"

"Judy was screaming when she ran outside. I thought sure she'd been burned. I ran out to help her. She ran all the way past the car before I caught her. It took me a while to calm her down. When I turned around, the house was already burning."

"I see. And do you still have any burn marks?"

Johnny lifted his T-shirt. There were burn marks all over his chest. The one on his sternum was very deep and still raw and seeping."

"Good God, Johnny," said his dad. "I didn't know about this."

"I never told you. And I never took off my T-shirt in the locker room. I always went home without a shower."

"And you played a football game with your shoulder pads laced over that burn?"

"Yes sir. It wasn't as bad as it sounds."

"No, I'm sure it wasn't. I'm sure it was worse. My God, we're lucky it didn't get infected."

"Wait a minute," said Horse. "Does this whole thing about that night have anything to do with you boys being benched for the Boulder City game?"

"Yes, sir, it does."

"I think I see the connection, but how about you explain it to me."

"We knew people would wonder why we weren't at the bonfire. Especially since Johnny and Judy were the homecoming king and queen and were supposed to light the fire. The three of us made up a story to protect Judy."

"And that story involved breaking a team rule?"

"Yes, sir. First, we told everyone Judy got sick after we picked her up, and so we took her back home."

"Weren't you worried that Judy's mom and dad would hear about the three of you not being at the bonfire?"

"No, sir. Mr. And Mrs. McPhearson don't talk to anyone in Smoke Tree, so we were pretty sure they wouldn't hear."

"But you boys had to make up a story about why you didn't go to the field after you took the young lady home."

"That's right. We told the guys on the team we had been across the river drinking beer."

"And the story got back to Coach Lucas."

"Yes, sir. But not right away. That's why we both got to play against Sunset Crossing. But somebody told him about our story the Monday after that game."

"And he came down hard on both of you."

"Very hard. He was real disappointed in us."

"So, Johnny was loyal to Judy, and Ade was loyal to Johnny, and you were both loyal to Coach Lucas even though he put you on the bench. Do I have it right?"

"That's about it, sir. What happens now?"

"That depends a lot on what I hear from Mohave County after the extradition hearing tomorrow. I suppose Mrs. Braithwaite told you about the hearing."

"Yes, sir, she did."

Horse leaned forward and lowered his voice.

"All right, gentlemen. I'm going to take you into my confidence, something I probably shouldn't do as a law enforcement officer. I know you two boys have been loyal to each other and to your coach. I'm guessing the apple didn't fall very far from the tree in that respect and that Mr. Snow and Mr. Quentin are cut from the same cloth, so I'm going to take a chance. What I'm going to tell you now, you must not repeat to anyone else—not even the McPhearson girl."

Johnny and I looked at each other.

"We won't tell her."

"Mr. Snow, Mr. Quentin, I can't ask you to not tell your wives because this affects their sons, but can I count on them being discreet?"

"My wife can keep a secret better than anyone I know."

"There is no Mrs. Quentin."

"Okay. The District Attorney and a couple of the judges in Mohave County don't much care for Mexicans and Indians, especially Mexicans and Indians from Smoke Tree. Sixto Morales had a bad reputation over there, and so anyone who was known to be his associate is not going to get much slack.

I know Charlie was with Sixto when Sixto robbed the liquor store and got himself shot. But I think Charlie just had the bad luck to be with the wrong guy because Sixto was not someone he usually hung around with. I don't think Charlie was any part of the robbery. The store owner pretty much admitted to me that it was Sixto's show all the way.

But that prosecutor up in Kingman may try to paint Charlie as a willing accomplice, and I'm not sure what that liquor store owner will say on the stand or even get a chance to say once he's been prepared for testimony. And I'm afraid there won't be any cross-examination because I think Charlie is going to go into this thing without a lawyer."

"Why won't he have a lawyer?"

"For some crazy reason, he thinks he doesn't need one. He says he won't be going to prison but won't tell me why he believes that. I can't get him to understand how serious this is.

Furthermore, the District Attorney may claim Charlie started the fire in that old house to cover up the fact that he finished off Sixto to keep Sixto from identifying him."

"That's crazy."

"You know it's crazy, and I know it's crazy, but crazy things get believed in courtrooms all the time. And if Charlie waives his right to a jury trial, which I think he will, he may catch a judge who already has a bad opinion of Indians.

I don't want to see Charlie get jammed up, so I may manage to put in a good word for Charlie when I testify for the prosecution. That's very unusual, unusual enough to get me in serious trouble if that prosecutor gets mad and writes a letter to my boss.

But here's what I'm working my way around to. Even if I do say something on Charlie's behalf, it's just a story I would be telling, and it would be hearsay because I wasn't there."

"But we were! We started the fire!"

"That's right. But you are juveniles, and no out-of-state court is going to make juveniles not accused of a crime in that state appear at a trial. That means I'm going to have to somehow get what you just told me on the record to save Charlie's hide."

"But how, since we're not going to be there?"

"I can call you to a hearing before the juvenile court on what would be a minor matter— the accidental fire. Now don't get nervous: juvenile hearings are very informal, and there would be no charges, even though I would have to serve you for the hearing. But that way, I could get your story on the record. I could then deliver that sworn testimony to the court during Charlie's trial, and the judge would have to at least take it into consideration."

"Heck, Lieutenant, I'd be glad to do that. I don't want to see Charlie go to jail. I know he's a good guy."

"I don't know him as good as Ade does, but I don't want him in jail either."

"And how about the McPhearson girl?"

"What would you need her for?"

"The prosecutor might claim that both of you boys are friends of Charlie's and were trying to cover for him. But the girl is different. Her family didn't move here until after Charlie graduated from high school."

"I see what you mean. I don't know whether Judy would want to help or not. And I don't know what her dad would do. But if we did have this hearing, when would it be?"

"Maybe never. Maybe we won't need to. Certainly not this week. I just want to be sure if it turns out Charlie needs your testimony for the record that you're willing to give it."

"Sure, Lieutenant."

"Mr. Snow, Mr. Quentin, I know this is something you might not want the boys to do, and I can't do this without your cooperation."

"You've got it," said Richard. "I don't want to see some young man get railroaded."

"Me either."

Horse got to his feet.

"Mr. Snow, Mr. Quentin, you've got some fine young men here. You should be proud of them."

"Thank you, Horse. We surely are."

"And thank you again for your permission to question them."

"Lieutenant, I have a question."

"What is it, Aeden?"

"I understand we're not supposed to tell anyone what you just told us, but is it okay for me to tell Mrs. Braithwaite and her son Billy that we started the fire? I asked Billy to help me find Charlie right after this happened, and Mrs. Braithwaite knows I know something about that night. Also, she's friends with Charlie's mom, and she's very worried about Charlie."

"I don't care if word gets out about you boys starting the fire. It's the part about the possible juvenile hearing you have to keep under your hats and especially away from the McPhearson girl. Okay?"

"Yes, sir."

"Lieutenant, I have a question too," said Johnny's dad. "How did you come to be at that meeting in uniform tonight?"

"Well, I came looking for the driver of a car described to me by Charlie Merriman. A black or midnight-blue Ford coupe with flames on the front fenders and hood. But before I could find the car, some good people found me first. Good night, gentlemen."

Chapter 27

AEDEN

When I woke up early on Tuesday morning, I was looking forward to meeting with Billy Braithwaite and his mom. I went down the hallway to the kitchen and made my coffee. Mom had an electric percolator, but I preferred making cowboy coffee just like at Lee's Camp.

I had the kitchen to myself. Dad had been called in the middle of the night, and Mom was still in bed. While I waited for the coffee to boil, I made toast and scrambled three eggs. I carried my breakfast to the table and found the previous day's L.A. Times from the living room. Even though Dwight Eisenhower was still president, the president-elect and his wife were getting all the press: JFK in the political news and Jacquelyn in the fashion pages. When I finished breakfast, I washed my dishes and went out the door to school.

I was early again, so I walked to the football field and looked out across the Mohave valley toward Boundary Cone and the Black Mountains. The late fall sky spread out above the valley, filled with cirrus clouds that looked like downy feathers. There was very little wind. I thought about everything that had happened in one short week. So much had changed so fast. I didn't feel like I was the same person.

I thought about Mrs. Braithwaite's discussion with me about going to college. I wasn't sure what I thought about it. I wasn't ready yet to sit down and discuss it with my parents because I was afraid I'd hurt my dad's feelings. He often talked about when I would be working for the railroad. The job had been good to him; it paid well, and he liked the people he worked with. College had never been discussed at our house. I didn't know what my mother would think about the idea. I thought she just shared my dad's assumption that I would go to work for the Santa Fe after I graduated.

I was a small-town boy. I thought of the wider world as a place I saw on television or read about in the newspapers: a place that was fun to think about but a place from which I was completely disconnected. I liked places that were wide and lonesome. I didn't know if I could live in a city. I didn't think I wanted to.

I heard car doors slamming. Students and faculty were arriving in the parking lot. I turned and headed across campus at a trot. Mrs. Braithwaite was already out of the car and dragging Billy's chair onto the sidewalk as I ran up.

"Thought you'd forgot about us, Ade."

"No, ma'am."

"I was afraid my college talk scared you away."

"I was just thinking about what you said."

"And?"

"Here, let me help," I said to buy time. I leaned forward and helped Billy out of the car. Once again, I was impressed by the strength of his upper body. I squeezed his shoulders.

"What have you got in there, rocks?"

"I made some weights out of coffee cans filled with cement. I lift them all the time, and I have a pull-up bar in the doorway to my room."

I helped him into the chair.

"To answer your question, Mrs. Braithwaite, I'm not sure yet."

"Well, don't wait too long to decide. Billy and I have planning to do."

"Yes, ma'am. And another thing: I wanted you both to know Johnny Quentin, and I talked to Horse last night. We told him every-thing that happened the night of the fire."

"And what is 'everything'?"

I gave her a shortened version of what we had told Horse.

"Thank you, Ade. Mrs. Merriman will be happy to hear this."

"Not much happier than I am to get it off my chest. I didn't like keeping this secret while Charlie was in so much trouble."

"I'm glad you told us. Now, you'd better get to class."

For the first time in a while, I was able to concentrate in my classes. The night we burned down the House of Three Murders was no longer bouncing around my head like a deranged jackrabbit. I thought that, for the most part, the events would become just a quaint memory: the kind of event I might recall at a class reunion as in, "Hey, Johnny, remember the night we burned down that house?"

I was very wrong.

That afternoon at practice, the guys on the team talked about the firing and re-hiring of Coach Lucas and his assistants. But the coaches themselves said nothing about it. It was almost as if it hadn't really happened. The only real difference at practice was that Superintendent Symington wasn't hanging around. That was a relief. The guy still made me nervous.

Practice was devoted to getting ready for the Friday playoff game in Riverside. We didn't know much about our opponent. We only knew they were a second-place team in their league and ran the same kind of offense as we did. But knowing what kind of offense they ran made preparation a lot easier. Despite that, we were nervous. A team from our town had never made it to the playoffs before, and we all felt under a lot of pressure not to let Smoke Tree down.

Chapter 28

CHARLIE

On Tuesday at noon, Charlie's mom came to visit him again. As before, Horse let them use his office. Charlie noticed Horse had let his mom keep her big purse with her for this visit. He also took the handcuffs off of Charlie. Horse closed the door to give them some privacy. After they sat down in the two chairs in front of Horse's desk, Charlie spoke first.

"Thanks for coming to see me again, Mom. But please, I don't want you worrying about me. I'm fine. I'm not worried about anything. The old ones are watching over me."

"I'm going to worry, Charlie. It's all I can do."

"Horse told me this morning he talked with Aeden Snow and Johnny Quentin. They admitted to him they set the fire. Horse also told me he hopes to get that into a trial if he thinks the prosecutor in Kingman is out to lay this all on me."

"I always knew Horse was a good man. He wants to help you."

"I know. And I'm grateful. I didn't know there were people like him with a badge."

"Charlie, I've got to get back to work, or they'll dock my wages. I was five minutes late when I visited you last Friday, and they took an hour's pay."

"Mom, I'm sure they're going to send me to Kingman. I want you to promise you won't try to drive up there to see me. Please, Mom."

"All right, my son. But I will be thinking of you all the time."

They stood up. His mother took his hands. She stared into his face without speaking. When she dropped his hands, she picked up her purse and held it pressed against herself.

"Be well."

She turned and went out the door. Horse was over at the dispatcher's desk, waiting to get his office back. She walked up to him and touched his shoulder. He turned.

"Thank you for your help. Will you tell me about the hearing?"

"Of course, Mrs. Merriman."

She turned away from him and walked out of the substation.

When she was gone, Horse told Fred to take Charlie back to his cell.

"No cuffs, Fred."

At two o'clock, he was in Judge Sherman's office with Horse. The court reporter, the bailiff, and the clerk of the court were the only other people in the room. The clerk called the case and handed Judge Sherman the governor's warrant.

Judge Sherman explained for the record that it was only a hearing regarding possible extradition to Arizona. He further explained no plea was to be entered because California was bringing no charges. The bailiff called Charlie to the witness stand, and Charlie rose from his seat. When he had been sworn in and seated, Judge Sherman spoke to him.

"Please state your full name and address for the record."

"Charlie Merriman, your honor. I live at the Mojave Village."

"Is Charlie your legal name. Not Charles?"

"Yes, sir, Charlie."

"Mr. Merriman, you are entitled to an attorney to represent you at this hearing. Do you have an attorney?"

"No, your honor."

"Mr. Merriman, if you cannot afford representation, an attorney will be made available to you by the court at no cost to you. If you wish to have an attorney, we will adjourn today's proceedings until an attorney can be appointed, and you can have an opportunity to confer with that attorney."

"No, sir. Horse explained all that to me, sir, but I don't want a lawyer."

"For the record, Mr. Merriman, 'Horse' would be Lieutenant Caballo of the San Bernardino County Sheriff's Department?"

"Yessir."

"Mr. Merriman, this is a very serious charge the State of Arizona may be bringing against you. You would be well advised to have legal counsel represent you in court or at least advise you regarding these proceedings."

"I understand, your honor, but I give up that right."

"So you are voluntarily in *pro se* on this matter? *'Pro Se'* meaning you are representing yourself even though this court has advised against that?"

"Yes, your honor, I am."

"Very well. Return to your seat. The hearing will proceed."

Horse was sworn in and told Judge Sherman what he knew about the case. He then asked the judge if he wanted him to play the tape recording he had made in his office.

Judge Sherman turned to Charlie.

"Mr. Merriman, since you are serving as your own attorney, you can object to the introduction of this recording if it was not made with your consent or if you were not aware you were being recorded when it was made."

"No, Sir. Horse, I mean Lieutenant Caballo, told me what he was going to do, and I told him it was all right with me."

"Very well, proceed, Lieutenant."

Horse got down from the stand and turned on the tape recorder he had placed on the court reporter's desk. The judge listened intently to the recording as the reporter entered it into the record.

When the tape ended, Horse turned off the recorder.

"Once again, Mr. Merriman, just so the record is crystal clear, this recording was made with your consent."

"That's right, sir."

"And there was no coercion involved in having you submit to this interview or during the interview itself."

"No, sir. Lieutenant Caballo asked me some questions, and I answered them."

"Mr. Merriman, do you have anything to add? Any statement you'd like to make?"

"I would like to say I had no idea Sixto was going to rob that place when we walked in."

"Mr. Merriman, statements as to your guilt or lack thereof are outside the purview of this hearing. This hearing serves only to determine whether you were indeed the person with Sixto Morales at the time of the alleged robbery of the liquor store."

"Yes, sir. I understand. I was that stupid guy."

"Then it is the finding of this court that there is sufficient evidence to establish your presence at Winslow Liquors with Sixto Morales Wednesday night, November second. That being established to the satisfaction of this court, the State of Arizona is hereby granted the right of extradition in this case. Mr. Merriman, you will be extradited to Arizona for whatever legal proceedings that state wishes to pursue. This hearing is concluded."

The judge rapped the gavel and left the courtroom.

Horse took Charlie back to the substation, then called Mohave County and told them the extradition had been approved.

That afternoon Charlie sat alone in his cell and thought about all that had happened. He was serene in the knowledge that everything had happened as it was destined to happen in order for him to have and then fulfill his *sumach a' hot*. He did not know how the rest of his path forward would be revealed, but he was sure it would become clear in due time.

He climbed into his bunk and ran through the dream again and again. Then he fell asleep and dreamed it again. This time it did not seem like a dream. This time it seemed like a memory of something that had already happened.

★ ★ ★

The next morning, a deputy from Mohave County came, cuffed him, and stuffed him none-too-gently into the back of his Plymouth Fury.

On the ride to the County jail in Kingman, the deputy told him with undisguised glee that on Friday morning he would be in front of Judge Emmet Watson.

"And boy, that man hates him some Indians. Hates them good. Especially you out-of-state Indians."

Nothing Charlie had experienced at the Smoke Tree substation prepared him for the Mohave County jail in Kingman. When he was delivered, printed, and booked, Charlie entered a world he had never known existed. First, all his clothing was taken from him. Then he was subjected to a full-body search. After that, he stood naked in front of a counter where he was issued prison garb. Perhaps "issued" was too fine a word. A trustee threw shoes, socks, underwear, pants, and a shirt at him. When he put them on, they didn't fit. When he complained, the trustee laughed and said to the guard, "Oh boy, we got us a new fish."

Charlie was led to a cell. As he walked past cells, prisoners yelled at him. Some of the remarks were lewd; some of them were just sounds he couldn't understand. The cell held four people, and there were three already there. They didn't look glad to see him.

The guard pushed him inside, locked the door, and left. Charlie moved to the corner of the cell next to the bars and sat down. His cell-mates stared sullenly at him. From time to time, they asked him questions. He never answered. In fact, he didn't speak to anyone all that day or the next.

Chapter 29

AEDEN

On Wednesday morning, I met Billy and his mom in front of the school. Mrs. Braithwaite told me the judge had agreed at the end of the hearing that Charlie could be extradited to Arizona. I was not happy to hear that.

The rest of the day was filled with ordinary events. I went to school, went to practice, went to work, did homework, and climbed into bed, happy with the subdued pace of my life. I had never known how much I could appreciate normal.

On Thursday, after practice, I hurried to dinner and then to work. The evening rush had been shorter than usual, and I had my books open on the desk when I heard a car ring the bell in the pump aisle. When I got up from the desk, I saw a red Corvette. As I walked outside, Judy McPhearson rolled down her window.

"What can I do for you, Judy?"

"What do you think? Fill it up with ethyl and get the windshield."

I rang the pump back to zero and started filling the tank while I washed the windshield.

"Would you check under the hood, please?"

While I checked the oil, I couldn't help but admire the small-block V-8. The engine compartment was immaculately clean. The valve covers, generator, and air cleaner had all been chromed. The engine gleamed under the fluorescents flickering overhead. A Corvette was my dream car, and this one was owned by someone I didn't like.

When I was finished, I closed up the hood.

"That'll be eight twenty-nine."

She handed me a ten-dollar bill.

"Keep the change."

"Can't do that, Judy. Boss doesn't allow us to accept tips."

"Well, I don't see your boss."

"No, he's not here right now."

"Then he won't know."

"I will."

"Aeden, Aeden, Aeden. You can really get on your high horse, can't you?"

I went in the office, rang up the sale, and brought back her change.

"Judy, what are you really doing here? Your dad takes his trade to the Standard station."

"I'm not my dad. Besides, I was wondering how you and Johnny were doing."

"I'm just fine, Judy."

"How about Johnny?"

"Go ask him."

Judy started up the car and revved the engine. She eased out of the driveway. When she got on the street, she burned rubber as she headed west. I guess she had figured out the clutch. I walked to the office and went back to work on my assignments.

A little before nine, the phone rang. It was Johnny.

"Hey, Ade. Guess who was here for the last hour."

"Judy."

"How did you know?"

"She stopped here first. Asked me how you were doing. What did she really want?"

"First thing she did was hide her Corvette around back. Then she told me she'd heard stories about us starting the fire. Wanted to know if we'd told the police."

"What'd you tell her?"

"Lied like a rug. Told her we hadn't. Told her we'd let it slip to some guys on the team about the fire but kept her name out of it."

"All right! Good for you."

"She almost got to me. She looked so good! Asked me all kinds of questions about my burns and getting benched for Boulder City. Part of me wanted to believe she really cared, but I could tell she didn't know Linda had told us the real reason she was worried. Even hinted we might get back together sometime.

I know she was just being nice so she could find out if the real story about the night of the fire was going to get back to her dad somehow, but she still made my heart ache. Just by being close to me. But once she figured out she was safe, she didn't want to talk anymore. She just walked out back, got in her car, and drove away."

"But you didn't tell her what the lieutenant told us. I think you passed some kind of test. Maybe this will get easier."

"I don't think it will ever be easy. I have pains in my chest all the time. I didn't know that was possible. I thought 'heartache' was only in songs."

"I'm sorry you're having such a hard time. I don't think I can say anything that will make you feel better."

"Just being able to talk about it to someone helps, Ade. And I can't imagine talking about this with anyone else."

"Well, anytime, Johnny. Anytime. Okay?"

"Thanks again."

"All right. Talk to you at school tomorrow."

Chapter 30

CHARLIE

Charlie Merriman was a little bleary-eyed on Friday morning. Everything Horse had told him about noise in Mohave County jail was true, and he had been unable to sleep much on Wednesday and Thursday nights.

After breakfast, they took him to the courthouse. When they called his case, he stood facing Judge Emmet Watson. Judge Watson was old, and it didn't seem age had mellowed him. He looked over his courtroom out of dark eyes sunk deep in his bony face. His expression was one of perpetual disgust. His unruly thatch of brown hair shot through with gray seemed to stand up in agitation.

His first words to Charlie were a challenge.

"Young man, where is your attorney? Is he late? This is not starting well. I have no tolerance for tardiness."

"I don't have an attorney, your honor."

"You are aware you will be provided an attorney by the court if you cannot afford one, aren't you?"

"Can't afford one and don't want one, your honor."

"You intend to represent yourself?"

"Yessir. The judge down in Smoke Tree called it 'pro' something."

"The correct term is *'in pro se'* young man. And that was a hearing. This will be a trial. You are charged as an accomplice in an armed robbery."

"Yessir. Horse told me that."

Judge Watson's eyebrows arched high as if they were trying to catch up to the hair sticking up from his head.

"Your horse told you that you were charged as an accomplice?"

"Not my horse, your honor. I don't have a horse."

"Then what *are* you talking about?"

"I'm talking about Lieutenant Caballo, sir. From the San Bernardino County Sheriff's Department. Everybody calls him Horse."

"Why in God's name do they do that?"

"Because 'caballo' means 'horse' in Spanish, sir."

"I don't speak Mex, young man. This is an English-speaking court. So when you refer to this fellow, you call him Lieutenant," he paused, "whatever you said his name is. Is that clear?"

"Yes, your honor."

"Now, about this *'in pro se'* matter. I won't allow it."

"Excuse me, your honor?"

"I won't allow it!"

"All right, sir, if you say so."

"I do say so. I'm not going to get overturned on appeal because I allowed some ignorant Indian to be his own lawyer."

"Your honor, I don't intend to be my own lawyer. What I mean is, I won't need one. I intend to plead guilty."

"Oh, no, you don't! No, you don't! Stop right there! I see what you're up to here. You're not sneaking in a plea before I can get you a lawyer. Uh uh! No way! You think you're clever, don't you, boy? Think you're some kind of jailhouse lawyer."

"Excuse me, your honor? A minute ago, I was an ignorant Indian. Now I'm a clever jailhouse lawyer?"

"Shut up! Shut up! Not another word out of your mouth! Not one more word!"

Judge Watson turned to the prosecuting attorney.

"You there, Mr. Samuels. Did you know this boy was coming in without an attorney?"

"No sir. I assumed he had counsel."

Emmet Watson slammed his bony hand down. His eyebrows went up even more.

"Stand up! Don't you ever talk to me from your seat. You may be the hotshot young lawyer from Phoenix, moved out here to show us country bumpkins how it's done, but you, by God, don't address this court sitting down. Let's get that clear right now."

Phil Samuels stood up, his face burning.

"I apologize, your honor. It won't happen again."

"It better not!"

He turned back to Charlie.

"Now, let me tell you what's going to happen. This court is going to provide you with an attorney. You may not want one. You may even be dumb enough to think you don't need one. But you're not going to appear in this court without an attorney again.

You are going to consult with this court-appointed attorney. That means you're going to listen very carefully to each and everything he has to say. You may then be a fool and ignore his advice if you want to. That's up to you. But you will have had benefit of counsel. Is that clear?"

"Can I speak now?"

"What? What do you mean, can you speak? I asked you a question."

"But you told me to shut up. You told me not to say one more word."

"Well, now I'm telling you to speak. But I don't want you saying a word about being guilty or not guilty or any other darned thing. All I want you to do is tell me you understand what I just told you."

"I understand what you just told me, your honor."

"Good. Very good. Excellent. Now we're making some progress. Now, you are going to confer with an attorney, and then you're going to be back in the courtroom on Monday morning. You're going to be arraigned on the charge, and then you're going to plead. Do you understand what I just said?"

"What does that word mean."

"What, 'plead'? You don't know what 'plead' means in a court of law?"

"No, your honor. The other word. 'Arraigned.' What does that word mean?"

"Just never you mind. Ask your attorney. That's what he's for."

He turned to the prosecutor.

"And you, Mr. Samuels. You'd better have your ducks in a row come Monday a week."

"Your honor?"

"What?"

"You want to start the trial a week from Monday?"

"You can't be ready? Is there something about this case you don't understand? Seems pretty darned simple to me."

"I suppose I could be ready, your honor. But I wasn't expecting to."

"You suppose? You suppose? Mr. Samuels, just what in the Sam Hill do you think we do here? This is a courtroom, man. We have trials. All the time."

"Yes, sir. I understand that, sir. But what if the defense is not ready to proceed? This man's attorney is very likely to ask for time to prepare his case."

"Are you positive he will ask for more time after he talks to this boy here?"

"Well, sir, not one hundred percent positive."

"Then you'd better be ready, don't you think?"

He turned to the bailiff.

"Now get this Indian out of my courtroom."

★ ★ ★

Charlie was brought from his cell to an attorney-client conference room at two o'clock that afternoon. He was cuffed and shackled. A portly young man with thinning blonde hair, wearing Levi's, a snap-button shirt, and cowboy boots was already in the room. There was a legal pad and a pen on the table in front of him and a large file case beside his chair at the table.

The guard pushed Charlie down onto the other chair.

"Lester," said the man, "how about unhooking my client."

"Nossir. This one is special. Everybody got it in for him. The judge, the prosecutor. No way I'm unhooking this boy."

Charlie sat awkwardly on the front right side of the chair.

"All right, Lester. You can leave now. I want to talk to my client in private."

"You sure you're going to be okay? I'll be glad to stay. I'll just stand over by the door."

"And report everything you can hear to the A.D.A.? I don't think so. I think the shackles and cuffs will keep him from jumping over the table and stabbing me to death with my pen."

Lester went out and closed the door.

"Hello, Charlie. I'm Calvin Hanson."

"Pardon me for not shaking hands, Mr. Hanson."

"'Calvin' will be just fine, Charlie."

"Yessir."

"Charlie, what did you do to get under Judge Watson's skin?"

"I don't know. I just told him I didn't have a lawyer and didn't need one."

"And he didn't like that?"

"No, sir."

Calvin's round face broke into a smile. "Charlie, these judges have to stand for re-election. The old-timers, like Emmet Watson, just hate to get reversed on appeal. Since you're facing a very serious charge that could get you a long term in state prison, he's not going to let you show up in his court without a lawyer beside you."

"I see."

"Charlie, I sense you don't really understand how serious this charge is. Are you aware this case has been in the paper up here?"

"Lieutenant Caballo said something about that."

"You also have a hotshot young prosecutor who wants to run for district attorney, and he wants to put you away for as long as he can."

"I guess that's his job. But he didn't look all that tough in there today. That judge jumped down his throat, and he just stood there and looked real embarrassed."

"Yeah, I heard about that. And there was a reporter there, so the story will be in the weekly paper that gets published this evening. So now he's really going to be gunning for you."

"What about the guy who killed Sixto? Won't anything happen to him?"

"In Arizona? Not a thing."

"Even though he shot him in the back?"

"Charlie, given Sixto's reputation in Kingman, the guy could've shot Sixto while he was sleeping and got away with it."

"I see. And they think that because I was with him, I'm a bad guy just like Sixto?"

"Now you're getting the picture. To top it all off, you have a judge who just hates Indians and Mexicans. A man who thinks only white people should live in this county."

"Yessir, the deputy who carried me up the hill told me about him. He didn't seem to care for me much."

"The deputy or the judge?"

"Neither of them, come to think of it."

"So, Charlie, will you answer some questions for me, even though you don't want a lawyer?"

"Why not."

"Ever been in jail before?"

"No, sir. Never."

"Ever been charged with a crime?"

"Nossir."

"None at all? Not even drunk and disorderly or driving while intoxicated?"

Charlie clenched his jaw, the cartilage crinkling at the hinge. He looked away and did not speak for a moment. When he did, his black eyes were staring intently into Calvin's face.

"You white people. That's the first thing you think of when you see an Indian, isn't it? 'He must be a drunk'."

"Sorry. Bad example. But I need to know if you've ever had so much as a speeding ticket."

Charlie shook his head. "Nossir. Nothing."

"Did you graduate from high school?"

"Yes. Smoke Tree High, 1958."

"Get good grades?"

"Real good."

"Play sports?"

"Ran track. Still hold the school record in the mile."

"Good. Any college?"

"No, sir."

"Okay, are you employed?"

"I was. Probably won't be after this. I was supposed to be back at work today. I've been on vacation."

"Where do you work?"

"Santa Fe Railroad. Track repair crew. Ever since high school."

"Good record at work?"

"Yes, sir."

"Okay. That all sounds good. That will help. Now, tell me everything that happened."

Charlie went through the whole story with him, from the time he left the Palms with Sixto until he turned himself in at the substation. When he was done, Calvin continued writing for a few minutes.

"Are there people I might talk to who would back your version of events?"

"Maybe. I think the guy at the liquor story probably knew I wasn't part of the robbery."

"I see."

"And Lieutenant Caballo. He seemed to believe me."

"I wouldn't count on him. He's going to be a witness for the prosecution."

"Don't you get to ask him some questions too?"

"Yes, I get to cross-examine, but these law-enforcement types tend to stick together. They don't want a prosecutor or a judge unhappy with them, so they give lots of 'yes' and 'no' answers. Won't elaborate. If I ask him questions about whether he thought you were part of this, the prosecutor will object on the grounds of 'calls for speculation.' If I press, the prosecutor will accuse me of 'leading the witness,' but maybe I can get something in."

"But he will be testifying out of his home state, won't he? I mean, he's probably never going to testify in an Arizona court again. So maybe he will say more than 'yes' or 'no.'"

"Interesting idea. No wonder you got real good grades in school. I'll talk to him, and I'll try to talk to the guy who owns the liquor store, this Brooks guy."

"Go ahead if you want to. But none of this matters, Mr. Hanson. I'm not going to prison."

Calvin flushed.

"Look, under the best of circumstances, this would be real hard to beat."

"I'll be okay."

"I won't. I don't want to be called down for poor representation. So, let's make a deal."

"What kind of deal?"

"You let me do a little work on this. Don't be so anxious to charge in there and plead guilty because if you do, there will be nothing I can do to help you. And you will go to prison. Guaranteed. If you plead guilty, the judge has to sentence you. You'll have a felony on your record forever."

"I don't care. My foreman at work said a judge would let you join the Army instead of going to jail."

"So that's why you haven't been worried? Look, Charlie, a lot of guys think that's true. But they're flat wrong. Army recruiters can't sign you up if you have a felony conviction. The rules won't let them. So if that was your plan for avoiding prison, it won't work. So please, Charlie, just tell me you're not going to jump up and yell 'guilty.'"

Charlie was silent for a long time.

"Mr. Hanson. You seem to be a regular guy, and you apologized for the 'drunk Indian' thing. I see what you're trying to do. I thought I could go to the Army instead of to prison, but now I'm worried. So if you really want to work on my case, see if you can figure out a way I can get into the Army instead of going to jail. If you can do that, I'll just sit there in court and not say a word."

Chapter 31

HORSE

Friday morning, Horse put together the duty roster. Then he caught up on some other paperwork. It was a quiet morning at the substation, and time seemed to pass very slowly. At noon he went down to the Jade for lunch.

When he got back to his office, he could contain his curiosity no longer.

"Fred. Get me Captain Taylor at Mohave County."

A few minutes later, Fred was on the intercom.

"He's holding for you."

"Good afternoon, Captain."

"Afternoon, Horse."

"Can you tell me what happened at Charlie Merriman's court appearance this morning?"

"It's quite a story. I think Merriman went in there to plead guilty, but Judge Watson wouldn't let him. Told him he was going to have the advice of a lawyer whether he wanted it or not."

"So what happened?"

"The judge had him taken back to his cell. The County sent a lawyer over to see him."

"A good one?"

"Yeah. Local boy who went off east for law school and then worked back there for a while before coming back home. Anyway, I hear he's good. We'll find out next week if Merriman listens to him. He's due in court to enter a plea. Word is the judge told the A.D.A. to be ready to go to trial a week from Monday."

"Charlie's lawyer will probably ask for more time."

"Maybe. If the lawyer can keep him from pleading guilty."

★ ★ ★

Horse thought he was done with Arizona, but at four o'clock, Fred buzzed him.

"A Calvin Hanson for you, Horse. Says he wants to talk to you about Charlie Merriman."

Horse picked up his phone.

"Lieutenant Caballo."

"Calvin Hanson here, Lieutenant. I've been appointed as Charlie Merriman's counsel. I'd like to talk to you. Got a few minutes?"

"I've got to tell you, this is the first time in my career I've been contacted by a defense attorney before a prosecutor talked to me."

"Maybe that's because I'm playing catch-up here."

"Is Charlie going to let you defend him?"

"At first, I didn't think so. Judge Watson told him he couldn't come into his courtroom without advice of counsel, so Charlie had to at least sit in a room with me while I talked. I think he wanted me to plead him guilty, but he changed his mind."

"Why?"

"He asked me if it was true a judge would let a guy convicted of a crime to join the Army instead of going to jail."

"So that's what he was thinking. What'd you tell him?"

"Told him it wasn't true. Told him a recruiter couldn't take a guy with a felony conviction, and the minute he pleaded guilty it would be all over, and he would go to jail."

"What'd he say to that?"

"He wants to know if I can find a way he can get into the Army instead of going to jail."

"Can you?"

"I'm still doing the research on that, but the short answer is 'yes,' I think it can be done. But it will take some cooperation from the judge and the prosecutor, and that may not be easy to get."

"So, what do you want to ask me?"

"Charlie thinks you might be, uh, somewhat sympathetic to his extenuating circumstances. Any truth to that?"

"I suppose so. Everything I have learned about Charlie in general and his actions, in this case, leads me to believe he was pulled into a situation beyond his control."

"Lieutenant, I know it would be very unusual, but is there any chance you could help me keep Charlie from even going to trial?"

"That's an appealing solution. It could keep me out of trouble with my boss. Let me think about it over the weekend. Call me after Charlie pleads on Monday morning."

"Thank you."

"Don't thank me yet. And one more thing. Lyndon Brooks is going to be the chief witness for the prosecution. Have you talked to him yet?"

"Headed down there tonight. It's a long shot. Prosecution witnesses don't have to talk to defense attorneys."

"Working a *pro bono* case on a Friday night?"

"Yes, there's something about this Charlie guy makes me want to do whatever I can for him."

When Horse hung up, Fred buzzed him again.

"Horse, I've got Phillip Samuels, Assistant District Attorney for Mohave County, holding for you."

Horse punched line two.

"Lieutenant Caballo here."

"Lieutenant, this is Phillip Samuels, A.D.A. Mohave County. I'm the prosecutor in the Merriman case. He's the young man ...."

"I know who he is. I arrested him."

"I'd like to set up a time to talk to you in person next week. Judge Emmett Watson wants this trial to go forward a week from Monday."

"Okay."

"How is Tuesday at one o'clock?"

"That'll be fine, barring some kind of emergency."

"See you then."

Chapter 32

AEDEN

I got to school early on Friday morning to meet with Billy and Mrs. Braithwaite. After we got Billy into his chair, I said, "Mrs. Braithwaite, I wanted to let you know I'm thinking about college."

"Have you discussed it with your parents?"

"Not yet. I'm going to do that this weekend. A lot is going to depend on how they feel about it."

"I understand. Billy tells me you have a big game tonight."

"Yes, ma'am."

"Good luck."

"Thanks, Mrs. Braithwaite."

Billy and I headed off to first period. When we got to the science building, I opened the door, so Billy could roll through. Ricky Stevens and Dick Herndon were coming out the door.

"Hey, Ade, what's with you and wheelchair Indian boy? You guys are together every morning. People are starting to talk. Is this love?"

Suddenly, all the frustration of the last few days boiled over inside me. "Hey, Ricky, why don't you shut your big mouth?"

"You want to try to shut it for me?"

"If you can spare five seconds, I'll re-arrange your face. It's bound to be an improvement."

"Big talk."

I dropped my books and started toward him. He hurried off as fast as he could without looking like he was running away.

"Big man, big football star," he shouted over his shoulder.

I gathered up my books, and Billy and I headed into class.

★ ★ ★

Fourth period was canceled for the pep rally. Afterward, the team had a special meal in the cafeteria. None of the other students seemed to think it was strange we were having steak (salmon for the Catholics) with baked potatoes and sour cream while they had soggy fish sticks. After the meal, we got on the school bus for the trip to Riverside. It was going to be a long, slow ride.

Johnny and I didn't have to sit next to coach this time, so we got our usual seat in the back of the bus. We talked about a lot of things during the long drive, including our fears about what might happen to Charlie Merriman. We had plenty of time to talk. Our driver kept the bus behind a big semi as we ground our way down the two-lane blacktop. I watched as one north-south trending mountain range after another appeared on the horizon, slowly grew larger, and then receded behind us as we entered the creosote-filled basins that followed each range.

When we left Victorville and Apple Valley behind and reached the top of Cajon pass, I thought there must be a fire somewhere below us. We were halfway down the hill before I realized it was just smog.

There were two reasons people from Smoke Tree did not go to the Los Angeles area very often. First, it was a long drive and a dangerous one. Highway 66 between Smoke Tree and Barstow was a narrow, two-lane road filled with a seemingly endless series of dips that could completely hide an oncoming string of cars from view. You never knew when an impatient driver, unhappy with following a long line of slow traffic, might fail to realize there were cars hidden in the dip up ahead and suddenly swing across the double line to pass.

Second, we were small-town people. Even though we complained continually about the "fools from L.A." and "L.A. drivers," we were intimidated by big cities. We felt unimportant, out of place, and out of rhythm with the world of urban life. I didn't realize it at the time, but this anxiety was reflected in our language. We referred to driving to the city as "going inside," as in, "we're going inside next week." It was as if we were going to be swallowed by some fierce monster.

Our bus was in Riverside by five o'clock. After a light meal, we drove to the Jensen Academy. The school was in the Arlington section of Riverside, close to California Baptist College. When we got off the bus, we had an hour before kickoff, so we dressed out and got on the field for some light jogging, followed by lots of stretching. The stands were already filling up. I was surprised by the number of people who had made the long drive from Smoke Tree and braved the big city to be at the game. It looked like we would have almost as many fans as the home team. We could see the smog hanging under the field lights like poisonous gas in a war movie as we stretched. It was so thick I could taste it on the roof of my mouth. It was a nasty, oily taste.

The game itself turned out to be a walk in the park. The Jensen Academy was badly over-matched. We were ahead 28-0 at halftime, so Coach Lucas emptied the bench at the start of the second half so more of the guys could get into a playoff game. By the middle of the fourth quarter, Jensen had closed the score to 21-35, so Coach put the first string back into the game. We scored twice in short order. He pulled us out again to keep our score below fifty.

By the time we showered, packed up, and got on the freeway, it was after ten o'clock. The team was in high spirits. Coach had the driver find KFWB on the radio, and we had rock and roll all the way to Victorville. When the station dissolved into static, almost everybody but Johnny and I went to sleep. As the bus rolled through the darkness, we talked quietly for a while. Then I nodded off too. I woke up when the bus started slowing down for a restroom break in Barstow. I noticed Johnny was awake and didn't look like he'd slept.

When we reached Newberry Springs, almost everyone was asleep again, but Johnny stayed awake, and I did too. As we drove the stretch between Newberry and Ludlow, I looked out at the few isolated houses marked by the weak glow of yellowish light from the windows. I wondered, as I always did when driving in isolated places, what the lives of the people living out there were like. I had no such curiosity about the people in the rows upon rows of houses sprawling beside the freeway in San Bernardino, Colton, and Riverside.

After Ludlow, there were no lights to be seen anywhere. Outside the windows of the bus were hundreds of square miles of desert empty of human beings. My kind of country. I don't know where we were when I went to sleep again: somewhere after Bagdad, I suppose. The next time I came awake, we were laboring up the west side of South Pass, the cholla cactus ghostly in the headlights. As we accelerated down the other side, the lights of Smoke Tree began to appear below us. I had to admit I was glad to be heading back to our familiar little town.

By the time I got to our house, it was 3:30 in the morning. I parked in front of the house instead of in the driveway so I wouldn't wake everyone, but when I went inside, Dad was having a sandwich at the kitchen table.

"Morning, Ade."

"Morning, Dad. Just get in?"

"Yeah, from the east. How was your game?"

"It was an easy one. They were no match for us. I almost felt sorry for their team, but Coach didn't try to run up the score."

"That's one of the reasons I like Coach Lucas."

"Me too. He's a good guy."

"So, off to bed?"

"No, I slept some on the drive. I think I'll head on up to Lee's Camp."

"Okay. I'm going to turn in soon. Got to get my rest. I've already marked back up. I'm trying to time these trips to be home on Thanksgiving."

"I'll try to get my stuff together without waking Mom."

"She might not be asleep yet. Might stick your head in and say 'hi.' She was sleeping on the couch when I got in, so I got her into bed."

"I'll bet she had a book open on her chest."

"You called it. I'm surprised there are any books left in the library she hasn't read."

I went to the carport for the food box, then to my room for my boots, jacket, sleeping bag, and homework. Once I had everything together, I went to the extra room for my guns. When I had them, I peeked into Mom and Dad's room.

Mom called out from the darkness.

"Hello, Ade. I thought I heard voices. How was your game?"

"We won."

"Good for you."

"I'm heading out."

"Off to the camp again?"

"Yes."

"Okay. Be careful driving up there. And don't step on any rattle-snakes."

"Try not to. See you Sunday."

"I love you, Ade."

"Love you too, Mom."

When I came back through the kitchen, Dad had filled the Stanley thermos with hot coffee for me.

"Thanks, Dad. See you Sunday."

It was still dark when I stopped at West End Shell for my hash brown breakfast. When I finished, I got in the car and drove all the way to Arrowhead Junction without seeing any signs of the dawn.

I wasn't sure Mr. Stanton would be up, but I pulled onto the apron in front of the station to check. I could see a dim light in his living quarters, so I turned off the engine. Mr. Stanton called to me from the screened-in porch.

"Morning, Ade. You're up and about early today."

"No earlier than you, Mr. Stanton. I've got some real good coffee here if you could drink a cup."

"My pappy taught me never to turn away a man bearing hot cof-fee. Step right on up here, son."

Mr. Stanton had an empty mug in his hand. I filled it from the thermos and poured a cup into the metal lid for myself.

"How was the game?"

"We won, Mr. Stanton."

"Good for you! When do you play again?"

"The day after Thanksgiving."

"How's your friend Johnny doing?"

"Hard to say, Mr. Stanton. He's been pretty quiet lately."

"I surely hope he's a healin'."

"I'll tell him you send your good wishes."

"Thank you, Ade."

"I should get going, Mr. Stanton. I want to be up in Vontrigger wash before the sun is above the horizon."

"Better scoot, then."

"I can bring you a couple more cottontail if you'd like."

"Thank you, Ade. I'd 'preciate that."

Forty minutes later, I was sitting above the corral in the wash. The rising sun was streaking the sky with pink. The rock I was sitting on held last night's chill. I was glad of my warm coat.

The desert was completely still, without the slightest breeze, something that happened only rarely, and then just before sunrise or at sunset. Slowly, slowly, as the sun rose above the horizon, the creatures that moved in the daytime began to be more active. Small gray birds flitted from creosote to bayonet yucca to desert willow. Down at the corral, the occasional antelope squirrel, tiny tail high, skittered across the sand, safe now that the owls had gone to bed and there were not yet hawks up on the thermals. A whip-tailed lizard streaked from one rock to another.

I began to hear the sounds of Gambel's quail talking as they fed just out of sight. They were on their way to get water at the cattle trough. I sat perfectly still, my shotgun cradled in my arms. The lead bird, a male with a drooping top knot, arrived and stood on a rock near the trough. He surveyed the area. Satisfied that all was clear, he called. The covey, about twenty birds, materialized from the brush on the east side of the corral and headed for the water.

Below me was a quail hunter's dream. All I had to do was stand up, and they would scatter all over the bottom of the wash. After that, I could hunt down the individual birds and shoot them as they broke cover. But as I watched them feed and take water, the hens talking and the cocks taking turn standing sentinel, I realized I didn't want to. They had to come in for water. It was the most vulnerable time of their day, and here I was, lying in wait. I left them alone so they could go on with their difficult lives.

After the birds had watered and moved on down the wash, I got up and walked back to the car. I wasn't sure why I hadn't hunted the covey, but I didn't feel I had missed anything. I also wondered what I would have done if I had been with other hunters.

When I reached Carruthers Canyon, it was still early morning. The east side of the big canyon was filled with long shadows; the right side was bathed in soft sunlight. In comparison to the creosote and white bursage flats around Goffs at the bottom of Lanfair Valley and the widely spaced Joshua trees standing like sentinels around Cedar Canyon Road, Carruthers Canyon teemed with life. In the lower reaches of the canyon, Joshua trees mingled with the junipers and pinyon pines that would dominate the landscape farther up. Big sage, chamisa, blackbrush, cholla cactus, desert willow, and cat's claw acacia crowded each other in what was, for the Mojave Desert, amazing profusion.

The dirt road crossed the bottom of the canyon from shadow to sunlight. I could see tailings left from the late nineteenth century by the Big Ledge Mine. Then the road ran along the west edge of the canyon until it hit the cut canyon where Lee Hoskins had built his adobe.

At Lee's Camp, the previous night's game and the long rides there and back caught up with me, and I was suddenly very tired. I unlocked the adobe and the root cellar and unloaded the provisions from the car. The day was still perfect: cold but very still. The sky above the cut canyon was blue, almost to blackness.

When I had finished unloading, I pulled a cot out of the sleeping room and set it up outside. I unrolled my sleeping bag, climbed under it, and immediately fell asleep.

★ ★ ★

I woke up sweating. The sun was directly overhead, and it was hot under the sleeping bag. I pulled the cot back into the adobe, pumped myself a big tin cup full of ice-cold water from the sink, and drank it all. Then I climbed up the steep side of the cut canyon to look out over the thousands of square miles of desert that surrounded me.

I sat in the bright sun on top of the hill, thinking about a lot of things. Thinking about my friend Johnny and his broken heart and damaged spirit. About Charlie Merriman sitting in the Mohave County jail, booked for accessory to robbery. About whether Horse would bring Johnny and Judy, and me in for a juvenile court hearing. About whether I wanted to go to college or stay in Smoke Tree so I could be close to these mountains. About Linda coming home from Santa Barbara for Thanksgiving. About the football game next Friday night, a game so important to the town, to the school and my teammates and suddenly so secondary to my friend Johnny and me.

The world of the desert continued on around me. The wind came up, and hawks and golden eagles began to ride the thermals. Down beyond the Pinto Mountains, a dust devil kicked up and began to scour the floor of Round Valley. A raven I could not see croaked loudly out in the main canyon. A small wood rat appeared on a rock five yards from me and stood on his hind legs, looking about and sniffing the air. He caught my scent and scurried away. By the time I was ready to scramble down the boulder-strewn hillside to the adobe far below, the sun was already beginning to tilt to the west.

After lunch, I thought about going out for a late-afternoon hunt, but decided to catch up on my homework instead. I spread my books out on the kitchen table and worked steadily until almost sundown. After I ate a salami and peanut butter sandwich, I read one of Lee's western novels for a while, then went to bed.

★ ★ ★

In the gray light of early morning, I took my .22 and started down the cut canyon. I had only gone fifty yards before I put up a cottontail. I shot it and dressed it out. Another twenty yards on, I shot another one. The daylight was growing brighter. As I cleaned the second rabbit, two pinyon jays scolded me loudly from a juniper tree.

I carried the two rabbits back to the adobe. I finished cleaning them in the sink, then filled a big pan with cold water from the pump and put the rabbits in to stay cool while I was gone.

I closed up the adobe, walked down the cut canyon to the main canyon and turned north toward the peaks of the New York Mountains. I climbed past the abandoned silver mines that dotted the south slope of the mountains, careful not to get too close to the shafts. By ten in the morning, I was in the saddle between the two peaks. Being very careful where I put my hands, I scrambled to the top of the highest peak, over 7,900 feet above sea level. There was a stiff wind at the top. It was very cold.

The sky was a cloudless, intensely deep blue. I could see Mount Charleston outside of Las Vegas to the northwest and Mount San Jacinto outside Palm Springs to the south. "God," I thought. "I love this place."

I would like to have stayed longer, but I wanted to get home in time to talk to my parents about college before I went off to work, so I started the long descent of the south slope.

At the bottom, I headed down the canyon. Arriving at the slot adobe around two o'clock, I put the rabbits for Mr. Stanton in plastic bags, cleaned up the sink and the rest of the house, and began loading up the car. I locked everything up and was headed down Lanfair Road by two-thirty.

I stopped at Arrowhead Junction and left the rabbits for Mr. Stanton. He tried to reward me with another soda pop, but I explained I was running late.

When I got home, Dad's car was in the driveway and Mom was frying chicken.

"You're back early."

"Didn't want to have to rush dinner before I went to work."

"Well, you're in plenty of time. You can unload the car, clean your guns, and take a shower before this will be ready."

* * *

When we were all at the table, I waited until dessert to bring up college.

"Mom and Dad, there's something I want to talk to you about."

"Uh oh," said Dad. "What have you burned down now?"

Dad could always make me laugh.

"Not a thing, Dad. I want to talk to you both about college."

"What about it?"

"I'm thinking I might like to go."

They looked at each other. Then my dad said, "Well, I have to admit you've surprised me here. Never heard you mention college before.

But if you want to go, I'm sure we can cover most of your expenses if you want to go to San Bernardino Valley College."

"Thanks, Dad. I really appreciate that. But I'm not talking about junior college. I'm thinking about a four-year school."

"Which one?"

"Central Coast."

"Where's that?" asked Mom.

"It's a private school in Cambria, north of San Luis Obispo."

Dad let out a low whistle.

"Aren't those private colleges expensive? I don't know that your mom and I have that kind of money. I hear even Doc Bergstrom and his wife are struggling to pay for Westmont College for Linda."

"I might be able to get a scholarship that will cover all my expenses."

"Where did you hear about this? From your counselor at the high school?"

"No, sir. Billy Braithwaite's mom told me about it."

"Betty Braithwaite? What does she have to do with this?"

"There's money for Indian students who show promise and other money for kids who are handicapped because of polio. Some of these private schools are especially interested in Indian students."

"But what's that got to do with you, Son?"

"That's what I asked her when she talked to me about it. She says Billy can't manage everything on his own if he goes to school there. He'll need a roommate who can help him. I've been helping her get Billy out of their car and into his wheelchair at school mornings, so she thought about me. She remembers Billy and I were good friends in elementary school.

Anyway, she's been talking to the college about me. They know about my school records in track, and they know I'm an okay football player. She says they seem interested in me.

But I don't know how you'd feel about me going off so far from home. And about me going to college in general. I mean, I don't know where it will lead. I always thought I'd work on the railroad after I graduated."

"Well, Son, the big question here isn't how we feel about it; it's how you feel about it."

"I don't want to do anything to hurt your feelings. I know you're very proud of working and taking care of Mom and me, and I don't want you to think that I'm not proud of that too."

"Ade, let me explain something. I was lucky enough to get this job just before the Depression hit and lucky enough to keep it all through those hard times. I like the work, and I mostly like the people I work with, but you shouldn't work on the railroad just because I did. If you think you might find something you would rather do, something that would make you happy, go ahead and do it. You're not going to hurt my feelings. I'll be proud of you no matter what you decide."

"Mom, how about you? What do you think about me going away to college?"

"I think it would be wonderful. Your father never had an opportunity like this, and I certainly didn't. When I was a young woman, it was very rare for girls to go to college. I would have loved to have gone, but at the time, it wasn't even a possibility for me. Maybe you could go for both of us."

"And Ade, one more thing. Thank you for coming to your mom and I with this. It means a lot to us. Some guys your age wouldn't have done that."

"Some guys my age don't have anyone who cares. I can't imagine Johnny asking his dad about something like this. I don't think he would care one way or the other."

"Don't be too hard on Johnny's dad. When his wife died, it knocked him to his knees. He's never been able to get all the way back up. I worry about him. My biggest worry is he'll get caught drinking at work and lose his job. He's barely hanging on by his fingernails now. Losing his job would finish him off."

"I never thought of it that way."

"It might be hard to understand love like that at your age."

"I don't think so. I think something just like it is happening to Johnny right now."

"Ah, it's probably just puppy love."

"I don't think so, Dad."

I left the table and drove to work. Since I had finished my homework at Lee's Camp the day before, I had all the slow time to think about college.

Chapter 33

CHARLIE

Early Monday morning, Charlie met with Calvin Hanson in the prison interview room. Once again, Charlie was brought in shackled and cuffed. Once again, Calvin asked the guard to remove the chains and cuffs. The guard refused and offered to stay in the room. Calvin told him to wait outside.

"I talked to Lieutenant Caballo on Friday. You were right. He does seem to be on your side. At least as much as I've ever seen a law enforcement type on the side of an accused. Help me understand something, Charlie. How do you convince a sheriff's lieutenant that you're a good guy, even though you're a suspect in an armed robbery?"

Charlie shrugged. "Tell him the truth."

"All suspects claim they are telling the truth."

"Turn yourself in."

"That's been done before."

"Have a real nice mother?"

"Maybe that's it.

I also went to Bullhead and talked to Lyndon Brooks. No luck there. When I told him I was representing you, he clammed up.

You and I are going to be in court together at nine o'clock. I wanted to talk to you before they took you over. This is going to be very simple and quick. The judge is going to explain what you're charged with and ask you to plead."

"Okay."

"And I'm going to plead you not guilty."

"Tell me something before I agree to that. How's that idea coming you had for keeping me out of prison?"

"It's looking better. But the whole thing is out the window unless you allow me to plead you not guilty."

"Then I'll plead not guilty."

"Good."

At nine o'clock, they stood at the defense table in front of the judge. Calvin entered Charlie's plea as 'not guilty.'

The judge asked Calvin if his client wanted a trial by a jury of his peers. Calvin said no. Then the judge asked if Calvin would be ready to defend his client by the following Monday. To the surprise of the judge and the prosecutor, Calvin said he would. The judge didn't bother to ask if the State would be ready.

"All right. Ten o'clock next Monday morning in this courtroom."

"One more thing, your honor. Since my client has pled 'not guilty to the charges, I request he be released on his own recognizance until the trial begins."

Phillip Samuels, who was still trying to figure out why Hanson hadn't asked for more time to prepare, started to speak, then remembered he was still sitting down. He got to his feet so quickly he almost knocked his chair over.

"Your honor, the State feels that an O R release would be inappropriate. This is a case of armed robbery where the victim was shot at multiple times with a high-caliber weapon."

"My client fired no weapon, your honor."

"That has not been established in this courtroom. This man is dangerous and should be held without bail for the protection of the citizens of Arizona."

"Your honor, Charlie Merriman has no criminal record. None. He has never been accused of a crime, much less convicted. He is gainfully employed and has an excellent work record. I am requesting bail of twenty-five thousand dollars."

"Gentlemen, gentlemen, don't get yourselves in a lather. Save the fireworks for next Monday. Bail is set at fifty thousand dollars."

Calvin Hanson spoke briefly with Charlie before he was led away. Charlie told him there was no way he could make bail.

Chapter 34

HORSE

On Monday morning at eleven o'clock, Calvin Hanson called Horse.

"Lieutenant Caballo speaking."

"Good morning, Lieutenant. Calvin Hanson here. Charlie pled 'not guilty' this morning to a charge of accessory to robbery."

"Thank goodness he took your advice."

"Judge Watson scheduled the trial for a week from today."

"You didn't ask for more time?"

"No."

"Did you ask for a jury trial?"

"That wouldn't be a good idea in Mohave County. I wouldn't be able to get a jury that would give Charlie a fair hearing. At least that's my opinion."

"You would know. I heard you grew up there. But what about Judge Watson? You must know he doesn't like Indians."

There was a brief silence.

"You didn't hear it from me, but that's true enough. However, he's an honest judge, and he knows the law. Also, there's been some tension between the judge and the A.D.A. Apparently, Watson thinks the guy is a city slicker. Since I'm a local boy, that might play in my favor."

"Before we go any further, Mr. Hanson, you should know that I have a meeting with the A.D.A. at one o'clock tomorrow."

"I expected that."

"How did you make out with Lyndon Brooks?"

"Not very well. When I told him I was representing Charlie Merriman, he wouldn't talk to me. He's the victim here, and he sees the prosecutor as the guy representing him. But I had to give it a try.

And while we're on the subject, I appreciate you being so forthcoming with me. That's a rare occurrence, in my experience."

"I'm sure of that, and frankly, it could get me in a lot of trouble if this goes to trial. So, I hope you're working on that idea you mentioned on Friday."

"I am, and it's looking pretty good. But I could use a little more help."

"I can tell you this much. When I meet with the A.D.A., I'm going to give him two documents. One may help you a bit, but the other is damaging. The one that may help is the autopsy report. It shows Sixto was dead before the fire started. So at least the prosecution won't be able to claim Charlie started the fire to finish his partner off, although he may still claim Charlie started it to cover the crime."

"And the damaging document?"

"The transcript of the extradition hearing. Charlie openly admits being with Sixto Morales and driving him away after Sixto was shot. Of course, he claims Sixto was pointing a gun at him, but that's Charlie's story. He also says he didn't know Sixto was going to rob the liquor store until it happened. But once again, that's Charlie's story. You'd expect him to say that."

"But there's something else, isn't there?"

"Yes. Now that I know Charlie is pleading not guilty, I'm going to set a juvenile hearing on Wednesday."

"What's that have to do with Charlie's case?"

"I'm going to get the statements of three young people who were at the fire at the abandoned house. One of them admits he accidentally started the fire."

"That would keep the A.D.A. from claiming that Charlie started the fire himself to destroy any evidence."

"That's right."

"That just might be the final piece I need to keep this from going to trial."

"I sure hope so, Mr. Hanson, because my neck is sticking out a mile on this one. This is the first time in my career I have ever cooperated with a defense attorney. If this ends up in trial, the A.D.A. may end up declaring me a hostile witness, something no law enforcement officer ever wants."

"I think we can avoid that."

After he hung up, Horse went to the juvenile court clerk and filed a petition of delinquency naming the three young people, something the law allowed him to do on his own authority. He was then lucky enough to catch Judge Brewster in his chambers and convince him to conduct the hearing. After that, he went back and waited while the clerk produced the summons for each juvenile to appear on Wednesday at noon.

Chapter 35

AEDEN

On Monday morning, after I helped Mrs. Braithwaite get Billy into his chair, I said, "Mrs. Braithwaite, I talked with my parents about going to college next year. I explained everything you told me. They said the decision was up to me."

"And what have you decided?"

"I'd like to go."

"Good for you. I'll talk to the people at the college. They'll send you information about the school and ask for your transcripts. What's your address?"

"2020 Buena Vista. Do you want me to write that down?"

"No, I've got it: perfect vision and a good view."

"Mrs. Braithwaite, thank you for thinking of me. This is getting exciting."

Billy and I headed off to class.

"So, Ade, we're going to be roommates."

"I hope so. Depends on whether the school wants me."

"They'll want you all right. My mom can be real persuasive."

During second period, Principal Flowers came on the intercom.

"Your attention, please. I just finished discussions with the California Interscholastic Federation. Our opponent for the semi-final round of the playoffs will be Saint Anthony High School of Garden Grove in Orange County. Since both teams have undefeated records, neither team will have home-field advantage. The committee has arranged for the game to be played in Barstow on Friday night. Congratulations to our boys for their win in Riverside, and best of luck to them in their next game."

★ ★ ★

That afternoon we began preparations for the game, but we knew very little about our opponent. Principal Flowers had learned their enrollment was over 1,200, almost three times ours. They were playing in the small-school division because they were only in their third year as a high school and had no seniors. They'd won a lot of games by lopsided scores.

Coach Lucas had no film of any of their games. He called Sunset's coach, but their coach was still angry about the game in Smoke Tree. Coach was sure Sunset Crossing had given Saint Anthony film of our game.

When I got home for dinner that night, Dad told me Horse had called and said he was going to set up the hearing we'd talked about at the diner. The hearing would be at noon on Wednesday.

That night at work, when the rush was over, I called Johnny.

"Hey, did your dad get a call from Horse?"

"No, my dad's out."

"When's he due back?"

"Early morning. Why?"

"He'll get a call. Charlie's going to trial next Monday. Horse said he's going to have the juvenile hearing he talked to us about. It will be at noon on Wednesday."

"Wonder if he called Judy's dad."

"I doubt it. I think he'll go out to see Mr. McPhearson in person."

"Boy, I'd like to hear that conversation!"

"Me too. Especially when he tells Judy's dad where we really were that night."

Chapter 36

LUCINDA

Wallace Sturges of Smoke Tree was a conductor on the Santa Fe. On Sunday, he was visiting relatives in Kingman and went to church with them. Before heading home, he went to lunch at the Hungry Boy Cafe, and he bought a copy of the Kingman Courier to read while he ate.

The lead story was about a court appearance by Charlie Merriman, a young Mojave Indian from Smoke Tree. He was surprised to read the man was an employee of the Santa Fe. Like most men on the train crews, he knew very few of the people who worked track maintenance

The article described Merriman as an accomplice in a robbery at Winslow Liquors in Bullhead City. There were several quotes from an Assistant District Attorney, Phillip Samuels. Samuels expressed outrage at the treatment the liquor store owner, Lyndon Brooks, had suffered at the hands of Sixto Morales and his accomplice, Charlie Merriman. Wallace read how Brooks, a veteran of World War II and Korea, had been made to lie on his face on the floor of the store. Brooks had been told he would be shot if he got up before the robbers drove away. Brooks told the responding deputy he decided he was going to shoot Morales the moment Morales stomped his new Stetson while Brooks lay helpless on the floor.

According to the story, after the two men left his store, Brooks got up, retrieved a weapon, and waged a gunfight with the robbers, mortally wounding one and forcing them to flee.

Wallace remembered reading a story in the Smoke Tree Weekly about a fire in the river bottom where the burned body of Sixto Morales had been found. Clearly, the writer of the Weekly story had not yet known about the liquor store robbery in Bullhead.

But something about the story puzzled Wallace, so he reread it carefully to be sure he had it right. The second reading confirmed that when Brooks opened fire on the two men, they were walking away through the parking lot with their backs turned. Phillip Samuels had said nothing about whether the shooting was justified.

The article concluded with a direct quote from the Assistant District Attorney: "Mohave County will not tolerate this kind of person from California coming over here. I will convict Charlie Merriman and protect the people of Arizona." Wallace Sturges kept the paper. It was still in the cab of his pickup when he hauled some junk to the landfill outside Smoke Tree the next day.

When he drove in, he saw Lucinda Morales picking through a pile of trash. He knew her only as "Landfill Lucy." He had no idea she was the mother of Sixto Morales.

He drove down one of the dirt roads inside the landfill, backed off the road, and got out. He left his door open. While he was unloading his trash, a dust devil tore through the dump, blowing smoke and grit in his face and snatching the Kingman Courier off his front seat.

After Wallace left, Lucinda went over to see if he'd left anything she could use. The paper was beside the trash. She glanced at it, and the headline caught her eye. *"DEFENDANT IN BULLHEAD ROBBERY IN COURT."* And below that, in smaller type, *"Smoke Tree Mojave man extradited from California."* She carried the paper back to her shack.

She retrieved a pair of scratched dime store readers and sat down on a wooden chair. As she scanned the article, Sixto's name leaped out at her. As she read it, she realized Lyndon Brooks had shot Sixto in the back! The article didn't come right out and say that, but that was clearly what had happened.

She dropped the paper on the dirt floor and pressed her hands to her face. Her breath came in ragged gasps as she cried. But the tears were not tears of sorrow; she had already cried those. These tears were tears of rage. Some cowardly gringo had shot her Sixto down like a dog in the dirt while his back was turned. She was very angry with Horse for not telling her that part of the story.

Lucinda sat in the chair for a long time. Then she got up to look for something in the chaos of her shack. Many years before, Sixto had brought her a handgun. He was worried about her living at the dump alone. It was a little Colt .32 automatic. When she asked him where it had come from, he said, "the guy who owned it don't need it no more, Mama."

She and Sixto had walked into the desert, and he taught her to load and shoot it. Lucinda didn't really think she needed the gun, but she kept it. Now, she was glad she had it. She found it wrapped in an oily rag. She removed all the cartridges from the magazine. She wiped them down and put them back in the clip. She pulled back the slide and chambered one of the eight rounds.

She sat in her falling-down shack in her scavenged chair with the gun in her lap. She knew what she had to do.

Chapter 37

HORSE

Horse pulled into the McPhearson's driveway at ten o'clock on Tuesday morning. Benedict McPhearson came to the door when Horse rang the Big Ben chime. When he saw who it was, he stepped out onto the porch and closed the door.

He smiled, but the smile didn't reach his eyes. "Hello, Lieutenant. Don't tell me Judy has been speeding again."

"Mr. McPhearson, since Judy is a minor, I've come to serve you with a notice for her to appear at a juvenile hearing tomorrow at noon. Either you or your wife or both of you should accompany her."

The color rose in Benedict's face.

"You mean you're going through with the reckless endangerment charge after you said you wouldn't?"

"No, sir. This is on another matter."

"Regarding ..."

"The night of November the third of this year."

"What about it?"

"It's about where your daughter and two of her friends were that night and what they did. This is important information in a trial in Arizona next week."

"And my daughter is supposedly guilty of what?"

"Not guilty of anything, sir. Nor will she be charged with anything. We just need to get sworn testimony on the record about events surrounding a fire that night."

"You mean the homecoming bonfire she went to with her boyfriend? She's already in trouble with her mother and I for coming home very late that night."

"Would that boyfriend be Johnny Quentin?"

"He was her boyfriend, yes. That relationship has been terminated."

"Yes, you made that clear the other day. And was Aeden Snow with them?"

"When they left the house, he was. He was also with them when they returned, but I suspect he wasn't with them all night.

Wait a minute! Is this about the fire I read about in the paper? The one where they found the dead body?"

"Yes, sir, that's correct."

"Well, I can tell you she was nowhere near it."

"I have conflicting information about that."

"From what source?"

"The two young men she was with."

Benedict McPhearson was silent for a few moments. Horse could almost hear the pieces of a puzzle clicking into place in the man's mind. When he spoke again, there was no longer even a pretense of friendliness.

"I can assure you, Lieutenant, my daughter will not appear at any such hearing. Being associated with that kind of incident could ruin her chances for a good life."

"Sir, I think you are over-reacting. As I said, there will be no charges. The hearing is for information purposes only. The contents of the hearing will be sealed when she turns eighteen."

"I know a thing or two about court records, Lieutenant, and my daughter will not appear in one. She will not be there."

Horse held out the document.

"This summons requires you and your daughter to appear at noon tomorrow in Judge Brewster's chambers. The address is on the order to appear."

Benedict McPhearson did not reach for the document.

Horse touched the paper lightly to the man's chest. For a moment, Horse thought McPherson was going to take a swing at him. He thought it might be interesting if he did. But McPhearson held his temper.

"By touching you with this document, I have served you with the summons."

Horse let go of the paper. It fell to the porch.

"Good day to you, sir."

As Horse walked down the steps, he heard the door slam. When he turned around, the summons was still lying on the porch.

★ ★ ★

At one o'clock on Tuesday afternoon, Fred brought Phillip Samuels into Horse's office. Samuels, a handsome young man of above-average height, looked fit and confident in his three-piece suit. He sat down and unconsciously ran a hand through his well-groomed, brown hair.

"It's a pleasure to meet you in person, Lieutenant Caballo."

"Likewise, counselor."

"Lieutenant, Captain Taylor tells me you did some excellent investigative work on this case. Mojave County is grateful."

"It wasn't all that hard. There was a pretty good trail of bread crumbs if you know what I mean."

"And you interviewed Charlie Merriman?"

"Yes."

"And it was a good interview?"

"Define 'good.'"

"No coercion. No withholding of his right to legal advice?"

"None. Charlie surrendered himself. We did not arrest him. Therefore, it was a non-custodial questioning. We arrested him when he was done."

"Very good. And you recorded the statement?"

"I did. And I told him I was recording it. He gave his permission. I have that on tape."

Horse slid a file across the desk.

"Here's the transcript of the extradition hearing. I played the tape at the hearing, and the contents are in the transcript, word for word. And I have one more thing for you."

He put a smaller file on top of the other one.

"This is the autopsy report prepared for San Bernardino County. It shows Sixto Morales was dead before the fire started. No smoke in his lungs."

Samuels opened the file and glanced through the contents.

"And I will have one more document for you by tomorrow afternoon."

"What document is that?"

"There will be a juvenile court hearing tomorrow. Turns out there were three young people from Smoke Tree at the house the night it burned. One of them set the house on fire by accident."

"I see. I'm not sure I can use that."

"But I will provide a transcript, and you should share it with the attorney appointed to defend Merriman."

"Don't tell me how to do my job, Lieutenant."

"Let me put it another way. It would be wise to share it because I've already told the defense attorney I will be giving it to you. I will have it in your office on Wednesday before close of business."

"So, when I put you on the stand, you'll testify to all of this?"

"Certainly."

"And I can count on you to be reticent on cross-examination?"

"Meaning?"

"Simple yes or no answers. No speculation. Not allowing yourself to be led anywhere we don't want the testimony to go."

"Mr. Samuels, I will testify to the facts as I know them. I'm getting the impression that if the defense asks me whether I think Charlie Merriman was a willing accomplice, you won't want me to answer."

"You won't have to. I'll object on the grounds it calls for speculation."

"Then it will come down to how the judge rules on your objection. You know judges allow latitude for defense attorneys on cross-examination. And if he allows it, it's only fair to tell you in advance I don't think Charlie Merriman knew this robbery was going to happen when he walked into that liquor store. I will say that in court."

Samuels leaned back in his chair and studied Horse.

"Then I might have to declare you a hostile witness."

"That decision would be up to you."

"Lieutenant, I'm sure you're aware that being declared a hostile witness by a prosecutor in a criminal case may not be good for your career."

"Is that a threat, counselor?"

"Just call it a dire warning."

"No, I believe I'll call it a threat. Let me tell you what I think is happening here. I hear you have political ambitions, and you're well aware of the attention this case is getting in your county newspaper. I think you've got a lot of people in your county who don't like Indians or Mexicans either, if the truth is known. I think you see this as one more step on your path to a successful run for district attorney and after that, statewide office. Tell me if I'm wrong."

"Believe what you will, Lieutenant. My job is to prosecute criminals. I think Charlie Merriman is a dangerous criminal who should be taken off the street. I intend to see that happens. I hope you heed my warning and we don't end up being adversaries. You and I are supposed to be on the same side."

"Let me ask you something before you go, Mr. Samuels. Have you interviewed Lyndon Brooks?"

"Yes, earlier today. A brave man who is going to make a great witness for the prosecution. A business owner and a veteran of two wars. Pretty good combination."

"And did you ask Lyndon whether he thought Charlie was in on this from the get-go?"

"No, I did not."

"Why not?"

"Because it's not important. Charlie Merriman was with Sixto Morales when Sixto pulled a gun and robbed the store. Charlie Merriman drove the getaway car. Charlie Merriman drove Sixto Morales to another state and helped him to a place of hiding. Therefore, Charlie Merriman was aiding and abetting a felony. That's all that matters here."

"You're not interested in finding out the truth?"

"I'm interested in prosecuting criminals. End of discussion, Lieutenant. I'll see you next Monday morning at nine o'clock in Mohave County Superior Court."

"Yes, you will. But since you have given me a warning, let me return the favor. This case could turn out to be a tar baby. You may wish you'd never got hold of it."

Chapter 38

LUCINDA

On Tuesday morning, while Horse was visiting the McPhearson house, Lucinda was putting on the only dress she owned, a green print. It hung loosely on her slight frame. She rummaged through a pile of clothing and came up with a wide, red belt. She put it on and cinched it tight. She considered searching for a better pair of shoes, but she had a long walk ahead of her and decided her red P. F. Flyers would do. Matched her belt anyway.

She put the gun in a big purse and walked out of her shack. There was no way to lock her door, but she wasn't planning on coming back anyway. She set off down the road to Highway 95, leaving the landfill for the first time in many years.

Lucinda walked to town and crossed the railroad tracks at the south end of the railyard. On the other side, she picked up the Bureau of Reclamation road that led to the bridge. By noon, she was on the Arizona side of the river.

She trudged along the road through the river bottom, turning and sticking out her thumb every time she heard a car. Dust and alkali kicked up by the north wind swirled around her as she walked. There were very few cars on the lightly-traveled road. None of them stopped for her. But finally, a truck from the Soto Ranch pulled over and waited for her.

"Hola, Senora. *A donde va?*"

"Bullhead, *senor.*"

"Climb in. I can take you part of the way."

The road turned northeast and rose up out of the river bottom into a series of low desert hills, barren of anything other than creosote and white bursage. When he reached the long driveway to the ranch, the driver stopped and let her out. She was a little more than halfway to her destination.

She ended up walking the rest of the way. It was not a pleasant walk. When the road turned directly north, Lucinda found herself walking into a strongly gusting, very cold wind. She wished she had worn a jacket. She was grateful when the road turned due west and dropped back down into the river bottom, where the mesquites and salt cedars gave some protection from the wind.

As she walked along the shoulder of the highway, she thought about what she would say to the man at the liquor store. Should she tell him what a coward he was for shooting Sixto in the back just because Sixto stepped on his stupid cowboy hat? And what was a man doing wearing a cowboy hat inside a liquor store anyway? Should she tell him that even though her son was an *hombre malo,* he was still her son and didn't deserve to be shot down without warning? Should she tell him to make peace with his Maker before she sent him into the next world?

In the end, she couldn't choose. She decided to just shoot him.

It was dusk by the time Lucinda reached Winslow Liquors. The parking lot in front of the store was deserted. Neon signs advertising Coors, Lucky Lager, and Olympia glowed in the window. When she pulled open the door, a bell jingled overhead.

A man looked up at her. He was older than she thought he would be, his face partially in shadow under what looked like a new Stetson. He had initially looked a little startled but seemed to relax when he realized a woman was coming in his store.

Lucinda walked to the counter and studied his face closely. There were crow's feet at the corners of his eyes. Frown lines slanted downward from the corners of his mouth. His eyes were a pale gray. He did not look like a friendly man. She was not going to feel bad about killing him.

"What can I do for you?"

Lucinda pulled the pistol from her purse.

"You can die like my Sixto died."

She emptied the pistol into him, continuing to shoot even as he fell. When there were no more rounds in the gun, she lifted the gate and walked behind the counter. He looked puzzled as the light went out of his eyes. She stood looking down at him until she was sure he was dead. Then she put the gun on the counter and picked up the phone. She dialed the operator.

"*Sacrame la policia.*"

"What?"

"Get me the police. There's a dead man here."

Chapter 39

HORSE

Wednesday morning, there was a knock on Horse's door.

"Come in."

Fred opened the door and leaned in.

"Captain Taylor for you on line one."

"Fred, why didn't you just buzz me?"

"Because I remember what you said about getting up and down to see if you could still move. I think I need to move around more. I just sit behind that desk all day."

Horse nodded and picked up the phone.

"Good morning, Captain Taylor."

"Morning Horse. Thought you ought to know this. Lyndon Brooks was shot and killed yesterday evening."

"Good Lord! Do you know who killed him?"

"We have a confessed killer. Lucinda Morales, mother of Sixto Morales."

"Lucinda shot Brooks?"

"Yep. Told my deputy she read an article in the Kingman Courier that said Brooks had shot her son in the back because Sixto stepped on his hat."

"Where is she now, and how did you find her so quick?"

"She's in custody here in Kingman. Booked for murder one. And we didn't find her. After she shot him, she called us and sat down to wait. She'll be in court a week from today. An attorney has already been appointed."

After he hung up, Horse sat thinking about Lyndon Brooks. A man who had been shot to death by a tiny, sixty-seven-year-old woman. Horse thought about Lyndon telling him he was afraid he was going to die on the floor of his business after surviving two wars. And now he had died on that floor. Would the fallout from the events of November second never end?

Which brought him to Charlie Merriman again. Phillip Samuels had lost his key witness, the victim of the crime. The victim who had given the description of Charlie Merriman to an Arizona deputy and to Horse. Horse wondered how the young assistant district attorney would cope with this.

Chapter 40

AEDEN

Wednesday morning, Judy McPhearson wasn't in school. Johnny and I thought she was probably getting ready for the hearing. By noon, we were in Judge Brewster's chambers with Horse, Johnny's dad, my mother and father, the judge, and a court reporter. Benedict McPhearson and Judy were not there. A well-groomed man in a navy blue suit was escorted in by the bailiff.

"Excuse me, your honor, are you conducting the juvenile hearing involving Judy McPhearson?"

"That's right. And who are you?"

"Stephen Dryden, sir. Hernshaw, Little and Dryden." He handed the judge his card. "I'm representing the McPhearson family."

"Long way from San Francisco, aren't you, counselor?"

"Yes, your honor."

The judge looked at the card again. "And are you the 'Dryden' of Hernshaw, Little, and Dryden?"

"No, sir. That would be my grandfather."

"And where is your client?"

"She will not be here, your honor."

"Well, where is she?"

The attorney looked at his watch.

"Somewhere over the Atlantic Ocean."

"Bound for where?"

"Switzerland, your honor."

"And when will she return?"

"That information has not been shared with me. I can tell you, however, that she will be completing her secondary education in a private school there. Now, if your honor will excuse me, I've got to hurry back to Las Vegas to catch my return flight to San Francisco."

And he walked out of the room.

There was a long silence. Then the judge spoke.

"Let's go on the record here."

The court reporter began typing.

"Let the record show counsel for Judy McPhearson has informed the court that Miss McPhearson is no longer in the United States. She is therefore beyond the reach of this court in any juvenile matter."

After that, the judge asked Johnny and me a number of questions about the events of November third. Johnny explained about accidentally starting the fire, and I confirmed his version of the events. Lieutenant Caballo also spoke for the record. When he was done asking questions, Judge Brewster announced, "Based on the evidence I have heard today, I see no basis for any charges in this matter. Therefore, there will be no further action by this court. When these young men are eighteen, the record of this proceeding will be sealed."

By twenty after twelve, we were outside. Horse thanked our parents for their cooperation.

"Lieutenant Caballo, will any of this help Charlie Merriman?"

"Hard to say, Ade. If this goes to trial, it would be a lot better for him if the McPhearson girl had been here today. The prosecutor could claim since you boys grew up with Charlie, you are lying for him. Judy didn't know him, and that would've given her testimony more credibility. But what we have may be enough because there's been a very strange turn of events. Last night in Bullhead, Sixto's mother shot and killed Lyndon Brooks."

"Killed the guy who shot Sixto?"

"That's right."

"I didn't even know Sixto had a mom."

"Her name is Lucinda. Locals call her 'Landfill Lucy'."

"The lady at the dump is Sixto's mom?"

"That's right. She was booked into the Kingman jail last night."

"The same place they're holding Charlie?"

"Yes. Strange world sometimes, isn't it?"

Johnny and I drove back to school. Johnny didn't say anything until we got there. When we pulled in the parking lot, he said, "Switzerland. Switzerland, for Christ's sake!" He didn't mention Sixto's mom or the man she had killed.

★ ★ ★

There was a pep rally last period, and then school was dismissed for Thanksgiving vacation. After the rally, Johnny and I headed off for our last practice before the game. Coach Lucas worked the offense on timing for the running plays and route discipline for the receivers. He told us if Saint Anthony's staff had reviewed the film of the Sunset Crossing game, they had no idea how good Smoke Tree could be when Johnny was throwing well.

The defense was pretty much in the dark about Saint Anthony, so they worked on tackling drills and pass coverage. Halfway through practice, Coach Lucas put me on defense so I could work against our receivers. I didn't enjoy trying to bring Seve Zavala down after he caught a pass; he usually shrugged me off as though I were a gnat. But I was glad to see how sharp Johnny was. His passes were once again hard and flat. I didn't even come close to picking him off. Saint Anthony's defensive backs were going to have a long night.

At nine-thirty that night, Linda Bergstrom walked into the '76 station and put down her suitcase.

"Hello, Ade."

"Hello, Linda."

" I walked straight here when I got off the train. Don't I get a kiss?"

"Sure."

She put her arms around me and gave me a very long, very enthusiastic kiss. Then she stepped back.

"I just wanted to show you how glad I am to see you again. Are we going to get together tomorrow?"

"Sure. I've got Thanksgiving dinner with my folks, and I'm sure you do too. How about tomorrow night?"

"That's a date."

"I'll call you tomorrow."

"Okay. Can I use your phone? I haven't talked to my mom and dad yet."

While we waited for her parents to come and get her, we caught each other up on the latest. She was amazed Judy McPhearson had gone to Switzerland. She was even more amazed to hear the story about The House of Three Murders and Charlie's upcoming trial in Kingman.

Mrs. Bergstrom pulled into the driveway. I carried Linda's suitcase to the car. Mrs. Bergstrom gave me a big smile.

"Nice to see you, Aeden."

"Nice to see you too, ma'am."

They drove away. I was glad business was slow because I wanted to think about how I felt about seeing Linda again. I didn't call Johnny and tell him about her visit. He was sad enough as it was.

Chapter 41

CHARLIE

That same Wednesday afternoon, Charlie was taken to the interview room to meet with Calvin Hanson.

"Charlie, I'm not sure yet how this is going to affect your case, but yesterday evening Lyndon Brooks was shot to death at his liquor store."

"Another robbery? That's crazy."

"No, not a robbery. Premeditated murder. Sixto's mother killed him."

"Sixto's mom?"

"Horse said her name is Lucinda, and she lived at the dump."

"Landfill Lucy? She's the only person in Smoke Tree poorer than us Mojaves."

"Do you know her personally?"

"No. I've never even seen her — just heard about her."

"So the prosecutor won't be able to say there was some connection between you? I mean, you were with her son when Brooks shot him."

"No. It's like I told you, Mr. Hanson. I didn't know Sixto other than to see him around town. And I sure don't know his mom."

"Okay. The fact that you've never seen her or talked to her is good news. I don't know if I'm going to be able to get her to confirm that or if the judge will believe her if she does."

"She's here?"

"In the women's section. She's going to be charged with murder on Monday."

"Are you going to be her lawyer too?"

"One pro bono case at a time is enough for this poor boy. Since the prosecution's star witness is dead, a lot of this trial will hinge on Horse and the statement you made when you talked to him. He tells me when he talked to Brooks, the man implied he didn't think you were a willing participant in the robbery.

And I have some good news. Lieutenant Caballo is holding a juvenile hearing in Smoke Tree right now to get testimony from three young people. As far as I can see, the only reason he's doing it is to help you."

"Who are they?"

"They're the people you heard at the house that night."

"What are their names?"

"Aeden Snow, Johnny Quentin, and Judy McPhearson. Do you know any of them?"

"I know Aeden. We were on the track team together when he was a freshman. And I know who Johnny Quentin is. He's the quarterback of the football team. Don't know the girl."

"Well, Lieutenant Caballo says they're going to admit they started the fire by accident. This will stop the prosecutor from claiming you burned it down to conceal evidence of a crime.

I'm thinking more and more this will never go to trial. I think I can get you into a uniform instead of a jail cell."

"Good."

"Unless you want to swing for the fences."

"What do you mean?"

"In light of these new developments, go to trial and try to beat the whole thing."

"Nossir. Just get me in the Army. That's all I want."

Chapter 42

AEDEN

Thanksgiving was cloudless, warm, and beautiful. As he often did on holidays, Lee Hoskins joined us. Dad roasted a ham on a spit over mesquite wood coals. He said he didn't want Mom stuck inside a kitchen on such a beautiful day. While the ham cooked, we sat out on the back patio. Starlings and sparrows flitted in and out of the three big mesquite trees we kept neatly trimmed in the yard. Roses were blooming on the white trellis Dad had built against the house. Birds took turns in the birdbath next to the planter by the carport. Mom and I drank iced tea with mint and lemon, and Dad and Lee were drinking beer.

As the sun began to tilt far enough to the west to dapple the backyard with shade, Dad told Lee about the hearing the day before: how the big shot attorney from San Francisco came into the judge's chambers and told us Judy McPhearson was on her way to Switzerland.

"How strange," said Lee, "to have that much money. To be able to put your daughter on a plane to Switzerland at a moment's notice."

"Not to mention making the arrangements for her to be met there and enrolled in a school a half a world away," Dad added. "Who has those kinds of contacts? And something I didn't think of yesterday. The whole family must have passports. I mean, you don't just land in Zurich and say, 'hi, I'm an American.' You have to have a passport to get into that country, and it takes a while to get one. It's not something you do in a day."

"Well, let's not worry about the McPhearsons or anything else," said Mom. "That ham should be perfect by now. Let's enjoy our Thanksgiving dinner and be glad we're together."

★ ★ ★

In the early evening, I picked up Linda, and we went to the movies. We saw Spencer Tracy in "Inherit the Wind." I thought it was a good movie for a guy to take his college date to.

Afterward, we drove out to the river and parked on a point like we used to. But something was different. It was clear, at least to me, that things would never be the same between us. Our romance was over and would not be revived.

Judy told me about her ex-boyfriend at Westmont College. She had been impressed with his little white Thunderbird and the fancy restaurants he took her to in Santa Barbara. He told her he was taking her to Carmel to meet his parents, but when they got there, the parents weren't home. The guy admitted they were in Europe. It was clear to Linda he wanted to impress her with the big house in the rich neighborhood and then get her into bed. She demanded to be taken back to school. He refused.

Linda walked out of the house and kept going until she found a place she could call a cab. The cab took her to the bus station in Monterey, and she took the Greyhound back to Santa Barbara. The guy never called her or came by the dorm again. At least that was Linda's version of events.

Our conversation that evening was mostly about events and not really about feelings. When I took her home and walked her to the door, she hugged me and gave me a kiss. This one wasn't as enthusiastic, but it was sweeter.

"Thank you, Ade. Thanks for the movie and the talk. Thank you for listening to my story. Maybe we can get together again when I come home at Christmas."

"Maybe. Time and distance change things, sometimes in a hurry. But I hope we stay friends."

"Me too."

"Bye, Linda."

"Bye."

★ ★ ★

By Friday night, the weather had turned again. At kickoff time in Barstow, the temperature was in the high thirties. The wind scouring out of the arid Mojave River bottom sent grit and debris twisting above the field lights. The dormant Bermuda grass between the yard lines was brown and stiff in the cold. The stands were full of people in warm jackets and knitted caps.

We played the best football we had ever played, but we had no chance. Saint Anthony's coach had borrowed his offensive scheme from a young man coaching at Whittier College named Don Coryell. We had never seen anything like it. We had no idea how to defend against it.

The first time they broke the huddle and got into their formation, there was only one running back behind the quarterback. There were multiple receivers flanked to the right side of the field, and one flanked to the left. I knew we were in trouble. They scored on their first possession. We scored right back, but we were no match for them after that. At half time it was 28-7, Saint Anthony.

Coach Lucas and the assistants devised a defensive scheme as the game went along, and at halftime, we went over it in on the chalkboard. But even though we understood what Coach wanted us to do, we couldn't stop Saint Anthony. I had told Mrs. Braithwaite there were guys at the coast who could run right past me. One of them was playing wide receiver for Saint Anthony.

But Johnny Quentin had a hot hand. The game film Saint Anthony's coaches had reviewed was of an injured Johnny who could hardly throw. On that night in Barstow, his passes were on target, and our guys were running good routes. Seve made believers out of Saint Anthony's cornerbacks. That set up our running game, and it clicked too, but there was no way we were going to win the game. We simply could not keep Saint Anthony out of the end zone.

Final score: Saint Anthony 56, Smoke Tree 42.

After the game, Coach Lucas thanked us for playing our hearts out the entire game. Some of the guys were in tears. Our great season was over. It was very quiet on the bus ride home. No one asked the driver to turn on the radio.

Chapter 43

CHARLIE

Monday morning, November 27, 1960, in Kingman, Arizona, the clerk of the court stood and said, "The State of Arizona versus Charlie Merriman, the honorable Emmett Watson presiding. All rise."

The courtroom was crowded. There had been a lot of interest in the case because of the newspaper coverage of the robbery. After the shooting death of Lyndon Brooks, interest had increased.

Judge Watson entered the courtroom from his chambers and ascended to the bench. Before anyone else could speak, Calvin Hanson said, "Your honor, permission to approach?"

"Come ahead."

Calvin spoke to the judge. Emmett Watson looked surprised but nodded his head.

"You'd better get up here too, Mr. Samuels."

As they stood side by side, the two made quite a contrast. Phillip Samuels in his perfectly tailored blue suit, white shirt, red tie, and wing-tip shoes: Calvin Hanson just formal enough not to earn a reprimand with his khaki pants, corduroy sport coat, snap-button shirt, bolo tie, and cowboy boots.

"Mr. Hanson seems to think he may have a way to save us all a lot of time."

"Is he changing his client's plea to 'guilty'?"

"Hardly. I'm going to recess the court and have both of you in my chambers to listen to his proposal."

While Judge Watson announced a brief recess, the attorneys returned to their tables and picked up legal pads. There were murmurs from the spectators. The reporter for the Kingman Courier leaned over the rail and asked the Assistant District Attorney a question. Samuels shook his head and walked toward the judge's chambers.

A few minutes later, the two men were in front of the judge's desk.

"Be seated, gentlemen. I don't know how long this might take. Mr. Hanson, let's hear your proposal."

"Your honor, first, let me suggest that this case is not as simple as it may once have been. The victim in the case, Mr. Samuels' key witness, has been killed. That changes things."

Phillip Samuels rose and started to speak.

"Sit down, Mr. Samuels. Sit down. I don't like you towering over me. Makes me nervous."

"But your honor, you told me not to address you while sitting down."

"That was in open court, you ninny. We're having a conversation here. I don't want you popping up and down like a jack-in-the-box."

"Yes, sir. Thank you, your honor."

"Well, what were you going to say?"

"That it doesn't necessarily change things that much. We have the transcript of the extradition hearing. In that hearing, Lieutenant Caballo of the San Bernardino County Sheriff's Department played what amounts to a voluntary confession on the part of the accused."

"Did the accused have the benefit of counsel?"

"Merriman hadn't been booked or charged. He came in and volunteered the information. He says that on the tape, and Judge Sherman, the Superior Court Judge, had him confirm that on the record."

"But your honor," said Hanson, "in the transcript, while Merriman admits he was inside the store with Sixto Morales, the man who committed the robbery, he states he had no idea Morales even had a gun, let alone that he was going to rob the place."

"Your honor," said Samuels, "a Mohave County Sheriff's deputy will testify that Lyndon Brooks gave him a description of Sixto's accomplice. Lieutenant Caballo of the San Bernardino County Sheriff's department will further testify that Lyndon Brooks gave him information that led to the identification of Merriman as the accomplice."

"That's true, your honor, but this is where the A.D.A. is going to have a witness problem," said Hanson. "The bulk of the work on this case was not done in Mohave County; it was done in Smoke Tree by Lieutenant Caballo. Based on his conversation with Lyndon Brooks and his follow-up investigation, Lieutenant Caballo believes Merriman's story. He is convinced Merriman didn't know Morales intended to rob the liquor store."

"But that's hearsay, your honor. And very conveniently, Mr. Brooks cannot be here to challenge the lieutenant's version of the conversation."

"Your honor," said Hanson, "there's hearsay, and there's hearsay. This is a reliable source. This is a witness with a letter of commendation in his file from the Mohave County Sheriff for his excellent work on this very case.

In addition to your honor, Mr. Merriman said there were other individuals at the house where Mr. Morales died. Lieutenant Caballo has now located those individuals, and they have admitted they started the fire that destroyed the house. Both Mr. Samuels and I have seen a transcript of a juvenile hearing in Smoke Tree in which the individuals made those admissions."

"Mr. Samuels, have you seen such a transcript?"

"I've seen it, but I'm not convinced of the veracity of these juveniles. They were acquainted with the accused. They could have been lying for him."

"Mr. Samuels, is this San Bernardino County Sheriff's Department Lieutenant, this Lieutenant uh, what's his name, here today to testify as a prosecution witness?"

"Yes, your honor."

"I'd like to get his take on this. It might save us all a lot of back and forth."

"Your honor, I must strenuously object. It would be highly irregular for a judge who's hearing a case to discuss possible testimony with a key witness before the trial begins."

"It may be irregular, but I intend to do it. We're going to go back to open court, and I'm going to announce I want to talk to a prosecution witness in my chambers. If you want to object for the record, that will be the time to do it. But you will look very foolish objecting to the presiding judge talking to a prosecution witness, your witness, in this case. It would be far more likely that the defense would object to such a conversation. Do you object, Mr. Hanson?"

"No, your honor. That conversation may lead to a solution that's good for everyone concerned."

"All right. Everybody out."

In the courtroom, the judge ordered the bailiff to bring Lieutenant Caballo to his chambers. He looked directly at Phillip Samuels. Samuels said nothing. Judge Watson then recessed the trial again.

Once again, the reporter for the Kingman Courtier leaned over the rail and asked Samuels a question. Samuels made no response of any kind.

The judge left the bench. The bailiff went out into the hall and brought Horse through the courtroom into the judge's chambers. In less than ten minutes, Horse came back out, walked through the courtroom, and out the double doors into the hall.

Judge Watson re-entered the courtroom. He declared the trial back in session.

"Counsel, approach the bench."

Samuels and Hanson came forward and conferred with the judge, then returned to their tables.

"I want to see counsel in my chambers again. The trial is once again in recess."

Samuels looked like he was going to say something but held his tongue. The murmurs from the crowd grew louder.

When both lawyers were once again seated in front of the judge, the judge spoke.

"Mr. Samuels, after talking to your key witness, I agree with Mr. Hanson. You have a serious problem. This trial, if it gets underway, could go very badly for the State, and the defendant could walk out scot-free. I don't want to see that happen, and if you give it some thought, you won't either. This lieutenant conducted almost the entire investigation, and he seems to give credence to Merriman's version. But I think Mr. Hanson may have a solution that will save us a lot of embarrassment. Mr. Hanson, explain what you have in mind."

"Your honor, my proposal is simple, and there is legal precedent to support it. You could make a stipulated dismissal of the charges against Mr. Merriman, with no objection to re-filing."

Phillip Samuels came out of his chair.

The judge waved him back to his seat before he could speak.

"Mr. Hanson, explain the stipulation."

"The charges will be dismissed with the stipulation that Mr. Merriman joins the United States Army."

"Do you see any reason your client would not be accepted by the Army, Mr. Hanson?"

"No, your honor. Mr. Merriman is a high school graduate. He is healthy. In fact, he holds the record for the mile run at Smoke Tree High. In addition, he has a clear record without so much as a traffic ticket. Any recruiter would be glad to have him."

"And if he can't get in? If they turn him down for some unknown reason, or he fails his physical because of some problem he is not aware of?"

"Then Mr. Samuels can re-file."

"Mr. Samuels, it's your case. What say you?"

"I don't like it."

"Why not? Your concern is getting this man out of the tri-state area. This does more than that. This puts him in the Army serving his country and fulfilling his patriotic duty."

"But sir ..."

"But nothing. We're going to go back in open court. Mr. Hanson is going to make a motion for a stipulated dismissal with no objection to re-filing. He is then going to explain the stipulation.

Mr. Samuels, you have two options. You can object and argue against the motion. Or, you can agree with the motion as the solution to a difficult trial complicated by the death of the principal witness. You can emphasize that the loss of this witness could lead to the complete acquittal of the accused. You can also explain this solution not only takes Mr. Merriman off the street but puts him in the Army, where he will learn some discipline and respect.

If you choose the first option, you will look like a fool because I am going to grant the motion. If you choose the second option, it will appear that all parties wisely reached an agreement that benefited the community and placed Mr. Merriman in the service of his country. And, you will have achieved a result tantamount to an admission of guilt. It will enhance your reputation as a tough prosecutor."

Phillip Samuels sat silently for a few minutes. Once, he almost spoke but thought better of it. He wrote some notes on his legal pad and then crossed them out.

"All right. I agree, your honor."

"Good. Now, one more thing, Mr. Hanson. Your stipulation will also state that Mr. Merriman must have signed up for the Army prior to Christmas. That way he will be in uniform shortly after the new year. If he has not signed up by Christmas, Mr. Samuels will re-file the charges."

"Certainly, your honor. I'd be glad to include that."

"You should be."

They went back to the courtroom. The judge re-convened the trial. Calvin Hanson made the motion, and Phillip Samuels made a face-saving speech supporting the motion and touching on the points the judge had raised. Emmett Watson granted the motion. Charlie Merriman was processed out of jail before noon.

Chapter 44

AEDEN

On Wednesday, Johnny and I went to Renée's for lunch. The sky was blue and cloudless, but it was very cold. The north wind was blowing straight down Broadway. One side of the "Go Scorpions" banner that had stretched across the street had come loose, and the banner was twisting and flapping in the wind. We each got a copy of the Smoke Tree Weekly from the vending machine and sat at the picnic table in the back of the parking lot. The cement block wall in the rear corner of the lot served as a windbreak, but the gusts above the wall blew chinaberries and twigs off the tree and sent them bouncing across the table.

So much had changed since the day we had searched the Weekly for details of the fire at the House of Three Murders. I was committed to leave Smoke Tree for college if Billy's mom could persuade Central Coast to give me a scholarship. My former girlfriend was now just a friend. Judy McPhearson was, as far we knew, somewhere in Switzerland. We had no idea if she would ever return to Smoke Tree.

Our local paper covered the game in great detail. Johnny had top billing. Nor had his performance against a superior team gone unnoticed elsewhere. There had been a big write-up about him in the San Bernardino Sun, and even the Los Angeles Times had an article that mentioned Johnny's 327 passing yards with no interceptions and no tackles for a loss. There was no doubt he would be receiving scholarship offers.

On the inside page, The Smoke Tree Weekly carried a brief description of Charlie Merriman's time in court. It was clear the writer of the article didn't understand exactly what had happened, but the story explained the part about Charlie having to join the Army to avoid a trial and possible prison time.

When we were finished reading both articles, we got burgers and fries at the window and carried them back to the table. As we ate lunch, I began to realize my path and the paths of my friends were going to diverge in a few months. I just didn't realize how soon.

"Some game, huh?"

"Yeah. Boy, those guys were good."

"So were you, Johnny. You were great."

"You weren't so bad yourself."

"I did okay on offense, but I was in way over my head on defense. That one receiver of theirs beat me again and again. I've never played against anybody that fast before. Made me feel like I was running in slow motion."

"Well, you intercepted one pass."

"My mom could have intercepted that wobbler. I'm telling you, Johnny, if their quarterback had been as good as you, they would have scored a hundred points."

"And Seve! Seve was great. He caught everything I threw his way. Never dropped one. And the way he ran right over their cornerbacks!"

"It was a great season, but it's all over now."

"Too bad all that other stuff was going on."

"You think we'll remember all this when we're old?"

"I suppose. I'll never forget Judy. I wish I could."

"Maybe that's a start. Wishing you could."

"Maybe. What do you think about what happened to Charlie?"

"At least he's not in prison."

"Yeah, but he has to join the Army? That's just not right. We get a little juvenile hearing. Judy doesn't show up, but nobody does anything because Benedict McPhearson has so much money, he can get her out of the country. But Charlie Merriman? Charlie has to join the Army! It stinks."

"It does."

"I want to talk to him. See how he feels about what happened."

"You'd better do it quick. He has to join up before Christmas."

Johnny hadn't eaten his French fries. He tossed them on the ground. The starlings descended. Sparrows showed up.

"You going to basketball practice today?"

"No. You?"

"No. I'm done with sports until track season."

"I may be done with them, period."

"I don't believe it. When Coach Sensabaugh hears he's lost his point guard, he'll be all over you. And baseball? You love baseball. You'll be out on the mound bringing the heat this spring."

"Maybe. Maybe, but I don't think so."

★ ★ ★

Johnny was right. By the first week in January, he was gone. After he talked with Charlie a few times, they drove to Las Vegas to see the Army recruiter. They joined on the "buddy system," which meant they would stay together through basic and advanced training and first duty assignment. Johnny's dad had to sign for him because he wasn't eighteen, but Johnny got no argument on that score.

I went on automatic pilot for the rest of high school. My social life, which hadn't been much anyway, simply ceased to exist. With Johnny gone, I was at loose ends. However, I studied hard, got my scholarship, and continued to work at the service station. I spent all my weekends at Lee's Camp.

Some nights when I was at the adobe, I would dream the dream I had dreamed when I saw Charlie Merriman's face. Sometimes, Johnny was running with us.

Chapter 45

AEDEN

I was home for Christmas vacation my freshman year in college. We were having breakfast when the phone rang.

"Aeden, it's for you. Johnny Quentin."

"Hello, soldier."

"Hi, Ade. I'm home on leave. Want to get together?"

"Sure. Come by."

Fifteen minutes later, my old friend was in our living room. He chatted for a few minutes with Mom and Dad before we drove away.

"Where we headed?"

"Remember the story we told the night of the fire? About being at Boundary Cone drinking beer?"

"Sure."

"Well, let's go do that."

We didn't talk much as we drove. Rattling over the washboarded road through the river bottom and up the side of the Black Mountains cut down on conversation.

Outside Oatman, we stopped at the place Seve Zavala called Zito's. The guy didn't even look at us when we brought the six-pack of Coors to the counter — just rang it up.

We sat on lava rocks at the bottom of Boundary Cone. Johnny told me about his year in the Army. He and Charlie had gone through basic and advanced infantry training. When they were done, Charlie decided he wanted to be an airborne Ranger. Johnny wasn't eager, but he went along anyway.

"What was Ranger training like?"

"Take Coach Lucas's worst August practice and multiply it by ten. Then do it all day every day for two months."

"But you got through it."

"Yeah, kind of surprised myself."

"What about Charlie?"

"Charlie? Charlie was born for that stuff. He was tireless. No matter how many miles they made us run, no matter how many pushups they made us do, no matter how many days we went with almost no sleep, no matter how much they screamed at us and harassed us, Charlie just kept smiling. Drove the guys training us nuts. I don't think they'd ever seen anything like it.

And one other thing. You could take Charlie out in the dark of a cloudy night, blindfolded, spin him around a bunch of times, take the blindfold off, and he would tell you where true north was! It was like he had a compass inside his head."

"So now what?"

"We're off to the 101st Airborne. Gonna be Screaming Eagles for a while. How about you? How's college?"

"I like it."

"And Billy?"

"Likes it too. And boy, does that guy study hard!"

"Play football this fall?"

"Yeah, freshman team."

"How was it?"

"The players are bigger and better. They hit harder. But I'm okay with it. I wouldn't be in college if it weren't for football and track. But I'll tell you this, our quarterback is not nearly as good as you."

We sat quietly for a long time, looking at the green-edged, silver ribbon of the Colorado River splitting the Mojave Valley below us. The sky was a deep blue, and a light breeze was blowing. I looked northeast at Spirit Mountain and beyond that to the Providence and New York ranges on the distant horizon. I was reminded again how much I loved this place. I realized I would rather stay here than go back to school.

"Did anybody ever hear from Judy?"

"Not that I know of."

"I drove by her house. It looks abandoned."

"It is, as far as I know. Not long after you left, the McPhearsons moved out. I don't know exactly when. One day the house was just empty.

I heard a rumor that someone saw Benedict in Las Vegas with the two guys who used to hang around their house. But you know Smoke Tree: always full of rumors."

★ ★ ★

The next time I heard from Johnny, it was Christmas vacation during my senior year. He showed up in front of our house one afternoon in a new Corvette Stingray. I heard him out front when he gave it a couple of extra revs before he shut it down.

Just as three years before, he came in and talked politely with my parents. My dad told Johnny how much he missed Johnny's father.

"Thank you, Mr. Snow. My dad told me once you were the only one who stuck up for him when his life fell apart."

When we got outside, I walked around the car.

"Nice wheels."

"Remember how much we wanted a Corvette when we were in high school?"

"Sure do."

"Bought it with my re-enlistment bonus. Charlie and I signed on for another four years."

"Why?"

"Why not? Too windy to roll stones, I guess."

I was thinking, let's take a ride out to Klinefelter and see old Mr. Stanton."

"He died, Johnny. Last year. They found him in his bed. Just wore out, I guess."

"What happened to his station?"

"Torn down. Nothing there now but an empty lot."

"Boy, lots of changes."

"Speaking of changes, I was sorry to hear about your dad."

"Yeah, left me the house. That's why I'm here. Came back to put it up for sale. I don't know if I'll ever be back here again."

He shook his head. "Tell you what, Ade, let's take a ride to To-pock. We can get a beer at Catfisherman's Paradise." He tossed me the keys. "You drive."

On the highway, Johnny told me about his tour in Korea.

"Cold, miserable place. No wonder they call it a hardship tour."

"You and Charlie still serving together?"

"Not for the last year. We've both been pushing recruits since we got back. Me at Fort Bliss, Charlie up at Fort Ord. But we'll be serving together again next tour.

And here's some news for you. Charlie used his re-enlistment bo-nus to get married. Some girl he was writing to in the Village. Says he wants to have some kids. Says this will be his last tour, and he's coming back here when he's done. Been saving his money."

"Good for him."

When we got to Topock, we got beer and sandwiches and went outside to a picnic table under a huge salt cedar.

"What about you, college boy? Still dodging the draft?"

"Yeah. Still have my college deferment. It will run out when I graduate next June. They'll get me pretty quick after that."

"Well, Charlie and I are headed to Vietnam next spring."

"Uh-oh."

"Yeah. Been there once already with the advisors. That place is a mess. This trip we'll both be with the First Cavalry. At least we'll be in the same division. Anyway, Ade, this thing is heating up fast. It's going to get bigger and nastier, and it won't be over for a long time.

"Wait a minute. I voted for Johnson. He's going to stop this, right?"

"I see college has developed your sense of humor.

Want some advice?"

"Sure."

"If they draft you, go to officer candidate school and get a commission."

"Why?"

"To be the guy making the decisions instead of some gung-ho West Point lifer. Maybe you can keep your guys from getting killed. And after you get your lieutenant's bar, go to Ranger school. You'll hate it, just like I did, but you'll learn things there that'll help you stay alive."

"Okay, I'll do it if I get drafted."

As we sat and talked, I realized time had opened a gap between Johnny and me. I was a college student. He was a man, a sergeant in the Army. His experience was far beyond mine. Unfortunately, it wouldn't be for long.

Chapter 46

AEDEN

When my ten-year class reunion rolled around in 1971, I was just beginning to emerge from the deep, debilitating, and relentless depression I had carried home with me from the war in 1969. A depression so deep there were times when I didn't think I could ever climb out of it. There were not many people in my class I wanted to see, but I had heard Johnny was back in Smoke Tree, and I knew Seve Zavala was a deputy sheriff working with Horse. Also, I wanted to see Billy Braithwaite.

The reunion dinner was at the Elks club. When I got there, most of the guys from our football team were standing at the bar, replaying every game of our senior season. I didn't want to do that. I walked away and was looking for Billy when a big hand clapped me on the shoulder.

"Aeden Snow! Long time, man."

"Seve! You're one of the guys I was hoping to see. How have you been?"

"Good, good, Ade. I heard you were in the green latrine."

"Heard you were too. Whereabouts?"

"Saigon, mostly. They took one look at me and said, 'M.P.'"

"So, that's why the deputy sheriff thing?"

"That, and wanting to work with Horse. Where were you?"

"Up in the central highlands. 1ˢᵗ Cav."

"Pony soldiers!"

"Yeah, with our flying steeds."

"Man, I couldn't wait to get out of the place."

"Me either. Sometimes I feel like I never left."

"Roger that."

"Say, have you seen Billy?"

"Over in the corner there."

"What about Johnny?"

"Johnny Q? We don't see Johnny in town very often."

"Where is he?"

"When he first got out, he went to work for the Santa Fe. That didn't last long. Fired him for drinking on the job."

"So, what's he doing now?"

"Wandering, mostly. He walks all over the desert. He built this contraption that looks like a big basket with bicycle wheels. Has all his stuff in it. Pulls it around behind him like a rickshaw."

"What's he do for money?"

"I guess he saved a lot of his pay when he was in the service. He still has some left from when he sold his dad's house, even though he gave half of it to Charlie's widow to help her with the twins. Gave her his car, too."

"Any idea where I might find him?"

"I heard some quail hunters saw him up by Wild Horse Mesa the other day.

Johnny's in bad shape, Ade. Not the Johnny you knew. He's losing it. Falling apart bit by bit. Has that cart he made full of books. Says he's trying to figure something out. Walks around talking to himself. Scares people a little."

"I think I'll go up in the morning and try to find him. Great to see you, Seve. You're looking good. Glad to hear you're working with Horse. He's a good man."

"Take care of yourself, Ade. Don't be a stranger. Come out and see us now and then."

I tracked down Billy Braithwaite, and we caught up. Billy had his law degree and was working for the tribe. He was head of the tribal council and was their chief negotiator. He told me the Mojave were finally getting full value for their leased farmlands. Life was improving for the tribe.

When I said goodbye to Billy, there was no one else I wanted to talk to. I went out the back door.

* * *

Early the next morning, I was in the Providence Mountains with a canteen of water and a pair of binoculars. It took me most of the day and a lot of walking over rough ground to find Johnny's camp. He had pitched a small tent among the big boulders at the base of Table Mountain just west of Wood's Canyon. The contraption Seve told me about was beside the tent, but Johnny was not there. I was wishing I had brought paper and pen to leave a note when I heard a voice behind me.

"You always poke around other people's stuff?"

Startled, I turned quickly. I hardly recognized my friend. Johnny was gaunt, bearded, and filthy. He wore stained canvas pants and a fatigue jacket over a flannel shirt. His long hair was greasy and uncombed.

"Johnny."

"Ade. What brings you to the wastelands?"

"Wanted to see you. Seve told me where I might find you – within a few square miles or so."

"Glad you stopped by."

"What are you doing up here?"

"Not much. Living. Thinking. Walking. Been doing it for a while."

"So I hear."

"Heard you ended up in 'Nam. When were you in-country?"

"Got there in time for the Tet Offensive."

"Lucky you. Where?"

"Central highlands."

"Cav, huh?"

"Just like you."

"You know Charlie was killed the year after I talked to you last?"

"Yes, I heard."

Johnny's voice broke. "He almost made it, Ade. We were so short we couldn't start a long conversation. One night a patrol got caught outside our wire and couldn't get in. He went out to help them and got killed. The man was a warrior.

I wasn't there, or I'd have gone with him. In fact, I wish I had gone out instead of him. He'd still be alive, and the twins would have a daddy."

"But you made it, Johnny."

"In a way. In a way. I was lucky to get out of the Army without a bad conduct discharge. Went a little *dinky dau* when I got back to The World."

"Well, they don't like to give bad conduct discharges to guys with the bronze star and two purple hearts.

So, how long are you going to stay up here?"

"As long as it takes."

"As long as it takes to what?"

"Make sense of it. All of it. The whole thing."

"The war? No one will ever figure that one out."

"The war and other things too. How we got onto that road."

"The country?"

"No, us. Remember?"

"Remember what?"

"That night. The night we burned down that old house. Everything went wrong after that. That's why Charlie had to go in the Army."

"But I never did really understand why you went. The world was opening up for you. You were getting scholarship offers."

"I went because I thought Charlie got the short end of the stick, and I thought it wasn't right."

"And you used to accuse me of being an idealist! And that was all of it?

"No, not quite. Benedict McPhearson got Judy out of the country, and even though I realized she had never loved me and never would, there was nothing left for me here once she was gone."

"You still think about her?"

"Hardly. It's like First Corinthians, Ade. 'When I became a man, I put away childish things.'"

"Well, it's all over now, Johnny."

Johnny shook his head. "You know better, Ade. You know it's never going to be over. It has twisted us up inside and made the world look ugly to us. We don't look at life in a good way anymore, do we?"

"No, we don't. But maybe someday we will again. Things change."

"Tell that to the crowd that sent us over there."

He looked at me for a long time, the setting sun tinting the side of his face burnt-orange, the north wind whipping his greasy hair around his face, and Gold Valley spread out below him. And beyond that, nothing and nothing and nothing and nothing, all the way to the Old Woman Mountains on the distant southern horizon.

Then it was as if I were no longer there. Something went out of his eyes. Johnny turned and walked away. I wanted to follow him and talk him off the mountain, but I knew I couldn't. He had cut to the heart of the matter. We had said all there was of importance to be said. I let him go, my heart breaking for the man who was my best friend.

He disappeared over the edge of Wood's Canyon. I turned and walked west toward my truck.

I never saw Johnny Quentin again.

THE END

"Men come and go, cities rise and fall, whole civilizations appear and disappear–the earth remains, slightly modified. The earth remains, and the heartbreaking beauty where there are no hearts to break…I sometimes choose to think, no doubt perversely, that man is a dream, thought an illusion, and only rock is real. Rock and sun."

—Edward Abbey

If you enjoyed this book, the author would be grateful if you would take the time to write a review. We independent authors lack the resources of the publishing houses to publicize our books. We rely on our readers to write reviews and recommend our books to others. Reviews and word of mouth are the best tools we have for selling our books.

When you reach the amazon product page that has the book, scroll down to just below the author photo will reveal a "write a review" button. Please click on it and leave your thoughts.

Thank you again.

Gary J. George

Many Thanks to:

Ginny Boyd George for her invaluable help in crafting this novel.
Her perceptive comments, suggestions, input, and editing assistance
were instrumental in producing the finished text.

Cover and formatting by 100 Covers.